Hood Girl, Good Girl

CYNTHIA MARCANO
INDIAN SPICE

URBAN
HOUSE
PUBLISHING

Urban House Publishing/Indian Spice Creations

Publisher's Note: This is a work of fiction. Names, characters, places, and incidents are a product of the author's imagination. Locales and public names are sometimes used for atmospheric purposes. Any resemblance to actual people, living or dead, or to businesses, companies, events, institutions, or locales is completely coincidental.

Book Layout ©2021 House of Cynthia Designs
Copyright © 2021
First Edition 2021 – Hood Girl, Good Girl
Author: Cynthia Marcano, Indian Spice
Library of Congress Control Number:
ISBN-13: 978-1-950913-08-4

For The City of Camden

Where it all started for two hood girls,
who are good girls hustling to reach their goals
and rising above stereotypes & prejudices.

ONE
Tianna

I shoved my head under the pillow trying to drown out the music playing loudly. Luther Vandross belting out *Never Too Much* over and over again was getting on my nerves. How did my parents expect to send me to bed, and for me to actually fall asleep while they were hosting Soul Train downstairs? I sat up frustrated and tapped on the wall above my headboard waiting for my little brother, Abe, to reply. He was my favorite person in the world. Way beyond his years. I often wondered if he bordered on genius. He was like a grown man in a boy's body. No tap back from his side meant he was asleep. The man-boy could sleep through a hurricane, so people laughing and carrying on surely wouldn't wake him.

I walked to my bedroom door and pressed my ear to it trying to make out what the adults were doing. That was what got me sent to bed in the first place; getting caught sipping on my fourth Hugs juice and loitering in the kitchen being nosey.

'Kids have no business in grown folk's conversation, Tianna. Let your mom enjoy her thirtieth birthday with just the adults. Tomorrow we'll all celebrate together as a family. Ok?' My dad, well stepdad, had a way of setting me straight without lifting a finger, or his voice. I didn't like it, but I respected his word and marched my 'narrow butt' upstairs to my room as my mom had suggested when I exhaled a little too forcefully for her liking.

Another round of the adults laughing all loud rattled my windows. Ok, that's a little overdramatic, but so were the 'grown folk.' Why were drunk people always either laughing or crying like they had no sense? My parents were born-again Christians and not

5

the partying type, but they knew how to let their hair down when they really wanted to. Apparently, turning thirty called for it. I'd seen *Mami* cry and laugh throughout the years without a drop of alcohol anywhere in sight. I much preferred her laughing, so I guess I shouldn't be complaining that she was having a good time.

The house went quiet for a moment before *Baby Come to Me* by James Ingram came on. Everyone began egging my parents on to start dirty dancing and singing to each other. That was their song and whenever it came on, they'd act like teenagers at an unsupervised house party. *Mami* always smiled when she recounted the story of how she knew she wanted to marry Pop the first time he sang it to her.

I could bet Pop was sauntering over to *Mami* like a cat hunting a mouse, and it made me unconsciously smile. *Mami* had an infectious laughter. I loved that about her, and no one could make her laugh like Pop could.

I couldn't help myself and sneaked out of my bedroom to watch them from the top of the staircase. Pop kissed *Mami's* neck and she smiled as she sang the woman's part of the song. He spun her around then kissed her lips before he put James Ingram to shame. My Pop had a voice that would make women blush. He was a fly dude. At least that's what all the women used to whisper when *Mami* wasn't close by. One day I wished to marry someone just like my stepdad. Pop really loved *Mami*. And although I wasn't his biological daughter, he loved me just as much as he loved Abe.

"Tianna, what are you doing out of bed?"

I jumped up startled by the unexpected voice behind me. Uncle Lou was standing there holding a beer, waiting for an answer. I looked down and fumbled my words before I found my bearings and used the charm Pop always said I had when I would talk my way out of punishment. He said I would make a good politician one day.

I folded my arms into themselves confidently and leaned my head sideways, eyeing Uncle Lou as if he were slow and I was the only one allowed to ask questions. "Uncle Lou. I was just watching *Mami* and Pop dancing. *Mami* and Pop wouldn't even care if they knew. And I like seeing *Mami* happy on her birthday. Oh, and happy birthday to you too. I still can't believe Grandma had y'all on the same day. But y'all not twins though. Was you mad that *Mami* stole your birthday? I'da been real mad if Abe had stole my birthday." I offered him the gapped tooth smile that adults always found cute wondering which question he'd get distracted with first.

Uncle Lou raised an eyebrow as he slowly took a sip of his beer. His reaction was a new one for me. I knew how to get my parents, teachers, most adults for that matter to just roll their eyes and laugh at my antics. Instead, Uncle Lou eyed me from head to toe. It made me uncomfortable, but I couldn't figure out why. As he continued to survey me, I uncrossed my arms and began fidgeting with the small hole at the bottom of my Care Bears t-shirt turned pajamas. I had outgrown it, but I refused to let my mom trash it, so I'd wear it to sleep.

I looked up and Uncle Lou was still staring at me. I followed his line of vision right to my budding breasts. The tight, worn tee left nothing to the imagination. Heat crawled up my neck. I covered myself with my arms and quickly dashed into my room, a goodbye to my uncle floating in the air I'd left behind me. I prayed he hadn't seen my nipples. I could never look him in the face again, I was so mortified.

I quickly changed into a nightgown and tossed my favorite t-shirt into the trash basket. A soft knock on the door scared me still. I didn't move a muscle but tuned my hearing to make sure I wasn't imagining things. A second soft knock propelled me to my bed. I quickly laid down with no time to get under the blanket. The hot summer night would be a good excuse if my parents were suspicious.

I turned my face toward the window, closed my eyes, and pretended to be asleep. I heard the door open slowly but didn't dare check to see who'd entered. I didn't expect my mom to check in on me until she was turning in for bed, as she had always done. Uncle Lou must've told on me and why she came to check in on me early.

Adults were always tattle-tailing. When the door click closed, I exhaled and let the calm of not being caught disobeying my parents lull me to sleep.

At first, I thought I was dreaming. I felt pinned down as if my bones had been replaced with steel. At the same time, I felt all of the hair on my body stand on end. I felt heat. I didn't understand what was going on. I felt pleasure but I also felt fear. The rancid smell of sweat, tobacco, and alcohol filled my nostrils, making me gag.

I opened my eyes and found Uncle Lou lying beside me on my bed fondling my breasts over my pajamas, his leg pinning both of mine down. I was too shocked to move or say anything. His hot breath reeked of cigarettes and beer. I fought back the urge to vomit. I slammed my eyes shut willing him to go away. Maybe he would just leave. Maybe I really was dreaming, and I could wake up and not remember this nightmare. Or maybe I was naïve.

His touch began to get more aggressive. He'd slipped his hand under my pajamas, and I reactively clenched my legs closed. He tried to touch what *Mami* always referred to as my treasure. I wouldn't loosen up my legs, so he stopped trying and went back to fondling my barely-there boobs. I kept my eyes closed and heard him unzip his pants.

I didn't know much about the ways of the world, but I'd seen enough of it to know that nothing good was going to come from this. I couldn't hold back the tears. He didn't seem to notice or care. I heard him moaning but I refused to open my eyes to see what he was doing. He grabbed my hand and placed it on his penis. Gripping his hand over mine, he pleasured himself. A few minutes later groaned and cursed then stopped, and I felt a warm fluid on my hand that made me want to vomit again.

A tap on the wall behind my bed brought me hope and anguish. Uncle Lou stood up quickly and zipped up his pants before wiping away most of what had covered my hand. A minute later I heard my door creak open and then close softly. After several minutes of quiet,

I dared to open my eyes. Uncle Lou had left my room, but disgust and shame had remained.

I didn't respond to my brother's tap. I didn't even have the courage to leave my bed to clean my hand. Never in my life had I wanted to shower so badly, but I couldn't move. I cried myself to sleep. The next morning, I showered longer than usual trying to wash away the dirt inside and out. I promised myself to not think about it. I'd take the shameful night to the grave if I didn't succeed in blocking it out of my memory first. That was the plan. Forgetting it ever happened.

Just as promised, we'd celebrated *Mami's* birthday as a family. We'd gone to a traveling carnival and gotten on rides. I saw a few of my friends and chatted with them for a while. On the way back to the car, we passed a photo booth. *Mami* insisted we all squeeze in and take a picture. As we were trying to make space, Pop pulled me closer to him telling Abe to squeeze in some more so *Mami* could fit in the booth. I recoiled at Pop's hand around my waist. He looked at me strangely but didn't say anything until *Mami* and Abe insisted on getting ice cream cones and I found myself alone with him.

"You ok, Ti?"

I had to stop being so fidgety or he'd know something was wrong. I nodded and gave him a hug remembering that Pop was nothing like Uncle Lou.

"Tianna, you know if something is wrong you can tell me, right?"

"Yes, but nothing's wrong, Pop."

"Ok, baby girl."

By the time *Mami* and Abe returned with our cones, all weirdness between him and I was gone. A week later my mom announced at the dinner table that she had gotten a new part-time job as a waitress at a diner a few miles down the Pike. For as long as I could remember *Mami* had been a stay-at-home wife and mom. I wondered why she'd want to work when Pop made enough money. We lived in a nice house, in a nice neighborhood. Pop took us on vacation every year. *Mami* had clothes with the price tags still on

9

them. Abe and I weren't spoiled but we had what most kids our age wanted. Why would *Mami* want to go to work when she had everything already?

Just as I had had reservations, Pop had as well. He didn't take to change well. A year or two ago *Mami* had cut off all her long dark hair and dyed it red. Pop nearly had a stroke. He didn't talk to *Mami* for the whole weekend. By Monday, he was back in the kitchen hugging her from behind and kissing her neck as she washed dishes. He even ran his fingers through her hair and laughed.

Sitting at the head of the dinner table and being true to who he was, he made his feelings known that a part-time job did not come before her duty as a wife and mother.

"Thomas Jefferson Leonard," *Mami* said her brow raised in defiance.

Abe and I looked down at our plates trying to hide our snickering.

"Now Tanya, why do you have to say all that? There is no need to use my whole name like that. And with that tone. No need at all." Pop shook his head and took a sip of his water. I would bet he was doing what he could to tame his tongue. Pop was such a chill guy you could've mistaken him for a corpse. I rarely saw him angry. But *Mami* had a way of getting under his skin like no one else could. He always teased that her passionate character both scorched and warmed him.

"Because you are acting like a caveman. I love being a wife and mother, but I need to do something that is just for me. It's only a few times a week. I have everything already taken care of and you guys won't even realize I'm gone." *Mami* picked up her fork and stuffed broccoli into her mouth before winking at Pop.

Pop cut into his chicken cutlet the least bit amused. "So, fill us in on this plan of yours."

"I'm working two dinner shifts a week and Saturday mornings. I'll make dinner early and leave it ready on the weekdays I'm at the diner. Y'all can warm it up. Saturday mornings the kids sleep in anyway, and that will give you time to play around in the garage with your toys in peace."

Pop chewed his chicken not amused by her remark. "Cute."

Mami smiled at him and didn't skip a beat continuing with her plan. "I told the manager that Sunday mornings and Wednesday evenings are off-limits, so we can still attend Sunday Service and Bible Study. Tommy, I have everything figured out. Trust me."

"Tanya, aren't you forgetting something? Who is going to be here to receive Abe off the school bus?"

"Pop, I'm seven years old, not a baby. No one has to take me off the school bus." Abe rolled his eyes and moved his broccoli around on the plate not having eaten a single bite of it.

"Abe, seven years old aside, it is required by your school that you are released to an adult. Ok, Champ?"

"I fail to understand why I know how to clean my own butt, but I'm still treated like a baby."

"That's enough Abe," Pop warned.

"But why doesn't Tianna need an adult to take her off the bus? It's not fair!"

Mami set her fork down and intertwined her hands, giving Abe the mom stare that used to freeze me in place. "Abraham Lincoln Leonard."

It took some effort, but I bit back my chuckle, not wanting to get caught in the crossfire of *Mami's* ire and Abe's tantrum. While *Mami* had inherited that loud, crazy, Latina trait, I had not. I'd learned a long time ago to make myself invisible whenever her eyes began turning green and She-Hulk would begin surfacing.

"The last time I checked there were only two parents at this table little boy. And neither one of us need to explain anything to you. Now no more backtalk, or you may not see eight years old. Got that?"

"Yes, *Mami*." It was barely above a whisper, but he'd forced it out. Abe was definitely *Mami's* child.

Pop motioned to *Mami* to calm down and not be so hard on Abe, but she just frowned her face up as if Pop had lost his mind telling her what to do. "As I was about to say," *Mami* continued. "Lou just lost his job and has been miserable. Mom called me worried that he was getting drunk every night and asked if you could find him a job."

Pop's eyes shot open to twice their normal size. "Me?"

"Don't worry. I'm not going to ask you to do that. But I figured he could fix some things around the house that you haven't gotten to yet and we can pay him a few bucks. While he's here, he can get Abe off the bus. That way we are helping him, and he is helping us. See? Everybody wins."

At the mention of my uncle's name, all humor had escaped me, replaced by crippling fear. In a flash, I was right back in my bed smelling his bad breath and praying for God to take him away. My fork crashed to the table, landing on the side of the plate breaking it. My hands were shaking so badly, I hid them under the table before sliding my chair out. "I'm sorry *Mami*. I don't know what happened. The fork slipped out of my hand by accident. I'll clean it up."

"No baby, I'll do it. I don't want you to cut yourself." She swatted me away and sent me into the kitchen for a rag and a small bag. I returned to the dining room, *Mami* now agitated.

"Tanya," Pop scratched his forehead. "Lou isn't at the top of my list of responsible adults. As a matter of fact, he actually ranks pretty low. Dead last if I'm honest."

"Tommy, don't belittle my family in front of the children. You are teaching them to disrespect their elders. Lou may not be Mr. Corporate America like you, but he knows how to fix things. Always has. It's only two days a week." *Mami* snatched the rag from me fixated on making her plan work.

With everything in me, I silently rallied behind Pop hoping he could convince her to keep everything as it was. *Mami's* hands moved quickly as she cleaned up the small shards of glass. She was pleading her case. She assured Pop that she had it all figured out and if we just worked as a team it could work. Pop refused, remaining firm on his decision. *Mami* angrily conceded and continued cleaning up in silence. She dismissed us from the table without dessert, not that any of us had the appetite for any, after all of that. I hated seeing her so disappointed but relieved that Pop had gotten his way. That was rare.

I took my glass into the kitchen and washed it along with a few dishes that were in the sink. I felt guilty about wishing against *Mami's* plan, but I couldn't lie that I was relieved. I dried my hands off and walked to the stairs ready to lose myself in my sketchpad when I heard *Mami* sniffling.

Pop heard her too. "Tanya, please baby, don't cry."

"I'm not crying," she said as she began refolding laundry that had already been folded, quickly wiping away her tears.

Pop took the towel from her hand and embraced her. "You and the kids are the most important things to me in this world. Nothing and no one come before you. I'm not going to allow anything, or anyone to bring trouble to my family. Please understand that. Now, I only wanna see tears of joy coming from those baby browns. Stop crying now."

Mami returned his embrace and sobbed on his shoulder. "I know Tommy. I know. I just really wanted something that was just for me. I love being a wife and a mom, but I'm more than that. I thought I was going to finally be able to prove that to myself. I never got to finish college like you. I have never really had a real job. I was excited about this. It's not about the pay or anything like that. I went out and found a job on my own. I was proud of myself. I can't remember the last time I've been proud of myself."

Pop wiped the tears from her eyes and smiled down at her. "You are definitely much more than that Tanya."

Pop exhaled deeply. "I'm sorry. You are right. A person's pride is important. I couldn't imagine not having a sense of pride in myself. And you should be proud of yourself. I never want to rob you of that chance. So, I think you should take the job."

Mami pulled away from him, her eyes wide and mouth gaped open. Pop smirked. "I'll have a talk with Lou about being responsible, and we can give him a chance."

"Really?" *Mami* asked Pop a smile widening on her pretty face.

"Yes, really," he mocked then laughed.

As *Mami* jumped up and down elated, I ran up the stairs to my room and crashed down onto my bed deflated. *Mami's* plan was to feel pride. Mine was to forget my shame. A shameful night I was determined to bury deep like stolen treasure, never to be found. Unfortunately, Uncle Lou found my treasure and looted it for several more years after that. And because two opposing plans can't both prosper, *Mami's* pride soared, and my hope plunged.

TWO
Bianca

My left hand was sweaty from my mom holding it so tight. I'm thirteen years old. Why does she have to hold my hand? I understand it's dark, but it felt a bit extreme and kinda embarrassing. Trying to keep up with her steps, forced me to walk faster. My mom was in a rush to get home to my dad because he was arguing about dinner not being done when he came home from work. I could hear his angry voice screaming into the phone and the next thing I know we were leaving her girlfriend, Myra's, house. I wiggled my fingers so she could release my hand or at least loosen up a bit, but it only made her grip tighter.

"Mom, you're hurting my hand. Can you please let it go? I'm not a baby."

"You're always going to be my baby. It's dark and I don't trust people, Bianca."

"We're almost home though. I can see our building from here. What could possibly happen, Mom?" I asked as I strengthened the pull, and broke free from her grasp.

"Girl, you better give me your hand. I'm not playing with you."

"Mom, you're overdoing it, dang. Can you please give me a little space? You are always crowding me. I'm right here, walking with you. You don't think holding my hand is too much?"

"I'm not going back and forth with you, Bianca. Give me your hand and shut up."

I spotted a few of the neighborhood kids hanging by the corner store alone and here my mom was trying to hold my hand. It was embarrassing. I just wanted to walk freely without feeling like I was chained down. Without thought, I ignored my mom's demands and defiantly ran into the street without looking, seeking freedom. I heard my mom call out my name.

"Bianca, no!"

I plunged ahead anyway. It all happened so fast. Lights quickly coming towards me. My mom pushing me out of the way. Me falling forward and hitting the ground. A loud crash. Voices hollering.

As I tried to clear away the fuzziness from hitting my head, I called out for my mom. She didn't respond. I forced myself up and stumbled. People around me insisted that I lay down and wait for an ambulance. Clashing voices made it hard to understand what was going on but the words, 'she looks like she's dead,' resounded in my ears with clarity.

The advice from strangers went in one ear and out the other as I fought the dizziness and got up to find my mom. The scene before me looked like one you'd see in a movie, and I had to concentrate to take it all in.

A car had crashed into a traffic light that was falling over. A crowd of people had gathered. Maybe my mom was among them. I squirmed through the crowd trying to see what everyone was staring at. I saw my mom's lifeless, bloody body laid in the middle of the street. I stumbled forward collapsing to my knees beside her.

"Mom." My voice was hoarse, and I could barely get it above a whisper. I touched her ivory hand to get a reaction from her. "Mommy, wake up." Still, she did not respond. Tears starting rushing down my face before I could even grasp what was happening. I began to shake her and cried out to her desperately. "Mom! Mom! Wake Up! Please wake up!"

I gasped when I noticed the pool of blood around her head. Her naturally blonde hair was soaked with it. I felt my stomach convulse. I turned to the side and vomited before my body become weak underneath me. I fell sideways into my vomit and landed beside her, darkness taking me under as I stared into her vacant hazel eyes.

I woke up to a horrible headache. My dad was sitting next to me, and I recognized I wasn't home. There were large windows and white walls everywhere. The accident rushed to the forefront of my mind as I tried to sit up.

"Dad, where's Mom? I need to apologize for running away from her."

My dad raced over to my bedside and said, "Bianca, calm down."

"I am calm. I just need to talk to Mom. Where is she?" I asked anxiously.

His eyes got watery, and he hesitated before he spoke. "Baby, your mom didn't make it." He collapsed into the chair beside my bed.

"What do you mean she didn't make it?"

"She's gone," he replied.

"No, she can't be gone! Dad, please tell me it's not true."

"I would never lie about something like that." He brought his hand to his eyes and rubbed. He looked tired and stressed.

"Dad, I have to apologize for running away from her?"

He set his hand down and exhaled as if he was half-listening to my ranting. "What happened, Bianca?"

I began to cry, "She was holding my hand so tight, and I wanted her to let go but she wouldn't. I ran off and the next thing I know Mom's gone and it's my fault."

He reached for my hand and held it. "No, you can't do that. You can't blame yourself. This was a terrible accident."

"If I didn't run away from her dad, she would still be here. She pushed me and saved my life and gave up hers."

"Bianca, stop. Don't do this. I won't let you. It's devastating enough to know your mother is gone. I refuse to listen to you blame yourself."

I stopped talking. My words were only adding to the hurt. I felt an excruciating pain that I had never experienced before. My heart felt like it had shattered into a million pieces inside my chest. My grief was so profound my body physically ached. I could see the pain on my dad's face, and it doubled my own. The traumatic loss of my mom and now the guilt for my dad's hurt was eating me alive.

It took weeks before I was ready to go back to school. I was hoping the loss of my mom would make the students ease up on the biracial jokes they'd often hurl at me. Oreo in particular. I suppose they thought that was clever because my mom was white, and my dad was black. I hated hearing such ignorance from people who had no clue who I was. It was fun for them but agony for me. I wasn't the same girl and definitely not in the mood to tolerate the ignorant jokes of my peers.

My dad started drinking almost every day after we left the hospital. His wife, and high school sweetheart, was gone. They'd been together so long he didn't know how to function without her. He didn't know how to cook so we'd eat at the pool hall a lot. He'd drink and play pool as I sat at a table doing homework. Then I started studying him instead of my school subjects. My dad was really good. Running men off the table like he was born to play. I watched him so much, I learned to play myself.

Months passed before I started grief counseling sessions. I knew counseling would get me to admit the part I played in my mother's death all over again, so I avoided it. Once I started failing all my classes, I had no choice but to seek help. My counselor, Ms. Mason, was very patient with me. There would be times when I just sat in silence for the entire hour of my session. I was so afraid to talk. I didn't want to be judged by her. One day, Ms. Mason explained to me that it wasn't her job to judge, only to listen and help me through my pain.

It wasn't long after that I began to slowly open myself up to her. She made me comfortable enough to talk to her and release the guilt that I was struggling with. Although it didn't stop the pain, I learned that it would be something that I had to adapt to as I moved forward in my life. Ms. Mason's main intention was to help me live my life without letting my loss paralyze my dreams, hopes, and goals.

My fourteenth birthday was a week away and I sunk into a depression. Remembering the plans my mom and I talked about to go get manicures and pedicures and go on a lunch date, broke me.

'Just you and me Bi-Bi," she'd said. 'A girls spa day.' The memory overwhelmed me. I missed her so much.

I would often get angry at my dad for drinking but now I understood. He was always saying how much he missed her. Drinking was his escape into another world. It was how he'd drown out the pain of missing someone who was never coming back.

I envied him. He had a way to forget. I wished I could create my own escape from the agony of missing the woman who gave me life. I would give anything to change running away from her, into running to her. A regret I would carry with me for the rest of my life.

I reverted to closing myself off from the path of healing and stopped counseling. Everything Ms. Mason had poured, and I learned, I soon forgot. I coped in my own way. Isolation and shooting pool became my therapy and I eventually mastered both without apology.

THREE
Justin

I laughed as I bounced the basketball between my legs keeping it out of Dad's reach. He swiped at it and missed. Again. At this point, I was just taunting him because I could. He stood upright, placing his hands on his sides, trying to catch his breath. He was all kinds of tired, but the old man was as stubborn as the day was long. At least, that's what my grandma used to say about him. He refused to quit. And so, did I. Go hard. Do right. Be better than yesterday. Never quit. That's what he'd been drilling in my head for as long as I could remember. About anything and everything in life.

So, I dribbled. And dribbled some more. Just as I knew he would, he tried to catch me off guard coming at me full force. I hit him with an Allen Iverson crossover breaking his ankles before taking it to the netless hoop and dunked it.

"Ohhhhh!" I gloated as I grabbed the ball and tucked it under my arm walking over to him. "That's game old man."

Dad was sitting on the ground with his arms resting on his raised knees. He looked at me as if he wanted to kick my ass, before his face split with a grin so wide I could damn near see every natural, pearly white tooth in his mouth. The smile that won Mama over no doubt. Grandma always said strong bones and teeth were a trait inherited from her side of the family, her dentures aside.

"The student becomes the master," Dad said extending an arm toward me. I helped him to his feet, laughing as he groaned all the way up. "Your old man's bones ain't what they used to be."

"I think Grandma was wrong and you're your father's son. I hear your bones creaking Old Man."

Dad chuckled. "Boy, if Mama were still walking this earth and heard you say that she'd smack you upside your head. Twice." He let out another hearty laugh. "That woman was a tyrant. God bless her soul."

"Nah. Grandma loved me too much."

"I may be the one with old bones, but obviously you're the one with memory loss. You don't remember that time she spanked you good for sticking your finger in all of her pies?" The smirk on his face reminded me of my little brother, Jordi. While I looked more like Mom, there was no denying Jordi was my father's son. From his bright white smile down to his bony legs and distinctive stride.

"Yeah, well after she spanked me, she snuck me into your old bedroom, and we ate an entire pie. She swore me to secrecy. I don't think I ever heard her laugh as much as I did that day. She tore that pie up."

The look of shock on Dad's face was hilarious. "Get outta town! That woman was full of surprises. Didn't even let me taste a single one of those pies neither." He shook his head disappointed over pies from over a decade ago.

"It was go-oo-od!" I cracked up, then ran off before he knocked me upside my head. I got to the building before he did and bounced the basketball against the wall waiting for him to catch up. He stopped to talk to Mr. Johnson from the tenth floor. And when Mrs. Diaz from the seventh floor walked past carrying some bags to her car, Dad waved goodbye to Mr. Johnson and hurried over to Mrs. Diaz to help her. A car rode past and honked and Dad waved. I had no idea who that was, but that was the norm with my dad. Everybody that knew him, loved and respected him. He'd worked for the Housing Authority since before I was born so he pretty much knew everybody in these parts.

He finally made it to the building and kicked me in my backside. "Boy, I know you saw Mrs. Diaz. Next time you help her, you hear me. No son of mine will behave like a neanderthal. My daddy didn't raise me that way and your Mama and I surely taught you better. Women are God's gift to this world. Where would I be without your mom?" He unlocked the door to the building and checked our mailbox in the lobby.

"I'm sorry Dad." I'd never thought about it much, but Dad was always opening doors for Mom. Carrying her bags. Grabbing stuff from the top shelf and kissing her on the cheek when she thanked him for the helping hand. He even brushed her hair for a while after she had sprained her wrist. He never let her intentionally struggle. He truly cared for her and about her.

"It won't happen again," I promised.

"I know son. Now when you get inside, go wash up for dinner. You smell like the dumpster outside with a side of onions. Damn!" He snatched the basketball from me and bounced it off my head, that smirk making a return.

I rubbed my head and stepped into the elevator avoiding the fresh puddle of urine in the corner. Mrs. Walker called out to hold the elevator. Dad quickly held it open and waited for her to enter before he did.

"How are you, Mrs. Walker?" I asked.

My dad winked at me and nodded approvingly. That was all it took for our elderly neighbor to let loose. She complained about the new rowdy neighbors that blasted their Spanish music too late at night and too damn early in the morning. The neighbors on the other side, never said hello. Damn foreigners. The tenants above her must run a zoo cause her ceiling was going to cave in from all the damn jumping. Bunch of unruly monkeys. On and on she went. Not that she cared if I was listening to her rant or not. She hadn't taken a pause long enough for me to respond had I wanted to. I imagined she would've complained to the elevator walls had no one else been in here with her.

Pressing the button to the eleventh floor I stepped back avoiding the puddle and remained quiet minding my manners and letting her rant. Before the elevator door slid completely closed, a quick hand waved in triggering the door to slide back open. In stepped a young man that I'd never seen before. My age. Maybe a year or two older. I had lived in this neighborhood all my life and thought I'd known just about everyone around here, even if just by recognition. New faces were a rare occurrence and not necessarily welcomed. Northside had its unspoken rules. Certain things just were. You didn't question it. You just went with the flow and kept it moving.

Growing up in the hood taught us to always be on guard around strangers and now was no different. I observed the guy standing in front of me with caution. I looked over at Dad who shook his head at me, raising a hand at me to be at ease. Where I was cautious, Dad was gracious.

The elevator began to rise when the stranger pressed the button for the fifth floor, leaving a streak of blood on it. He didn't seem to care. Only Mrs. Walker's complaining chatter filled the cabin. Dad must have noticed the streak too. He slid in between me and the stranger pushing me back against the wall, my Jordan's now standing in pee.

"Young man," Dad said to the stranger. "You seem to be bleeding. Are you ok? Do I need to call an ambulance?"

Silent and foreboding he continued to face the elevator door, not acknowledging Dad at all. The elevator slowed then stopped. As the door began to creep open, the man finally removed his hand from his pocket and opened a switchblade in one quick motion.

Mrs. Walker gasped then began hollering in a panic. Still, the young man didn't so much as flinch. He exited the elevator and looked down the hall in both directions.

Dad told Mrs. Walker to calm down and that everything would be alright. "Son, go down to Darrel's and call the police."

"Wait, Dad. What are you going to do?"

"There's no time for questions, Justin. Go do as I said, now. Hurry."

I nodded and watched Dad turn right as I turned left. I ran to Darrel's and pounded on the door. Then pounded again. His mother thrust the door open visibly upset.

"Why the hell you banging on my door like that? Thought you was the damn po-lice banging like that. Darrel ain't here."

"Mrs. Thompson, I'm sorry. I'm not looking for Darrel, I need to use your phone. It's an emergency."

"What emergency?" She asked raising an eyebrow not moved by my words.

"There's someone with a knife and my dad told me to come here and call the police."

Ms. Thompson sobered her temper quickly. "Your dad?" She looked past me down the hall then moved aside to let me in. "Alright. Come in. Come in. Phone's in the kitchen." Ms. Thompson had left the door open and had gone down the hall to investigate. Or maybe just be nosey.

I quickly called 911 and told them what I'd witnessed and that my dad had told me to call so they wouldn't think I was prank calling. The operator didn't seem to care and said she'd dispatch someone over. I hung up and ran out of Darrel's apartment.

When I got to the other side, there were a few residents in the hall crowding the door to apartment 509. I heard the scuffle within, sounding as if the furniture were being thrown against the wall. I searched for my dad amongst the neighbor's chattering and waiting outside the door but didn't see him.

"Ms. Thompson, have you seen my dad?"

"No, baby. He wasn't here when I walked down but someone said he was inside."

"Inside?" Inside the apartment that sounded like a warzone? I pushed my way through the crowd attempting to go inside, but Leroy held me back.

"I can't let you go in there, Justin."

"Move. My dad's in there!" I shoved Leroy but he'd barely moved. A stint in prison had him built like a bodybuilder who'd popped steroids like candy.

"He's the one who told me not to let you in."

"Well, then you go in! Damn! You can't just leave my dad like that! That kid had a knife and who knows what else!"

Leroy looked at me and I could see the anguish in his eyes before they hardened like steel. "I can't do that either. I'm not going back to jail. Not for you and not for nobody. But I do respect your dad, so I'll do what he asked. He said for you to stay out here, so you gonna stay out here. Now, don't make me knock you flat on your ass boy?"

I yelled and punched the wall. I felt the pain shoot up my hand for an instant, but I didn't care. I paced the hall until there was just silence. And then just more silence. "Come on Leroy! He could be dead in there!" I yelled before the door creaked open.

My dad walked out hunched over, looking exhausted. "Someone call an ambulance. Someone is bleeding heavily in there and the other is knocked out cold. I'm not sure if he's alive or not."

"Dad! Are you ok?" I put his arm around my shoulder and helped him walk forward and away from the crowd that was too busy looking into the apartment but not stepping inside.

He nodded. "Go tell your mother I'm going to the hospital. Tell her not to worry. Just tell her to meet me there. She knows how much I hate doctors." He removed his arm from around me and winced.

"Dad, are you sure you're ok?"

He put his big palm to my face with the same smirk and tapped my face a few times. "You just worry about your mom, you hear me?"

"Of course, Dad. I'll go with her to the ER, so she won't worry."

"Now that's the young man I raised." He coughed and continued holding his stomach, a dark stain beginning to show on his tee-shirt.

"Dad? Your shirt!" I began to panic.

He snatched me by my shirt and pulled me closer. "You focus on your Momma, Justin. Do you hear me? A man's word is his honor and his integrity. I'm trusting you with her." It was rare the time Dad ever got physical. He had earned my respect and obedience without having to ever physically discipline me. A slap to the head and kick to the butt was always done in love and fun. But right now, I knew he wasn't kidding.

25

"Ok, Dad." I gulped the fear lodged in my throat and nodded quickly.

He released me and smoothed out my shirt. "You're a good son Justin. Now, go on Son."

Not bothering to wait for the elevator I ran as fast as I could up the stairs and into our apartment. Mom was serving dinner and as soon as she saw me started complaining we were late and to go wash up. I was so out of breath it took a full minute before I could tell her about Dad. She quickly took off her apron and grabbed her purse.

She yelled for Jordi to wait at Aunt Tee-Tees down the hall until she came back to get him. Jordi opened his door, his game controller in his hand. "What about dinner?" He whined.

"Boy, I said go. I don't have time for this."

I snatched Jordi by his collar, my hand stinging a bit, and told him to stop giving Mom a hard time. I told him there was an emergency but didn't mention Dad. Jordi huffed and did as told, snatching a drumstick from the table before walking down the hall.

When we got to the emergency room, my mom inquired about Dad from the woman at the reception desk.

She was polite and calm. "What is his name?"

"Michael Earl Saunders."

She tapped into her computer then looked at her ringing phone. She raised a finger signaling for us to wait a moment while she took the call.

I wanted to snatch the phone from her hand but refrained. Apparently, she was one of those 'gifts' dad mentioned, and I ought a remember that and behave accordingly. She hung up and looked up at my mom.

"That was actually referring to your husband. He's been taken into emergency surgery." She handed us two passes and gave us directions to a waiting room on another floor where the doctor would come out and talk to us. My mom turned to me in a panic and began to berate me with questions. I answered her as best I could before my hand began to throb.

Mom noticed me wincing and took a look at my hand. "Why is your hand swollen?"

"I punched the wall when they wouldn't let me in to help Dad."

She marched me back down the ER reception desk and signed me in to be seen. She'd told them that Dad was also in surgery and to please come and search for her down here to update us.

It took forever before I was taken to the back to be examined. They needed to perform an X-Ray. Mom wanted to go check in on Dad while I was being X-Rayed but didn't want to leave me alone. I insisted I'd be ok and practically pushed her out the door. I could see how worried she was and wanted her to find a measure of relief.

Turned out I'd sprained my hand, but nothing was broken. They'd splinted it and gave me care instructions and Mom still hadn't returned. I was released and headed straight back to the surgical waiting room to find her, but she wasn't there. I asked the woman sitting at the computer and she pointed me down the hall. I walked around the corner and saw my mom sitting on the floor her head between her knees sobbing.

The air rushed out of my lungs. I couldn't move. I didn't want to know why she was sitting on a hospital floor crying. She rested her head back against the wall and turned in my direction. When she noticed me standing there, she shook her head side to side and let out a wail that haunted me for years. I fell to my knees knowing I'd never talk to my father again.

FOUR
Tianna

I hurried out of the shower, my hands shaking furiously as I dried myself off. I quickly slipped into my pajamas, gathered the blood-stained sheets, and shoved them into the black trash bag. Looking around, I found my panties and shoved them in the bag too. I couldn't chance leaving any evidence behind. I stuffed the bag under my bed until trash day and then I'd slip it in with the other trash. I clumsily redressed my bed with fresh linens. I heard Pop's car pull into the driveway, him and *Mami* just arriving home from bible study. The sound of the car door closing lit a fire in me to get the deed done fast; didn't matter if it was done right.

Turning off the light, I hopped into bed pretending to be asleep, trying hard to steady my labored breathing from all my running around. Not a full five minutes passed before I heard a knock on my bedroom door. I didn't respond but heard my door creak open anyway. If *Mami* was anything, she was predictably consistent. I was fifteen, and she still checked in on me every night before she went to bed. She walked over and felt my forehead. Presumably checking for a fever. I'd stayed home from Bible Study not feeling well. She mumbled that I was clammy rather than hot and assumed that the fever broke. If she'd known it was my hymen instead, her hand would be around my neck rather than on my forehead.

After uttering her nightly prayer of protection and blessings over me, *Mami* left as fast as she'd come. For the millionth time, I couldn't help but wonder if her nightly ritual was pointless. It didn't work when I was ten and it surely wasn't working now.

At the sound of the door softly clicking closed, I released the breath I hadn't realized I'd been holding. My heart was pounding so hard, how *Mami* hadn't heard it was beyond me. I turned and faced my window and finally let the tears fall. Too ashamed to pray, I laid in silence vowing to never let myself get caught up in such an intimate situation again.

Although I had experienced many sexual encounters, this was the first time I'd participated willingly and actually lost my virginity. The treasure I had been taught to save and share only with my husband had been gifted to Bryson Long instead. He told me he loved me. I'd wanted to believe him but deep down I knew it was said in the heat of the moment. Trying to assuage my guilt I tried convincing myself that maybe Bryson and I could end up as one of those couples that started as teens and stayed together until they were old and gray. God would forgive me if I'd lost my virginity to my future husband, wouldn't He?

My tears flowed harder at the disillusion. I knew good and well that loves like that didn't exist anymore. *Mami* had married the last good man on earth. And if I were honest with myself, even if Bryson did love me, I didn't love him. Yeah, he was all that and a bag of chips. I couldn't lie about that. All the girls in school wanted to get with him but he'd chosen me. It felt good to be wanted. Bryson would walk me to class and home after school. He was cool to hang with. He knew how to make me laugh and smile. I liked him. But that couldn't be what love was. It had to be bigger than that.

Not bothering to wipe my tears, I let them soak my pillow. After a while, the tears had ceased but my guilt continued fiercely. Memories of Uncle Lou flashed in my head like a channel being switched every second, each recollection making me sick to my stomach. Would it ever go away? I doubted it. For years I'd worn shame like a shiny badge. Over time it had only seemed to blaze brighter. I longed for the day I could extinguish its burn. The soreness between my legs reminded me that today wasn't that day. The thought brought a fresh wave of uninterrupted tears.

"I'm sorry, God." My soul wanted to shout out the repentance, but it escaped as only a whisper. "Forgive me."

Easter Sunday always brought new faces and the regular irregular churchgoers to church. Amidst the mass of people, I was surprised to see Bryson's. I hadn't seen him in school for a few days and when I had paged him, he'd never called. I figured his beeper was either broken or out of service because the alternative was that he was avoiding me, and I refused to believe that. Sure, he didn't truly love me, but we did like each other. Of that, I would bet my virginity if I'd still had it.

I weaved my way through the crowd to go over and say hello. Before I reached him, he pulled his beeper from his belt and checked it. I could see it blinking so vividly it stopped me as if I'd crashed into an invisible wall. The smile on his face made me want to slip through the floor and hide in the darkness. There was no mistaking that kind of smile. That kind that makes the butterflies in your stomach flutter and your face blush.

No. I wasn't going to assume. There was a good explanation why I hadn't seen or heard from him since the night he told me he loved me and accepted my virginity. I took a step, and then another, forcing my feet to be courageous first. After I tapped him on the shoulder, I ignored how his radiant smile diminished when he turned and faced me.

"Hey."

"Tianna. Hey." Bryson looked around baffled. "What are you doing here?"

"This is my church."

He nodded. "Right. You are a church girl. I forgot."

I smiled and tried not to read too much into his awkwardness. "I haven't seen you around school. Have you been sick or something?"

"No. I've been at school." He didn't look me in the face and every second that passed made me regret walking over to him.

He didn't elaborate and I couldn't hide my surprise or disappointment. "Oh. Ok. Well, I paged you. Did you get it?"

Bryson looked at his shoes, then back at me, red-faced. "Tianna, listen. I think you're cool and all, but I have a girlfriend. I don't think she'd like me calling you or hanging out with you."

"A girlfriend?" I replayed my question in my own head. I perused my memory quickly looking for a sign I may have missed or a conversation that I may have forgotten that would make this revelation make sense. But I found none. I got stuck on 'I love you' and 'trust me' right before he devirginized me. A girlfriend was never mentioned.

"Yeah. Alexis."

He had the nerve to say it as if it were public knowledge or something and I was an idiot for not being in the know. Truth was he'd never once mentioned Alexis, Mercedes, BMW, or a girlfriend. Not when he kissed me between classes. Not when he dropped me off at my doorstep. And certainly not when he came to my house and began to take my clothes off.

"I don't know an Alexis." For the life of me, I don't know what possessed me to stand there and say something so stupid. Of everything I could have said, should have said, that had to be the dumbest. As soon as it left my mouth, I wanted to reel it back in like a fish caught on a hook. And then it got worse.

Lexy Carstarphen sidled up beside Bryson, pecking him on the cheek. "Hey, Babe. Took you long enough. I paged you wondering where you were."

Lexy. Alexis. I stood corrected. Apparently, I absolutely knew an Alexis. The Pastor's niece, he'd adopted a year ago along with her little brother. If kindness and purity were a person, Lexy Carstarphen would be it.

31

"Happy Easter Christianna." She greeted me with a warm hug. "I didn't know you two knew each other."

"We go to school together," Bryson said quickly. He narrowed his eyes at me in warning.

Did he think I was going to admit to the Pastor's beloved saintly niece that I had lost my virginity to her boyfriend? That I would publicly embarrass myself even more, right there in the church lobby on Easter Sunday?

"What a small world," Lexy said, her smile beaming. Or maybe it was her halo.

I wanted to hate her but what for? She hadn't done anything wrong. In fact, I had always admired her. Her sweetness could frost cinnamon rolls. I wondered what it must be like to be so wholesome and pure. Untainted.

Standing in front of them both, I could guarantee she hadn't let Bryson get past second base, and yet he had still chosen her. No sex required. It made me feel that much more shameful and stupid.

"Yep. Definitely a small world." I returned her smile and excused myself. "I need to get into my choir robe before service starts. Have a Happy Easter."

"You too! And hug Abe for me. He is so adorable. And funny," she chuckled before giving her full attention to her cheating boyfriend, as I waved and walked away.

I battled between being angry and sad. I felt stupid. I felt cheated. As if I had been robbed of something that was meant to be precious. But who was I kidding? I was to blame more than Bryson. Yeah, he was a liar and a cheater, but he hadn't forced me to have sex with him. I freely gave it. When he called me to ask what I was doing, I didn't have to accept his suggestion to come over. I didn't have to invite him up to my bedroom. And I certainly didn't need to let him take it beyond kissing.

I ran to the women's restroom in the back of the church where the classrooms were and set my tears free for a few minutes before I channeled the version of Tianna that learned to not feel anything. The Tianna that taught herself to be numb when Uncle Lou was over and *Mami* was at work and Pop wasn't home yet. The Tianna that ignored the whispers in my soul that I was ugly, disgraceful, and trifling. I let the Tianna that let her heart go cold, take over. She was my protector.

I marched myself onto the altar and sang melodically. I clapped energetically. I swayed from side to side rhythmically. When the choir director motioned for the choir to go louder and longer, I raised my voice loudly. When the Pastor prompted us to greet our neighbors, I did so kindly. During prayer, I bowed my head reverently. I did everything required, effortlessly. Thoroughly. Convincingly.

And I did every bit of it emotionlessly.

A few weeks later, I arrived at youth bible study a few minutes late. Now that *Mami* had begun working full-time as a shift supervisor at a restaurant near the mall, she would sometimes get stuck later than she was scheduled. Pop never said a word in front of us, but they'd had plenty of private arguments. *Mami* wasn't exactly the quiet type, so I'd only ever hear her side of the argument and it was always the same. She was sorry she was late but that was her job, and there was nothing she could do about it.

Class had already begun when Abe and I walked in. I sat in the back row not wanting to disrupt the class. Abe had no issue whatsoever drawing attention to himself as he uttered 'excuse me' a dozen times, apologizing for putting his butt in people's faces as he squeezed into the row where his friends sat. The disgruntled look on their faces as he passed them by made me laugh to myself. That boy was something else.

Turning to give my attention to the teacher, I made eye contact with Lexy. I waved. She did not. She pretended she hadn't seen me and quickly turned away. I found it strange as she had always been bubbly and kind. After service, some refreshments were served as always and everyone was either chatting with their friends or playing a game on the recreational side of the youth chapel.

Abe walked over to me stuffing the rest of a chocolate doughnut in his mouth. "Ti. Something's going on. I don't know what, but Melvin said some rumors are going around about you and asked me what was going on. Said his sister was pissed."

"Melvin, Lexy's brother? And don't say 'pissed' in church."

"Whatever. And yeah, her brother. She snapped at him when he went to grab a second doughnut and told him to get lost. He was so mad. Said she'd been acting like a b–"

"Watch your mouth baby brother," I interjected.

"Brat," he finished. "Stop doing that? You're worse than Tanya. At least with her I actually do something wrong before she flips out."

"You know if *Mami* ever heard you call her Tanya, she'd flip you?" I teased.

"Whatever. Anyway, Melvin said Lexy has been real crabby since she broke up with her boyfriend and that it had something to do with you."

A part of me began to panic. The other part of me didn't care if Bryson fell off the face of the earth. Tianna, the protector, took over and kicked fear out of my system. Feeling nothing was better than feeling everything. "Let's go. Pop and *Mami* are probably waiting for us."

I opened the door to exit the youth chapel and bumped directly into Lexy. I excused myself and stepped around her.

"You can play innocent Christianna, but we both know you are far from it," she said so only I could hear. "What's done in secret always comes to light. You best believe that."

I said nothing and walked away. I could feel a battle waging within me. Tianna, the protector, and Tianna with the big heart warred. As much as I tried to tune Lexy out, her words cut like a knife. I wanted to not care, but my heart still bled. Not for Bryson. Not even really for myself. I didn't care about Bryson's reputation or what was good for him. I didn't even really care for myself. But I did care that Lexy was the one unintentionally hurt. I hadn't been the one who had put her in harm's way, but it was still my decision that brought her pain.

Tianna, the protector could swing a sword and cut down the Uncle Lou's and Bryson's of my life, but she waved a white flag to the Lexy's of the world. The innocent victims of sick, cheating, lying and dishonorable people were not her enemy.

Yeah, I could've explained to Lexy that I didn't know that she and Bryson were together. Yeah, I could've explained that he told me he loved me and that he'd lied to me too. I could've explained I lost my virginity to him and that I wasn't some fast girl that was trying to steal him away. But none of it would have mattered. She had already tried and convicted me, and I was guilty in her eyes. So, I'd have to live with reaping what I had sown, no matter how unfair it seemed. I had learned a long time ago that innocent people didn't live life unscathed and when trouble came knocking on their door, justice sided on what appeared true, not always what actually was.

Pop and *Mami* were waiting for us in the car. I could tell they had been arguing again. *Mami* stared out the window, not saying a word. Pop did all the talking asking us about class and what we'd learned. Abe went on and on about the doughnuts served after class. The fact that Pop didn't redirect Abe about actual bible study and let him complain about not enough doughnuts, meant he was pretending to listen, even throwing in a mumbling sound here and there.

When we got home, Pop and *Mami* went their separate ways, not saying a word to each other. Abe didn't seem to notice but I could feel the tension. I hated seeing my parents mad at each other. Their love for each other was a lifeline for me. Proof that I could one day find someone to love like that and would love me back the same way. But I supposed marriage wasn't perfect and couples fought.

It took a few days but hearing *Mami* giggling in the kitchen and Pop standing behind her kissing her neck was gross, but I'd take gross over separation any day of the week.

FIVE
Bianca

My adrenaline rushed as I ran home enraged, blood pouring from my nose. The four girls chasing me finally stopped and ran off in another direction. When I reached my apartment building, I zoomed through the doors, passed the elevators, and into the hallway that led to the stairwell. I needed to catch my breath. I lifted the bottom of my black t-shirt and wiped the evidence of a fight still dripping from my nose.

I jetted up the steps until I reached my floor. I was still trying to figure out why I'd gotten jumped. The laughter and taunting as those bitches pounded on me played on repeat in my mind. I was angry and wanted to call my girls Darcy and Vy so we could find them and square up. I opened the stairwell door onto the fifth floor to the daily cacophony of screams and cussing from the young couple who lived a few doors down. I'd learned to tune it out a long time ago, otherwise, they'd a drove me crazy.

I approached my front door cautiously, unlocking it and entering quietly. I tip-toed inside so my father wouldn't hear me. His snores eased me. I wasn't surprised when I peeked into the living room and saw him passed out drunk in his chair, several beer cans scattered on the floor. I bolted to my bedroom and locked the door.

I was pissed as I paced back and forth talking to myself and vowing revenge on every single one of them punk asses. I gave it to them, though. They fucking got me real good. But only 'cause it was four of them and only one of me. Best believe had it been a one-on-

one, I woulda beat a ho down. There was no use in being mad about what I couldn't change.

After I showered, I managed to calm down. I pulled out my journal to write. It was how I released everything I was feeling without interruption or judgment. More times than I could count, I wrote about the car accident that took my mom's life. Most times I wondered if death hadn't stopped with hers. Dad had become a full-blown alcoholic and practically a stranger to me. He was rarely sober enough to leave the sofa for more than enough time than it took to go to the liquor store so he could feed his addiction. I can't remember the last time we laughed together or had a meaningful conversation. I was basically raising myself. He was physically present but that did nothing to mollify the idea that I was in the world all alone.

The next morning, I left the apartment before my dad could see my battle scars. I met up with Darcy and Viola at Viola's house after her mom left for work. We planned to play hooky from school for the day and chill in the house. As soon as I walked in, they noticed the bruising on my face.

Darcy put her hand up to stop me. "Whoa. What hell happened to your face?"

I moved her hand aside and walked in not wanting to make a big deal about it. "I got jumped by four girls last night while I was walking home from the store."

Viola's quick temper erupted. "What! Why didn't you call us?"

"Because I handled it. I'm bruised, but I'm aiight. Two of them left probably needing some stitches over their eyes."

"Yo! I wanna know who the hell jumped you. For real. And for what though?" Darcy asked.

"Just because they felt like it. I was minding my business. Y'all already know how I am." I sat on the edge of the couch with my legs spread apart like a dude would.

"That's exactly why I'm pissed." Vy kicked my feet together, always reminding me that I was still a girl no matter how much of a tomboy I was. "Nah, we gonna find them."

I rolled my eyes and closed my legs. "I ain't pressed no more. I gave them a good fight all by myself."

"That's not the point dammit! They need to know they can't be just jumping people because they feel like it." Vy, the ghetto ass mother-hen.

"They gonna get it. They fucked wit' the wrong one this time." Darcy high-fived Vy before she took a blunt out of her backpack and lit it.

I wish I would have lied about the bruise because I didn't want any more trouble. I had to convince them not to leave the house, wait it out, and let me see if I could find more information so we wouldn't be roaming the neighborhood looking crazy. They calmed down and agreed that being strategic was better than being impulsive.

Later that day, when I got home, my dad was sitting in the living room guzzling down a beer. I could tell he was drunk. His speech was slurred when he finally caught his breath and spoke to me. One side of me was so angry at him for turning into an alcoholic, but the other side of me felt bad for him.

I walked into the kitchen to get a bowl of cereal and realized there was no milk. I dashed to the first-floor *bodega* of our apartment building. As I entered the store, I heard the cashier, Pedro, telling a customer that his sister Milly was in the hospital with a serious brain injury. Milly was older than me by a few years, but she was my home skillet, so that caught my attention. I slowed my pace a little so I could hear what happened to her. Pedro got emotional and began talking in Spanish. I didn't know a lick of Spanish except for some cuss words Milly had taught me a few years ago when she was outside blunted out her mind. So much for being nosey. As I reached the counter with my gallon of milk, a few boys walked in. I recognized two of them from my building and school. They were a year or two older than me.

"Hey, Pedro, what's up with your sister, Homie? How is she? Did they find the girls who did that to her?" One of the boys I recognized asked him as he paid for his *empanada*.

"Someone told me it was a *muchacha* her name Angelica, but I no know." Pedro threw his hands up giving up on trying to explain in his broken English.

"Yo! I heard that name too. If it's the same girl, she down with this girl posse. It's like four or five of them. Supposedly that's Robin's crew. They jumped some girl out East, around the corner from me," the Spanish kid added.

The more I listened the more it piqued my curiosity. A girl posse jumping girls? Nah. That was too familiar to be a coincidence.

"I'm sorry about your sister, Pedro," I chimed in while handing him my five-dollar bill.

"Hey Bianca," one of the boys said.

"Hey," I paused trying to remember his name, "Justin."

He laughed and nodded. "Yeah, Justin. "And this is Manny and Corey."

I didn't respond. What was I supposed to say? I shoved my balled-up fist through the handles of the plastic bag and thanked Pedro.

"You want me to carry that milk for you?" Justin asked.

"I got it. Thanks for asking though."

"You sure? I'll walk with you to your door. It's not a problem."

It felt like a million eyes were on me waiting to see what I'd say or do in response. I started feeling a bit of anxiety coming on. Justin grabbed my bag, then grabbed my hand and said, "Come on."

It caught me off guard, but I didn't reject him. I don't know why but I went with it and let him walk me to my door. We walked in silence until we reached the elevators.

"Don't think I'm givin' you some just because you carried my milk. Aiight? You can get ta steppin'."

"Well dang! How you gonna say that?"

"I just need you to know, so you won't be expectin' nothin' from me."

"Why can't I just be nice to you because I like you?" Justin asked as the elevator doors opened.

"Like me?"

"Yeah, girl. I like you." Justin stepped inside the elevator and held the door to keep it from closing. "Come on. Get in."

My heart began to race, not knowing what to say. His confession was so unexpected, so rather than say something wrong, I didn't say anything at all.

"Are you okay?" he asked as he pushed the button to the fifth floor.

"Yeah, but I didn't tell you what floor I live on. How did you know that?"

"I've been living here just as long as you Bianca. Plus, I said I like you, so that means knowing a few things about you," Justin laughed.

"Are you like, stalkin' me?"

"Stalking you? For real?"

"Yes, I'm for real."

"It ain't that serious. I'm not a stalker."

When the elevator reached my floor, I wanted to jet at top speed. All of it was so awkward, and I still didn't know what to say. I reached for the bag, but Justin pulled it back away from me. "I'm going to walk you to your door. You don't have to be that way with me."

"Like what?"

"You seem nervous."

"Just not used to being speechless like this."

"Nobody ever told you they liked you before?"

"Well yeah but more so in passin'. Guys riding by in a car honking or grabbing my hand when I walk to the corner store. Guys I don't know but I just keep walkin' and mind my business."

"Oh, so now you have nowhere to run. That's good. I don't want you to run. I've been waiting for a long time to try and kick it to you. Today seemed like the perfect day."

"For real?"

"Do I look like I'm joking?"

"Um, no. I don't know what to say. I've never actually talked to a boy on that level."

"For real? Aiight then. No pressure."

We reached my front door, and I felt the perspiration on my forehead, my anxiety had elevated so high. "Thank you for carryin' my milk and walkin' me to my door. That was nice of you."

"Any time," he said as he gave me the bag. "Maybe we can hang out sometime."

"Well, I guess that would okay." I shrugged not really caring one way or the other.

"That's way better than a no."

"You're persistent. What if I would've said no?"

"Sometimes no means you have to work harder for a yes. I don't give up if it's something I want."

"I'm not a somethin',"

"Okay, dang." Justin laughed and rubbed his head. "You're right. You're not a something but a someone. A little feisty someone."

"Just lettin' you know I'm no one's somethin' or thing."

"It wasn't trying to offend you. My apologies."

"Ok. No worries and thanks again," I said as I turned the doorknob.

"You're welcome beautiful." Justin smiled and took a few steps backward before he turned around and left.

I shut the door and wiped my forehead relieved that was over. Justin had seen right past my rough girl image and saw up close and personal my nervousness. It was completely embarrassing. I lost my appetite and forgot all about the cereal. I leaned against the door and closed my eyes trying not to panic. I wondered if he'd tell everyone how I was sweating and that I'm not as tough as I make myself seem. The last thing I needed was more people busting on me.

After I put the milk in the fridge, I went to my room and mentally beat myself up for showing weakness that would leave him to question my strength. I spent the rest of my Friday evening in my room wallowing in self-blame and what-ifs.

The following morning when I woke up, I decided to take the bus to Philly and roam the Gallery for a little while. A change in scenery was exactly what I needed. As the bus pulled up, I heard a woman screaming to hold the bus while running down the street. I stepped onto the bus and paid my fare. "There is a woman running for the bus, asking you to wait for her," I said to the bus driver.

She tilted her head down and looked over her glasses as she chewed her gum. "She better hurry up. I gots to stay on schedule."

I walked to my seat just as the women boarded. She was breathing heavily from running and frantic trying to get out what she was trying to say between breaths. "Pull off, please! A man is chasing me!"

"A man is chasing you? Oh no. Wait a minute now. This is not how that works. Where is your money?" The bus driver asked her.

"I don't have any. The man just took it from me."

"What? Oh no. You gots to get off, Honey. I get conned all day long for rides. You gotta get off."

"Please. I'm not tryna con you."

"If he took your money, why is he chasing you? Shouldn't he be running in the opposite direction?" The bus driver stared at the woman as she popped her gum waiting for a response.

I felt bad for the woman and walked to the bus driver and handed her fare money. "Here, I'll pay her way."

"Oh my God! Thank you so much," the woman said and hurried to the seats in the back.

The bus driver eyed the woman through the mirror as she walked back in a hurry. "She know damn well ain't nobody chasing her, but okay. That will be two dollars and ten cents."

Even if it weren't true, I didn't care. I just wanted the bus to pull off and leave the city. My beeper started going off. I thought about ignoring it, but if it were my dad, he'd get pissed. Turned out to be Darcy's house number with 911 at the end of it.

"Wait a minute! Don't pull off yet! I need to get off the bus!" I hollered.

The bus driver sucked her teeth and opened the doors back up just as she was about to pull off. "You know what? Y'all getting on my nerves already and I just started my shift! First her. Now you. Come on now. I gotta get over this bridge!"

"Sorry!" I hollered as I ran off.

I went back up to my apartment to use the house phone, but my dad was on it. He was arguing with someone who owed him money from a tune-up he had done a few months ago. When he started searching for owed money, it meant he drank up all his money. I called Darcy as soon as he hung up.

"Hey. What's wrong?" I asked.

"I found out who those skanks are that jumped you. Terri, Angelica, Jessica, and Robin. I know where they be at. Let's go!"

"Go where?"

"Out Cramer Hill. They out there now. I just got a call from Vy."

"Word?"

"Yeah. Come on."

"Okay. I'm on my way."

I went into the top drawer of my dresser and grabbed my brass knuckles and darted out the door. I made it to Darcy's in a flash, then we picked up Vy and went to Cramer Hill. We sat on a bench across the street from Voneida Park. We were there for a half-hour before we spotted Robin's crew. It was about to go down. We walked toward the park to approach the girls. As we got closer, we overheard them bragging about how the last girl was crying as they beat her.

"They don't know they about to be doin' the same damn thing," Darcy mumbled, and we laughed in agreement.

They spotted us getting closer and lowered their voices. When we were a few yards away Darcy pointed at me. "Y'all remember her?"

"Nope. Who is she and why do we care?" Angelica answered. She was the one who swung on me first. I owed that bitch one.

"Oh, y'all about to care in a minute." Vy retied her hair into a bun and took off her jacket. "B, put that crazy-ass hair up before they snatch that shit up," she whispered to me.

"She looks like an Oreo to me," another one joked. That shit pissed me off. The girls looked at each other and laughed.

"We don't care." Robin stood up and I could see she was ready to bring it. "Now what?"

Before I could say a word, Darcy charged Robin and slammed her into the bench then started kicking on her. Angelica jumped in and pulled Darcy back by her hair. I went after Angelica and started punching her on the top of her head so she could loosen her grip on Darcy. It was hard keeping track of fists being thrown, names being called, hair being pulled, and faces being kicked.

I felt a wet substance on my hands and saw red everywhere. "What the fuck?" I checked myself but only saw blood on my hands. Blood was pouring down Angelica's arm and she yelled out that she had been stabbed.

Robin was on the ground screaming in pain from stab wounds. The other two girls ran off. I looked over at Darcy and Vy, and they both had knives in their hands.

"Why did you stab them? What the hell! We ain't say nothing about stabbin' people!" A few people had come out of their houses, so it was time to jet before we got caught. "Come on! Let's get out of here before the cops come!"

We ran off, and the entire time my mind was in such a confused state as to how things went wrong so fast. After we ran a few blocks away, we slowed down.

"What was that? Why did y'all stab them? Y'all didn't mention anything about stabbin' anyone! Why did y'all do that?" I screamed furiously.

"We did that for you, girl!" Darcy screamed as she got in my face.

45

"Yo! You betta get the hell out of my face, Darcy. I ain't scared of you!"

"Come on y'all! We not doin' this shit! And stabbin' them was Darcy's idea. I told her it was not a good idea," Vy admitted, "but what's done is done."

"So why did you do it? Y'all know y'all gonna get charged? They gonna tell." I paced back and forth my adrenaline still rushing.

"All the shit they been doing, they ain't tellin' on nobody. I bet they say they don't know who did it," Darcy said with confidence.

"Yeah, well my name better not come up in shit. I ain't down wit' gettin' no charges for stabbin' nobody. That's strictly y'all doing. You didn't mention anything about that to me because y'all know I ain't down for that."

"I don't want to go to jail." Vy began to panic a little bit.

"Girl ain't nobody goin' to jail," Darcy intervened.

"You're crazy. Y'all just stabbed people and you think you ain't goin' to jail. The one thing I do know is, I'm not!"

I was angry and silent on the rest of the way home. I could hear whispers from the two as they walked behind me. Our plan for revenge turned disastrous. I wish I would have just stayed on the bus and went to Philly.

I stayed in my apartment for the next few days, scared out of my mind. The stabbing made the news, and they were on the hunt for suspects. I felt like it was only a matter of time before they came knocking on my door. My butt cheeks flinched every time I heard a knock at one of my neighbor's doors. My dad didn't need any more stress in his life, and neither did I. I was so angry with Darcy and Vy that I couldn't bring myself to talk to them. I felt so deceived.

The doorbell rang and I almost jumped out of my skin. I looked out of the peephole and saw it was Justin. I was hesitant but I opened the door not wanting to act suspicious. "Hey, Justin."

"Hey, Bianca. Was wondering if you were okay. Haven't seen you."

I stood in the doorway hoping to get rid of him quickly. "Yeah, I'm fine."

"I heard they think your girlfriend Darcy stabbed some girls the other day. Is that true?"

I stood at attention and looked behind him to see if anyone was within earshot. "What? Wait. Come in." I pulled him in by the arm and shut the door. "When did you hear that? Today?"

"Yeah, like twenty minutes ago. Were you with her?"

I thought about not saying anything. I didn't know him from a can of paint, and he could've been setting me up but at this point, I needed to tell someone. "Justin, I was with her, but I didn't stab anybody. You have to believe me.

"And wherever Darcy is, Vy is too. Did she stab someone?" He looked at me waiting for a response. The truth of my confession didn't shock him.

"Those girls jumped me, and we went to fight them. We girls and that's what we do, but I didn't know Darcy and Vy had knives and was going to stab them. They didn't tell me because they knew I wouldn't agree with that. I was down with fighting but not the stabbin' part."

"Wow." He scratched his forehead. "That's crazy. You better hope they say you didn't know anything or they gonna charge you too."

"I told them that I didn't have anything to do with stabbin' anyone. I hope so too. I'm scared." I couldn't believe that I admitted that to Justin. I was kicking myself the week before for showing him that I was nervous and now here I was admitting I was scared. I don't know why I felt I could trust him, but I did.

"I would be too. Get you a lawyer just in case though."

"A lawyer?"

"Yes."

"I hope it doesn't come to that."

"I hope not. You out here fighting. You need to chill. You're too good to be out here acting crazy with those girls. They a bad influence on you Bianca."

"Those girls jumped me right before they jumped Pedro's sister. I don't be out here looking for trouble but if it comes my way. It is what it is."

"I understand you have to defend yourself, but you don't go looking for trouble. Look what happened. And then your friends got you all jammed up. What kind of friends do that?"

"I know. I'm so mad at them."

"Well, I was on my way to the store for my mom. I just wanted to check on you and make sure you were okay. Can I come back to see you tomorrow?"

"If you want to."

"Cool. I'll see you tomorrow. And here. This is my pager number and house number if you need me or want to talk. I'm here for you Bianca." Justin wrote down his digits and handed me a small piece of paper.

"Okay. Thank you."

I felt like a weight had been lifted off my shoulders when I confessed what happened to Justin. I'd been holding it in and going crazy on the inside. If he had heard about Darcy, then I knew shit was about to hit the fan.

That night, to clear my mind, I went to Ricky's bar, owned by my dad's friend growing up. He'd always been like an uncle to me and would allow me in to shoot pool. Everyone there knew me and considered me the neighborhood niece or granddaughter to all the older men. They were all my unofficial bodyguards. Over the years I'd beaten a lot of them at pool. They'd taught me the hustle, not just the game, and if ever I needed to make quick cash, I'd go there and rack up. I observed for a long time before I began to play and then my daddy taught me the mechanics and skills personally.

"Hey, Uncle Ricky. Do you mind if I shoot a few games? Need to clear my mind."

"Go ahead, Baby Girl. The table is all yours. You wanna drink?"

"Huh?"

"Only joking. Just making sure you don't say yes." He joked.

"You had me going for a second there, Uncle Ricky. But trust me. With what I'm seeing with my dad, I don't think I want to ever drink."

"Good. I'm glad you're paying attention. He needs you to keep being strong, Baby Girl. I know it's a lot of pressure, but I've watched you grow into a strong young lady, and I know you're going to grow into a responsible woman."

"That means a lot to me, Uncle Ricky. I'm not feeling so responsible now though."

"Want to talk about it?"

"Not really. I'm going to shoot some pool to take my mind off things for a bit. Hopefully, someone comes in and wants to play me. I could use a few bucks."

"You know I'm here whenever you need to talk or need anything. I know I can't replace your daddy but he's like my brother so that means you're always in good hands with me."

"You don't have to say that. I know that already. You family, and I'm grateful to have you in my life. I know my dad feels the same way."

"Sometimes things need to be said. You can't just assume people know. Especially, when it comes to young folk."

"You know what? You're right. Thank you for letting me know. Now, let me get over here and do something to this table."

"Don't hurt nothing!" Uncle Ricky laughed.

I laughed as I walked away, "You know I am!"

I played a few games and even wound up playing a few people who had to pay up. Something about a man's pride wouldn't let him walk away from the challenge of a teenage girl beating him and pretty soon a few men had lined up to try and put me in my place. After winning my third game, I called it a night. I was distracted for the time being, but as soon as I left, I became swallowed up by the reality I was trying to run away from.

When I got home, my dad was sitting in the living room talking to two police officers.

"Bianca, what the hell is going on?"

"Wait. Dad, let me explain-"

"You stabbed some girls?"

"No, Dad. I didn't stab anyone."

"Mr. Williams, we need you and your daughter to come down to the police station to answer some questions. We didn't say your daughter stabbed anyone. What we did say is your daughter was at the scene of the crime."

"Okay, okay. Bianca, let's go," my dad said followed by a loud burp from his many empty beer cans sitting on the floor next to his chair.

"Dag Dad. No excuse me. No nothing. That's so embarrassing."

"I'm the one who should be embarrassed. The police are here for you. I can burp in my damn home! Excuse that!"

For the first time since my mom was gone, my dad raised his voice at me. The nerve of him to be embarrassed by me. All the times I've seen him pissy drunk, in the house, walking the streets, or in the bar, and he's the one embarrassed? Shit! He's the neighborhood drunk that all the kids make fun of. But okay, Dad.

We went to the police station, and I was asked to tell my side of the story, no doubt to see if it matched up with Darcy and Vy's who'd already been there. They told their side of the story and made sure that I wasn't implicated in the stabbings. I was so relieved yet scared at the same time. They were charged with third-degree assault and criminal possession of a weapon. Luckily, the injuries to the victims were not life-threatening and both were released from the hospital with stitches.

Of course, we confessed why the fight took place to begin with and Robin's crew faced charges of people being assaulted in the city by a group of girls. So not only did Darcy and Vy get arrested, but so had Robin and her girls. Justice on all ends. I was glad it was over.

When we got home, Dad apologized to me for saying he was embarrassed by me. I'm glad he did because that really hurt my feelings.

The following night, Justin and I chilled in my living room. My dad wasn't home. Most likely at Uncle Ricky's bar so it was a perfect time to have company.

"I know you're glad they told the truth. You could have been in big trouble with them."

"I know. I'm still in shock that they actually stabbed them. Seeing all that blood freaked me out."

"Have you talked to them?"

"No. This destroyed our friendship. I think Darcy is mad because she made a statement that they stabbed the girls for me. I didn't know anything about anyone getting' stabbed. We were only supposed to throw hands, not sling knives."

"You need to stay out of trouble. All that fight stuff is gonna get you locked up or dead. You're too pretty to be out here fighting wit' ya' little self."

"They jumped me. What was I supposed to do? Nothing? You're not in my shoes so you can't tell me nothin'."

"Attitude. Attitude. I was not judging you. I was just saying you can make better decisions, that's all. Calm down, girl."

"Don't tell me what to do, Justin."

"I'm not your enemy, Bianca. Damn."

"Whatever."

"You've been through a lot. I can understand you're angry on the inside. But you need to stop tripping on people who want good for you."

"Don't say you understand my anger because you don't."

"I'm sorry, you're right. I don't. I still have my mom. I can't imagine what it feels like to lose her."

"Please, I don't want to talk about that."

"Why? It's a part of you. It's a part of me too."

"And how the hell is it a part of you too?" I was half annoyed with his nonsense.

"I was out there that night the accident happened. I saw you and your mom laying in the street. I saw when you got up, went over to her, and passed out. It was a horrible night. I'll never forget it."

"You were there? You saw what happened?"

"I saw the car hit her."

The memory rushed to my mind, and I got very emotional. "It was all my fault. My mom was gone because of me. I ran from her, and she chased me and pushed me out of the way to avoid me getting hit."

"Bianca, it was an accident. The man was charged with vehicular homicide. He was drunk and speeding. This was not your fault. Is that what you've been doing these past years? Blaming yourself?"

"Yes. If I hadn't run away from her, she'd still be here."

"How can you say that? Would if you didn't run away and both of you crossed the street together? You both could have gotten hit. Stop blaming yourself."

"Every time I try, I go back to thinking about that night all over again. It's so hard not to. I hate this feeling." My mom's lifeless eyes flashed in my memory. I slammed mine shut hoping to make it go away. It had been years and it was still as vivid as the day it happened. I doubted I would ever forget.

Justin stood up and extended his arms. "Come here."

I got up from the couch and drew to him like a magnet. The moment we locked into each other's embrace my tears felt free to stream down my face. He wiped them away, lifted my chin, and kissed me.

I wasn't expecting it, but I liked it and kissed him back. Before I knew it and we were making out heavy. Scared my dad would walk in, I took him to my bedroom. We made out some more and before I knew it our shirts were off.

"Do you have a condom?" I asked nervously. I had never had sex before and I wasn't even sure what to do but health class popped in my head.

Justin looked at me surprised and nodded quickly. He took his wallet from his back pocket and took one out, showing it to me. "My mom gave it to me a few months ago when she caught me staring at you."

I laughed then covered my face blushing. I couldn't believe he had just admitted that. He laughed too and stuffed his wallet back in his pocket.

"Does that mean, you've never done this before?" I asked.

He hesitated. "No, but I mean I know what I'm doing," he said bragging.

"You don't have to lie. And it's fine because I've never done this either, so I won't even know if you doing it right."

Justin narrowed his eyes at me trying to act all hard. I rolled my eyes in response and began fidgeting with my nails, staring at the floor. Why were males always so prideful? Here we were in the dark half-dressed worried about the wrong things. Maybe this wasn't the right time. I picked my shirt up off the floor ready to put it back on.

"Ok. I admit I don't know what I'm doing."

I stopped and stared at him. "Neither do I."

"I promise to try not to hurt you though. And we can go slowly. I just want to be with you." He stepped closer then kissed me again. And just as he promised, Justin slowly and lovingly took my virginity and gave me his. That night a bond formed between us and connected us on a level I never expected.

SIX
Tianna

I furiously wiped the angry tears streaming down my face with as much vigor as I used to scrub my name and phone number off the wall in the boy's locker room. I knew I had no business being in there. I'd be in some serious trouble if I got caught. But what other choice did I have? If I didn't get it off the wall, no one would, and it had to come off. Besides, my friend Morgan was keeping watch outside the door in case anyone showed up. I mean, it wasn't a perfect plan, but it would have to do.

After a few minutes of scrubbing, my hand started hurting. I sat back to get a better look at my progress on the wall or lack thereof. The writing had faded a little, but not nearly enough for all the effort I'd put into it. That marker was definitely freaking permanent. My hope exhaled out along with my frustration. I let the tears run freely now, not bothering to wipe them away. My shoulders sagging, I stared at the fat droplets that landed on my jeans leaving dark wet spots.

As I sat there a pathetic lump of tears and torment, I had the urge to scream at the top of my lungs and release all my pent-up anger. How did I always end up in these humiliating situations? Maybe if I could learn to keep my legs closed, I wouldn't be. I tossed away the self-condemnation too much of a coward to look at myself too closely. I was without a doubt a Monet and the closer I examined me, the messier I appeared.

But how would screaming help right now? If anything, it would bring unwanted attention and a definite detention if not suspension. My name on a wall wouldn't save me from punishment. Throughout all my life, the right thing never seemed to prosper and wrong always managed to succeed. Then again, I probably couldn't tell you right from wrong if my life depended on it. Getting through the day was my only focus. I was so glad this was my last year of high school. I seriously hated it.

I painted a portrait of myself on my mental canvas. I imagined the strokes and colors it took to recreate this scene of me on the floor. It had become a habit of mine whenever I wasn't within reach of my artisan tools. It had become my escape. I hated the portrait I was conjuring up in my imagination of me sitting on a dirty floor in tears. A small fire burned within me refusing to be pathetic. I slid my black Jansport closer to me and rummaged through the front pocket. I pulled out a yellow highlighter then set it aside. That wouldn't help. Same for the pens and pencils. At the very bottom, I found my black Sharpie. Without hesitation, I ripped the cap off and began to scribble over my name and phone number. With every letter and number that disappeared into the black cloud I was doodling, relief grew, and my tears ceased.

"Well, look whose here."

I recognized the voice behind me and willed myself not to panic. I turned to see Leon Thompson and a few of the other varsity basketball players standing behind me. The mere sight of him made my stomach clench. I began to feel around for the cap to my marker but couldn't find it. Not bothering to collect my pens and pencils, I snatched my backpack from the floor and quickly stood up. As fast as I could I headed toward the exit. So much for Morgan standing guard.

I wasn't blessed with speed and before I could take two steps, Leon raised his arms like a barricade, blocking my path.

"Whatcha doin' in here Tianna? Making sure your name and number don't fade? I knew it was you that wrote that on there. Don't worry. Your ho status ain't goin' nowhere."

His dumb friends chuckled and hi-fived each other, making my mouth go dry and my palms sweaty. I wiped them on my jeans before stepping to the side, attempting to go around him. Unlike me, Leon had been favored with athletic ability and easily matched my step, placing his hands on my arms to keep me from leaving.

"Aht, aht, aht. What's the magic word, Tianna?"

I remained quiet and avoided eye contact with him. Immediately I thought back to the last time we had been so close to each other. The memory made the blood rush to my face and the sudden warmth in the room was beginning to make me feel sick.

"Come on now, Christianna Faith Leonard!"

Regret washed over me like the ocean waves at Wildwood. Another boy I thought I could trust with my innermost thoughts, secrets, and body brought me nothing but heartache and shame. As if I were still there, I could see Leon sitting on the park bench beside me. His smooth dark skin was velvety like chocolate and his dimples so deep, a girl could dive into them. Leon's smile had the power to reel me in like a fish took worm bait. And when I told him that my middle name embarrassed me, his face sobered, and his flirty gaze turned gentle. He promised to never tell anyone, and I believed him. Like a guppy, my mouth gaped open at his tenderness and understanding. Stuck on stupid he kissed me so good I'd forgotten what my own middle name was. It wasn't long though before a fish reeled out of the water couldn't breathe. That's exactly what I felt like waiting for Leon to gut me open as he shook his head in a mocking tone.

"Where are your manners, young lady? I know ya holy-rolla moms taught you better than that, girl. Then again, if you take after her, probably not. Y'all think just because y'all go to church that that can just erase your past and makes y'all innocent and shit. Nah. Y'all sling in the gutter just like everybody else."

His words swirled around inside my head not knowing where to land without detonating. What could he possibly know about my past or even my mother's? Shame began to flood me at the thought of anyone knowing my past. Did he know Uncle Lou? Had I let that slip out hypnotized by his smile?

Leon put a finger to my chin gently and turned it toward him, dragging me away from memories that had begun to resurface only to transport me to different ones I just as soon wanted to forget. I was back to our first date when he moved in on me so slick Michael Jackson could've busted out on my lawn in a white suit calling me Annie and asking me if I was ok. I had been hit by a smooth criminal alright. Leon had driven me home and we'd sat in his car for a few minutes laughing and talking before we kissed so tenderly then intensely before I gave in to his whispers of how good he could make me feel. It was the first time I had had sex in a car. Wasn't the last time though.

Leon quickly disrupted my memory with his taunting. I couldn't decide which was worse; Leon in recollection or reality. "Jesus wouldn't approve of you vandalizing school property or being rude Tianna?"

The mention of Jesus unsettled me even more. I did not want to think of my faith or what was supposed to be, any more than I wanted to be in Leon's presence. And I was pretty sure Jesus felt the same about me as I had about Him. "Excuse me," I uttered hoping to finish the ordeal with as much dignity as I could scrape up.

Leon lowered his arms, a cocky grin as wide as the Delaware River spread across his face. "That's what I'm talking about."

He stepped aside just enough that I still had to brush up against him to escape.

"Yeah. You excused, Beautiful."

Out of custom, as opposed to genuine faith, I sent up a quick prayer up to the heavens, relieved I had gotten past him. Not wanting to show fear, I took a steady step, then two. I refused to let him see me run although everything in me wanted to. Maybe Jesus did care after all.

I didn't make it to the third step before Leon tugged at my backpack strap halting my progress. Or maybe Jesus didn't want to have anything to do with me, just as I'd thought.

"Tianna?"

I stopped but said nothing. Leon gently played with the tip of my ponytail, and I could feel the warmth of his breath on the back of my neck.

"Don't you worry Lil' *Mamí*. The whole team got that number saved. When we want some easy ass, we know exactly who to call."

I was so sick of the bullshit and didn't know how much more I could take before I snapped on somebody. "Yeah. They can call your mom."

The words left my mouth before I even processed the thought. I suddenly felt myself pushed up against the wall, my hands gripped above my head. Leon's nostril's flared and his usual Mac Daddy expression had hardened. I could tell he was fuming mad. Tianna, the protector was trying to surface. I was pinned up against that wall and a part of me didn't care.

"Oh! You got mouth Lil' *Mamí*?"

I struggled but broke free from his grip. When he came at me again, I used the sharpie as a sword and lunged at his face marking up his face as I had done the wall.

Leon jumped back. His eyes widen as he frantically touched his face. "You crazy bitch! You tried to cut up my face!"

I exhaled deeply, my adrenaline pumping before holding up the Sharpie in my defense.

"You wrote on my face?" He yelled as if that were worse. He rushed to the mirror hanging on the side of lockers nearby and assessed his reflection. I snatched up my backpack that had fallen to the floor and this time ran toward the exit! Butchie and Ray snatched me back and pinned me to the wall again, covering my mouth and cutting off my attempt to scream for help. The sinister look in Leon's eyes made me want to vomit. I thought I'd never see that look on a man's face ever again, but here it was on someone not even a man yet. I thought I had outrun that part of her life, but it had somehow found me and followed me without permission. Leon grabbed my backpack and tossed it across the room.

"You owe me something for this here, Ti," Leon said pointing to his marked-up face. With every step closer to me his voice softened. "How you gonna repent for your actions, girl?"

I swallowed the lump in my throat but couldn't speak. He leaned in and whispered in my ear. "We can do this the easy way or the other way. You decide." He untucked my shirt from my jeans then slid his hand up under my T-shirt. He began to fondle me over my bra. I turned my face and closed my eyes.

Every nerve ending in my body stood at attention. The contents of my lunch were rumbling inside, and the room felt as if were closing in all around me. I gasped to breathe, but like a clogged vacuum, no matter how much I tried to suck in air, I couldn't inhale enough. The room began to spin as I broke out into a cold sweat. "The easy way," I said barely above a whisper. If I chose to participate then at least it was a choice. Anything but force.

Leon cracked a smile and slowly removed his hand from under my shirt. "That's a good girl," he said before kissing me on the cheek. "Tonight, at seven. Don't be late Tianna."

After Leon and his boys left the locker room, I ran to the bathroom and vomited. After a few minutes, I cleaned myself up, grabbed my belongings, and walked out the back door of the gym. I needed to escape. I had never ditched school before, but I couldn't seem to find the strength to care. As I reached the trees that separated the school property from the neighborhood houses, the sound of voices arguing made me stop. It was Leon. I didn't want to be seen by anyone but especially by him.

"Stop telling me to calm down! That bitch wrote all over my face with a damn marker! This better come off or I'm gonna make her regret the day she grew a brain."

"Baby, it'll come off with some soap and water."

The sound of a female's voice caught me off guard.

"Come on. We can go to my house. My mom and her new boyfriend are away on vacation or something. I'll clean your face and make you something to eat. Then we can go to my room to hang out. I'll deal with Ms. Goody-Two Shoes tomorrow."

It was Morgan. Hundreds of times she's called me Goody-Two-Shoes, but never with disgust. At least not to my face. I nearly choked at the betrayal. I won't lie. It hurt, but I'd been through enough betrayal and hurt in my sixteen years of life that high school girl drama didn't have what it took to bring me to my knees. As fast as it hurt, it dissipated. Tianna, the protector had fully engaged. Morgan lying and playing me out was my norm. If anything, bonds and friendships were strange to me. I never seemed to quite get that right and preferred solitude. In solitude, I only had my own mind to battle with.

Footsteps approaching made me cut through the trees that led to the street. I don't know why but I began running. I hated running, but my body needed to release everything that had built up. So, I ran until I couldn't breathe. Maybe I'd pass out from lack of oxygen and die. Embarrassingly enough it took only a block and a half before I decided living wasn't so bad and how much I valued air. I bent over holding my side gasping for it, my backpack crashing to the sidewalk

"You alright?"

I jumped up straight, my hand flying to my chest as if it actually had the capability of keeping my heart from bursting out. I noticed the large cardboard box before anything else. My gaze rose slowly to meet the eyes of the culprit that nearly left me heartless. A bootleg version of one of the Wayans Brothers, minus the fame, stared back at me from behind the picket fence that used to belong to the Turner family. I was too winded to speak and just nodded still trying to catch my breath.

He shrugged his shoulders and went about his business. Only after he walked away did I notice the moving truck parked in the driveway. I snatched my backpack up from off the ground and situated it in on my shoulder. I didn't even take a step before I was snatched back and spun around. Leon grabbed my backpack and in one swift motion put it on his back.

"You'll get this back tonight," he said.

Alarm set in. My house keys were in the side pocket. My sketchpad was in there. I didn't want him going through my personal stuff. "You don't have to take my backpack. I'll show up," I said as nonchalantly as I could.

"Just an insurance policy Lil' *Mami*. You'll get it back."

I looked down to the ground trying not to let my emotions overrun. "Please give it back, Leon."

"You real hardheaded Tianna. I don't want your corny little backpack. Relax."

"Yo. Why don't you give her back her stuff? She said please." Shawn Wayan's understudy was standing at the fence, a lamp in his hand this time.

"Who the hell is you and why you in our business? This don't got nothing to do with you, fake ass Devante Swing."

The stranger chuckled. He exited the fence and handed me the lamp. My heart started pumping overtime. What was he doing?

"Actually, my name is Elijah. Nice to meet you." Elijah stuck out an open hand to Leon waiting for him to shake it." It caught me off guard.

Even Leon looked at him puzzled. "Man, get outta my face with that." Leon slapped Elijah's hand up and before I could make sense of it, Elijah had grabbed Leon's hand twisting it behind him. Leon was cursing and struggling in vain trying to get free from Elijah's hold but couldn't.

Elijah pushed him forward and pinned him up against the tree, Leon's cheek pressed against the bark. "Are you going to give her back her stuff?" Leon cursed again. Elijah pressed him against the tree harder. "What was that?" he asked.

Leon hesitated but nodded. Elijah released him and snatched my backpack from Leon's back. Leon touched his face, and I could see he was fuming. "You can have that shit back. Trust me, Tianna, this ain't over." He took a few steps back, stumbling. "And Devante, you got an ass beating coming your way. Watch your back." Leon ran down the street furious.

I was stuck on stupid not knowing what to do or say. Elijah handed me my backpack and stared at me, his eyes opening wide.

"What?"

He smiled and pointed at my hand. I looked down at my hand. Duh, the lamp. "Oh, my bad." I handed it to him quickly and stepped back.

"You ok?" He asked. I nodded and put my backpack on. He smiled again. "Cool. I better get back to unloading then."

I nodded again and moved aside to let him by. He closed the fence and walked toward the house.

"Thank you," I said loud enough for him to hear before bolting down the street. Every step got me closer to home and all I wanted to do was get lost in painting.

"Hey! Hey! Hold up!"

I turned to see Elijah running to catch up to me. I waited, squinting against the sun in my face. When he finally made it, he was tall enough that he blocked the sun from my eyes. I waited for him to say something.

"I thought I'd walk you home just in case that guy decided to follow you."

This kid kept surprising me, and it made me uncomfortable although I knew he was just trying to be nice. I started walking, afraid to stay there too long in case Elijah was right about Leon. He walked alongside me quietly and when I reached my house, he waited for me to go inside.

The following morning at school, I saw Elijah walking with one of the student volunteers that gave the new students tours and helped them get adjusted. It hadn't even crossed my mind that he would be attending school here, but there he was. I said a silent prayer that he and Leon wouldn't get into anything before the announcements over the loudspeaker came on interrupting my prayer.

Later that day, as had become my custom, I sat at a table close to the cafeteria window alone, sketching as I listened to my Discman. My mom would have a stroke if she knew I was listening to Biggie Smalls, so I kept that CD in my backpack and only listened to it at lunchtime.

A shadow fell across my sketchpad blocking the natural light. I looked up to see Elijah towering over the table, his backpack slung on one soldier and a lunch tray in hand. I saw his lips move but didn't hear what he'd said. I slide my headphones off and waited for him to repeat it. "Is this seat taken?" I looked at the entire table where I sat alone and then back at him wondering if he was being sarcastic. He actually waited for a response.

"No."

"May I?"

I shrugged. I didn't care where he sat. He began to eat his lunch and I went back to sketching. I left the headphones off my head but could still hear the music. I wasn't sure how much time passed before I signed my name to the bottom of my finished pencil sketch.

"You're good."

I'd forgotten Elijah sat at the table. I looked up and smiled. "Thanks." There were no signs of his lunch or trash. I was a little surprised how'd much I'd tuned everything out that I hadn't even noticed him get up to toss his trash.

The bell rang and we began to exit the cafeteria. "Could you point me toward room one seventeen? I have Computer Technology and I'm still learning how to get around."

"I'm headed that way. I'll walk with you."

We walked in silence, and I pointed toward the door once we were near it before I kept walking. He thanked me and headed off. After a week of him sitting with me during lunch in silence watching me sketch and me walking him to class afterward, he'd finally interrupted me and began small talk. I'd mostly just listened. Answering an occasional question with as few words as necessary or smiling at one of his stories even though sometimes I wanted to laugh.

After a few weeks, I rarely sketched during lunch too engrossed in the stories Elijah would tell. His dad was in the military, and he'd moved all over the world. Up until his parents divorced last year and his mom moved near her hometown. Every when I spoke about sad things, he had a way of making everything sound purposeful and lively. He had a way of making me feel like I was right in the midst of each story.

I started answering his questions in more detail and had finally told him the full story about Bryson and Leon. Even the ones in between. Two of which I'd forgotten their names. Yet Elijah never judged me. Just listened.

SEVEN
Justin

I woke up from a dream and the first thing I remembered was seeing my dad's face. I instantly smiled, but then the reality of him not being here snatched it away. It had been a few years, and I still couldn't believe he was gone. My mom was a strong woman and pushed through her grief. Jordi seemed to be a bit withdrawn at times. And other times he acted out. I knew it was because he didn't know how to deal with our dad's death. I tried being the best role model for him, but I felt like I was not succeeding. Me leaving for college concerned me that no one would keep him in check and on the right path. The last thing I wanted was for him to give Mom a hard time and stress her out.

Later that day, I met up with my friends, Manny and Corey, to play basketball. I wasn't into the game like I normally was, so I cut it short.

"What's wrong bro? You don't seem yourself. You aiight?" Manny asked.

I grabbed my bottled water and hesitated to answer the question, but the words rolled off my tongue anyway. "I had a dream about my dad. Well, we didn't talk but I saw his face."

"I had a feeling it had something to do with your dad," Corey added.

"It is that obvious?"

"I notice almost every time you're not in a good mood it's because of your dad," Corey answered.

"I noticed it too but didn't want to assume this time. You know you can always talk to us bro," said Manny.

"Thanks. I just keep a lot of stuff to myself. Don't want to bother anybody with my stuff."

"It wouldn't be a bother. We're friends. We've been knowing each other since daycare. C'mon bro. Don't do that," Corey said.

"Okay, okay. You got that. Maybe that was just an excuse, so I don't have to talk about it. It's still hard to accept. I know he's gone but it just doesn't seem fair. I'm trying to live my life the best way I know how. I can't help but think about him every day. I'm about to graduate and he's not here to witness it."

Every time something good happened in my life my dad was the first person I wanted to tell. Making the varsity basketball team. Losing my virginity. Being accepted into college. Yet, he wasn't here for any of it. Why did he have to interfere in other people's business? Maybe if we would've just stayed on the elevator, he'd still be alive. I put the cap back on my water and stopped tormenting myself with the what-ifs just I had told Bianca to do.

Manny eyed Corey before he filled the silence. "I honestly don't know what to say because I still have both my parents. I can't imagine that pain, but you can always talk to us."

"Thanks, Bro. I appreciate that." And I meant it. I grabbed my hat off the bench and slid it on my head backward.

"Let's go grab something to eat at the *bodega*. I'm hungry." Corey slipped his backpack on his back and tightened the straps.

"I think I'm gonna go to the *Chino's*. I want some fried rice." Manny said.

"The *Chino's*?" Corey asked mocking Manny. "You so damn Puerto Rican. "*Chino's*? That sounds like some hick shit. It's Chinese Take-out. And ain't you tired of eating rice all the damn time? Shit, bro."

Manny threw the ball at Corey hard, but Corey caught it. "Kiss my ass. It's the damn *Chino's*, and I'm getting some muthafuckin' fried rice. Y'all can keep them nasty ass Jamaican beef patties. Bootleg ass *empanadas*."

"Yo! Don't be crackin' on my beef patties. They good as hell."

I laughed at them busting on each other and we left the courts. "I'm good y'all. Dinner's probably already done so I'm just gonna go straight home." Corey and Manny didn't pass up the opportunity to make fun of me telling me to eat all my peas and keep my elbows off the table. I laughed it off. Most times they'd beg to come over for dinner because they'd tasted first-hand how Mom could burn. Today we parted ways and went about our own lives.

As I got to the outside of my door, I could smell my mother's fried chicken. The aroma made me greedily close my eyes, smile, and rub my stomach before opening the door. When I walked inside, my mom was in the kitchen cooking while listening to her R&B from the Seventies CD grooving. "Hey, Mom!"

"Well, hello my son. *What's going on? What's going on?*" She sang Marvin Gaye to me and laughed.

I just shook my head at her and smiled. "Didn't start off too good but I'm feeling pretty good now."

"Is that so? What made it pretty good? Yes, I'm being nosey," she laughed.

"Bianca and I are together."

"Really?"

"Yes. I really like her, Mom."

"Keep in mind, you're about to leave for college Justin."

"I know, Mom."

"I think that girl has issues. I saw her almost get into a fight not too long ago, and her little tail was fired up."

"Mom, who doesn't have issues?"

"Well, excuse me. I'm not judging her. I just want you to be careful."

"That's exactly what you're doing. I can take care of myself. I'm not afraid of her. I see something that you don't."

"Listen to you, sounding like your daddy. Okay. I'm going to mind my business, but always know, that you are my business, Justin. I only want what's best for you."

"I only want what's best for me too, Mom."

"You're growing up so quick, it scares me. Such a great young man you are."

"Yeah, yeah, yeah," Jordi says as he walks into the kitchen.

"Hello to you too baby brother."

"Jordi, that was rude," Mom said.

"Great. I'm getting double-teamed," Jordi said and immediately turned to leave the kitchen.

"Whoa. Wait a minute. Stop right there." I exercised my older brother tone.

"You're not my dad. I don't have to listen to you!" Jordi shouted and continued to walk toward his bedroom. I followed behind him.

"What is wrong with you? Why are you being such a mean-ass?" I asked.

"I'm not."

"You are. And you're upsetting Mom. I know I'm not your dad but I'm the closest one you've got. I know Dad would want me to step up and make sure everything is okay, and that includes making sure you're okay too."

"I don't want to talk about this."

"There may come a time when you do. I'm here when you're ready but until then, please don't take your attitude out on, Mom or me. For that matter, anyone. I love you, little brother."

I left Jordi's room and went back into the kitchen. My mom was visibly upset. "Mom, I don't think I should leave for college. I can enroll in community college. Jordi needs me here."

"No. Absolutely not. Your Dad wouldn't have any of that and neither will I. He will be fine. We will be fine. You've been excited and waiting for the day to leave for college and you will. That is the end of this conversation. Do you understand me, Justin?"

"Yes ma'am."

"Okay. Wash up and get ready for dinner. And let Jordi know too."

"Ok."

"Thank you."

It was quiet as we ate dinner. I'd never experienced being so uncomfortable at my own dinner table with my family. I wanted to grab my little brother and tell him that I understood his hurt and anger. Yet at the same time, I wondered if I needed someone to hug me and tell me the same, just as much as he did.

EIGHT
Bianca

I was hype that I had had enough credits to get co-op and work part-time at a nursing home in Cherry Hill. I worked so hard to get my grades up after nearly failing last school year. I had to give my mom something to smile about. I reached a point in my life where I refused to let the past stand in my way. I can't lie that Justin had a lot to do with that. Since we'd been together, he'd made a great impact on my life. He was always telling me to be better and do better and it resonated with me. He had goals and dreams and it didn't sound corny or impossible to want more out of life. I envied that about him and others. In particular, my cousin Tiffany, my dad's niece.

We'd always gotten along but since my aunt hadn't ever liked my mom, Tiffany and I didn't see too much of each other growing up. We'd gone to the same middle school but never in the same class or the same circle. One day Tiffany surprised me and had asked to hang out. I jumped at the chance. Ever since I had had a falling out with Darcy and Vy, I had only ever hung out with Justin and his homeboys occasionally. I missed female companionship.

Over the summer she and I had started to get close. Even more so when I transferred to Woodrow Wilson High School from Pennsauken Vocational after my grade point average dropped so low that I'd had a zero before the decimal point.

It was cool though. A new attitude. A new school. A new friendship. I was living life better. I was excited. Because we had the same last name, Tiffany and I were in the same homeroom and even had one class together. I thought it was fly graduating with my first cousin. It wasn't long until everyone knew we were down with each other. We were cousins and best friends. Double bonded.

Everything was going smoothly until Thanksgiving at the high school Turkey game. Every year the two inner-city high schools played against each other. It was a rivalry that had been going on for decades and an honored tradition in Camden. As every year, current and alumni students repped their schools hard and talking trash to each other.

Tiffany and I had on new clothes and had our hair done. You couldn't tell us nothin' sporting our orange and black, Woodrow Wilson High's colors. I was anxiously waiting to see Justin so he could see that I had his name spray-painted on my hoodie. He was home from college for Thanksgiving.

There was a group of girls walking by Tiffany and me, and one of them was an old friend of mine named Sandy, from middle school. She was now a student at our rival high school, Camden High.

"Hey, Bianca," Sandy said all smiles and dimples.

"Hey, Sandy! It's been a while! How are you girl?" She had always been cool people.

"I'm good. And you? I'm so sorry about your mom. She was such a nice lady."

"Thank you. I'm better. I miss her but I'm taking it one day at a time."

Sandy offered a smile before it flattened. She looked at Tiffany then back at me trying to hide her surprise. "Can I speak with you for a minute B?"

"Yeah. What's up?" I walked off to the side with her.

"I don't want to start anything but why are you with Tiffany ?"

"What do you mean? That's my cousin."

"Your cousin?" She couldn't have looked more surprised had I said Tiffany was Lil' Kim.

"Yeah. How do you know her?"

"Well, I remember her from middle school. And she my sister's homegirl."

"Who Lesley?"

"Yeah. They used to hang real tight for years. I was never close with her. I have my reasons, but after all the trouble she caused you, you're okay with her?"

"What trouble? What the hell is you talkin' about?" I asked in confusion.

"Wow. You don't know, do you?"

"Know what?"

Sandy hesitated before looking back at Tiffany again. She pulled me away a little further. "Do you remember in school how kids would pick on you, calling you Oreo?"

"Yeah. Something I will never forget. It was one of the most horrible times I had in school. Why you bringin' that shit up?"

"It was Tiffany who started that. She always spoke wit' jealousy when it came to you. Especially your hazel eyes and light hair. I thought you knew about it."

"Wait, wait, wait. You're tellin' me that Tiffany started that racist name? Why didn't you ever say anything to me?"

"Because Tiffany was a bully then and I was scared of her, shit. You know she was always beatin' somebody up. I wasn't trying to get jumped. Plus, I didn't even know she was your cousin."

"Why tell me now? That was years ago."

"Because that ain't the worst of it. She down with Robin's crew and she the one that had them jump you. I thought you knew that and that's why you and your girls retaliated."

"Nah. She wasn't there the day we brawled." I said thinking how all of this was just too crazy for words.

"I'm just warning you B. She a snake. There is definitely undercova' hate goin' on. Be careful."

It all clicked. That was why the girl called me an Oreo at the park the day we fought them. And all this reaching out to me to be friends was just her setting me up for Robin and her crew to pay me back.

The truth smacked me in the face, and I saw red. "Yo! I'ma beat the breaks off her ass. For real."

"Wait B. Please don't do nothin' crazy. I just wanted you to know so you can watch your back."

"I appreciate that, but hell nah. You know I'm pissed, right? I ain't letting this shit slide." Sandy may have been scared of Tiffany, but I sure as hell wasn't.

"Yeah, I know. I'm goin' to catch up to my girls. My parents still have the same phone number. Call me some time," Sandy insisted.

"Bet."

When I walked back over to Tiffany, my entire demeanor was different. So much so, my silence spoke volumes.

"What's wrong with you?" Tiffany asked.

I looked Tiffany right in the eyes and asked, "Where did the name Oreo come from?"

"The cookie? Don't you think you need to research the company for that answer Bianca? Why you askin' me that?"

"I'm not talkin' about the company. I'm talkin' about when I was in middle school and the kids started callin' me Oreo. Where did it come from, Tiffany ?"

Tiffany stuttered. "I, I, don't know what you're talkin' about."

"You're goin' to lie in my face like I'm stupid?"

"Bianca, you need to chill. Is that what Sandy told you? You gonna believe her over me? Your blood? For real?"

"I'm tired of people always hollerin' about blood when they are the same ones doin' devious shit! Yeah, I believe her!"

"Oh wow, you trippin'!" Tiffany tried to belittle me and play it off. "Sandy just hate me 'cause I took her man. I ain't even want him like that."

"Nah, you trippin' if you think I'ma believe you."

"Don't believe me then! I don't care! Take that white attitude and kiss my ass!"

'That white attitude.' Ironically, I blacked out. All I could hear in my head was Tiffany's mom calling my mom white trash. I was so tired of never being black enough. Never being white enough. Never enough.

Next thing I knew, I punched Tiffany in her mouth, and we started fighting. I wanted to pay her back for all the trauma she had caused me in school. She had no clue what I went through, being harassed by the constant racial bullshit. I was miserable, barely wanting to show up. I pounded on her without holding back. It took four guys to break up the fight. Justin was one of them.

"Bianca, stop! What are you doing?" Justin hollered.

"It was her! This whole time!" I screamed.

"You're dirty and ugly just like your mom! Crazy bitch!" Tiffany yelled.

"Bitch what? Oh no. Let me go, Justin. I'ma fuck her up! Let me go!" I cried as I tried to break free from Justin's grip.

"No! Let's go! Come on!"

Justin walked me to his mom's car and took me home. He was angry at me. When we pulled into the parking lot, there was silence for a second.

"Why do you have to fight all the time? It's getting old and tiring Bianca. I'm sick of it."

"She deceived me and pretended to be cool with me."

"That's your cousin, Bianca."

"She had those bitches jump me!" I couldn't contain my fury. "She's nothin' to me! I can't be connected to people who secretly hate on me. All this time. I'm such an idiot. I should have known. She never liked me from the beginnin'. Just like her mom never liked my mom. How can you not see my side, Justin?" Angry tears streamed down my face.

"That's what I've been doing for how long, Bianca?"

"I'm so sorry. I lost it. Damn!" I screamed as I punched the dashboard.

"I can't deal with your blowups. We may have to take a break from each other. You need some type of anger management. I've been telling you this for a while now. You're going to hurt someone, or someone is going to hurt you."

"So, you're breaking up with me?"

"We need a break."

"I don't need a break. You need a break. Speak for yourself."

"Okay. I need a break then. Is that better? And please, don't turn this around on me. I've been patient and trying to get you to see that you need help. Playing pool is not going to fix your anger or anything else."

"Fine!" I got out of his car and slammed the door. "Fuck you and everybody else!"

"See what I'm talking about? You just proved my point!" Justin hollered and then pulled off.

My mind was all over the place as I made my way back home. I was prepared to walk past my dad and straight into my room, but I saw his body lying still on the living room floor. I ran over to him, "Dad! Dad! Wake up, Dad!"

I checked his pulse. He wasn't breathing. I became a frantic mess and ran to the telephone to call 911. I couldn't lose my dad too. I administered CPR as instructed. Although he wouldn't wake up, I had to believe with everything in me that he would. I was not giving up on my dad. It seemed like forever before the paramedics arrived. When they did, they immediately took over CPR and rushed him to the hospital.

A few hours later I was told he'd suffered a severe stroke. They couldn't tell me the extent of the damage until they ran more tests. I wanted to turn to Justin, but he'd just broken up with me. It had been a while since I had felt all alone in the world and wanted nothing more than for Dad to wake up.

Later that night, Tiffany and her mom, Aunt Charlene walked into the waiting area where I was sitting.

"What's going on with my brother?" Aunt Charlene asked.

"He had a stroke."

"How bad is it? Is he able to talk? Is he awake?"

"They mentioned nothing about him being awake, so I'm assuming, no. And they won't know how bad it is until they run more tests. I've been waiting for a while. They should be coming out soon to let me know something."

"Do I need to sign any paperwork for him?"

"No. I'm eighteen now. We already handled paperwork just in case anything happened to him." I wanted to laugh when her face cracked but I let that knowledge piss her off and celebrated in silence.

"What? Well, I want to see the paperwork."

"Aunt Charlene, I don't have to show you anything. The doctors here know and that's all that matters." My fuse was short, so I snapped and rolled my eyes. Silent celebration was over.

"Don't talk to my mom like that," Tiffany interjected.

"Girl, shut up. Ain't nobody payin' you no mind. You and your mom can leave. We don't need y'all negativity up in here."

"You better watch how you talk to me," Charlene snapped back. "Your mom never knew how to discipline you and that's why you so disrespectful and why you ran out into the street. Still haven't learned to check that nasty-ass attitude of yours. But I ain't your mom and I'll smack that mouth of yours!"

"And guess who's gonna get smacked back!" I shouted.

A nurse walked into the waiting room, "Hey! We do not condone this type of behavior. This is a hospital. Please, lower your voices. We can hear you all the way down the hall. Who are you waiting on?"

"I've been here all day waitin' to see my dad, Calvin Williams. He was brought in earlier today, suffering a stroke. I've been waitin' to get more information on his condition, and I want to see him."

"Okay, I'll check. But you cannot raise your voices in here again or security will be called. Okay?" The nurse looked at us demanding cooperation.

"I understand. I'm goin' to wait in the hallway. I don't want to be around them anyway," I explained to the nurse as I walked away and gave Tiffany and Charlene the evil eye.

"Whatever," Tiffany said.

When I walked into the hallway, I heard someone call my name and I turned around.

"J-Justin?" I stuttered in surprise.

"How is he? Is your dad okay?"

"Oh my God, you're here. Thank you so much for comin'," I said as I walked over to hug him. "I don't know how bad it is yet. They should be comin' out soon to tell me somethin'."

"My mom told me they rushed your dad to the hospital. I didn't want you to be by yourself."

"Thank you. You being here means a lot."

"I'm mad at you but not that mad to let you go through this alone. You know I wouldn't do that to you. Did you eat?"

"No. I don't have an appetite."

"At least drink something. You have to take care of yourself."

"I left my water in the waiting area. Tiffany and her mom are in there and we started goin' back and forth, so I left."

"I'll go get it." He volunteered. He was back in a hurry. "The doctor is in there updating your aunt. Come on."

"What?" That woman was asking for trouble. Her and her trifling daughter. I rushed into the waiting room and interrupted the doctor. "I'm here doctor. You can give me an update. Just me. I'm his next of kin and power of attorney. No one else is allowed to be told about his medical condition. Including her." I put my hand all up in Charlene's face.

"Bianca, just talk to the doctor. Ignore them," Justin admonished.

I would've but Tiffany decided to take it to the next level. She slapped my hand away and shoved me in the back of the head. I turned and lunged for her. Justin pulled me back and I was only able to grab a handful of hair, but I yanked it hard, not letting go. She was screaming so loud staff ran out to the waiting area. Tiffany bit my hand until I released her.

"Biting me just like a bitch would. Go crawl on all fours female dog!"

I spit at her, and it landed on her shoes.

Justin yanked me back. "Enough! You two need to leave!"

Charlene was outraged. "You ain't nothing but dirty white trash just like your mom." She pointed at me with chipped fingernail polish and a wrinkled finger. "You probably ain't even my brother's real daughter. I'm going to get a lawyer. I'm his sister and I have every right to know what's going on! This ain't over little girl."

Security had shown up and removed them both and warned me I was next. I gave Charlene my back and faced the doctor as if she didn't exist, but the doctor had left. I was so caught up in rage I hadn't even noticed. I cursed. I needed to know what was going on with my dad.

Justin grabbed my hand and we walked up and down the hallway soothing me and being supportive as if he hadn't just seen me go off. He was trying his best to keep me calm and pull a few laughs out of me. That was one of the reasons why I loved him so much. He always made the best out of a bad situation.

Two hours passed before Dr. Heinz came out to update me about my dad. "You are Mr. William's daughter, correct?"

"Yes." I was mortified when he gave me a stern look.

"While you were out here sorting family situations, we ran a few more tests. He needed more than anticipated."

"Is that a bad thing?"

"Well, we wanted to make sure that we covered every area to give us an idea of how bad your dad has been affected. It looks like some brain damage could cause short-term memory loss, and there is some paralysis on the right side of your dad's body. It may be temporary. We'll see how he progresses before we can know for sure. The next forty-eight hours are critical. As far as his speech, we will need to assess impairment if any once he wakes up and talks. If he can, that is."

"If he can? Oh my God, Daddy!"

"I'm just stating the worst-case scenario to better prepare you. Nothing is certain. We have to wait until he wakes up to know for sure," Dr. Heinz calmly stated.

"Doc, when can she see him?" Justin asked.

"The nurse will be out to get you when it's time. Hopefully, not too much longer."

"Okay. Thank you, so much for the information Dr. Heinz."

We walked the hall until it was time to go see my dad. Seeing him lay there helpless broke me even more on the inside. After sitting with him for an hour, Justin took me home and stayed the night with me to make sure I was okay.

A few days later I was informed that my dad would need to go to therapy, and it was possible that he would have to live in a nursing home if his condition didn't improve enough to take care of himself. All I could do is pray to God to help him. Justin vowed to be my moral support and that he'd be right by my side through it all.

NINE
Tianna

One day after school, Elijah was waiting outside and when he saw me, he began walking beside me finishing a story he hadn't finished during lunchtime. A girl fight had broken out at an inner-city high school his cousin attended during the Thanksgiving football game. The closest I'd ever come to a fight was when Elijah gripped Leon up and that wasn't much of a fight. I just walked alongside him listening as if we had been doing this all our lives.

The following Monday, he was waiting outside for me to walk to school. I was surprised to see him but just as everything else with him was effortless, so was this. It became our routine. We walked, talked, and walked. He became my best friend. The closest friend I'd ever had.

A few weeks into December, Elijah asked if we could stop by his house on the way to mine. He invited me inside and sat me at the kitchen table. His dog gave him a warm welcome that he returned. He ran upstairs for a few minutes and returned with a box wrapped in Christmas paper and handed it to me.

I looked at it confused. "You got me a Christmas present?" The grin on his face was so childlike I wanted to laugh. "But Christmas is still a few days away and I didn't get you anything. I can't accept this." I slid it across the table back to him.

He laughed. "You better cut that out and open it. It took me a half-hour trying to figure out how to wrap it right."

I grinned. I could picture him creasing the paper and measuring the pieces of tape. He was the neatest teenage boy I'd ever met. "Ok, but I owe you a gift." He winked in response and something inside of me made my stomach clench. I ignored it and unwrapped the gift. A wooden box was filled with an assortment of brushes, pencils, and paints. All the brands that I liked and used. In the center was one of my sketches, professionally printed and framed. My eyes shot open before they began to tear. I couldn't even tell you why. I wasn't a sappy person.

He chuckled and grabbed my hands helping me to my feet. "You're supposed to be excited, not crying."

I couldn't even look at him in the face I was so embarrassed. I wrapped my arms around him. He hugged me and let me cry without teasing me. When I finally eased up, he lifted my chin and smiled down at me. "You are gifted. Always remember that."

Overcome with emotion I reached up on my toes, closed my eyes, and pressed my lips to his. He didn't kiss me back. I opened my eyes confused. Sadness was written all over his face. I had never seen that expression on him before and it slapped by across the face. I backed up mortified tripping over the chair. "I'm sorry. I shouldn't have done that." I grabbed my backpack and dashed toward the door, opening it clumsily.

He pushed it closed and turned me around. The sadness still haunted his eyes. I tried to turn around again trying to escape but he wouldn't let me. I stopped fighting and leaned against the door letting the tears I tried to hide run free.

He wiped them away and kissed me on my cheek. Then my other cheek. Then he kissed me, but I was as stiff as a statue. I was confused. He chuckled then kissed me again. This time I kissed him back. It intensified. Within minutes we were undressed and on the couch. I hadn't intended for it to go all the way, but we had. Afterward, he walked me home holding my hand and carrying my wooden box telling me another story as if it had been the most natural thing in the world.

Several weeks later, Elijah had invited me to his house for dinner. His Mom wanted to meet the person he had been spending so much time with. I was nervous but it was important to him, so I agreed. I showed up with a dessert my mom taught me how to make wondering if that had been a stupid idea.

Elijah answered the door and grinned at my lopsided cake. "Ti you didn't have to bake something. Like you really, really shouldn't have," and cracked up. I slapped him on the arm and he laughed harder, pulling me in for a side hug, pecking me on the lips. "Come on. Momzilla is waiting."

I pulled him back. "Momzilla?"

He laughed again and winked. "Chill. She don't bite."

I relaxed realizing he was joking.

"Much," he added just as we walked into the dining room. By then it was too late to panic as she had been in the dining room setting a salad on the table.

"Mom, this is Christianna. She baked a cake," he said his eyes wide open and a disgusted look on his face, teasing. "Christianna, this is my mom, Marvette."

Marvette chuckled. "Boy, stop teasing that girl." She extended her hand, and I shook it. "I have heard a lot about you. It's nice to finally put a face to a name. And thank you for the cake. It looks delicious."

"I thought you told me lying was a sin." Elijah faced his mom his mouth hung open.

"Eli, don't be rude. I raised you better than that. Now go take that into the kitchen. We'll slice it after dinner." She turned to me and shook her head. "Boys. I'm glad I only had one."

"I heard that," he yelled from the kitchen.

We both laughed. I sat down at the table, waiting quietly and patiently. My nerves had settled some, but I regretted bringing dessert without asking first. I spotted a pie that looked ten times better than my cake and now she probably felt obligated to serve my chocolate mess instead of hers.

She asked about my family as we ate. I told her about my parents and Abe. She asked about school. I told her about my grades with as little fuss as possible. Elijah chimed in raving about my 'exceptional grades and numerous school accolades. He sounded like a proud mother. I felt phony being praised for just doing what came naturally to me.

The smell of the collard greens turned my stomach, although I usually liked them, so I politely turned them down when offered. I pretended to clear my throat covering my mouth and nose with the napkin just to avoid the smell. I don't know if Marvette noticed but she took the bowl of collards into the kitchen and brought out a pitcher of lemonade.

I felt a hand under the table and looked up to see Elijah wink at me. We held hands for a bit before Marvette brought out slices of chocolate cake. She complimented the taste and Elijah agreed, eating two slices. I barely touched mine, my nerves getting the better of me. I wondered if they were just being kind about my baking. It wasn't something I pretended to be good at.

I helped clear the table and offered to help Elijah wash dishes. He rinsed and I loaded the dish washer. My school night curfew wasn't too far away so I thanked Marvette and Elijah for inviting me to dinner. She thanked me for coming and wished me a good night.

Elijah walked me home and thanked me for coming. He could tell I was nervous. "I'm sorry about the greens. My mom had asked me what food you liked, and I thought you said you ate collard greens, so I suggested it."

I quickly apologized. "No, I do like them. It wasn't your fault or the collards. I was just nervous and couldn't eat anything. My stomach was in knots. I've never met someone's Mom before."

He twirled his finger in my ponytail as he looked at me lovingly. "I love you, Tianna."

All the blood rushed to my feet, and I could feel a cold sweat breaking out. I shook my head no. He was seventeen. What did he know about love?

He laughed. "No?" He pulled me closer to him. "I love you."

I broke free from his embrace and vomited in my mom's rose bushes. I ran upstairs and vomited again. I took a shower and stared at the ceiling for an hour replaying his words over and over in my head. He loved me. I wanted his love for me to be real. I prayed and drifted off to sleep with a smile on my face with the faintest hope that it was.

"Christianna! Christianna!"

The yelling is normal with *Mami*. She's Puerto Rican. It's how she talks. But when *Mami* says my name in Spanish, I already know I did something wrong. I walked down the stairs to the kitchen, my migraine from throwing up all night making me dizzy. I would have rather gone to school than be yelled at.

"Yes?" I opened the cabinet and grabbed some graham crackers pretending to not notice her mood. The sight of the crackers made my stomach rumble, so I put them back.

"I'm making a grocery list and I just realized something. You haven't asked me to buy you maxi-pads last month or this month?"

I relaxed my shoulders and calmed myself. I thought I was in actual trouble for something. "I had some leftover from before. And last month I didn't bleed a lot. But it should be coming soon, so yeah, I need some. And something for my migraine, please."

"There's some pain medication in the medicine cabinet. And what's 'soon' Tianna? Do you even know when you are due for your period?"

"No, not really but that's because it's always changing. Sometimes it skips a month. Sometimes it's seven days long. Last month was just one day. And not even a lot."

Mami stared at me for a second then rose from her chair, grabbed her car keys, and left the house without a word. Or her list. It was strange but lately, *Mami* had been very tense and jumping down everybody's throats for no good reason at all. Abe had mentioned menopause as if he even knew what that meant. I took a few pain meds with some milk and forced down a cracker since it said to take with food. I went to my bedroom and pulled out a small canvas and my pallet. I set up my paints and brushes when Abe knocked on my door. "Elijah's on the phone."

He handed me the cordless phone. Elijah had called to see if I had been feeling better and that he'd missed me at school. He felt terrible that his mother's cooking had made me sick. I laughed and assured him I was fine. It was a case of nerves and nothing more. I didn't mention the migraine.

He went quiet and I could tell he had something to say but couldn't get it out.

"Ti?"

"Yeah."

"All I want you to do is trust me."

"I do." At least as much as I could ever trust someone that wasn't *Mami*, Pop, or Abe.

He seemed glad to hear it and told me he loved me again. I didn't know how to respond to it. I didn't know if I loved him back and I didn't want to lie to him.

"I'll pick you up tomorrow for school," he said not seeming to care if I'd said it back or not.

We ended our conversation right after. I began painting two hands intertwining. The idea just sprung up in my head, so I went with it. A little later *Mami* came into my bedroom without knocking and tossed a bag onto my lap. She crossed her arms and stared at me. I can see she was upset but I had no idea why.

"What is this?" I asked confused. She didn't respond. I pulled out a box from the bag surprised to see a pregnancy test. Was this why my mom had been acting weird and moody? Was she pregnant? "Are you pregnant?" I asked not sure how to feel about it.

"Don't play stupid Tianna!"

I shook my head trying to loosen some sense in my head that could help me understand what was going on. I held up the test and looked at her. So, if she wasn't pregnant, was the test for me? I nearly choked on my own saliva.

"*Mami*, are you serious?"

"Are you a virgin?"

The question knocked me upside my head. I wasn't a virgin ten times over. Bryson had been my first and Elijah my last but in between, I had tried to find fulfillment in at least four other guys including Leon. I wasn't a virgin. I wasn't even a vir.

I got up from the chair and walked to the bathroom without answering her. I had no idea how pregnancy tests worked. I opened the box and read the instructions three times and still didn't know what to do. My mind had begun to wander, thinking of the several times Elijah and I had had sex. The first time was so unexpected I couldn't remember if he'd worn a condom. After that I never paid attention. I had just always let the guy handle that part.

I began to panic. I thought about why *Mami* would even think to buy me a pregnancy test. My period. I must have said something that triggered her. I had been irregular last month. I counted how many days since my last period and thirty-five days had already passed. My panic increased. I read the directions again, paying full attention. I followed the instructions to the letter. Two minutes would have been torture but I didn't have to wait that long. I snatched the box from the counter confirming what a positive test looked like and made sure I wasn't seeing things.

I took the second test out of the box and repeated it. Once again, two minutes wasn't needed. I lowered myself to the floor staring at the tests through blurred vision. I don't know when *Mami* came into the bathroom, but she was standing in front of me, her small feet pacing. I heard her, but I don't know what she said. I finally looked up and saw her staring at the test, her hand to her forehead. She walked out of the bathroom and didn't say a word.

I got up from the floor and put on my coat. I took my old bicycle out of the garage and rode it a few miles down to Pop's office. By the time I got there, the parking lot was nearly empty, but his car was still there. The receptionist was gone but I knew where his office was. I took the stairs too anxious to wait for the elevator. I reached the third floor and opened the door, taking a minute to catch my breath.

It was only a few minutes past five o'clock and the sun had already set. Most of the lights on the floor had been turned off but Pop's office was still on lending me some light. I walked toward his office nervous about what to say. Between him and *Mami*, he was the one I trusted to be calm and rational. He'd always been the steady person in my life. *Mami* loved me of course but she wasn't good at keeping her emotions at bay. I wanted to explain to him I was pregnant before she did.

I stopped and took a breath, bracing myself. He was more rational but that didn't mean he wouldn't be upset. Before I took another step, I heard a woman's voice in his office. She was asking about travel plans and I could see her writing notes on a notepad. I stepped back into the shadows. I couldn't talk to Pop in front of her. She stood up and I was relieved she was getting ready to leave. I didn't know how much longer I could take the anxiety.

I peeked inside the office to see what was taking her so long and saw her massaging Pop's shoulders. I straightened at the sight, something in me snapping. He loosened his tie and kept reading over a document on his desk. She kissed him on the neck, and he smiled but kept reading. She whispered something in his ear that got his full attention and he swung her around onto his lap and started to kiss her.

I had been through many things in my life. I had suffered many heartbreaks and betrayals. I had been used. I had been abused. I had been abandoned. But nothing prepared me for the hurt that my father's infidelity rocked me with. I walked out of his office without letting him know I was there. I thought about riding to Elijah's, but Marvette was home, and I wasn't allowed in his bedroom when she was home. Instead, I went home and locked myself in my bedroom. Not once did *Mami* or Pop come looking for me.

After midnight, I snuck out of the house and went to Elijah's. I knocked on his window for a full twenty minutes before he woke up. He let me in and snuck me into his bedroom. At the sight of him, I burst into tears. He hugged me and consoled me until I was calm. I told him about my dad first. His dad had cheated on his mom, so he knew all too well how that went.

I composed myself scared about how he'd react to what else I had to share, but there was no turning back. "Elijah, I took a pregnancy test today." He pulled back and looked me in the face. "It was positive," I whispered.

He jumped up and began to pace. "Are you sure?"

"Yes. I took two tests, and both were positive."

"Both were positive." My words stopped his pacing. He lowered himself to his bed in shock. Then let himself fall back with a thump.

"Elijah," I couldn't hold the tears back, "I'm scared."

He sat up and waved me over to him. I sat on his lap, and he rubbed my back. "I know Ti. It's going to be ok. We'll work it out."

"Ok. I trust you, Elijah." He smiled at me and kissed me on the lips. We laid in his bed and fell asleep.

I woke up to his mother standing over us, anger on her face. "Elijah!" She yelled. He stirred but didn't wake. I elbowed him lightly but that didn't help. "Elijah!" She yelled it louder.

"Dang, Mom. I'm up. I'm up."

"What is Tianna doing in your bed, Elijah?"

I quickly got up from his bed, fully clothed, and put my sneakers on as he sat up on his bed still groggy wearing nothing but boxers and a wifebeater. The state of her son's undress tipped her over the edge.

She turned to me and called me all kinds of trash, fast ass, whores, and everything in between. Elijah rubbed his eyes not seeming to be concerned. I grabbed my coat and headed for the door.

"Tianna, wait. Don't leave." He walked over to me and held my hand. "Mom, stop talking to her like that. She's not like that."

"Not like that? What kind of girl is asleep in a boy's bed while he's in it practically naked? And boy you know better than to be having some girls in your room! I don't care how smart she is or what church she goes to!"

Elijah just let her rant, not seeming to care much. He slipped a T-shirt on over his wifebeater and went back to holding my hand. I wanted to leave but every time I tried to free myself, he held on tighter.

Marvette took a breath and Elijah used the opportunity to speak. "Mom, I love her. And she is pregnant. You going off for nothing because what's done is done."

"Pregnant?"

"Yes, Mom. She's pregnant."

"Not again. Boy, do you not learn your lesson. How many times is it going to take for you to learn to put a damn condom on! I'm not going through this again Elijah! Do you hear me? I'm not."

Marvette removed the pin from the grenade, tossed it on the floor at Elijah's feet, and walked out of his bedroom. I tried to slip my hand from his grasp, but he held it tighter.

"Tianna, it's not what it sounds like."

I yanked my hand free. I didn't care. I ran out of the house. He chased behind me but didn't go beyond the yard with no pants or shoes on. With no other place to go, I ran home. Pop was in the kitchen drinking coffee and stopped me.

"Tianna! Are you just getting in the house?" He was stunned. "Where have you been all night?" He set his coffee down and tuned up the rarely used dad tone. "And more importantly what were you thinking? If your mother found out, I'd have to pull her off your ass."

"Yeah, well maybe you should give yourself this speech." Never in my entire life had I talked back to Pop, but I didn't care. He wasn't my real father anyway. That loser abandoned me. And this one was a dog like all the rest.

"And what exactly is that supposed to mean young lady?" I turned my back and walked away. "Christianna Faith Leonard, get your ass back here, now."

I stopped and faced him. "Christianna Faith Cruz."

I hadn't laid a hand on him, but the verbal assault wounded him. He jerked back at my words and said nothing more. For a split second, I wanted to apologize and take away the hurt I could see I caused, but the image of him kissing a woman that wasn't *Mami* reared its head, and my remorse dissipated. I didn't want his last name. I didn't want him as my dad. And I didn't want him as my safety net.

I locked myself in my bedroom. When *Mami* finally got the door unlocked, she talked until she was blue in the face asking me a million questions. I answered none. For two days I imprisoned myself in my bedroom. I turned down every call and visit from Elijah. Abe snuck me some crackers to help settle my stomach. Suddenly the bouts of nausea made sense.

On day three, my mom caught me sneaking to the bathroom and waited for me to come out, and dragged me to Elijah's house, hell-bent on talking to him and his mother about his responsibility as a father. *Mami* knocked on their front door like she was Po-Po. Had I the energy to care I would have wanted the ground to swallow me whole, but they could all go to hell for all I cared.

Marvette answered the door calmly and collected and when *Mami* demanded to have an audience with her and her son, Marvette politely declined.

"Elijah is not here. He moved with his father to Colorado. And as far as we're concerned, my son is not that baby's father. I'll drop dead before you try to shackle my son to your daughter with a baby that isn't his."

I looked up at Marvette. The woman had the unearthly ability to blow up my spot. Bomb after bomb as if I were Baghdad and she was the US Military. I saw nothing in her expression. Not anger. Not sadness. Not contempt. Nothing. She opened her mouth to say something else, but I didn't even bother to listen. I casually walked away listening to *Mami* going off on Marvette, right past *Mami's* car and down the street, not caring what they argued about.

I eventually ended up at school and climbed up to the highest level of the football field bleachers. I can't tell you how long I sat out in the cold staring out into the field. After a while, flurries began to fall, my cue to go home. I stood up and took a step, but too late I realized my legs had gone numb and I couldn't feel them. I went tumbling down the bleachers.

I lost the baby and found sorrow. I lost Elijah and found a new level of loneliness. I lost Pop and found Tommy, my mother's husband. I lost the ability to love or trust anything or anyone and found bitterness. I lost Christianna, Faith, and Leonard.

TEN
Bianca

Two Years Later

I had two morning classes to attend before I could go visit my dad in the nursing facility. It had been two years since his stroke and the mobility on his right side was extremely limited, as was his impaired speech. Dad barely spoke not wanting to bother with the struggle of forming words. He'd get so frustrated he'd bang his left hand on the table then would quit trying. It ate me up seeing him that way. Yet, I could be nothing but grateful that he was still alive and here with me.

I could relate to him on some level. He hadn't been the only one frustrated with impairment. My traumas constantly triggered my anger and impulsivity. I'd overreact and blow up at the smallest things. I was beginning to annoy myself as much as I had annoyed Justin.

I just wanted to be a better person so bad that it made me cry because I just didn't know how. Justin was right. Pool hustling couldn't fix me, no matter how much I loved the game or that it made me feel good about myself.

Truth was, no matter how much I loved Justin, he couldn't either. Relying on him and his advice to fix the brokenness inside was failing and not fair to him or me. I knew I needed more but I hadn't changed much since the days of therapy with Ms. Mason. I was still afraid of facing the truth. I'd been avoiding it for years.

I had finally accepted that in order to get through it, I first had to face it. That realization alone was significant. It was slow going but even an inch of progress was still progress. The funny thing about taking steps to make your life better is that the determination pours over into other areas like spilled juice. I felt the need to do better and be better in all parts of my life just as Justin had always encouraged.

I told myself to just try a college course or two, just to see if it was a good fit for me. One or two turned into a full-time nursing student. With Dad living in the nursing home full time and Justin away at school, it had become my main focus. It was also my biggest secret. At first, I hadn't told anyone in case I failed, I'd do so without anyone knowing. After I'd kept up with my studies, I kept it a secret just for my own peace and purpose. I protected myself from the haters and doubters and didn't have to explain my actions to anyone. It felt good to succeed on my own without Justin having to push me or Dad having to scold me. It was something that I wanted to keep just for me.

I needed to prove to others as well as myself that I was capable of doing good in my life and with my life. I knew many people saw me as this angry person who wanted nothing more than to be bitter for the rest of my life, but they were so wrong. I wanted more from life and aimed to prove it. Yeah, it was hard as hell. I'd never been a person that liked school, but I stepped up, one challenge at a time. I needed my mom to be proud of me as she looked down at me from heaven.

I zipped my backpack closed and grabbed my house keys off the table. As I was about to walk out the door the phone rang. I quickly snatched up the cordless from the kitchen wall.

"Hello."

"Hey, Babe. How's your morning going?" Justin asked.

"Pretty good. About to leave out. I have some errands to run before visiting my dad."

"Oh okay. Where do you have to go?"

"Um, well, just to snatch up a few groceries and pay the cable bill."

"I thought you got groceries yesterday."

I smacked myself in the forehead. "Oh, I did. Forgot some things." I could have made up a better excuse than that. I was a master at avoidance, but I'd never been good at deceit.

"You know I know you, right?"

"Why you say that?"

"You sound like you're not telling me the truth. What's going on B? What are you not telling me?"

"I love that you know me so well, but this time I kinda wish you didn't," I laughed.

"What, what do you mean?"

"It's nothing bad. Please just trust me. I'll tell you soon." There was no point in continuing the charade but hopefully he'd just let it go.

"So, I'm right. Tell me. What is it?"

Or maybe he wouldn't. "Aww, man. It's supposed to be a surprise, Justin."

"You know you have to tell me now. Come on. What?"

"Okay. I'm on my way to class."

"Class? What? You finally taking anger management classes? That's great, Baby."

"Noooo."

"Okay. Now I'm confused," Justin said.

"I go to community college." I closed my eyes and listened intently wondering how he'd respond.

"Wait. What did you just say?"

"Yes, you heard me correctly. I'm taking classes at Camden County."

"Whoa! When did this happen? I'm at a loss for words right now. I wasn't expecting to hear that."

Even though I had wanted to keep it private it a little longer, I was proud of achievements and had nothing to hide on that front. "Right after I graduated high school. I'm about to get my associate degree."

"You've been in college for almost two years Bianca?" He practically yelled over the phone.

"Yeah." I dragged it out a little embarrassed I'd kept the secret from him for so long.

"You have me speechless right now."

"Are you happy for me? Is it a good speechless?"

"I'm a little irked you kept it a secret but I'm so happy to hear you're in college I'll let that go. I never expected to call home and hear you say that."

"And why is that?"

"Well, you seemed too comfortable being in the hood and the past few years you have been so engulfed in your past, dealing with your anger issues. I just couldn't see you going to college."

"Wow. Thanks, Justin." That stung my pride.

"No, no. Please don't take it in a bad way. I'm just being honest. I didn't know if you wanted more for yourself out of life, even though I did."

"Well, as you can see, I do want more."

"Yes. Shockingly, I do."

I expected him to be surprised but how much so was a little insulting. I stayed quiet rather than start an argument. I had come too far to let negativity bring me down.

"Bianca, I've always known you could do and be so much more. I didn't mean to come off doubting you. I'm actually blown away right now. God answered a prayer. I don't even know how to explain how relieved and happy I am."

"Really?" And just like that, he smoothed my ruffled feathers. I didn't even have to say a word and he read my mood over the telephone. I loved the deep connection we shared.

"Of course, really. I'm proud of you. I love seeing your progress, Baby. You were made for something bigger, B."

I smiled from ear to ear. "Thank you for believing in me, Babe."

"We need to celebrate. Better yet, we'll have a super special Valentine's Day next month. I'll come home just for you."

"Aww, thank you. You have no idea how I'm feeling right now. I'm so motivated and proud of myself."

"I am too. Hey, what are you going to school for? What's your major?"

"Nursing."

"You just keep surprising me! A nurse?"

"Yes. Helping take care of my dad and working in the nursing home really inspired my decision. I believe helping people is what I'm supposed to be doing."

"Woman, now I know you need to handle your anger issues if you're going to be working with people. You don't want a patient to piss you off and you clockem' out of anger," Justin laughed.

I laughed and said, "No, I wouldn't do that."

"Nah seriously B. How do you know? You know you be snappin' and I really do understand why. And I know sometimes you are provoked but it's your reaction that scares me. You lose control. Baby, I'm only saying this because I love you and I want you to succeed but you really need to stop dodging and get the help you need before something bad happens."

"I hear you, Justin, and thank you for caring. But please trust me. I'm fine for now. Eventually, I will though."

He exhaled deeply. "Ok, well it's about time for my next class, I have to go."

"Yeah, me too."

He laughed. "You too, huh? I love it. I'll call you tonight. And I'm still in shock. You made my day, B."

"You still make me blush after all this time, Babe. Thank you."

"That's my job."

"And you do it well.

"Damn right. Ok, I have to go, and you get your ass to class. I'll talk to you later. I love you."

"I love you, Justin."

After I hung up with Justin, I went to class and knocked out my assignments before heading out to see my dad. When I got there, I noticed dried-up tears streaked down his face. My intuition was immediately disturbed. I kissed him on the forehead and went straight to the nurses' station where four nurses were talking and laughing.

"Excuse me. Who is the nurse for Calvin Williams?" I was short and to the point. I needed answers.

"That would be me. My name is Laura. I've been with him since seven this morning. Is everything okay?"

No. Everything was not ok. I held in my frustration and tried to keep calm. "My dad looks like he was crying. Did something happen?"

"Not that I know of. He wasn't in such a good mood when the LPN went to bathe and change him."

"Did you ask him?" Her blame-shifting irked me. How the hell was she his nurse and hadn't noticed he'd been crying? Maybe if she was doing her job rather out her laughing with the other staff, she would have noticed that something was wrong.

"He's asleep. I didn't want to wake him but will most definitely ask him when he wakes up."

"Okay. Well, what's the LPN's name?"

"Dana."

"Dana what? Dammit?" I snapped tired of her giving me half-ass answers.

"Dana Witherspoon. Why? What's going on? Watch your language."

"You ain't my mom. I can say what I want. I want to speak with her to see if she knows why my dad was cryin'. I'ma black out in here if I find out she did somethin' to my dad!"

"Can you please lower your voice? I'm sure Dana did not do anything to your father. Calm down and we will straighten this out. We will be in to talk to you shortly."

"Yeah. Do that. Thank you."

"Of course."

When I got back to my dad's room, he was awake staring at the ceiling.

I walked over and rubbed his head, "Hey Daddy. How are you? I brought you some protein shakes."

He blinked his eyes as an answer for okay instead of trying to verbalize it.

"Daddy, were you crying? I see dry tears on your face," I asked as I touched the left side of his cheek.

He blinked again.

"Why? What happened?"

The door opened and the LPN, Dana walked in.

"Hello, my name is Dana. You wanted to see me."

"My dad looked like he was crying, and I wanted to know what happened."

"Nothing happened. I didn't see him crying. He may have cried after I left. I'm not sure, but I didn't see him crying. Nothing happened while I was with him."

I looked over at my dad. He eyed Dana with terror in his eyes.

"Well, somethin' happened dammit," I said not believing her bullshit.

"And again, nothing happened while he was with me. I have to go and see to my other patients. You can talk to his nurse if you have any other questions or concerns."

Her passive-aggressive attitude pissed me off. After she left, I tried to get my dad to tell me what happened, but he laid there in silence, not even blinking his eyes. I wondered if he was afraid to tell me.

When I got home later that night I went through the mail and opened a letter regarding my dad's partnership in the garage he'd worked at for many years before his stroke. With him no longer being able to work and his partner wanting to retire they'd finally sold the business. Not knowing anything about selling a business I'd left the details to my dad's partner and friend, trusting him to be fair and honest. A check with Dad's share of the profit had shocked me. A larger amount than we had originally thought stared back at me.

What was I going to do with that kind of money? I felt like I was about to be rich! Hood rich anyway. I didn't care though. This could help me catch up on bills, do some things for dad, and put some money away. I could finally spend more time studying instead of having to hustle pool a few times a week to make ends meet.

I'd thought about my Dad crying in that facility and vowed to use the money he'd earned to try and make a better life for him. The day had been a rollercoaster of emotion, but I was grateful for the blessing that sparked hope.

ELEVEN
Tianna

I walked into my Visual Arts classroom excited. Basic courses bored me although learning came easy to me. I was finally able to add more creative courses to my schedule. I hadn't yet chosen a major and knew I needed to. I longed to start life doing what brought me joy but was nervous about declaring art as my major. I put off thinking about it as I searched for a seat. I chose the middle seat in the back row and took out my notebook and pen. Waiting for class to begin, I felt like a full-on nerd reading over the syllabus the professor handed me as I walked in. Art was woven into my soul and brought me peace, so I devoured every bit of teaching and opportunity to learn.

Once class began, the professor had asked a few questions about our previous knowledge of various art forms. A lot of what he referenced I had known of or at least heard of, but I didn't raise my hand to speak on any of it. I preferred to blend in with the background like camouflage; soak up the knowledge and go on about my life. These days, I kept to myself for the most part. No friends. No social life. Just me and Vin Easel, my painting easel.

After I had lost both the baby and Elijah, I homeschooled the remainder of my senior year of high school. I had stopped attending church altogether. That year I'd rarely left my bedroom or the house. I'd escape to the backyard at night when everyone was asleep to get some fresh air and a change of scenery.

One night during the summer, I was rocking back and forth on the patio swing looking up at the stars, and heard *Mami* and Pop arguing in the kitchen with the window open. She'd found lipstick on his collar, as cliché as that was. He remained quiet while she verbally annihilated him. When he did finally speak, his response was calm. "Tanya, you ruined our family when you chose your job over us."

It angered me to hear him say that. What a coward. He didn't even have the courage to admit he ruined our family too. *Mami* didn't force him to cheat. Not that she was any better. He wasn't entirely wrong. I often wondered how different life would be if *Mami* hadn't started working. Uncle Lou touching me flashed in my head and I willed it out of my consciousness. The hate I'd built up for him had festered so deeply I never visited *Mami's* family just to avoid him altogether. And when they came to visit, whether he was with them or not, I locked myself in my bedroom. The first few times, *Mami* got on me about being rude and not going down to say hello. Eventually, she stopped insisting I be well mannered and pay her family some respect.

Pop moved out of the house a few months after that. He and *Mami* reconciled a few times and broke up a few more times but he never moved back in. Abe began to split his time between *Mami's* house and Pop's adding to my lonely existence. I never stepped a foot in Pop's place. I'd rarely spoken more than a few words to him at a time since I saw him with that woman. *Mami* assumed I was just caught up in hurt and taking it out on everyone. She was wrong. My anger at him was intentional and direct.

I walked out of class and headed to the coffee shop on my way to an art studio I began spending time in. It was a hole in the wall and small, but it was quiet, and the owner was chill. With the unexpected money I received from my biological dad's passing, I rented a small space in the back of the studio big enough to paint in and store all of my supplies. It was my own little world and I loved it. I spent as much time as I could there.

On the wall by the one drafty window, I hung up the framed artwork that Elijah had gifted me for Christmas years ago. I don't know why I kept it. I suppose it reminded me of a short period of joy in an otherwise painful life span. Like a small island in a vast ocean.

A year after he'd left, I contemplated taking my own life. Not because of him. Not because of Pop. Not even because of the miscarriage.

I had always believed that a child's life was supposed to be carefree and innocent. Adulthood was what caused stress and required fortitude. I had barely survived adolescence. How much worse would adulthood be? I didn't want to find out.

In my breakdown, I began screaming, crying, and tossing things around my room including the framed sketch. It crashed against the closet door before landing face down on the carpet. The glass broke, as had the frame. I removed the sketch and examined it. The broken glass had caused a tear in the corner, but it was otherwise fully intact. I had never known why Elijah chose that particular sketch to frame, but it didn't matter. He had once told me I was gifted and that stayed with me. I emptied the bottle of painkillers into the toilet and flushed. I had a small spark of joy still left in my life. After that night, I promised myself to live out my dreams no matter what. School, volunteer work, and art consumed my entire life since. My already good grades, upgraded to highest honors. I had become so driven and focused I'd earn several full academic scholarships including to the University of Colorado. I had applied on a whim and later regretted it. I declined it, determined to burn any bridge that led to a haunted past.

After leaving the studio I went home purposely avoiding dinnertime. I saw Tommy's car in the driveway and was glad I hadn't had to break bread with him. Once inside, I headed straight for the stairs not wanting to be bothered with his attempt at small talk.

"Ti? Is that you?" *Mami* called from the kitchen.

I let out an irritated breath before responding respectfully. "Yeah, *Mami*. I'm gonna go shower and study before bed. I have an early class tomorrow."

"Come in here for just a minute," she called out.

I hung up my coat and unraveled my scarf as I walked into the kitchen. "Hey." I didn't direct the greeting toward anyone in particular. Tommy sat on one of the island barstools quietly. That was fine by me.

Mami looked over at him and when he didn't move a muscle to speak, so she did. "Abe was taken to the police station for disorderly conduct."

That grabbed my full attention. "Wait. What?" I looked back and forth between them looking for details. "What happened?"

"He got into a fight in the mall food court that escalated into a brawl when one of the kids involved picked up a chair and tossed it. It hit an innocent bystander and narrowly missed a baby in a stroller."

"Is he ok? Where is he?"

"He's in his room. He didn't get charged or arrested but he had to get released into our custody."

"What was he thinking?" I asked annoyed at his immaturity.

"Defending his sister," Tommy finally spoke frustrated.

His voice irritated me, but I asked him to clarify his remark anyway.

"I don't know the specifics. He refused to tell me." Tommy stood from the island upset. "This family has had its fair share of issues, but I won't be disrespected and I sure as hell won't have Abe turning into some lowlife punk. Tianna, we have our issues, but keep my son out of it."

His son. I don't know why that felt like I was stabbed in the heart, but it had. I refused to cry though. I hadn't cried since the day I promised myself to reach my goals. And I wouldn't do it now.

"Tommy, as far as I'm concerned, my brother," I stressed, "will never be a lowlife punk like his father."

I felt *Mami's* hand across my face and it stung. I left the kitchen without saying another word, *Mami* behind me telling me how disrespectful I was. I heard Tommy trying to calm her down but on and on she went. I climbed the stairs with the little bit of warmth left in my heart reserved only for my brother. And that too was on the brink of being snuffed out. Not because I didn't love him, but because a small flame can't survive in a tundra of ice.

I tapped on the wall above my headboard, and Abe replied in code permitting me to enter his domain. I walked over to his bedroom and tapped twice so he knew it was me. I closed the door behind me and tossed myself back on his waterbed imagining I was floating in the ocean.

"I know I say this every time, but it's really weird that your dad bought you a waterbed. Definitely, a guilt-trip gift."

Abe paused his video game and turned his chair to look over at me. "My dad? That's a new one."

"So is getting into a fight at the mall. What gives Abraham Lincoln? You're the most peaceful person I know. Well other than your obsession with boxing and martial arts."

He shrugged and turned back to the video game. "Boys just being boys."

"I call bullshit, baby brother. Tommy said you were defending me. What's he talking about?"

Abe yelled out a few expletives after being gunned down in the video game, losing a life. He started again, concentrating fully on the game. I watched for a bit, waiting for him to be ready. After twenty minutes, he removed the headset and tossed the game controller on his desk.

"I see you aren't leaving which means you are being annoyingly stubborn."

"And since we already know I'm very good at it, we mind as well just skip the appetizers and get to the meat of the issue. What happened?"

He rested his elbows on the chair's armrests and twisted from side to side. "A few of my friends and I were walking in the mall, and we came across a few other dudes." Abe avoided eye contact with me. "Do you remember Bryson?"

A blast from the past that I'd chosen to forget. "Unfortunately."

"The guy's a real dick. Anyway, he got stupid and asked if the line for Tianna's Whoris Wheel had shortened some so he could get a free ride. Then he said, 'Probably not. Tianna's legs stay open twenty-four seven like 7-11.' So, I clocked him in the chin before his boys jumped in and then Melvin got in it. Before I knew it chairs were flying. But because I box, the little pussy wanted to press charges on me."

My eyes widened. "So, what happened? Why didn't he?"

"I'm not a pro boxer so his claim didn't hold up. Besides, he's the asshole that was throwing chairs."

Hot shame burned me from the inside out. I thanked Abe for coming to my defense and apologized that he had experienced that on my behalf. Life kept on teaching me that the consequences of our actions didn't stop at just ourselves. The connection we share with others are likes cords that carry our good and bad vibes and has the potential to flow into others. Although I had taken a vow of celibacy years ago, my choices back then were still affecting me now.

"Ti, don't apologize. He's an ass and deserved the broken nose."

I hugged my baby brother who wasn't a baby anymore. Tommy got one thing right, Abe was not even close to being a lowlife punk. He'd grown into a strong young man, inside and out. I was proud to be his sister. I smacked him in the back of the head to keep balance between us before I left him to his video games. Too much mushy stuff irritated him. And when he told me I smelled and needed a shower, I saluted him and grinned before I exited his sanctuary.

For the first time in a long time, I prayed. Not for myself. I wasn't worthy of receiving anything from God. Frankly, I didn't think He liked me too much. But I prayed for Abe. Bias aside, he really was a great guy and I wanted God to protect him from the levels of misfortune and self-loathing I had endured in my life. Granted some of my screw-ups were my own doing but others were not.

Yeah, I know no one goes through life without pain, suffering, and trials and I wasn't asking God to keep Abe from any of that. That wasn't realistic. I just wanted Abe to be able to cope with whatever life threw his way and not lose the goodness in him because of it. I had lost my goodness many moons ago. I often wondered if I ever had any to begin with. It was too late for me, but not for Abe. Exhaling a deep breath, I stopped that line of thinking that would lead me directly to a pity party and let it go.

Sitting in Philosophy class was like sitting on a seesaw. Emotions ran up and down. The class was intended to stretch our critical thinking muscles. Debate was encouraged and many of my classmates lived to argue. I preferred observation as opposed to being heard. But since the course required participation, every now and again I'd chime in on a topic that the students seemed to be neutral on. I had no desire to debate with anyone. Until today.

He raised his hand and argued that Affirmative Action in the United States was necessary and gave all of his reasons why. After he was done, you could hear a pin fall, it was so quiet. Not one person, including the twentieth century Plato that argued everything, spoke up to debate his point. I hadn't noticed until now that our class was predominantly white males. An Asian here and there. A few white young women. Then there was him and there was me. Two brown people.

He sat back in his chair pleased with himself for eloquently stating his point that no one seemed to challenge. I could only assume that no one wanted to challenge a black man on a topic entangled in racism. Especially if you weren't a minority. Fear of offending or looking like a bigot was real, I suppose. But fear based on stereotypes of angry brown people was even more so.

I admit I raised my hand not only because I disagreed with this particular black man's stance, but also because his cocky attitude grated on my nerves. The professor's eyes widened a fraction before he permitted me to rebut. When the young brother turned around to see who dared combat his point, my hands got a little sweaty. I hated confrontation and arguing so I tuned him out as I had done everyone else in my life.

"Affirmative Action is not the solution to diversifying the workplace and classroom. It only perpetuates the idea that the color of a person's skin should determine who belongs where. For no other reason than the color of a person's skin, a job is awarded, or a classroom seat is assigned is just as damaging to our society as not hiring someone because of the color of their skin or admittance into a school.

The root of the problem that has kept this country segregated is ignorance and fear. Until ignorance is eradicated, nothing will diversify us. Not only does awarding a job to someone who may not even be qualified because of the color of their skin jeopardize the efficiency and success of that business, but more importantly it potentially subjects that person to an environment that isn't conducive to their own personal success. Co-workers would resent him because of how he received the job. If unqualified, he is setting himself up to fail. And when he fails what do you think the response to his failure will be? 'I told you so.' And the "I told you so' wouldn't be a reflection of his individual failure but categorizing an entire group of people to be labeled as failures as well. And unfairly so.

And I will even go as far as to say that employers would intentionally hire an unqualified minority under Affirmative Action just to have them fail in order to coerce a result in their favor. They want to say, 'I told you so.'

Affirmative Action is not balancing the scales. It is a hindrance and a slap in the face to our people. We deserve equality, not a hand-out that sets us up to fail. We should never settle for anything less than that. Award me for my merit, not because I have more melanin in my skin or because my eyes slant more than yours. Hire me because I am qualified not because my hair curls a certain type of way or because my nose spreads wider. Choose me because I earned it and learned it not because I have an accent."

I exhaled.

The silence afterward made me uncomfortable, and I could feel lots of eyes on me. I hadn't intended to get so emotional. But I had spoken my piece and meant every word. I dared look up and caught his eyes still on me. He smiled, nodded in approval, then faced forward. I don't know why, but his reaction settled me, and I contained my smile. Pride was a double-edged sword. Too little damaged self-esteem. Too much made you arrogant. But it was the only word I could find that fit my mood. I couldn't remember the last time I was proud of myself.

I was suddenly ten years old again watching *Mami* cry to Tommy about going back to work and that all she wanted was to feel pride in herself. I felt her sorrow for a second before I buried it deep. Those memories led to others that I'd rather not think about.

After class, I took my time packing my bag. I wasn't in any rush to go back home, and Sarah was holding a private teaching session at the studio, which meant the subject was nude, so I couldn't go there until later. I decided to go to the student center and read the assigned chapters. Philosophy was ok to participate in, but the reading always put me to sleep when I was at home. Maybe here I could manage to get it done.

I slung the strap to my messenger back over my shoulder and slipped my gloves on. One of the female students smiled as I walked by her, and I returned it. One of the males moved aside as if I were going to bite his head off. I smiled at him too. Ignorance and fear. Fear and ignorance. All I could do was control my part in it. Love as I wanted to be love. Treat others as I wanted to be treated.

As I walked down the hall, I heard someone behind me calling out. "Hold up!" I could hear the footsteps gaining on me, so I moved aside to let whoever it was, pass by in their rush. I was surprised when instead, Mr. Affirmative Action began walking beside me. "Hey," he said.

I was taken back by his sudden appearance and attempt at conversation. "Uh. Hey."

He was out of breath and juggling a coat, backpack, and some paperwork. He pinched the paperwork between his lips and the backpack between his knees while he slipped his coat on. I kept walking. I had no desire to continue our debate.

He caught up again, still slightly out of breath. "Dang girl, you can't hold up for a sec?"

I stopped and turned to him. I blinked slowly and pressed my lips together a little agitated. "My name is Christianna. Not girl. And whatever your rebuttal is, you can save it for class. Debate is not something I enjoy."

"I can't tell," he joked.

I didn't share in the humor.

"So do people call you Chris?"

"No. My friends and family call me Tianna." I stopped and remembered I had no friends. But the Tianna part was true enough.

"Ok cool. So, Tianna, I just wanted to give you your props on your rebuttal. I still don't agree completely but you opened up my mind to seeing things a little different. A different perspective."

I didn't know how to respond so I nodded and thanked him for the accolades he'd given me.

"I had no idea you had all of that in you. Thought you were one of the potheads that sat in the back and only showed up for credit."

I could tell he was trying to be funny and not offensive. He needed to work on that, but I gave him credit for trying and couldn't help but taunt him a little. "Who said I'm not?"

He put his hands up in mock surrender. "Ok, Method Man. I ain't judging you."

I shook my head playfully. If I kept responding to his nonsense, with my own, he'd keep it going. Seemed like he was well-versed in nonsense. I kept the funny thought to myself. He put his hand out offering me an introduction. "Hello, Tianna. I'm Justin Saunders. My family and friends call me Justin."

His big bright smile and polite manners made it hard to be intentionally standoffish toward him as had become my way. I shook his hand and toned down the amusement that tickled me. There was no need for him to know that I found him charming. In fact, quite the opposite. I erected my walls at the first sign of an intruder alert. "It was nice meeting you, Mr. Saunders."

He laughed out loud and let me be on my way. "I'll see you later Tianna," he yelled as I walked away. I put my hand up in a nonchalant wave goodbye and decided to go straight home after all.

TWELVE
Bianca

A night out shooting pool at Uncle Ricky's bar was what I needed. With the money Dad had received, I hadn't been around to hustle in a minute, and they were happy to see me.

"Hey, where ya been baby girl?" Uncle Ricky asked.

"Busy with school Uncle Ricky."

"School? What school?"

"I go to Camden County College."

He stopped and looked at me like I had ten heads. "Why am I just hearing about this?"

"It was a personal goal and I ain't wanna tell nobody. Please don't take it personal Unc."

He frowned his face before he nodded in approval. "Never. You have your reasons." His smiled broadened. "I have a niece in college. Hey everybody! Baby Girl is in college!"

"Uncle Ricky, no. Please, stop. I was only telling you," I whispered forcefully.

"Oh, I'm sorry Baby Girl. I got excited."

The cheers throughout the bar embarrassed me but I smiled and gave thanks even though I seriously didn't want the attention. I quickly changed the subject ready to step out of the limelight. "I'm going to play a few games Unc."

"Hey, you haven't been here in a while. I had the room upstairs fixed up. There's a pool table up there if you want to shoot in private for a bit."

"Really? Bet. That's perfect."

"Go ahead, Baby Girl. You got a few hours. There's a tournament starting later if you want to make some money."

"Oh okay. Thank you for letting me know. This might be my warmup session," I laughed.

He took the cigar out of his mouth and pointed at me. "Exactly. That's why I told you. You always leave here with these jokers' money." His laughter sounded like an old radiator about to burst before he started to cough, the result of smoking for more years than I had been alive. Every time I heard him laugh, I had the urge to clear my throat. I loved him though.

I went upstairs and spent some time on the pool table alone. After my third round, a few of the people in the tournament began showing up with the same idea of getting some practice in beforehand and an audience began to form. I heard a few haters critiquing my skills and trying to psych me out mentally before the competition started. Usually, I'd take the bait and show off, but Justin's words had lodged themselves in my mind and I chose to avoid drama rather than entertain it. I decided against competing and didn't stick around. Instead, I went home, showered, and ate dinner before going to bed.

The following day, I decided to catch the bus to Philly to roam the Gallery before going to visit my dad. The gum-smacking bus driver from years prior pulled up looking over her glasses at me.

"Come on girl! I aint' got all day!" She hollered. She hadn't changed a bit either.

"Well dang," I said to myself as I boarded. I let it go immediately not wanting to get into it with her. I wasn't even up the steps, and she was already frowning and shaking her head adamantly.

"Uh-uh. I'm not taking any dollar bills today. Exact change only."

"Well, how am I supposed to know that when you normally take bills?"

"Look. Do you have exact change or not? Ain't nobody got time to explain NJ Transit rules to you." She placed her index finger on the brim of her glasses and pulled them down to give me a stern look.

Oh! She was buggin' looking like Shirley from *What's Happening*. "What's your name?"

"Sharon. S to the h, to the a to the r, to the o, to the n. Now, why you wanna know?"

"Because you're being rude Shirley. I just want to get to Philly. Can you give me change so I can pay my way, please?"

"Shirley?" She asked appalled. I wanted to laugh but I didn't. "Rude? Little girl, I'm not being rude. I'm simply telling you I don't take bills and I need exact change. Something is wrong with the machine. See here? It ain't working right." She obnoxiously tapped on the fare machine that looked like it was turning on and off by itself.

"So, I guess I ride for free then?"

Her eyes opened wide, and she adjusted herself on her seat like she was ready to snatch me up. "Give me your bills, with your little smart mouth. You wanna start reporting people and stuff and trying to get out of paying. Here. Here go some change."

"Thank you. That's all I wanted." I handed her my money and waited for my change.

She went to hand it to me then pulled it back. "Wait. You that little girl that use to get on my bus, right? Where you been, girl? I didn't know that was you with that baseball cap on."

"Yup, it's me. And you still chewing that gum and chewing people up, I see." She was something else, but I actually liked her. She handed me my change and I had to laugh.

"Girl I have to stay on point. People be trying to play me and get over. I run into all types of people driving this bus. Child, I had to call the po-lice last week because this girl wanted to fight 'cause I wouldn't let her ride for free. Caused a whole scene. Thought I was gonna lose my job that day 'cause she stepped way over the line. Her wig was about to be on the floor somewhere. Okay?" she said while pulling off.

"Wow. They be trippin'."

"Yes, girl."

She talked until I got off at my stop. I was looking forward to gazing out into the water and getting lost in my thoughts as I rode over the Ben Franklin Bridge. It always humbled me. I was a small dot in such a big world. Hopefully, I could do it on the ride back home.

I got off the bus on Ninth and Market Streets near the Gallery's main entrance. On my way inside a group of guys blocked the entrance and I excused myself as I weaved my way through them.

"How you doin' Shorty?"

"Good," I said as I kept walking.

"Can I speak wit' you for a minute?"

"Really don't feel like talking," I answered as I went to open the door. Before I could blink, he had stepped in front of the door and blocked me.

"Do you know who I am?"

I stopped in my tracks. "Nope."

"I'm part of the group Black Sheep."

"So?"

He licked his lips and tilted his chin up quickly. "So gimme your number, Beautiful."

"I'm supposed to just give you my numba 'cause you a rapper? I don't think so. Now move outta my way 'cause you can't get with this or get with that."

"Ohhhhhh!" The guys with him began laughing and shoving each other, giving each other pounds and making a scene, embarrassing him even more.

"Fuck you bitch. You ain't all that anyway."

"I was thinking the same thing about you." I stepped around him and entered through the other door. I didn't let him see that his arrogance pissed me off. Why were people always trying to get me to blow my top? I just wanted to be left alone.

I went into the Gallery, did some shopping, and ate lunch at my favorite spot. As I sat in the food court, I watched a girl eating a slice of pizza while her parents talked to each other.

I don't know why, but I watched them for a long while. After she was done, she got up and put her trash in the can, and waited for her parents to do the same. A moment later she slipped her hand into her mother's, without fuss. I tore my gaze away from them, my heart suddenly heavy.

I shook it off quickly and focused on why I had come to Philly in the first place. Felt good to finally break away and have some me time. School kept me busy. Every time I turned around, I had to write this and do that. I got it done though. And I couldn't complain. It had kept me out of trouble.

When I got home, I'd had a voicemail from the nursing home asking for a return call. I called immediately and was told that my dad had had an accident. For some time now, my dad had been going to therapy to help him walk again. He'd made very little progress due to his lack of effort. So, when his nurse was walking him to the bathroom, and he fell and hit his head, it was logical that something like that could happen.

Instead, my intuition kicked in again. I knew accidents happened but the frequency in which my dad had accidents couldn't be a coincidence. Today's fall had made the third accident in a month. That I had known about anyway. I was tired of my dad always getting hurt while in the care of the people who got paid to take care of him.

I freshened up and left out to go check on my dad. As I exited the elevator, I heard two dudes arguing over money. That was nothing new around here, so I ignored it and walked toward the door. Gun fire erupted in the lobby, and everyone began to run. I immediately fell to the floor and covered my head. Moments later I heard a little girl screaming for her mommy. I looked over and she was holding her arm, blood dripping onto the floor.

Assuming she'd been shot I ran over to her. She'd been grazed. Her pregnant mother was laying on the floor not too far from us, blood gushing from her neck and beginning to pool around her.

I wasn't squeamish but my stomach jolted at the sight. My mom's body flashed in mind, and I staggered at the memory.

The little girl began to cry, and I quickly shook it off and eyed the lobby to see if I could find something to wrap around the little girl's arm. With no luck, I took off my shirt and used it to stop the bleeding. People started coming back in the lobby panicking at the sight of the pregnant mother lying dead on the floor. Several people began yelling to call 911 and I focused on the little girl. It was too late for her mother.

"What's your name sweetheart?" I asked the girl trying to take her attention off her mom.

"My mommy. I want my mommy," she cried.

"I know baby. I know. We have to wait for help to come. Stay right here with me. Help is coming."

As I tried to console her, I avoided looking at her mom. I fought against the trigger of my past seeing my mother lying dead in the street and didn't know if I could do it again. I didn't want to make this about me but instead, help the little girl I could, unfortunately, relate to.

The sound of the ambulance sirens drew closer and within a few minutes, the EMT crew came running into the lobby. Some went over to the pregnant woman and others came to me and the little girl. She was taken to the ambulance without hesitation. The police came in and asked me questions, but I couldn't give any info on anyone's identity.

I didn't get a chance to see the men who were arguing. Everything happened so fast, I was still in shock from what I had seen. When the police told me I was free to go, I went upstairs showered, and changed my clothes. I wanted to see Dad now more than ever.

When I arrived at the nursing home, my dad was staring into space, looking past the television. I stood in the doorway for a few minutes and watched him. I missed hearing his voice. I missed walking into our apartment and seeing him sitting in his chair. I was overcome with emotion and stepped out into the hallway.

I walked to the nurses' station and the nurse filled me in on the fall. Overall, my dad was okay. I was grateful to hear that, but I still wanted to know the full name of the LPN that was with him when it happened. Suspicious of his care, I had begun to document everything from names and dates to what, when, where, how, and why. When I went back to his room, there was an LPN in the room. Just as I was walking in, I saw her hand in the air as if she was about to hit my dad.

"What the hell are you doing?" I asked.

I startled her and she dropped her hand quickly. "Nothing."

"Looked like you were about to hit my dad. What's your name?"

"Wasn't nobody about to hit him. I was stretching my arm before I lifted him up."

She must've thought I was some little stupid bitch. I walked over to her wishing she would pop trash. "Let me find out you in here hitting my dad or hurting him in any way and it's gonna be me and you. Best believe that."

Her microbraids swung as she shook her head at me and pressed her big lips together before rolling her eyes. "Why are black people always threatening someone? Just so ghetto all the time. Leave that mess in Camden and come here and act like you got some sense. For real."

"What?" I said as I sat my purse on my dad's bed and stepped closer to her.

"Oh! You heard me. Don't let these scrubs and my proper grammar fool you. I can be professional, but you are not about to be in here threatening me and think I'm just supposed to take it. I'm from the hood too. Trust me. I ain't no punk," she said and took a step toward me like she wanted some. Then she had the nerve to smirk at me.

I lost it and mugged her. We started fighting. I got a good grip on her hair and pulled her away from my dad's bed. Her yell alerted people in the hallway, and two of her co-workers ran into the room to break up the fight.

I was out of breath and could feel my ponytail was lopsided, but I didn't care. I looked over at my dad and terror filled his eyes as he looked back at me. My rage surfaced again, and I wanted to lunge at her. "Stay away from my dad! You know you was about to hit him! I caught you! I'm gonna have you fired!"

"I didn't do anything to your dad!" She was holding her head and I laughed because I knew I tore her head up. "Shut up and get out of his room," I said more calmly. I looked at her co-workers and pointed at her. "Y'all better take her out of here before I hook off on her again. Ain't nobody gonna hurt my dad and think y'all gonna get away with it! Fuck that! I ain't having that! Trust me!" This time I yelled so they could all hear me. I'd fight each and every one of them!

The employees began whispering amongst themselves and stepped aside to let someone in. A serious-looking woman stepped in looking around at everyone. "What's going on?"

"Who the hell are you?" She could get some too.

"My name is Ramona Childs and I'm the nurse manager. Now I repeat; what is going on in here?"

"Well Nurse Manager Childs, I'm about to sue y'all asses. When I walked in, she was about to hit my dad." I pointed at the Brandy wannabe who'd fixed her ponytail. "Her hand was up in the air. If I hadn't walked in, she would have hit him. I want to sign a complaint."

The nurse manager looked over at the LPN who shook her head denying it. "She's lying."

Mrs. Childs looked back at me and straightened her shoulders. "I need to speak with Angela as well to get her side of the story. There will most likely be a complaint filed by her as well."

"A complaint by her? She was about to hit my dad and was popping shit!"

"Did she hit you first?"

"No. I mugged her because she got too close to me and was taunting me. I don't play that invading my personal space. And she told me I was ghetto. Y'all write up what y'all want. I'm going to get a lawyer and sue y'all. As soon as I can, I'm getting my dad outta here."

"Wait. We need to come together and talk so we can straighten this out. We don't need to involve lawyers."

"Oh, you wanna' talk now? Nah, I'm good." The police walked in but I did not give two fucks.

"We got a call that a fight broke out in here."

"Yes, it's under control officer," Ramona said.

"Who was fighting? Someone called, so we need to know what's going on? You can't just act as if nothing happened. If we leave and someone gets hurt, we're going to be liable. So now, who was fighting?"

I spoke up ready to blow up everybody's spot. "Me and some girl who work here."

"Where is she?"

"She just walked out," I explained. "Looking like Brandy just sitting up in her room. Her ugly as braids."

"Ma'am I'm gonna need you to calm down. Now, what was the fight about?"

I ignored his reprimand, my adrenaline still pumping. "I caught the woman who is supposed to be taking care of my dad, about to hit him."

"What?"

"Exactly. I walked in and her hand was in motion, and I scared her. Then she had the nerve to step in my face and was slinging all kinds of stereotypes and prejudice shit at me."

"We need to speak with her. What's her name?"

"Angela. Ask her boss for her last name," I said as I looked at the Nurse Manager.

"Rivers. Angela Rivers. We really don't need to do this here," Ramona said. "Could we go to my office? We are disturbing our patient."

The older officer ignored her and took out a notepad and began writing names down. "Can I have your name ma'am?" He asked me.

"Bianca Williams. B I A N C A."

He finally acknowledged Mrs. Childs. "Can you locate the other individual so I can get this paperwork done?"

She hesitated before she nodded and sped out of the room. She wasn't too happy about the police being involved. Seemed like she was about to brush the entire incident under the rug to protect her raggedy-ass employee. I sat with my dad while the officers spoke with Angela. Eventually, everything got straightened out and Angela was not allowed in my father's room or to be involved in his care. It was too late though. She'd done her damage. I was still moving forward with finding another facility for my dad to go to. I no longer felt comfortable leaving my dad there.

I sat with him for a while before I went home. I just wanted to take a hot bubble bath and relax. After I finished up a few assignments, I ran my bath water just as the phone rang.

"Hello."

"Hey B. What are you doing?" Justin asked.

"About to take a bath. I had the worst day ever."

"My mom told me about the shooting in the building."

"I was there, Justin. Right in the middle of it. I was scared."

"Why didn't you call me?"

"It was one thing right after another. I got a call about my dad falling and then the shooting happened as I was leaving. I had to rush to the nursing home afterward. It was a crazy day."

"What else happened?"

"That's it."

"You sure?"

"I went to Philly for lunch, but other than that, yup, that's it."

"Oh, so we lie to each other now, B? I got a call a few hours ago. You got into a fight at the nursing home?"

"Who told you that?" People were so damn nosey and didn't know how to mind their business.

"Did you forget that you put me down as a contact for your dad? They called me to complain about you. I missed class and an exam because I was on the phone with them for over an hour. They wanted to ban you from the facility and wanted to kick your dad out. I had to talk them out of it and promise that you wouldn't cause any more trouble. Damn! Was you really in there fighting the staff taking care of your dad, Bianca?"

"Yes. But it wasn't like the other times, Justin."

"You were fighting again. That's my entire point. I'm sick of hearing about you fighting. I thought you grew out of that. You're a young woman and still out here fighting. And now it's directly affecting me."

"Justin, let me explain."

"No. I'm tired of hearing the same thing. I had to convince them not to press charges on you. Why are you not understanding that this ain't no joke?"

"Press charges on me? She was about to hit my dad! I should be pressing charges on her! Why are you making me out to be the bad guy?" Justin was straight buggin' and I was ready to explode on him.

"You hit her first. At her job. What did you think would happen, Bianca?" He yelled.

"I can't believe you are fucking taking their side! You go off to college and now you think you better than the rest of us? You think you above the hood? Well, not me! I ain't letting nobody disrespect me or my dad."

Justin went quiet for a moment before he spoke. "I want some time apart. I can't do this no more."

"Do what?"

"Us. This."

"What? But it's not like that." I instantly regretted coming at him. He had just made me so mad. I wanted him to be on my side. I had had enough of people coming at me.

"Good night, Bianca. Take care of yourself," Justin said before I heard the dial tone.

He didn't even let me explain or apologize. Maybe I could have walked away to prevent the fight but to be honest, yes, I was angry. Seeing her hand in the air, knowing she wanted to make contact somewhere on my dad's body set off the crazy within.

I was hurt that Justin just cut me off. I knew he wanted better from me. I wanted better from me. A part of me felt so lost and longed for peace. I dissected the situation and tried to see it from Justin's point, but I couldn't get past the anger. No matter how I tried, all roads led to rage and me wanting to hurt that woman. Maybe I did need help. Hell, I was pretty sure I needed some serious counseling. But despite accepting that, I was adamant that I would not ever apologize to Justin or anyone else for protecting my dad. Not now. Not ever.

THIRTEEN

Justin

I hung up the phone and yanked the cord from the wall. I loved that girl, but damn she robbed me of peace and a man without peace was a man without control. A man without peace was a man living on the brink of destruction. Why couldn't she see the damage she was causing? Not just for our relationship, but for herself. All that ghetto shit was just not cool, not to mention immature. Too many times was I stressin' about her getting into something and my studies and grades suffered. And now I'd missed an exam. I'd have to go beg the professor for a makeup exam. Even with the slim chance she would've granted it, I wouldn't get full credit.

What was the point of working my ass off in school to try and build a better life if B was just gonna drag the life I was trying to leave behind, with her and invade mine? I let out an angry growl like a vicious pit. I promised her better. I promised I'd never leave her. But what about her promises to me? She didn't care about those. No. Just her hurt. Her pain. How could we ever trust each other if we kept shitting on each other?

She basically called me an Uncle Tom because I was trying to do more with my life. The hood wasn't what was ghetto. It was that mentality. My people trying to pull each other down when one of us had the audacity to try and rise up without rap or sports. I wasn't ashamed of my beginnings. It made me who I was but that didn't mean that's where I had to stay. Should I have stayed there with her just to prove I was hood enough?

Nah. I couldn't do it. I had to leave. There and her. I loved her but I couldn't let that stop me from doing what I had to. I promised my Dad I'd 'bring my mom'. The more I thought about my dad's last words to me, the more I was convinced he wasn't talking about bringing her to the hospital. He was talking about bringing her out the ghetto. And if it was the last thing I did, I'd keep that promise to him. I owed the hood nothing. My mom and brother were what mattered. I couldn't abandon my dad's legacy to make others feel better about themselves for not wanting and doing more for themselves.

Not to mention Jordi. I had to get my little brother out of there too. Those streets were calling his name something serious. He didn't have Dad there to watch his back and teach him to rise above the hustling game that only landed you in jail or a coffin. That fast money was tempting. I know. Half my boys from the hood were either hustling or strung out and I remember wanting to be like the ballers that was just faking the rich life.

I be damned if I let Jordi end up like that. I couldn't fail him. I refused to. I had to give my focus to school and success. I loved Bianca. I did. But my love was not enough. She needed to find a way to love herself enough to get the help she needed. I wished she would have, but you can't force a person to do anything no matter how much you love them and want the best for them. I wasn't no Uncle Tom or thought I was better than anybody. I was the strong black man my dad had raised me to be. Do better. Be better. And I wouldn't apologize to Bianca or anybody else for rising up. Not now. Not ever.

FOURTEEN
Tianna

A scheduled head-to-head debate with Justin made me want to skip class. Weeks after the Affirmative Action class, Professor Glassier had pinned a list of topics to the wall. Each student had to sign up to research one, with no more than two students per topic. I didn't much care which topic I had. I would have to research any topic regardless of what it was. I was the last one to sign up and was left with the last topic available. Population control. As I signed my name next to it, I saw Justin had already signed up for it first. As I walked back to my seat, I could see some of the students staring at me, but I wasn't sure why until Professor announced that we would be required to debate our topic in front of the class. It encompassed a large part of our grade and we had just two weeks to prepare.

I finally understood why no one had signed up for Justin's topic. He was a very vocal student oftentimes radical in his point of view but very convincing. I didn't always agree with him, but there was no denying he was a thinking man. Many times, he got me to take a step back and reevaluate my position. A few times I wanted to knock some sense into him, but I refused to be the token brown girl in the class with an attitude, cutting black men down to size. Our people were at each other's necks enough.

Today, however, I was determined to hold my own. If I dragged his ass all over class, so be it. I kept telling myself that just to build up some confidence. Truth was, he was a formidable opponent and not one I could dismiss so easily, and I wanted to vomit I was so nervous.

Everyone showed up for class that morning, coffee cups and breakfast in hand. Even the Professor introduced us as if a Pay-Per-View boxing match were about to begin. Talk about pressure. Justin walked up, his expression focused. I knew he meant business, so I tuned everything out and set my index cards in front of me. I'd read them hundreds of times. Justin looked down at my cards and quickly smiled before he masked it. He had no index cards.

The debate began and I matched every reason he gave for population control with a statistic or finding that combatted his reason. We had been evenly matched. Professor Glassier turned to the class and opened up the floor for them to ask us questions. He hadn't done that in any previous debate. Justin and I looked at each other presumably thinking the same thing. Why us?

We turned toward the class and took their questions. Their questions and comments weren't too thought-provoking until someone asked Justin if he believed that mandatory birth control and restrictions on family size in Africa could solve world hunger, where the problem existed the most.

I didn't know Justin well, but I felt tension radiate off him in waves. His assignment was arguing in favor of population control. I couldn't imagine what answer he could possibly give but I waited anxiously for his response.

He leveled his shoulders and spoke up. "Population control for the benefit of the world as a whole shouldn't fall on the shoulders of just one continent. Or just one group of people. It is a global issue that requires a global solution. We must all do our part."

"That seems like more like a dream than reality. The truth is that Africa has the highest poverty rate in the world. It is not a global issue, but the world is supposed to be responsible in solving an issue that isn't entirely theirs?" The young man, Ryan, sipped his coffee, and I could see the smirk behind his Styrofoam cup. He came prepared to test Justin.

Justin didn't skip a beat though. "Morality aside, parts of a whole all have a responsibility to work for the common good of the whole. Africa has only recently become the poorest continent and not even the entire continent. India and Southern Asia were once the leaders in poverty. The recent economic boost in those areas aided in reducing the level of their poverty but they both still come a close second and third to Africa. It is not solely an "Africa" problem. Exports and imports from foreign countries aid in keeping our economy and the global economy at large, stable. Ebb and flow. You give and you get back. So, it is in fact a global issue. And it requires a global solution. Yes, population control is a small part of the solution, but economic growth is the true answer to end world hunger."

Professor Glassier cut off the student who looked ready to spit out another fireball at Justin. Professor Glassier thanked Ryan for his questions and ended his one-man war against Justin opening the floor to other students. I peeked over at Justin who had fire burning in his eyes. When no one else asked a question, Ryan once again fired off a shot.

"Christianna, being against population control how do you justify poor African women that have little to no food, fresh water, or suitable dwellings to be free to have as many children as they want? Sometimes as many ten to a family. Why should we be responsible for feeding them because they don't know how to control themselves?"

It was subtle but I heard Justin's humorless laugh. "Wow, man." He looked over at Ryan who'd set his cup down and crossed his arms waiting for Justin to react. I did instead.

"Thank you, Ryan, for your question. The average birth rate per woman in Africa is a little over five children per woman. In both Latin America and Asia, the average is the same. However, in Africa, other factors contribute to why population control is neither ethical nor practical. Firstly, the mortality rate in Africa among children is significantly higher. So while they are birthing more than the average amount of children, many do not survive. Having larger families is how they ensure to keep their bloodlines going since the death of children isn't uncommon. Secondly, the death rate related to AIDS is also higher, once again reducing the population.

Aside from the fact that some women choose to have larger families, some are not given the choice. Many virgins are raped by men who have been infected with HIV and AIDS with the misguided belief that sexual relations with a virgin would cure them. Lack of education, ignorance, and fear leads to women being raped and impregnated.

And lastly, in poorer countries, there are more children because frankly, what other means of entertainment do they have? There is no electricity to watch television. There are no pubs to go hang out in. Once the sun goes down, they are left in darkness. None of us here are children. We all know what happens in the darkness between a man and a woman. Here in the USA where we have every luxury available to us to keep us entertained, frat boys still only focus on beer and getting laid. But Daddy's money keeps those abortions nice and quiet."

"Thank you, Ms. Leonard. That is quite enough" Professor Glassier cut in. "Class is over for today. I'll see you all next week. Read chapter eight for Tuesday's class discussion." He tossed a few papers into his briefcase, snapped it shut, and winked at me before he disappeared through the door.

I felt the tension release and was happy class was over. I hated confrontation now more than ever. My studio space was calling out to me something serious. I haphazardly stuffed my index cards in my back pocket and wrapped my neck up in my scarf. February winds were no joke.

"Daddy's money huh?" Justin chuckled as he slipped his arms into the sleeves of his Philadelphia Eagles coat and zipped it up.

I laughed. "I kinda slipped out of debate mode there for a minute there, didn't I?"

"Slipped? Girl, you were ice skating all on that fool's head."

I bust out laughing. "I should've ice skated over his lips."

"Damn you violent. You must be a Latina."

That whole statement was extremely racist but yet it was comical to me. I was far from violent, and I lacked that whole crazy vibe Latinas were stereotyped as. "Actually, I'm half Puerto Rican and half Black. My biological father was Black."

"Was? What did he bleach himself like MJ?"

I kept my desire to laugh out again under control, but I swear this dude could have me cracking up all day if I let him. But for now, I'd just keep him at bay. "No. He died a few months ago."

"Aww, man Tianna. I'm sorry. I shouldn't have said that."

"It's ok. I didn't know him. Met him twice my entire life. He left my mom when he found out she was pregnant."

"My dad died too. He was a great man. Still miss him a lot. And I mean no disrespect, but it was your dad's loss."

Justin was turning down Sappy Street and I wasn't rolling with him down that road. I steered the conversation sharply left and kept on trucking. "Speaking of loss. Ryan must have lost all sense coming at me like that. Ouhhh, he made me so mad."

"Uh oh. That Boricua coming out. You talkin' bout you ain't crazy like that. Yeah right. You're just a late bloomer."

This time I let my laughter loose. Justin was usually corny funny, but his sarcasm and smart mouth were what drew me more and also raised alarms. The attraction was not physical. Not that he was a bad-looking guy. But his personality was magnetic. I wasn't offended or sensitive to his remarks. I would sometimes even bait him just to measure his quick wit. He rarely disappointed. Of course, I'd never let him know that. I refused to allow myself to remove a single brick from my fortified soul. If we'd met at a different time or in another life, we probably could have been best friends.

Just like Morgan or Elijah.

Whoa. Pause button. That revelation was like a punch to the gut and had me adding a layer of brick and mortar to my Rapunzel high tower faster than the prince could say—"

"Tianna, let down your hair."

My gaze darted to Justin in a flash. "What did you just say?" I asked freaked out.

"I said, Earth to Tianna. Are you still there? You look like you were in another world there for a minute."

I seriously needed to get out of this classroom and quickly. The cold air should do me some good. Or at the least, take my mind off everything besides staying warm. I bundled up and headed out. Justin walked out with me, and we continued to talk about class, Ryan being the bulk of the conversation. Justin did admit that he had been nervous about debating against me and when I told him the same, he grinned so wide all I saw were his big ass teeth.

"Don't go putting too much air in that big ass head of yours. Some of my nerves were stage fright. I don't like being the center of attention."

"That's kinda hard with that face don't you think?"

I pretended to let the compliment fly over my head. Laughing was cool. Flirting I wouldn't entertain.

"I mean, you probably scare children and shit."

Well ok then. I had just played myself thinking he was complimenting me, but at least I hadn't done so out loud. I cracked up, nevertheless. His clown self always found a way to make me laugh at myself and not take everything so seriously. It was a safe place to just be me. I was relieved that he wasn't trying to cross a border I didn't want to venture past. I was beginning to find a friend and wasn't ready to give that up.

Justin and I began discussing Philosophy after every class. A few times we grabbed a slice of pizza and talked about life and how we'd change the world if we could. Today was one of those days. A young kid was handing out flyers advertising Karaoke night at a favorite local bar amongst college students. Justin took a flyer and dismissed it, tossing it aside without even looking at it.

I picked it up and read it. "We should go."

Justin looked at me as if I had lost my mind. "I don't do Karaoke. He altered his voice to sound like Carlton from *The Fresh Prince of Belair*. "Tryna have me up in there singing Backstreet Boys or Elton John." I chuckled at his goofy self. "Nah, I'm good, Pocahontas. I'm gonna keep my black ass right here in Where-I-Belong-Ville."

I tugged at his coat. "Come on. I'll buy you a drink."

"I'm not much of a drinker."

"You're not much a looker either, but I'm still willing to be seen in public with you. Come on. It'll be fun." I shoulder bumped him. Then bumped him again.

"What is wrong with you? Stop doing that. We are not *Laverne and Shirley*. And yo ass need to go hang out in the hood a little more. Find some soul or something. You black, girl. Act like it."

"Ok. I'll make a deal with you. You come to Karaoke Night with me tonight and I'll go to any place you choose whenever you invite me."

Justin thought about it for a second then winked. "Bet. And you buying me a burger and fries."

I agreed and once there, he'd stuffed his face with a burger and fries. While he was scarfing down his food, I signed us up to sing a song without him knowing. When they called us up, his nostrils flared, and he was about ready to have a tantrum. Then he relaxed and nodded in surrender. We walked up to the stage and the MC handed us our microphones. Justin leaned in and whispered, "You better enjoy this because I got something for yo ass. Trust me. Payback's a bitch."

I ain't gonna lie. I instantly regretted Karaoke Night for a second then figured I mind as well make the best of the situation since he was dead set on getting revenge. The song began to play, and he lightened up, bopping to the beat.

"Thank you!" He yelled above Lauryn Hill's 'oohs.' "At least it's Hip Hop!"

131

If only he knew what was about to happen. Right on cue, Justin and I both put the mic up to our lips to rap the first line of Nas's *If I Ruled the World* but only my mic worked. While I rapped *'Imagine going to court with no trial'* Justin tapped his mic and held it up signaling that it didn't work. I winked at him as I rapped *'Days are shorter. Nights are colder,'* and he crossed his arms at me and grinned catching on to what was happening. When I finished the first verse and Lauryn began to sing, I pulled the mic from my lips pointing at his mic to let him know it was his turn to use it. He looked at the microphone then back at me and covered his face.

The crowd started cheering him on encouraging him to sing the chorus. He burst out laughing and shook his head refusing to sing. I rapped verse two, this time looking right at him. He laughed then got into it encouraging me as if he were my hype man. He lifted his hands encouraging the audience to stand up and dance, and they did. Probably because they were drunk or maybe just because Justin was entertaining. By the time Lauryn was singing the chorus again, Justin was on the mic singing and the audience went nuts.

Of course, he ate that up. The man loved charming people and making them smile. I backed off and let him rap the third verse and he did so effortlessly as if he were the headliner on tour. I sang Lauryn's part and when he walked up to me, looked me in the face, and *'If you could be mine, we'd both shine,'* I stopped singing. He winked and kept the show going. I came back to myself and finished singing. We walked off laughing and out of breath. Familiar faces from school and some new ones patted him on the back and pointed at me in salute.

Back at the table, I gulped my water and fanned myself. Anything to avoid looking directly at Justin. I couldn't get those lyrics out of my head. But even more so I couldn't pretend that he hadn't just planted a seed in my heart that I was afraid was about to take root. When had my hardened heart softened? When had walls come down? I specifically remember hanging the Love Don't Live Here sign, prominently for everyone to see.

Like a knock upside the head, it dawned on me. He snuck in through the friendship door. Just as Elijah had. Back then I hadn't cared. This time I was careless. The security guard at the friendship door was asleep and let this damn intruder in. Justin wasn't allowed in. No one was allowed in. I wanted to kick him out, but the problem was I didn't want him to leave. I impulsively ordered a shot and choked on it.

Justin left the booth and came back with my coat after I had started gagging like a fool. "Let's go Sister Mary Clarence."

I had no idea what he was talking about. He pulled me up by my hand and let out a little sigh. "You ain't never see *Sister Act*? What the hell. You been living in a bubble?"

He teased me all the way back to his dorm where my car was parked. I removed the keys from my pocket, and he snatched them.

"What are you doing?"

"I can't let you drive without making sure you're ok first."

"I had one shot. It ain't that serious."

"You didn't eat dinner. Yeah, I noticed. And you aren't a drinker. The way you gagged on that whiskey you've probably never had a shot in your life."

He was right, but he didn't need to know all that. "I'm fine. Not even tipsy. See?" I stood on one foot and touched the tip of my nose with my finger without stumbling.

"Man, Corey's dad can do that after two forties and two shots. That ain't no real test."

"Well, what is a real test Detective Williams?"

"Who?"

I snatched my keys back and shook my head. "You ain't never see *New York Undercover*? What the hell. You been living in a bubble?"

I turned to unlock my car door when he spun me around and pressed me up against the car, his face just inches from mine.

I think I stopped breathing. I stared at him unsure what to do. He lowered his eyes to my mouth, and I gulped. He got closer, then halted. A few seconds later he pulled away from me. I was both relieved and disappointed that he hadn't kissed me.

"Ok. Your breath smells bad but not like alcohol, so I think you're safe to drive." I slapped him on his arm, and he pretended it hurt as he laughed. "Damn girl. You sure you don't got that Boricua temper?" I hit him again twice for good measure. He laughed again teasing me that my hits were like little baby fists pounding on him.

I laughed even though I didn't want to. "You get on my nerves."

He pulled me close and gave me a bear hug before he opened the car door and watched me drive off. As I pulled away looking at Justin through my rearview, I tucked away the realization that the whiskey hadn't affected me nearly as much as that man just had.

FIFTEEN
Bianca

Weeks passed, and my life was awkward without talking to Justin. Although I didn't regret defending my dad against Angela, I couldn't deny the fact that I did need help with my anger. I'd been putting it off for years, hoping one day it would magically disappear. I was hurting and feeling lonely. I had to somehow find a way to accept the help that I needed to release the built-up anger inside of me. I was tired of it having so much power over me and my life. I wanted to learn self-control and not react or blow up.

One Saturday afternoon, I opened the phone book and looked through yellow pages to find an anger management program and broke out into a sweat. I closed the book and sat for a few seconds paralyzed before I gave myself a pep talk. *C'mon, Bianca. You can do this.*

I closed my eyes, inhaled and exhaled, before opening the phone book again. I turned page after page until I saw the words, Free Yourself. That was exactly what I needed. Freedom. Was that a sign? I grabbed my pen and wrote the number down. I got up from the kitchen table and began to pace, contemplating calling. Why was is it so freakin' hard to reach out for help! I began to hyperventilate and rushed into the living room to sit on the couch. I began rocking back and forth, tears rolling down my face.

After twenty minutes passed, I wiped my face and mustered up the courage to dial the phone number. I spoke with a counselor named, Lisa Bivens. She was extremely nice and sounded concerned about me wanting to come in for anger management. I was under the impression that it was a one-on-one thing, but she informed me that it was a combination of one-on-one therapy and group sessions. I immediately shut down, and she understood my silence.

"Hello, Bianca, are you there? I know finding out that this is a group setting, may have frightened you. Do you know how many times, I've had this conversation with first-timers? Many. So please, talk to me. Come back out of your shell, and let's finish setting you up for your intake. There's never any pressure to participate. Sometimes it helps to just listen to others."

"Ok." I was hesitant but I had to at least try.

"Great! Will Tuesday at 6 pm work?"

"I'll be there."

"Wonderful. You took a huge step today. Congratulations, Bianca. I'll see you on Tuesday."

"Thank you. See you then."

For the first time since my mother had died, I finally felt like it was time to face my issue with anger and defeat it. I was tired of running. I was tired of pretending that I was okay. I was tired of the battle. I'd lost a great man that I loved because of it. I'd nearly gotten my dad kicked out of his care facility because of it. I thought about the day I fought Angela and the terror in his eyes when he'd looked at me and wondered if that terror was also because of me. Had I embarrassed and disappointed him? Shame flooded me. He was the only person in the world I had left. I cried thinking I had let him down.

I wiped my tears and refused to feel pitiful. It was time for me to focus on being a better woman in all areas of my life. I didn't want to continue to pick and choose where I needed growth. I needed to be whole. I would no longer pretend like my problems didn't exist. I prayed my mom was watching over me and that I'd make her proud of me. Shit. What a smack to the face. I was twenty years old and nothing had really changed since my mom had died. I was still as stubborn as I was when I was thirteen years old.

Just as Justin had said I needed to grow up and change. And I loved him, but I wasn't changing for him. I wasn't even doing it for my mom or dad. I was doing it for myself. I accepted that I truly did need help.

I felt like a weight had been lifted off me. I hadn't even started counseling yet and I was already feeling the effects of freedom. Growing pains brought about freedom and healing. I was ready to go through it.

Part of those pains was missing Justin so much. I wanted to call him when I hung up with Lisa ready to share my good news, but I didn't. He wasn't a part of my life anymore and I had to come to terms with that too. I was starting a new chapter in my life. I embraced it. I was going to do what was best for me, and that was focus on the new journey ahead, facing my anger and putting it to rest.

The next morning, I went to see my dad and shared the great news about going to anger management. He got teary-eyed and smiled at me. "I, I'm pr pr proud of you B." It had taken him some time and a few tries, but he'd gotten it out.

"Oh my God! Dad! You spoke!" It felt so good hearing his voice although raspy. I cried as I hugged him.

That's all he said, and that was enough for me. It had made my whole day. Laying the foundation for healing had me motivated and focused. Getting my anger under control was added to my list of priorities along with Dad and school.

I walked into my building floating and feeling free. Life was headed in the right direction. Finally. When I approached the elevators, I looked to the right and saw two people through the back glass doors, shoving each other as if they were about to fight. I did a double-take when I saw one was Justin's little brother, Jordi. I thought about pretending I hadn't seen it but I couldn't so I went outside to intervene.

When I got there, I recognized Talib, a kid I used to go to high school with. He wasn't someone I feared but who he hung out with was no one you wanted on your bad side and here Jordi was pushing on him like he ain't have no sense.

"Hey. Hey. Jordi, what's up? What's goin' on? Stop. Stop pushin' him. Talk to me," I said as I touched his hand.

"Nah. He keep runnin' his mouth. Talkin' trash." Jordi pushed my hand away and lunged at Talib.

"You betta get him before I hurt him out here. I wasn't even talkin' to him. He on some I-hate-the-world shit. I'm too old to be fightin' this little boy. I'm a grown-ass man," Talib laughed.

"Jordi, come on. You heard him. He's not tryna fight you. Do I need to go get ya mom?"

"You don't have to get my mom. You should really mind ya business. You ain't even my brotha's girl no more."

"You need to listen to her, young boy. For real." Talib's patience looked as if was coming to its end.

"I'm doin' what's right. It don't matter if I'm not wit ya brotha no more."

Jordi quickly walked past me pissed off. The wind slapped me in my face as he went into the building, and I followed behind him. We both got onto the elevator, the silence between us louder than words. When the elevator stopped, I got off and trailed behind him.

"I don't need a babysitter," Jordi said as he walked.

I remained silent as I followed him. When he opened the door, his mom was standing where we both could see each other. Jordi became more irritated. "Great. Oh boy." He rushed past her and disappeared into a room.

"Bianca?" Mrs. Saunders asked as surprised to see me.

"Hello, Mrs. Saunders. Uh, Jordi was about to get in a fight and I kind of stopped it."

"What? Jordi, get back out here!"

He huffed as he walked back out to her. "Mom, I didn't fight. She stopped it. Okay?"

"No, it's not okay. What is with this I don't give a shit attitude, Jordi? I'm tired of it."

Now that I had seen Jordi home safely, I didn't need to stay around. "I just wanted to inform you about what I saw and walk Jordi home."

"Thank you, Bianca. I appreciate your help." Mrs. Saunders replied.

"You're welcome."

I took a deep breath, went to the elevator, and made my way to my apartment. The incident with Jordi stayed on my mind for the rest of the night. I wanted to reach out to Justin but at the same time, I knew it was better for Mrs. Saunders to fill him in on what happened. We hadn't communicated in months, and I didn't want to disrupt his time away with troubling news. I stayed to myself as I had been doing. I knew that that was the best thing for me and that helped me move on.

SIXTEEN
Tianna

Blue acrylic paint slipped from my hand and crashed to the floor splattering on my white Keds. "Damn it," I let out in a whisper. I grabbed some towels and wiped up the mess before taking off my shoes. I began to wipe them down with fresh towels when I felt inspired to turn my accident into purpose. I chose some muted colors and painted abstract art on my shoes. What started as a quick project turned into hours of peace doing what I loved.

As had become my habit, I made it home past dinnertime. I parked on the street, a car I didn't recognize in my usual spot. I wondered if Tommy had bought a new car. Then again, he'd never parked in my spot before and preferred parking behind *Mami*. The house was quiet when I entered, but I heard voices in the backyard. I wasn't surprised *Mami* was outside enjoying an unusually warm Spring night. I had no idea who was in the backyard with her, nor did I care to find out. I went into the kitchen to grab a bite to eat, not bothering to turn the light on. I didn't want *Mami* to know I was home.

I lifted the lid to the crockpot to investigate. Chicken stew. I wasn't in a stew mood. I rummaged through the fridge looking for a yogurt that I'd seen in the back that morning, when I felt someone behind me reach into the fridge, their body pressed up against my backside. I jumped and turned to find Uncle Lou about to open a cold beer. He popped the tab and smirked at me before taking a sip.

My flight response kicked in. I walked around the island to avoid walking by him. He took a few steps to his right and blocked my path. "You left the refrigerator open. Go close it. The beers are gonna get warm." He took another casual sip.

My mind kicked into gear. If I played this smart, I could probably get to the knife drawer in time to open it and pull one out before he reached me. I backed up slowly, my hands trembling. I got to the fridge and closed the door. I took a few steps over and put my hand to the drawer and pulled it, never taking my eyes off him. He hadn't moved an inch and just watched me like I was his weak prey. I slid my hand in the drawer and pulled out the first knife I felt, holding it up for him to see. He laughed then set his beer down on the island that separated us.

"You better put that knife down before you cut yourself. All kinds of accidents can happen when we play with knives little girl."

"I'm not a little girl anymore."

"I see. You all woman now." He surveyed me up and down and bit his lip. "I haven't seen you in a long time, Tianna. Where you been? You been hiding from me?"

"Leave me the hell alone or I will cut your balls off." I don't know where the courage came from it, but I meant every word.

He mocked me. "Look at you all grown up and feisty. I like that. A woman who fights back turns me on. Scared little girls are boring."

"You are sick and disgusting. If you take one step closer to me, I will scream and tell everybody what you did to me."

He stepped closer. "You think they don't already know?" He laughed and his lack of regard for being found out raised my fear. I'd learned that a person that feared nothing, was capable of doing anything.

"I will tell Grandma and *Mami* everything you did to me," I threatened.

His expression sobered. He almost seemed bored. "You that stupid Tianna? They all know. They just don't say anything because that's what families do. We keep each other's dirty little secrets and make-believe they never happened. That's loyalty. That's *familia*! We stick together no matter what. That's why you never told on me. Or maybe it's because you liked it."

Mami knew? Everyone knew? My stomach churned and I wanted to vomit but I had nothing to eject. I dropped the knife feeling helpless and hopeless. Uncle Lou took a step closer and then another until he was standing close enough that I could smell his breath. The stench reminded me of years ago and I heaved but only bile made its way up burning my throat. I covered my mouth and closed my eyes. I felt his hand caress my cheek down to my chin.

"*Bella*. And your breasts were beautiful too." His hand began to works its way down.

All I could see was that shy, naïve little girl of my past trembling in fear. Her innocence stolen. I wanted to protect her and vindicate her. Anger surged within me. I lifted my knee swiftly and kneed *Mami's* brother in his groin with all my might. He crouched over in pain. I grabbed the crock pot of lid and hit him on the head. He fell to one knee, and I knocked him over, before running as fast I could.

I jumped in my car and drove without a destination. My vision was blurred, as I kept wiping away the tears that flooded my eyes. I saw the exit for school and headed that way ending up at Justin's dorm.

After I buzzed him, alarm shot through me. What if his roommates were there or if he had a girl over? I walked back to my car and sat there, tears streaming down my face. No place to go. I remembered the studio and turned the ignition when I heard a tap on my window. It was Justin. I shook my head at him. He opened my car door and reached over to the ignition and turned the car off.

"Come on. Let's go upstairs." I sobbed unable to leave the car. He picked me up and carried me. I shoved my face into his chest and cried all the overdue tears I'd pent up for so long. He didn't say a word and tried to set me down on his bed, but I gripped onto him as if I were drowning and he was my life raft. And still, he said nothing. Instead, he lowered himself into his lounge chair and nestled me in his lap. As I cried, he rested his cheek on the top of my head and rubbed my back until I fell into a fitful sleep.

I woke up and could feel the swelling around my eyes. I felt lost for a moment until I looked up and saw Justin asleep, his arms still around me. I squirmed, my legs sore from sleeping in the fetal position for so long and he instinctively hushed me soothingly and began rubbing my back again. Then I remembered everything; from him carrying me from my car to him holding me close. I hadn't removed a stitch of clothing and he hadn't touched me inappropriately, but fear and shame crept up my spine and shook my core. Intimacy was far scarier than the aftereffects of lust. I could not and would not allow myself to be vulnerable again. There wasn't a single soul on this planet that I trusted other than Abe. The idea of letting my guard down made me want to jump from his lap as if it were lit with hell's fire.

Eyes still closed, Justin continued soothing my back his voice soft and mellow. "Relax Ti. We didn't do anything wrong. Lay back down. It's ok. You're safe here. I promise." He pulled me toward his chest and leaned his cheek against my head again. I could hear his steady heartbeat and it calmed me. Before I knew it. I was asleep again.

When I woke up again, I found myself in his bed, a blanket covering me. Justin sat at his desk reading a textbook. "Good morning, Ugly." His smile was brighter than the sun shining through the window.

I sat up looking for my shoes. "Good morning," I said sheepishly. Once again, I felt the discomfort of such familiarity. Hadn't I learned my lesson already from waking up in a bed that wasn't mine? "Ummm…"

Not looking up from his reading, he sipped from a cup then set it down and turned a page. His mood changed instantly. "Your shoes are in the closet. Your jacket is too. I put your car keys in the pocket."

I quickly stood and went into the closet and grabbed my things. I gathered myself quietly. After I was done, I stood behind him shuffling my keys not knowing what to say. When he didn't turn around, I headed for the door.

"Just like that. Gonna leave without saying goodbye, huh?"

With effort, I stopped myself from reaching for the doorknob and bolting. My emotions were high, and I couldn't trust anything in my head or heart. I was a jumbled mess of anxiety, hurt, and disbelief. And to make things worse I also felt safety and comfort from someone I didn't allow myself to trust. But I kept all of that hidden underneath a thin layer of self-control. "I didn't want to disturb your studying," was all I offered as an excuse. He turned and faced me. I thought I saw anguish in his eyes. But it was most likely frustration.

"What did I do or say that would make you think you are disturbing me?"

"Nothing. I know I just dropped in on you unexpectedly and a wreck and I'm sorry about that. You've been nothing but kind. I am very grateful."

Justin stood and walked over to me slowly. I wanted to erect a wall to keep him from coming closer and knocking down the fragile barrier I had surrounded myself with. It was as fortified as the bubbles kids blew into the air during summer. He lifted my chin and kissed me on the forehead before he wrapped me in a hug that I thought I'd lose myself in.

Part of me wanted to tear away. Another part wanted to hang on. Chaos within made me want to run and hide but every time I took a step away, he brought me back physically and emotionally.

"I'm always here if you need me. To talk. To cry. To just sit. To rap battle." Despite my turmoil, I laughed. He always had a way of bringing me down off the ledge without even trying. I felt safe in those moments. "You never disturb me, Tianna."

"Thank you." Words couldn't express the amount of gratitude I felt toward him. I didn't know how to say so without sounding needy. The last thing I wanted was to be needy or someone to see me as such.

He released me and tapped my nose. "Anytime beautiful." He went back to his desk to study, and I quietly walked out.

Last-minute I decided to attend my morning classes although unprepared, but I much preferred that to going home. I could already hear *Mami* lecturing me. The last thing I wanted was a lecture from her. Her brother's words echoed in my ears. Everyone knew. They all knew. The back of my eyes burned, and I blinked it away. I wasn't going to cry today. I had already given them too much of me.

After class, I stopped by the studio. I painted a silhouette of a woman reaching heavenward. I used only black paint. No other color seemed to match my mood. I felt darkness and suffocation. I thought about the scripture that truth sets us free, and I couldn't understand how that was true. Knowing my mother and family betrayed me wasn't freeing. It imprisoned me. But what did I know about scripture? I was the whore. I was the fornicator. I was the one God allowed to be molested. I looked up at the framed sketch and Elijah's words echoed in my heart.

'You are gifted. Remember that.'

I may not have been worthy in God's eyes, but I refused to believe I wasn't valuable even if just a little. I don't know why I hung on to the words of someone who also hurt me but, in my recollection, I couldn't remember any other time words were spoken to me in kindness. It was a sad truth that did its fair share of imprisoning me.

I leaned the canvas up against the wall and stared at it. I looked around at all of my work and wondered the point of it all. What purpose was there in mixing colors and spreading them on canvas? It all seemed meaningless. Life seemed meaningless. How sad that the only thing that brought me joy had no worth to anyone but me. Is this all life really had to offer? Where was the justice of losing my innocence? I was a little girl. Naïve and carefree. Where was the love and comfort of a mother? Where was the loyalty and protection of a father? Friends and enemies were one and the same.

In anger, I swept everything off my table sending it crashing to the floor. I ripped every canvas and screamed out. But no one could hear me. And no one would care. I sat in my colorful mess of paint and tattered art and cried. I wanted to end the misery of my lonely life.

So many times, I had been told how pretty I was. Girls envied my face. A face I had no control over creating. Men wanted my body. This body was a curse that attracted perverted men before my curves had fully developed. This face was a curse that brought me unwanted attention and hate for simply being born this way. From the minute I was created in my mother's womb I was cursed. I sat in my mess for so long that the paint had dried by the time I stood up. I refused to go home. That was no longer my home.

I went to the Karaoke bar for a drink, taking a seat in the back booth where no one would see me. I took a few shots and just sat there a perfect representation of who I was. A broken, painted-up mess. I thought I was imagining things when Justin slid into the booth across from me. "Hey, Sister Mary Clarence." Just looking at him made tears stream down my face. "Ok. That's enough. Let's take you home," he said.

I shook my head like a frightened little girl, my eyes wide with fear. He looked at me strangely. "Ok. We'll go to my place. Is that ok?" I hesitated before I agreed. He helped me to the car and drove to his dorm room. I refused to be carried like a child and insisted on walking. After falling down three times, he picked me and tossed me over his shoulder. I felt too sick to fight him physically, but he heard an earful of words just as colorful as my ruined clothes.

He plopped me on his bed and shook his head at me. I could tell he was upset. I started to cry again. The one person in the world other than Abe who genuinely liked me for me, even if just a little, was upset with me. I panicked and apologized. He waved it off and told me he wasn't upset but I could tell that he was. When he came over to help me take off my shoes, I apologized again. He nodded but didn't look me in the face. I leaned forward and tried to kiss him, and he pulled back away from me. I tried again but this time he stood up aggravated.

"Stop it, Tianna." He let my shoe fall to the floor. "I'm going to grab us dinner and give you a few minutes to change." He opened a dresser drawer and pulled out sweatpants, a T-shirt and towel, and set them on the bed beside me. "The shower is the door across the hall. You can change into these. Don't let anyone see you, ok? I'll be right back."

I picked up the garments and nodded. He walked me to the bathroom and made sure I had everything I needed before he left. I showered for a long while just letting the paint run off my body and the pain wash away with my tears. He rejected me. Twice. My humiliation was hotter than the shower.

The water turned muddy and gray for a while before it ran clear. I lathered myself and shampooed my hair with Justin's masculine hygiene products. I was still a little dizzy and nauseous, but I was beginning to sober up. I dressed and snuck across the hall back to his room, making sure no one saw me. I wasn't sure why I was hiding but I just did as he asked.

When I entered, he was placing a can in a small refrigerator. "I was just about to check in on you. Your food is getting cold."

The smell of Chinese food made my stomach turn. "No thank you. I don't feel so well."

He pulled out a box of saltine crackers from a plastic bag and handed them to me. "Chew on these slowly. Too much too fast will make you throw up."

I sat on the edge of the bed and brushed my hair, forcing small bites of the dry crackers. I closed my eyes to keep the room from spinning when I felt Justin take the brush from my hand. He straddled himself behind me and gently began to brush my hair. Every nerve in my body stood on end. Intimacy. I craved it like it was air and I was human lungs. Yet, I repelled it like water did oil. A constant war within myself.

Justin stopped brushing and I instantly missed his ministrations. "I don't know how to tie it," he said his voice soft and raspy.

"That's ok. Thank you." I left it loose and waited for him to stand up and free me from the cocoon of tenderness that he'd surrounded me in.

"Come," he said. He slid back on the bed and invited me into his arms. I accepted his invitation and nestled up to him, my head on his chest listening to the rhythmic pounding of his heart. It lulled me into a trans. Is this what safety felt like? For the first time in years, I fell asleep without a worry in the world.

SEVENTEEN

Justin

Her hair was so soft I couldn't keep from running my fingers through it, knowing I shouldn't let myself go there. She looked so peaceful when she slept. I smiled down at her. How was she here with me? The warmth I felt in my heart gave way to questions. Why was she here with me? The question crept into my mind, and I had a hard time letting it go. If for no other reason than to be a supportive friend, I wanted her to confide in me, but I wouldn't push her to tell me what was wrong.

If there was one thing I knew about Tianna, it was that she was headstrong but not impulsive. She was a thinker. Yeah, she'd gotten drunk at a public bar but that was a rarity, and not at all like her. It concerned me that this brilliant woman felt she needed to do that. What pain was she looking to forget? She wasn't the overdramatic and attention-getting type. In fact, the opposite. She was the one you found holding up a wall at a party or behind stage producing instead of starring in the show.

Then again, what did I know? She and I had had some deep conversations that left me thinking about her thoughts and ideas hours after we'd parted ways. She made me see things in ways I never had. She made me believe if we worked smarter and harder, we had a chance to succeed in life. That was all great but in retrospect, we'd never really discussed anything about our personal lives. Every time I would bring up family or my future, she'd very subtly change the subject. I didn't catch on to it right away but eventually, I had and tried to stay away from that road. She avoided it for a reason, and I aimed to be a place of safety for her and respect her privacy. When the time was right, she would be free to share if so chose.

She exhaled deeply bringing my thoughts back to her beauty. The natural kind. A harmonious mix of cultures in one beautiful creature. Her wavy hair must have been inherited from her mother. It was long, full but not tightly curled or course. Her mouth reminded me of my ancestors, wide with full lips. I wondered if they were soft. Her skin, the color of cinnamon, could have been passed down from either or even both. It was smooth and clear, minus two faint beauty marks by her temple.

She wrapped her arm around my middle, cozying up to me even tighter than before. It was strange that it felt so natural. As if we had been doing this for years. But I knew all too well it was someone else altogether who I'd done that with. I shut out the thought not wanting to think about Bianca. Nothing good came from mindless wandering through memory lane.

Tianna's eyes fluttered opened and she looked up at me bringing me back to where I belonged. In the present. The sadness I'd seen in them when she returned from her shower had given way to peace. The corner of her mouth upturned timidly and everything virile in me rushed to the surface.

I broke eye contact and rested my head against the wall staring up at the ceiling. In my head, I replayed the last conversations I had with my dad. 'Women were a gift.' I couldn't take advantage of a woman under the influence. I wouldn't. I fought everything in me that wanted to devour her yet make her feel safe and wanted.

I grabbed the novel I kept by my bed and began to read it aloud to her. I'd read *Black Boy* by Richard Wright so many times the book was merely a tool to guide the story along as I'd already known it so well. Tianna didn't say a word and just listened. I read to her for an hour before I closed the book.

"You're a good reader."

"Thank you. I'd thought I'd put you to sleep."

"No. I like listening to you read. It's soothing."

I laughed. I'd never heard that before. Then again, I hadn't read aloud since middle school.

"You should find a job just reading books aloud all day long." Tianna chuckled and sat up detangling herself from our embrace. A cold draft took her place, and I missed her warmth instantly. She excused herself to the bathroom and came back in search of food. She ate a bit of her Chinese slowly, her thoughts seeming to be a million miles away. She set the platter down on the desk and cleared her throat, sitting upright and straightening her shoulders. "I'd like to tell you why I'm here."

I nodded and listened to her for a very long time. A story that recounted her life from a little girl to the present. Fury rose within me. I balled my fists wanting to punch something. No. Someone. A very specific someone. But I listened and allowed her to vent in safety. Afterward, I pulled her up to her feet and hugged her, offering every ounce of comfort I possessed. I promised myself to always be a person she could rely on. To be someone she'd never had before. A real friend.

EIGHTEEN
Tianna

I leaned against the edge of my makeshift table and watched anxiously as Justin explored my studio, gazing at the pieces of art I hadn't completely destroyed in my meltdown and had since hung on the wall. My gallery was humble, but it was mine. As my slow R&B mix played in the background, he studied each one intently, his face expressionless, as if he were an enthusiast in his element. I had never cared much about getting the opinions of others for my work, but I respected and valued Justin and I found my stomach turning in knots waiting for a reaction. Any reaction.

He thumbed through my sketchbooks and smiled a few times. It made my heart leap. There was something about his smile that reverted me to my tween days crushing on celebrities. The fact that I had a pleasant memory of that time in my life surprised me. Justin bringing it out in me, didn't. That's who he was and what he did without even trying. He was light and goodness and joy. I was content when I was with him. I was different when I was with him. I liked me when I was with him. So, I removed one layer of my wall and spent as much time with him as I could. He became my closest friend. My only friend actually.

"Anytime you're ready to say something, I'm ready to hear it." I walked over to my bureau and opened the top drawer removing my brushes and palette. I had started a new painting and was anxious to add to it.

After I had grabbed the paints I needed, I turned to Justin, curious as to why he was so quiet. He was staring at me, his smile subtle and sweet.

"What?" I asked nervously.

"I had no idea." He motioned to my artwork. "About any of this. Ti, you are so talented. Why didn't you say something sooner?"

I shrugged my shoulders. "I didn't know I was supposed to. Art has always been a part of my life. I don't talk about it much. I just paint."

"Woman, you do more than just paint," he laughed. "This shit is really good. Like you should be in galleries. Have you ever had someone look at your pieces before?"

"I don't show my art to anyone. It's just always been a passion, but I've never seriously considered showcasing it."

His jaw dropped. "No one has ever seen your artwork before?"

I began adding paint to my palette. "Yeah, of course. My parents. My brother, Abe." I thought of Elijah but couldn't force his name out of my mouth. "A friend I had in high school used to like my sketches."

"That's not what I meant, and you know it, smartass."

I grinned at his remark as I loaded a flat brush and blended colors until the cinnamon hue, I wanted had emerged.

"How long have you been sketching and painting?"

I put paint to the canvas and let my hands move on their own accord as I recollected my childhood. "My mom said I've always loved crayons and coloring books, but I was about six when copied a coloring page on a blank sheet of paper. My stepdad asked if I had traced it and made me prove I hadn't when I told him I hand-drawn it freehand. He chose a different coloring page and watched as I sketched that one from scratch, praising my amateur skills. He urged me to keep practicing.

I just remember art being different for me. It was fun for me. I actually wanted to practice. I asked my mom if I could quit dance and take up art instead. She refused to let me quit anything and made me continue dance classes until the Spring Recital. After that, she never brought up dance again. Thank God. I hated wearing all that makeup and those glittery outfits."

I heard him chuckle, but I had already begun to lose myself in the strokes and shading. There was something about that piece that had enraptured me. I angled my head from side to side, dabbing coloring here and there. I don't know how much time passed before I took a few steps back to survey my work only to bump into Justin. I hadn't realized he'd been standing behind me. He put his hands to my waist to help steady me. I thanked him, but he didn't let go. Instead, he stepped into me, wrapping an arm around my waist.

Janet Jackson cooing *Any Time, Any Place* in the otherwise silence prompted me to let my head rest against him. Justin moved my hair aside and placed a soft kiss on my neck. I closed my eyes and embraced the affection. When his kisses began to trail upward, I dropped my brush, reached up, and caressed his head encouraging his exploration.

He turned me around, removed the palette from my hand, and kissed me as if it were the last thing on earth, he'd ever do. Paint covered his head and face, but he didn't seem to care so neither could I. His tenderness infiltrated every cell in my body making me want to reciprocate his enthusiasm with my own. And for the rest of the night both in my studio and in his dorm room, we got lost in the exchange of each other.

A few days later Justin stopped by my studio just as I had completed the piece. I had stared at it for so long before he had arrived, I had gotten lost in it. It had been so long since I had been so emotionally invested in my own art. I couldn't help but feel as if I had painted my soul on that canvas. He sat on my stool and nestled me between his knees, leaning his chin on my shoulder.

"What did you name it?"

"I haven't. I feel like I won't do it justice. It needs to be fitting."

"Well, no matter what, it's amazing Ti."

I turned to him and pecked him on the lips. "Thank you. So are you."

"Oh, is that right?" Justin wrapped his arms around me and kissed me back a few times before he stood to his feet to check his vibrating pager. "It's my mom."

I took Justin to Sarah's office and let him use the phone. Within a few moments on the line, he became frantic and started shooting questions off like a machine gun. He quickly apologized to his mother and exhaled deeply trying to calm himself. I excused myself from the office and went back to my space and cleaned up. I had just finished putting away my brushes when Justin returned. It looked like he carried the weight of the world on his shoulders.

"Everything ok?" I could see worry tormenting him.

"Not really."

"If you want to talk about it, I'm here to listen."

He stared at me strangely before he plopped on the stool and waved me over. I walked over to him, and he brought me before him and rested his forehead on my chest, and gripped my shirt by the waist. "My little brother Jordi is rebelling. My mom just told me that a few weeks ago he was picking a fight with an older guy that I went to high school with and yesterday he'd gotten into a fight at school. I don't know what to do. Sometimes I want to quit school and go home to make sure he doesn't get himself kicked out of school or shot. But I know my Dad wouldn't want me to quit school."

"What would your Dad want?"

"To make something of myself so I can take care of my mother in brother long-term."

"And that requires you being here I assume?"

"That requires me getting an education and getting a degree and making something of myself and I want to do that here."

"So, you feel torn between two places?"

He looked up and I could see the sadness in his eyes. "Something like that."

I hugged him tightly. "I can't do much, but I'll pray for him and you." Maybe God would hear my prayers if they were sent to help someone else.

Justin pushed aside my bangs and caressed my face slowly. "You are the amazing one. Thank you. Your prayers are more than enough." I reached down and kissed him. He returned my kiss so tenderly and sweetly, I wanted to join myself to him. There was such comfort with Justin, I couldn't wrap my mind around that he was real and in my life. As if he was reading my mind, he set out to show me how real he was and did so for hours until he left the following morning to go back home and check in on his family.

NINETEEN
Bianca

A celebration wasn't what I had been expecting when I arrived at therapy, but I walked into a room filled with balloons, a congratulations banner pinned to the wall, and a chorus of voices yelling "Surprise!"

They scared the shit out of me. "What? What's going on?" I asked alert and confused.

"It's your three-month anniversary and one we consider a milestone. And here we celebrate milestones." Lisa smiled demurely.

"Really? I had no idea."

"Yes. Today is an important day, Bianca. We celebrate you and your progress. You have come a long way and we are proud of you."

Everyone in the room clapped and cheered. I was so overwhelmed that I teared up. There was a table set up with food, beverages, and a cake that read, Congratulations Bianca! After a group session, the Misfits gathered for dinner and cake to celebrate. I was so overjoyed I felt like my mom was in the room with me. It was such a surreal moment.

Afterward, I went home to study for my finals and stressed about all the reading I had to do when a knock at the door broke my concentration. No one ever visited me I was sure whoever it was had had the wrong door. I looked through the peephole and Justin's entire face was in my view. I hadn't seen him in months and our last conversation had gotten ugly. I didn't know what he could want now after so long, but my heart raced, nevertheless. I quietly stood at the door for a moment bracing myself before I opened the door.

"Justin. Hey. What are you doing here?"

"Hey. Bianca. I'm sorry, I didn't mean to interrupt you."

"You aren't interrupting. I'm just surprised to see you." I opened the door wider. "Come in."

He hesitated then looked back behind him before turning back toward looking sheepish. Had we become that estranged that he'd preferred waiting outside? I wish I hadn't invited him in. Just as I went to recant the offer, he took a step forward.

"Uh yeah. Sorry about that. I should have called first. I just wanted to stop by and thank you for what you did a few days ago. My mom told me what happened with Jordi and how you stepped in."

I closed the door behind him. "Oh, no problem. You're welcome. I'm just glad that I broke it up before it got physical. Talib didn't really want to fight Jordi, but he would have. Know what I mean."

"Yeah, I know. I spoke with Talib. Me and him have always been cool. He told me how you got Jordi to back off. It surprised me."

I walked into the living room and sat down on the couch. "Why? Jordi isn't a bad kid. He's just going through some stuff. Cut him some slack."

"I didn't mean my brother. I meant you."

"Me? Why me?"

He removed his ball cap and scratched his head. He always did that when he was nervous. "Never mind."

Justin and I had known each other for years and while our romantic relationship hadn't worked out, I was hoping we could at least be friends. I guess I was wrong. His demeanor wasn't much friendlier than a stranger's. It bothered me that he couldn't even be straight up with me, but I chose to just let it slide. Life was going well for me, and I wanted to stay on that path. "Um ok. Well, no thanks are necessary. I was just doing what was right."

I picked up my book and continued reading where I'd left off. He could see himself out. He lingered and when I looked up, he was staring at the helium balloons I'd brought home from my celebration.

"Congratulations?" He asked.

I looked at him not wanting to reply. How was it that this fool couldn't clarify his cryptic comment to me and was now low-key all in my business? I chose to answer because I had no need to be short with him as he was with me. At my core I was still B from the hood and proud of it. But more so because I was proud of my accomplishment.

"I reached a milestone and completed three months of my anger management class."

He turned to me abruptly. "Anger management class?"

"Yeah."

"Word? What made you do that?"

I was hesitant but spoke my truth anyway. I had nothing to be ashamed of. "Losing you made me see that I needed help."

His eyes opened a fraction, and I could tell he wasn't expecting me to admit something so personal.

"I don't know what to say."

"You don't need to say anything. That was a reason but not the only reason and now that I have been going for three months, my reasons to keep going are different. I am different."

"What does that mean?"

"Don't get me wrong. I'm still B, but I'm learning to see things through without anger tainting them. I'm learning to be calm and patient. Not to be impulsive or think the worst. I feel like I'm being freed, and I need to see this through for me and my dad."

Justin's gaze locked on mine for a moment before he cleared his throat and looked down to the floor breaking the connection.

"My brother may need some anger management. He's been in such a bad place since our dad died."

"In all the time we've known each other, I never brought up your dad. Mostly because it would lead to talking about my mom and I didn't want to go there. And I assumed you were like me and didn't want to talk about it."

"That's funny you say that. I never brought up my dad because I didn't want to remind you or your mom. I didn't like seeing you sad."

My heart swelled at his words. I hadn't spoken to Justin in months, and I thought I was getting over him. It was very clear I hadn't. Not even a little. I composed myself and reminded myself that he'd broken up with me and sought out to be friendly.

"I remember your dad. He and my dad used to chat all time. I don't think I ever said so but I'm sorry for your loss. He seemed like a nice man."

"He was a good dad and a good man. I miss him."

I could see Justin fighting the emotion, but I didn't save him from it. Lisa had said our feelings were real to us and there was no shame in feeling. It was just up to us to not those feelings rule over us.

Justin checked himself quickly and I wasn't surprised. He'd never been an explosive person. He stuffed his hand in his pocket and looked at me again. "I understand the anger you harbored because I see my brother struggle with it. I never want you to think that I didn't understand."

"Thank you and I hope Jordi gets the help he needs because it's very liberating winning yourself back from that dark place."

"I am very happy for you Bianca."

"That's very nice of you to say." I felt the love I had for him bubbling up to the surface refusing to stay suppressed, so it was my turn to check it and I did. I said nothing more and waited for him to say goodbye but instead, he lingered.

"Well besides that. What else have you been doing?"

"Just focusing on me. Studying. Taking care of my dad. Occasional pool."

"You're not dating anyone?"

"Nope. Haven't dated since our breakup and I'm cool wit' that. Healin', gettin' my anger under control, and findin' my center is all I've been focused on. I've lost a lot but gained some great things and friends in the process. Romance is not on my mind right now." And I meant it.

"Right. I understand." Justin readjusted his hat and began to walk toward the door. "Well, I don't want to keep you from whatever you were doing. Again, thank you. My mom and I appreciate you."

"You're welcome. I hope everything works out with Jordi."

"Me too. Have a good day, B. It was good seeing you."

"Thank you and you too," I smiled as I shut the door.

I was proud of how I handled the entire unexpected situation. I kept cool, calm, and collected. I saw my own growth. I admit that his lingering, and strange reaction to me not wanting romance right now brought out the giddy teenage girl in me, but I told myself to stay focused. He only came to say thank you and I'd leave it at that.

I picked up my notes and settled back onto the couch but for a moment I let myself glow. For months, I had wondered how Justin would react to my transformation, and here he unexpectedly popped up when he wasn't even on my mind, and I'd gotten my answer.

The following morning, my alarm didn't go off and I was late for my last class of the semester. I managed to finish my final exam on time but worried that I may have rushed through some of the answers. What was done was done and I was pretty sure I'd done well anyway. Afterward, I took the bus to the Cherry Hill Mall for a change of scenery. I was tired of being inside studying. I was glad school was over and I had two weeks of relaxation before my summer courses started.

Hours after browsing the mall I grabbed some Bourbon Chicken from my favorite spot. As I was eating Isys had beeped me. I finished my food and called her back on one of the payphones by the bus stop.

"Hey, girl. What's up?"

"Bianca, girl. I have some bad news," Isys cried.

"What's wrong?"

"Brandon got into a fight. He was jumped by a group of guys. They beat him badly. They rushed him to the hospital. It doesn't sound good B."

"What are you talkin' about? What happened?"

"Brandon was being Brandon."

"What the hell does that mean?"

"Apparently Brandon was at a pub and some guy accidentally bumped into him and spilled his beer on him. When he didn't apologize Brandon called him out on it, but the guy just laughed it off and kept walking. So, Brandon followed him poppin' shit the whole time. The guy swung on Brandon, and they started fighting. It got broken up but Brandon being Brandon wouldn't let it go and kept going. The guy was there some friends and they jumped him when he called them all out. One guy grabbed a bat they had hanging on the wall and took some swings on him before the rest stomped on him."

I was furious. I wanted to take a bat to someone's head. Bunch of fucking cowards. What kind of a man didn't square up and take an ass beating or giving one fair and square? I growled trying to keep my anger at bay. I wanted to knock some sense into Brandon myself. What the hell was he thinking? He wasn't. That was the damn problem. Still, he didn't deserve any of that.

We all kept in contact updating each other and found out Brandon had suffered some broken bones including his ribs, contusions, internal bleeding, and cerebral edema. He had been found unconscious and still hadn't awakened.

When I got home, I cried so hard and released all of my pent-up frustration. It was crazy how easily a person's life could change in an instant. I had just seen him yesterday laughing and joking and twenty-four hours later he was fighting for his life. We are all on edge, hoping and praying that he pulled through. For a moment, I thought about picking up the phone to call Justin, but I didn't and chose to keep to myself as I had been doing. I had already proved to myself that I didn't need him.

The unknown regarding Brandon's prognosis made the days that followed hard to go through. In the meantime, I spent more time with my dad now that school had ended. The small progress he had made was better than none and I was grateful for any type of improvement. My mind wandered and I wondered if Brandon would need the same type of care for the rest of his life.

I sat with my dad for an hour before a CNA walked in the room to bathe my dad and dress him in clean clothes.

"It's about time. My dad should have been had his bath."

"Excuse me?" Alicia asked.

"I said it's about time someone came in here to clean up my dad. He has on a diaper and should be cleaned first thing in the mornin'. Why aren't y'all doin' that?"

"Unfortunately, we're a bit short-staffed today and running behind schedule. Your understanding and cooperation would be much appreciated."

"And you doing your job would be much appreciated." I snapped.

The CNA shook her head and exhaled deeply. "Can you please step aside so I can do what I need to do?"

"You know what? You go right ahead. I'm gonna take a walk and cool off a bit. Dad, I'll be back." I said and left the room. Walking away was one of the techniques I learned in anger management. I knew I was hurting because of what was going on with Brandon and leaving helped me prevent one unrelated unfortunate situation from causing another one. I'd learned that I had the power to control my emotions and that made a hell of a difference in avoiding drama. Checking my impulsivity was far more effective in getting the right result than wanting to beat somebody down.

After walking down the hall and overhearing another CNA saying how much her feet hurt from all the mandatory overtime, I realized I had come off aggressive in Dad's room and felt bad. When I returned my dad was looked and smelled clean and fresh. I thanked Alicia and apologized for coming at her when she first came into the room. Holding myself accountable for my actions and the things I said was also something that I needed to work on. Granted, it was a process, but I was trying.

When I got home, I'd had a voicemail from Leah saying Brandon had finally awakened.

TWENTY
Tianna

After one of the rare times I'd eaten dinner with *Mami* and Abe, I trudged over to the couch and propped my feet up on the coffee table. Abe soon followed with a bowl of ice cream. He picked up the remote and clicked through the Pay-Per-View Channels. That was the last thing I remembered before I woke up hours later, now lying comfortably on the couch, my shoes off, feet up and covered with a blanket. Abe was gone, but *Mami* sat in the single chair sipping from a mug and reading a book. She looked peaceful with her feet tucked under her, engrossed in her book. At that moment I realized I missed my mom. Or at least, the mom I thought she was.

She looked over at me and closed her book. "Hey. Did you have a nice nap? You looked so comfortable I didn't want to wake you."

I stretched and sat upright. "I'm sorry. I didn't mean to doze off. I guess all my late-night studying for finals caught up with me."

"Time spent wisely. I'm proud you did well this semester."

What was she talking about? I did well every semester. I let the thought go and tried not to be so cynical. I avoided tension with my mother at all costs. All of my anger and hurt toward her were pent up behind a carefully constructed dam. Any opportunity that could potentially put a crack in it, I sidestepped. A broken dam released an unstoppable force that could not be controlled nor taken back. There would be no coming back from that.

I stood up still groggy and longed for my bed. "Thank you, *Mami*. I'm gonna head to bed. Enjoy your book."

165

"Someone named Justin called. I told him you were asleep, and he said he'd call you tomorrow."

I nodded. Between both of us studying for finals, Justin and I hadn't talked much, and I missed him. "Ok, thanks." I haphazardly folded the throw blanket and tossed it on the couch ready to head upstairs.

"Tianna, wait. Please sit for a minute."

Sometimes sidestepping trouble required patience, keeping quiet, and enduring the unexpected. I readied myself with all three weapons and sat down facing *Mami*. She'd tried mending our relationship several times in the past few months, but her words never penetrated past skin deep. How could they? Nothing she said could change her betrayal. But every time she attempted a reconnection, I listened and extended grace. I did not wish to disrespect her. I just simply no longer trusted her. It was impossible to have a meaningful connection with someone you didn't trust. Family or not. Mother or not.

"It's been a while since we've talked. I just wanted to catch up. How are things at the studio?"

I couldn't remember the last time *Mami* had asked about me. I tried to hide my surprise. "The studio is good. I finished a painting. I haven't done that in a while. I like how it turned out." I didn't know what else I could say.

"And are you all set for summer courses?"

I nodded. "Yes." Again, what more was there to say?

"So, are you and Justin dating?"

Our chat had suddenly become twice as awkward. "We like each other." I left it there. My love life felt too private to share with her. "*Mami*, I'm really tired. I'm gonna head to bed."

"Ok. But I wasn't trying to pry Ti. I just miss talking to you. And there is something I've been wanting to tell you for days and it never seemed like the right time."

I sat back down on the couch and gave my mother a pleasant smile as my way of offering a listening ear although everything in me wanted to escape. Yet once again I endured.

"I guess the best way to say this is to just say it."

My anxiety began to rise.

"Tommy and I have been going to couple's therapy and we want to give our marriage another try. A real try. We are going to renew our vows."

My anxiety gratefully plummeted. I found I didn't care. *Mami* and Tommy's marriage was no concern of mine. They'd broken up and gotten back together more than the big-piece puzzle Abe was obsessed with as a kid. And just like his puzzle, their marriage was missing pieces to make it complete. Fidelity came to mind. "If that's what you two want to do, no one else's opinion should matter."

"Telling you was a courtesy, Tianna. I do not need anyone's permission or validation to honor my commitment to your father."

There was so much wrong with her statement I couldn't wrap my mind around it to make it make sense. Firstly, Tommy was Abe's father, not mine; and committed was not a word I'd use to describe him. Like at all. *Mami* was no better. She was the spokesperson for emasculating a husband every time a wife didn't get her way. Where was the honor in that?

I could sense *Mami* getting defensive, and I almost fixed my lips to bring her down off her blushing bride high horse, but I stayed quiet. I did not need to hate on her life. If she was happy, how stupid was it that I'd hold a grudge? I hated how cynicism had become my initial reaction to things. I refused to be a bitter person. Don't get it twisted though; no matter how much my relationship with *Mami* had changed, I could never just stand by and watch her get hurt. That was not who I was. So, I'd mind my business and stay out of marital affairs, but I wouldn't keep quiet to Tommy's infidelity again. For now, all I wanted was to go to bed.

When they said they were renewing their vows, they'd truly meant it. A month had passed when I had slipped into a pale pink satin dress before walking over to *Mami*'s room to attend to my Maid of Honor duties. She was applying mascara and beamed when she spotted me through the mirror's reflection. "Christianna!" She set the mascara aside and turned to me inspecting me from head to toe. "You look so beautiful."

I blushed at her praise. I couldn't remember the last time *Mami* had complimented me. It surprised me that I soaked it up like hot concrete did raindrops. "Thank you, *Mami*. But today is all about you. So, let's get you ready. Your husband is in the backyard waiting for you and Ms. Nelly did a beautiful job decorating."

Mami put her shaking hands to her cheeks and blew out a loud breath. "I don't know why I'm so nervous. It's not like we aren't already married."

"Just focus on how much you love him and I'm sure the nerves will go away." I sat *Mami* down and fixed the back of her hair that she'd missed before I touched up her makeup. Once she slipped into her simple beige dress, I zipped it up for her. Abe knocked on the door a few minutes later just as I placed flowers in *Mami's* hair. She refused a veil.

"Is the bride ready yet?" Abe asked from the door covering his eyes.

I laughed at him. "Only the groom isn't allowed to see the bride before the wedding. You can uncover your eyes, dodo bird."

Abe dropped his hands from his eyes and walked into the bedroom closing the door behind him. "You calling me a bird because I look so fly." He spun around showing off his suit like he was a member of The Temptations.

Mami cracked up so hard she smacked him on the arm for nearly making her cry and messing up her makeup.

"*Mami* now how you gonna hit me for something I *almost* did?" Abe exaggerated his bewildered expression.

"Boy, hush up, looking like your father." *Mami* adjusted his tie and tapped his chin, her smile big and wide.

Abe sobered for a minute. "*Muy bella, Mami*," he complimented, looking down at her. This time *Mami* did cry, and Abe dabbed her tears before they streamed down her face. "Ok, ok," he said. "Stop all that. You gonna look like a raccoon walking down the aisle and I ain't gonna let the bride of Frankenstein steal my shine when I walk you down."

Mami chuckled and walked over to her dresser, searching for something. I rolled my eyes secretly amused by my brother's nonsense. I grabbed the bouquets from atop the dresser and for good measure, I popped Abe in the back of his head with mine sending a few petals floating to the floor. "Clown."

"Ow! Tianna why'd you do that? Ma, Ti hit me in the back of the head." Abe tried not to laugh and kept the Abe Show going. "Come on now. We too old for this. Grow up, Tianna. In college and still acting like you in pre-school."

Mami checked her earrings in the mirror and chastised me. "Tianna, I told you to stop picking on your brother."

Abe winked at me proud that his foolishness had an audience. Eighteen years old and still acting like a brat. I flared my nostrils and narrowed my eyes in overdramatic fashion promising revenge without even saying a word. He mocked me pretending to be trembling in fear. I burst out into laughter. Sometimes, that boy did not have the good sense God gave him. I waved him off and got back on track.

"It's four o'clock. I'll go tell everyone to take a seat and have them start the music."

Mami exhaled and nodded. She straightened her dress more from nerves than for appearance. I handed her, her bouquet and exited her bedroom. At the bottom of the stairs, I spotted Ms. Nelly and asked her to have all the attendees sit down so we could get the ceremony started. She gushed and did my bidding for me. Truth be told, I had been avoiding going downstairs. Especially the yard where the ceremony and reception were being held. I wanted to be a dutiful daughter, but I had no wish to see anyone from the past. Not *Mami's* church friends. Not my mother's family. Especially her brother.

Justin promised to sit where I could see him and told me to keep my eyes focused on him. He was always doing that. Thinking of ways to help me and live life contently. He was steady. As I grew to know him more, it became my favorite thing about him.

Ms. Nelly returned just as *Mami,* and Abe had reached the bottom of the stairs. Everyone was seated, waiting on the bride. Outside I could hear *Baby, Come to Me* playing. I positioned my bouquet and walked out first. I followed the open path and looked straight ahead. In my peripheral I could see people seated to the left and right of me, but I didn't dare turn to see who filled the chairs. When I made it to the arch serving as the wedding altar, I turned and faced the patio doors where the bride would exit. Although I didn't look at Tommy, I saw his presence filling the space at the altar waiting for *Mami.*

'You look beautiful, Ti,' I heard him say before everyone stood to their feet and turned in search of the bride. All but one person. Justin sat two rows back facing me, a big old smile on his face. He winked and his eyes conveyed a message I didn't need to hear to understand. He was there for me. The thought calmed me.

I focused on the bride walking down the aisle. When she made it to the altar, Pastor Carmichael asked who was giving the bride away and Abe stepped up, kissed *Mami* on the cheek, and handed her off to Tommy doing their secret handshake. They added a few outrageous turns and slaps to it, and everyone laughed at their antics including, myself. It almost felt like I had my family back. In that moment I realized how much I missed them. Us. Even Tommy.

He and *Mami* exchanged vows, and both cried. I admit I teared up too. The ceremony was short and sweet and after all of the chairs were cleared away, the guests stayed for a BBQ reception and music. I found Justin laughing with Abe as if they'd known each other all their lives. I didn't interrupt but walked over to the refreshments table and palmed some Ritz crackers. Although my nerves had settled, I couldn't stomach anything heavy.

Pastor Carmichael's eyes shot open when I inadvertently made eye contact with him. I tried to turn away, but it was already too late. "Tianna, I hardly recognized you! Look at you all grown up. How are you, sweetheart?"

"Pastor Carmichael, I'm well thank you. How are you and the family?" I hadn't seen Pastor Carmichael or anyone from my former church since high school. Religion was one of the many things I removed from my life. I still prayed and believe God existed. I just didn't fit in with church folk. I found no comfort there.

"Everyone is wonderful. Mrs. Carmichael is around here somewhere. Jr. is now stationed in San Diego. The Mrs. and I are going to go see him in a few weeks and then stopping to visit with Lexy at UNLV. You remember my niece Lexy don't you?"

I smiled and nodded politely. "I do. I hope she and Jr. are making you proud." Wrong choice of words for they opened the floodgate of every good thing they'd done in the last five years. Pastor C. began running down all of Lexy's accomplishments. He ended it all with how thankful he was that she'd found herself a nice handsome Pastor's son that had proposed to her.

Pastor C. shook his head and grinned. "In Las Vegas. Sin City of all places. Isn't it amazing how God will send blessings out of the unlikeliest of places, people, and situations? My, my, my He is good!"

"All the time," a male voice chimed in. Justin tapped my arm. "I'm sorry to interrupt Pastor. Beautiful ceremony by the way, but

Tianna is needed inside for something important. Do you mind if I steal her away?"

Pastor Carmichael put his hands up in gracious surrender. "Of course, of course. Go on ahead. And Tianna, I hope to see you back at church soon. Don't be a stranger too long."

I waved back at the Pastor as Justin ushered me into the door through the kitchen and into the dining room. "What's wrong? What's going on?"

He pulled me close and kissed me. I laughed and kissed him back then tapped him on the arm. "You had me nervous. I thought something was really wrong."

"There was. Abe said that the Pastor was going to talk your ear off, and you looked ready to bolt so I'd thought I'd come to save you. I think that deserves another kiss. Like those princes in fairy tales. The chicks stay letting those cats kiss them."

He always found a way to make me laugh. I kissed him then rested my forehead against his. "Thank you for saving me."

Soft little voices interrupted the moment.

"You ask her."

"No, you ask her."

I moved away from Justin a respectable distance and gave my attention to two little girls whispering in each other's ears. "Hi girls." They must've been Mrs. Perez's two new foster children.

The taller one shoved the chubby one forward volunteering her to be the spokesperson. She stepped back and shook her head just as unwilling as her sister. The taller one then spoke, "Jazzy needs to go to the bathroom." Both kept their eyes trained on their feet shuffling in place.

As soon as I directed them to the upstairs bathroom, they shot up the stairs in a hurry, the chubby one dragging the taller one behind her.

I'd never had a sister or a female best friend, but I probably would have been the one being dragged. I cuddled up to the only best friend I had and joked with him about the girls. They were so adorable. Justin kissed the tip of my nose then moved to my cheeks. He coiled a fat tendril around his index finger over and over and again. "You owe me. You know that right?"

"I owe you? What are you talking about?"

"I told you you'd pay for that whole karaoke bullshit you put me through. It's time to collect, *Boricua.*"

I cracked up. "Oh boy. What are you up to?"

"After this reception, you gonna find out. I hope you know how to drive fast and ain't a snitch. I'll cut you in on it too."

My eyes widened and I felt my palms begin to sweat. I leaned in closer to Justin. "You better not be thinking of doing what that sounds like."

He pulled me closer and whispered, "You got my back or not, Ti?"

"I got your back and your front, Justin. That's why I won't let you throw away your future on some craziness. I'll handcuff you to my bed if I have to."

His hardened expression softened, and a smile spread across his face then gave way to his laughter. "Damn girl. You ready to sex slave me to keep me outta trouble huh? I like that."

My creamed coffee-colored face must have turned ten shades of red. I looked around to see if anyone had heard him before I shushed him. "I didn't say anything about sex. And I can't believe you'd play around like that. You scared me, Dumbass."

Justin laughed and hugged me tightly. "I was just teasing you, Mrs. Leonard."

"Mrs. Leonard is my mother."

"Exactly."

He had the nerve to laugh at his own joke. I rolled my eyes and ignored it. I was nothing like my mother.

"Relax, Ti. I'm just joking around." He kissed my neck and rubbed my back. "Can you come to spend the night tonight? I've been living in the summer housing dorms for two weeks and you still haven't been by. I miss you."

I wrapped my arms around him and exhaled. I missed him too. "Yeah. I'll go pack some clothes and put them in the car. We can leave in a bit. I gotta do the picture thing and mingle for a bit first."

"Sounds good. Aiight. Go pack and I'm gonna go get something to eat and introduce myself. That barbeque is making my stomach growl and I can't let this fly suit go to waste." Justin spun around peacocking his clothes before he kissed me. "Pack for a few days." Then he disappeared into the backyard.

I climbed the stairs on light feet. Life was far from perfect, but Justin had become a bright light in an otherwise dim world. I told myself to cut out the pity party. What did I have to complain about? There were people far off worse than I was. I went into my bedroom and pulled out my gym bag from high school. I discarded the memories that tried to surface. Those days, those people, those times were far behind me. Memory lane was inviting me to visit but the only place I wanted to travel to was Justin's.

After I packed, I closed my bedroom door behind me and down the hall I strangely saw the linen closet door close on its own then crack open again. I set my things down and walked over to the closet where a little girl was peeking out at me.

"Come on out sweetie. Why are you hiding in there?" I opened the door and she cowered into the corner frightened. "It's ok. I won't hurt you." I extended my hand out to her and lowered myself to her level so she wouldn't feel threatened. "It's ok. Come on out." She hesitated but stepped forward. "What's your name?" I asked the chubby one of the two girls I'd seen earlier.

"Melanie."

"Melanie, where's your sister?"

She began to cry and eyed the bathroom door. Alarms went off in my head. "Is she in the bathroom?"

She nodded.

"Is she hurt?"

Melanie eyed me with no response.

"Is she by herself?"

Quickly Melanie shook her head, and I could see the fear back in her eyes.

"Ok, I want you to go downstairs and get my friend for me, ok? Do you remember my friend?"

Melanie nodded. "The boy you were kissing?"

I smiled at her more to comfort her than anything else. "Yes. Can you tell him to come upstairs as fast as he can?"

She nodded again and I sent her rushing. I closed the closet door and headed to Abe's bedroom to grab his *Nunchaku* sticks to use as a weapon, but his door was locked.

"Shit." I ran into my room next, but I couldn't find anything. I rummaged through my closet and grabbed the leather belt I barely wore. It was better than nothing. I rushed back to the bathroom and quietly opened the door.

Melanie's sister was sitting on Lou's lap. His hand was up her dress and his pants down. She trembled so fiercely I could see it. Suddenly I saw ten-year-old Tianna sitting on his lap instead. My stomach began to churn, and I wanted to vomit. When she saw me, the little girl burst into tears and ran through the open door right past me.

Had I been in a stable mindset I would have been grateful that I had been able to rescue her the way no one had rescued me, but all I could see was scared Tianna too afraid to run. Too afraid to tell. Too afraid to fight back.

Lou stood up, his penis hanging free, and he didn't seem to care. Slowly he pulled up his underwear and pants, leaving himself exposed. With a disturbing grin, he palmed himself suggestively. "I guess you taking her place since it's your fault she's gone."

I tightened my grip on the belt. "You disgusting bastard."

As if I hadn't said a word, he looked past me smiling, put his penis away, and continued. "You miss playing with me, Tianna? I used to miss playing with you but then you started whoring. Yeah, the whole family knows you fuck anybody that comes along. We all know Little Ms. Goody-Two-Shoes got pregnant, and the boy left you. Nobody wants a used-up fast-ass girl like you. Even when you were little you were a little skank. Standing in the hallway showing me your little titties. I should've told your mom. Maybe she could've set you straight back then and beat your ass for being a ho."

Hot, angry tears streamed down my face in a torrent. "I hate you."

"You don't hate me. You liked when I touched you. Yeah, Ti. I heard you moan. I felt you orgasm when I played with you. You liked it. You wanted it. You remember all those nasty little things I taught you, and now you do them to all those boys you fucking."

"Tianna." Justin was standing behind me. The agony I heard in his tone when he called my name meant he'd heard everything. Every single dirty word that bastard had said. Shame swallowed me whole and I wanted to beat Lou with the belt, but I wanted to disappear even more. I couldn't turn around and face Justin. Of every human on the planet, his was the only opinion of me that mattered. Seeing disgust in his eyes would break me.

How? How did I let someone gain that power over me? I backed out of the door and felt his hands on my back.

"Tianna." His voice was hoarse as if he could barely stand to utter my name.

I broke free and ran.

"Tianna! Wait!"

I didn't stop. I ran down the stairs, snatched my car keys from off the hook, and sped out the door. At first, I drove around in circles. Then I got on the highway and followed it without a destination in mind.

I ended up at the shore. Summertime at the shore was always busy. It didn't matter though. I felt like I was on the Boardwalk alone despite all the attention I was getting from being in a bridesmaid dress. I took my shoes off and walked onto the sand. The sun was beginning to set, and the beachgoers were packing up and leaving. I walked along the shore before I plopped myself in the sand and cried. I watched the waves lapping back and forth and eventually it calmed me.

Tianna the Protector was trying to take over, but I fought her. She ruled with an iron fist. For the first time in a long time, I saw a glimpse of happiness with someone who genuinely cared about me. I had already started to embrace it and wasn't ready to let it go. I didn't want her to shut Justin out.

Until I heard Justin saying my name over and over again in my head. Every disgusting word that my mother's brother spoke cut me, but it was Justin's one word that fatally wounded me. 'Tianna.' I couldn't stop hearing it.

Did Justin believe that monster? While I'd told him about being molested, I'd never admitted that I had climaxed. I hadn't even known what that was until years later. I began to cry again. I could never face Justin again. Ever.

I couldn't hold on any longer and Tianna the Protector took over. She shut everything down. Every emotion. All the love. All the hope. She took no prisoners. No one penetrated her defenses. I transitioned into numbness. I wasn't sad. I wasn't mad. I wasn't anything. I felt nothing.

I returned home the next morning to a quiet house. Party cups were scattered about, evidence of a recent party. I never realized how much of a prison this house had become to me. Almost everywhere I turned a bad memory accompanied it. Yet, even in those memories, I didn't feel anything. I walked into the kitchen to grab a glass of water. I was so dehydrated my lips were cracked and I felt queasy. I hadn't eaten in nearly twenty-four hours, and it was catching up to me.

Mami sat at the kitchen table, still wearing her wedding dress. She stared into a cup oblivious that I had walked in. The way she drank from her cup, I could tell it wasn't coffee. Most likely something stronger. My keys rattled against the countertop grabbing her attention. She looked up at me and said nothing. She began to sob. Her smeared mascara and raccoon eyes told me she'd been sobbing all night.

She covered her mouth to keep her sobs from escaping, and when her shoulders began to shake uncontrollably, I didn't know what to do. I felt nothing. I cared about nothing. Logically I knew I was supposed to care, but sorrow, sympathy, and compassion weren't logical. They were emotional and that part of me had been shut down like a blown fuse box. It wasn't a choice. I had no control over it. I was a walking Zombie.

I drank my water and walked out of the kitchen. Sleep and studying were my only goals. I climbed two steps when I heard *Mami* behind me.

"Tianna."

I stopped and faced her but didn't speak.

"Please wait."

Still, I said nothing. I turned and took a few more steps.

"Tommy is in jail. Lou is in intensive care."

I made it to the top of the staircase, walked into my bedroom, and locked the world out. I spoke to no one for three weeks. Not even Abe. Justin had called several times, but I rejected the person at the door trying to hand me the phone, and the caller.

One morning, I woke up to birds chirping. I couldn't remember the last time I had heard them. Not that they had stopped singing. I had just been unable to hear them. Emotional suppression robbed a person of every sense. There was no joy to be had in anything. Colors were dull. Love was non-existent. Even hatred and disgust were far from you. It was a state of nothingness.

I closed my eyes and focused on the bird's melody. It made me smile. I wasn't ready to do cartwheels, but it was a small step to coming alive again. I appreciated every millimeter of progression out of the pit of numbness.

I got dressed and could smell bacon cooking. It made my stomach queasy. I ran to the bathroom and vomited. So much for hoping for a brighter day. I brushed my teeth again and gargled mouthwash. When I stepped out of the bathroom Tommy was waiting outside the door. He was surprised to see me.

"Tianna." He scratched his head and avoided eye contact with the misguided notion he had to say something. He didn't. And I wouldn't. *Mami* and Abe had attempted to give me the account of what happened after my encounter with Lou in the bathroom, but I refused to hear a single detail.

My mom hadn't attended a funeral, so I assumed Lou was still alive. And hopefully, Mrs. Perez had had him arrested. Several times I had thought about that little girl. I was sorry I hadn't made it to her sooner. If I hadn't been downstairs playing love doctor with Justin, I could have saved her sooner. I tried to bury the guilt. I had already carried enough wounds to last a lifetime. At least Tommy had played her hero and she was able to see that she was victimized. That it was not her fault. I was glad she had at least gotten that. I hadn't prayed much, but I had prayed for her to not end up as I had.

I stepped around Tommy and walked to my bedroom, relieving him of phony pleasantries.

"You'll always be my baby girl, Ti."

His words halted my steps. I heard the bathroom door close before a single tear escaped. Over the next few days, my nausea had increased as had the tears. I went from feeling nothing to feeling everything in heightened fashion. From one extreme to the next, I missed everyone in life that I loved. I had spent most nights awake sketching just so I wouldn't experience night terrors. Now I wanted nothing more than to sleep all day if just to avoid the smell of food. I began stuffing towels under my bedroom door to keep the odor from seeping in.

Sometimes it worked. Today, it hadn't. My mouth was salivating, and I could feel my stomach pumping. The smell of chicken had wafted in and sent me running to the bathroom. The bathroom door was locked. I tried to make it back to my bedroom to use my wastebasket but didn't make it in time. Outside of Abe's bedroom, I fell to my knees as the contents of my stomach escaped. The sight of chunks and its rancid smell had me adding a second layer to the hallway carpet.

Abe opened his door. "Ti, you ok?"

I shook my head and held my stomach willing it to cooperate and stop churning.

"Aww man, that's nasty!" Abe covered his mouth as if he were ready to contribute to the pile.

"What's going on?" I heard *Mami* ask behind me.

"Ti's sick."

Mami helped me to my feet and sent me to shower while she cleaned up the mess. Afterward, she checked in on me and brought me some crackers and a glass of Ginger Ale telling me to take small sips. I was grateful although I kept my words to a minimum. I thanked her before I dozed off. I woke up a short while later and found a pregnancy test on my nightstand.

Mami may have been a lot of things, but stupid wasn't one of them. And for the second time, she had been right. I tossed the positive test in the trash and cried myself back to sleep; the spark of contentment doused and sending me back into darkness.

TWENTY-ONE

Justin

Never in my life had I ever wanted to take a man's life. A part of me still wanted to finish the serious hurting I had put on that fucking pervert. He had been damn lucky Mr. Leonard broke it up. But thinking back on it, I should have left the trash alone and chased the treasure. Tianna had run out of there so fast I didn't think and just reacted to my anger. On some level I wondered if this was what Bianca felt like all the time. So angry you just wanted to hurt something or someone. A part of me broke inside. Bianca had deserved my understanding not criticism. Crazy how perspective can completely change how you see circumstances.

After two weeks of calling and stopping by Tianna's house with no luck, I had decided to give her space. Hopefully, she could see how her uncle had just been trying to manipulate her. Anyone who knew her at all, wouldn't have ever believed that she was at fault or enjoyed her abuse. That man was sick.

I felt my blood pressure rising again and couldn't focus on my studies. I got up and picked up the phone. My roommate looked up at me annoyed.

"For real bro? Man, get over it. She don't wanna be with you anymore."

I ignored him and listened as the phone rang. Abe answered. "Hey, Justin. Let me walk the phone up to her. Hold on."

I cringed at his immediate response. Maybe I had been calling too much. I listened and waited patiently.

Abe's voice could be heard loudly. "Oh good. You saved me a trip upstairs. Justin is on the phone for you."

And for the first time in a week, I had heard her voice. "Abe, I already told you that I don't want to talk to anyone. Especially Justin. Tell him I'm not here."

"Damn Ti," I heard Abe say before I assume he covered the phone with his hand. A few minutes later, he came back on and apologized on her behalf, but she couldn't take his call right now. No other explanation. Not that I needed one. What she said had been enough.

I finished my summer classes and had seen Tianna twice on campus, but only from a distance. I went out of my way to avoid her each time. I felt bad for her but getting shut out when you really cared about someone and only wanted to help, was not cool. I had feelings too. So, I focused on respecting her wishes and getting over her. I won't lie, I missed her, but I couldn't let anything, or anyone disrupt my peace or get me off track. I said my goodbyes to her from a distance and hoped that maybe one day she could heal, and we could be friends again. If she ever needed me, I'd be there for her.

For now, I had a family that needed me and that's where I turned my attention. I thought about Jordi and how to fix things between us. I called my mom, and we decided a guy's trip to go visit Auntie Wynn, my dad's sister, in North Carolina for a few weeks was just the ticket. New scenery, places, and faces were exactly what Jordi, and I needed.

TWENTY-TWO
Bianca

S trawberry milkshakes were Brandon's favorite, so I picked one up on the way to his house. He'd been home for a few days and all of the Misfits had visited him except me. Leah told me he'd asked about me several times already. I couldn't deny I had been avoiding the visit. I was tired of seeing people I cared about hurting. But friends were there for each other so I pushed aside my own drama and did what I should as a friend. His brother let me in and showed me to his bedroom.

When I walked in, he had been asleep, and I let him rest. I set the milkshake down on his nightstand and looked at him. It had been almost two weeks since I'd last seen him and I was hoping he'd miraculously be ok but in reality, I knew that was impossible. Even still, it broke my heart to see him laid up. An arm and a leg were in a cast. His midsection was bandaged up, looking like a mummy. The bruising on his face had faded to yellow in some areas. The cuts on his lip and eyebrows were scarred.

I couldn't help myself and I cried. How could people be so damn heartless? Yet at the same time, I was grateful he was still alive. He opened his eyes, looked up at me, and smiled.

"B. Where you been?" His voice was raspy, and he tried to clear it.

"Don't talk. Just rest."

He winced. "Shit. All I do is rest. I'm ready to go to Leah's and get in the pool."

I quickly wiped the tears and laughed. "Sounds good to me. But first, you gotta get healed up 'cause your ass'll sink to the bottom with those casts on and my ass don't know how to swim. You'll be shit outta luck."

He laughed then coughed. I felt bad for making him laugh and in turn causing him pain. "Oh, my bad."

He shook his head and dismissed it. "You aiight. I'm glad you came. You staying for a bit?"

I nodded and took a seat. We chatted for a bit until he dozed off. Effects from his pain medication. I thought about leaving while he was asleep but didn't want to just disappear. Instead, I waited and studied my course notes for class the next day. When I looked up, he was staring at me."

"You stayed."

"Yeah, I didn't just want to leave without saying goodbye."

"I'm sorry I fell asleep."

I looked at him like he was stupid. "How you apologizin' to me for gettin' rest? Stop talkin' crazy."

He didn't laugh but stared at me. "I'm sick of bein' in here B."

I sympathized with him, but I cared more about him getting better than him out there acting wild. "Bran, just rest and don't stress nothin' else. You gotta get better. Focus on that. Don't make this harder than it already is."

He huffed like a kid having a tantrum and turned his face away from me. I hadn't meant to be so hard on him. I felt awkward and decided now was the best time to go home. The last thing I wanted to do was make his recovery worse.

"I'm gonna head out now. I have some more studying to do before class tomorrow. I hope you get some rest."

He looked at me and nodded. I grabbed my bag and walked to the door.

"B?"

I turned toward him. "Yeah?"

"Please come back soon."

I beamed a smile his way. "You couldn't keep me away even if you wanted to." He didn't respond in words or expressions. I walked out and went home thinking about his sad eyes for the rest of the night.

A few days later I returned and heard laughter coming from his bedroom. Some of the Misfits had been visiting. Leah sat by his bedside feeding Brandon applesauce while Dani sat at the chair by the foot of his bed reading him a book. The cover had a woman and man half-naked on it making out so I could imagine what had them laughing like they were stupid. Leave it to Dani to read him porn.

When I walked in, Leah yelled hello and Dani repeated it in her sing-song voice.

"Hey B," Brandon said sounding a little less depressed than the last time I had visited.

"Hey. How's the patient and his private nurses?"

Leah laughed. "Just trying to keep his spirits up."

"Amongst other things," Dani added holding up her book. I expected nothing less than for Dani to make everything perverted.

"That is disgusting." Leah set the applesauce down and stood up. "And that's my cue to leave."

Brandon shook his head. "Ain't nothing wrong with me there. Oh! believe that."

"That ain't none of my business," Leah replied before she kissed him on the forehead. "Be good. I'll be back soon."

"Define good."

She cracked up and hugged me on her way out. "Keep an eye on him. He's been moody," she whispered before she disappeared out the door.

Dani continued reading and ten minutes later I interrupted her when the story got too nasty for me. "Dani, ain't nobody trying to hear all that."

She rolled her eyes and set the book down. "Fine. Party pooper. I gotta go anyway."

"Where you going?" Brandon whined.

"To work."

"Work?" Brandon and I said it at the same time.

She narrowed her eyes at us. "Yes, work. I got a job. At a restaurant. As a waitress."

"Congrats Dani! That's cool." I was happy for her.

"Thanks! Let's hope this one lasts," she joked as she walked up to Brandon and tapped him on the nose. "I'll finish reading this to you on my next day off."

Brandon winked at her. "I can't wait. Good luck at your new job."

"Thanks, Bran." She kissed him on the cheek loudly and sashayed out the door.

With Leah and Dani gone, the room got quiet, and I opted for the seat Leah had sat in. "Do you want to finish the applesauce?"

He shook his head no. "I'd rather you tell me about school. How's it goin'?"

"It's goin'."

He smiled. "That bad?"

"No. I'm doin' well actually. Just lots of studying. Can't wait to be done."

He asked me a few more questions about school and then he asked me to tell him about my mom. It was strange and random, but I told him. For the first time since her death, I spoke about it without the anger I once had. It still hurt like hell to recall it, but I didn't have the urge to punch the wall or drown myself in my regret.

I heard him wince and realized I had lost myself in storytelling and hadn't been paying attention to him. "Are you in pain?" He shook his head no in an obvious lie. I wanted to knock him upside his head. "Bran, when are you due for your pain meds?"

"At six."

I checked my watch. "Brandon it's 6:45!"

"I didn't want to take them and fall asleep. I was ok."

I forced him to tell me where the pills were and made him take them. Afterward, I chewed him out for being so stupid. He ignored me and told me to finish my story. I talked until he fell asleep.

It became a routine. I'd visit and feed him. Sometimes I'd shave his face and brush his coarse hair that had since grown out, losing its shapeup. He'd ask me to tell him a story about my life and he'd listen until he fell asleep. It was weird but if it helped him cope, then I'd do what I could to help.

One day he'd asked me to tell him about my love life. I smirked. "Well, that's easy. I don't have one. The end."

He wasn't amused. "You ain't ever been in love B? Come on now. You too cute. I know you've hooked up with somebody."

I thought about Justin. "I had a boyfriend, and we were together for a few years. He went away to school, and we grew apart. Me getting in fights all the time pushed him away. He broke up with me."

"Did you love him?"

I hesitated before I answered him. "Yeah, I did."

"Do you still?"

I didn't respond. I didn't want to think about Justin or what wasn't healthy for my mind or heart. He had been a part of my past and I had accepted that and moved on. I changed the subject and asked him about the many women I was sure he'd hooked up with. He was a big-time flirt. He was happy to tell me about the women he'd loved and lost. Mostly because of his temper, making a joke about it. It pissed me off.

"You think your temper is funny? Look at you right now."

"I didn't beat myself with a bat, B."

"No. But you didn't walk away either. You chased trouble. You coulda gotten yourself killed!"

"So, this my fault?" He looked stunned.

"You don't see how this is just as much your fault as it is theirs? For real? When you gonna start takin' responsibility for your shit Bran?"

He faced the wall and didn't reply.

"I'm gonna go. I didn't come here to fight with you. You're due for your meds in forty-five minutes. I'll tell your brother on my way out."

I returned two days later unsure if he'd want to see me. I braced myself for backlash but found none.

"You came back."

"Was I not supposed to?"

"I thought you were mad at me."

"Who said I'm not. But what does that have to do with being a good friend? I called your brother to check in on you and he said he had to go out for a while, so I volunteered to babysit." I smirked.

"Babysit?" Brandon didn't hide how offended he was.

"Yeah. You act like a baby. Tantrums and all." I frowned my face up mocking him.

He finally laughed and just like that, we were back to being good. After dinner, I put my textbook back in my bag ready to go after being there for a few hours.

"B?"

"Yeah," I said as I moved his rolling table closer to him and refilled his cup of water adding a fresh straw.

"That guy is stupid."

"You gotta narrow that down cause most guys I know are stupid. Including you." I cracked up at my joke.

"Very funny. But I'm serious."

By the tone in his voice, I could tell he was trying to be sincere. "What guy?"

"The one that broke your heart."

I'm sure my face turned red. I cleared my throat and straightened his sheets to keep from facing him.

He chuckled. "Don't worry. I'm not kicking game. I'm just letting you know you deserve somebody who'll appreciate you. You can stop blushing now."

I cleared my throat. "Ain't nobody blushing." I was never any good at compliments or showing vulnerability. It made me uncomfortable.

"Yeah, you are. You look cute when your face turns red and your hazel eyes squint."

I covered my face irritated. "I do not. Stop staring at me like that. Weirdo."

Justin laughed out loud and then held his ribs. "Don't make me laugh like that." He groaned in pain.

I felt bad. "My bad."

He asked for water, and I held the cup for him and placed the straw in his mouth to help him sip.

"Thanks, B."

"You're welcome." I wiped the dribble from his chin.

"If you love him, you should tell him."

I stared at Brandon wondering why he kept insisting on talking about Justin. "Where'd that come from?"

"Laying in bed all day, I ain't got nothing to do but think about shit, and one thing I know for sure is. Life's too short to waste."

I left Brandon's with his words playing on repeat in my mind. I didn't know if I wanted to put myself out there with Justin, but Brandon was right. Life was definitely too short to waste.

The fire alarm's constant loud noise refused to be ignored and when I began to smell smoke, I realized it wasn't someone playing with the alarm. I swiftly jumped up from my bed and slipped on some clothes so I could get the hell out of there. When I opened the door to the hallway smoke had filled it. I began to panic because I knew I couldn't get on the elevator and had to find my way to the stairway. I started to cough as the smoke-filled my lungs. I covered my mouth and walked with everyone who headed to the stairwell.

Right before I got to the end of the hallway near the door to the stairwell, I heard a woman hollering for help. When I got to my neighbor Rita's door I peeked in her apartment, and she begged for help with her four children. I went inside and heard one of the kids crying. Rita quickly ran into her bedroom then rushed back out with a bag on her right shoulder and carrying her five-month-old baby.

Hysterically she pleaded for help. "Please help me. I can't carry them all down the stairs." She was frantic and making me nervous. Another one of her children started crying causing more panic.

"Calm down. You're making them panic and that's not helping nobody. I'll get two and you carry your baby and grab one of their hands. Okay?"

"Okay. Yes. Thank you, so much," Rita eyed me her eyes filled with fear.

We grabbed the children and exited the floor through the stairwell. People were running past and pushing through causing others to panic. As the smoke got heavier, it was harder to breathe and carry the children. We finally made it to the lobby and firemen rushed past us, some helping us out while others were trying to get to the fire.

Outside, a huge crowd of residents had been evacuated and were waiting across the street watching in awe and talking to each other. We walked as far away as we could get from the building, crossing to a less crowded part of the street. Further down the street, I saw Mrs. Saunders sitting on the ground, and Justin and Jordi were huddled over her as if something were wrong. I hadn't even realized he was back from school. I made sure Rita and the kids were ok before I ran over.

"Hey, what's wrong?"

"She twisted her ankle rushing down the steps," Justin answered.

"Can you move your ankle, Mrs. Saunders?"

"No. I'm in a lot of pain. It hurts when I try."

"She may have broken it or have a bad fracture. Did anyone call for help?"

"No. We had to rush past the phone booth," Justin answered.

When emergency services pulled up, I ran over and pulled a medic to come check on her. After evaluating her, she needed to be transported to the hospital for a possible broken ankle. Those not needing medical attention stood outside for three more hours before we were cleared to go back inside the building.

That afternoon Justin stopped by my apartment to let me know that his mom had suffered a bad fracture and thanked me for the help with the medic.

"You know you don't have to keep thanking me for doing what's right."

"And you do know you can just say you're welcome, right? I'm thanking you for caring. There were a bunch of people out there and you were the only one that even bothered coming over to see what was wrong. We're grateful."

"You're right. My bad. You're welcome. And if y'all need anything just let me know."

Justin winked then cocked his head back before poking his head in the door. "Is that smell coming from in here?"

I mushed his head back out the door. "Dang, you nosey. And, yes it is."

"What's that? Like a Stouffers frozen meal?"

I frowned my face up at him. "No, it ain't no damn Stouffer's."

"B, you in here cookin'?" Genuine shock filled his face before it looked like a lightbulb turned on over his head. "Was it you that started the fire?" He frowned his face up like a disappointed father.

I almost punched him in the mouth. Instead, I dismissed his ass by closing the door right in his face. He pushed it open before I could shut it all the way. "Wait," he said laughing.

I opened the door and gave him the evil stare.

"You really in here cookin'?"

I raised my eyebrow and pursed my lips together losing my patience.

"Don't get mad. I didn't know you knew how to cook, damn. And for real, when did you learn 'cause you never knew how to cook when we was together?"

I let my irritation subside a little. He was right. It had only been recently that I had learned and was still learning. Isys had taught me a few things and I liked learning. I had only mastered a few things but whenever I had time, I would learn something new and then take it to Brandon to try. He had been my guinea pig.

"I have been learning for a few months now."

He peeked inside again. "It smells good."

"It's baked mac and cheese. I was getting ready to fry some chicken."

"Oh snap! Fried chicken? Oh, I gots to taste this," Justin laughed and tried to bulldoze his way in.

I put my hand to his chest. "Slow ya roll. Ain't nobody invite you in."

"Oh, it's like that?"

"Yeah, it's like that. I haven't seen you in months. And from what I remember, the last time you was here, you was acting corny like you ain't know nobody." I waited for him to deny. He didn't.

"Yeah, that was awkward. You can't blame me though, B. We had broken up and hadn't seen each other since before then. What I woulda looked like coming up in your apartment acting like nothin' happened?"

I was getting tired of him always having a point. Even still, that changed nothing. "And you ain't just gonna walk up in here now and act like that either."

He backed up and nodded. "You right. Me and Jordi just back from down South and my Auntie fed me good. That shit just smells good as hell and I reacted. My mom is resting her foot and Jordi and I haven't eaten dinner yet. I was trippin'. My bad."

He was laying it on thick. I rolled my eyes at him. "I do pretty damn good on the fried chicken tip. It took more than a few tries to master it, but I got it. I'll bring some up to y'all in a bit. Tell Mrs. Saunders not to worry about dinner tonight."

"Yo, word?"

I shook my head yes and smiled. "Yeah."

He reached in and tapped the tip of my nose. "Thanks, B."

"You're welcome."

An hour later I packed up some food and hauled it upstairs. Jordi answered the door, more interested in the food than in the company. I served everyone, including Mrs. Saunders who looked at me cautiously. She thanked me for helping them out the night before but eyed the food like I had poisoned it or something. Jordi didn't care and tore into it.

"Yo, I thought this was gonna taste kinda nasty but it's slammin'."

"Damn bro. Why you gotta be so damn ignorant?" Justin turned to me and apologized. "I'm sorry B. We are grateful for the food. You didn't have to."

"Michael Saunders, mind your manners." Mrs. Saunders eyed Jordi and still hadn't touched a bite of her food.

"You're welcome. I'm glad I could help. I'm gonna go. Y'all enjoy." I sped outta there and went back to the solitude of my apartment, ate my own dinner, and showered. I began looking through my DVDs in the mood to watch a comedy. The knock on the door surprised me but only one person knocked on my doors these days, so the person on the other didn't.

"Hey. My mom asked me to return your dishes and to thank you again."

I grabbed the cleaned dishes from him and took them into the kitchen. "Did she finally eat after I left? She looked like she was scared of my food."

He laughed. "Don't mind her. You can't blame her. Don't nobody cook for her family but her. Her pride was a little bruised but after Jordi told her that your chicken was better than hers, she gave in and tasted it. And then tasted it some more. Damn near ate the plate. Then said her chicken is still better than yours."

I cracked up. The fact that she'd eaten it was compliment enough for me. "That's funny. I'm glad she liked it."

"I did too. You got any leftovers?" He looked around the kitchen.

"No. I packed up the rest for a friend."

"She's a lucky friend."

"You mean he. He's a lucky friend."

Justin cocked his head back surprised. "Oh. I thought you said you weren't dating. My bad."

He looked disappointed and it made my heart leap. I remained quiet though. He was fishing for information, and I wasn't telling him nothing. Mostly because there was nothing to tell, but he didn't need to know that.

"Well, let me get outta here. Thanks again, Bianca." He walked to the door.

I wasn't telling him anything, but I didn't want him to leave either. Life was too short to waste. I closed my eyes and exhaled before I spoke. "What are you up to right now? I was about to watch a movie. Do you want to stay and watch it with me?"

He turned back. "Yeah, I'm not doing anything."

He sat on the couch as I put on a Martin Lawrence stand-up. Only a few minutes into it, and our laughs echoed throughout the apartment. I got up to go to the kitchen and tripped over Justin's foot. I fell to the floor feeling so small. Within a few seconds, Justin helped me up to my feet. Without any reservations he brought me close to him holding me close, burying his face in my neck.

"Justin, what are you doin'?

"You smell so good. That's my favorite perfume. Sand and Sable, right?"

"You still remember my perfume?" I could hardly concentrate with him so close and probing.

His voice was heavy with seduction. "How could I forget it as much as I used to kiss on your neck? That smell is a part of me. I brought you a bottle of it for our first Christmas together."

"Yes, you did," I said my voice raspy. I pulled away and he held my waist not letting me get far. I stared at his neck to avoid looking up at his face. He lifted my chin and stared at me. He hesitated before he leaned down to kiss me. My lips making contact with his answered his silent question.

He broke away and I didn't want it to stop. "Kiss me again."

After our steamy kisses, I slowed things down and took a walk to the kitchen to calm myself down. I didn't want to take things too far so soon. I didn't want a summer fling before he went back to school. That situation was dead and gone. Remembering how we ended before brought me right back on track. I never wanted to feel that heartbreak again. I walked back out to the living room and stood by the door.

"I'm about to go review some of my notes for class tomorrow and get ready for bed. It's getting late."

"You kickin' me out?" Justin teased.

"Don't say it like that." I tried not to laugh but I wasn't a great actress and cracked up.

Justin walked over to me and kissed me on the cheek before opening the door. "Thanks again for dinner."

I nodded and smiled, the whole time wanting him to stay and make love to me, but I was learning how to control my impulses and I had nearly failed but I pushed through.

"And dessert," he added. I chuckled and shook my head at him as he walked out and shut the door behind him.

I went to visit my dad for a few hours before I went to check in on Uncle Ricky. Figured I'd shoot a few games of pool while I was there. When I walked into his bar, he was throwing back a shot.

"I thought the doctor told you to stop drinking," I said as I approached the bar.

"One isn't gonna hurt. I've been doing good," he explained.

"You sure it was only one because you don't look like you had only one. You know I know how you look when you have shots of Tequila."

"C'mon Bianca. Don't interrogate me."

"How's your symptoms? Still feeling tired, thirsty, and going to the bathroom a lot?"

"Yeah."

"Are you takin' your insulin?"

"I hate needles."

"So, does that mean you're not takin' your insulin?"

"I've been okay without that shit. I don't like takin' medicine. I don't trust these doctors. We're like fuckin' guinea pigs to them. You take somethin', then it messes wit' somethin' else. Those muthafuckas. Everything is about money."

"Do you realize that your diabetes is serious? You can develop CVR from having it and especially when you're not taking your medicine and takin' care of yourself."

"What da hell is CVS?"

"CVS is a pharmacy, Uncle Ricky. I said CVR. You're being a wise guy. This is not funny. CVR is cardiovascular disease and ultimately can cause a myocardial infarction."

"What da hell did you just say? Speak English Bianca. Using that terminology shit. I didn't understand nothin' you just said."

"Basically, you can have a heart attack. Is that want you're aiming for?"

"Now you know damn well I don't wanna have no heart attack."

"Well, that's the road you're travelin'. I'm already dealin' with my dad's long-term damage from a stroke. You think I want to get a call sayin' you had a heart attack? No. I do not! Can you please stop bein' so selfish? You have people here who love you. You have to take betta' care of yourself."

"Okay, okay. Damn. It's hard stoppin' somethin' that you love doin' out of nowhere. This diabetes shit is in the way."

"Yeah, well, you betta' straighten up before it puts you out the way."

"That wasn't funny, Bianca."

"It wasn't meant to be funny. I am dead serious."

"Why you had to say dead?"

"Uncle Ricky, that's your guilt messin' wit' you. Stop. You're makin' me laugh and I'm tryna be serious," I laughed.

"You usin' a poor choice of words at the wrong time, shit. Scarin' the hell outta me."

"You ought to be scared the way you movin'."

"I'ma try to do betta Baby Girl."

"You promise?"

"Yes. I heard you. I promise. I'm not tryna die any time soon."

"Thank you."

"I see school got you in here talkin' like a doctor. You must be doin' pretty damn good."

"I am. I'm so excited about graduatin'. I've been goin' all year long so I can graduate quicker. It's almost here. Then nursing school."

"Wow. Look at you. I'm proud of you and I know your dad is too. I was up there with him for a while yesterday. He's still funny. Don't let his slow slurred speech fool you. He still talks shit," Uncle Ricky laughed.

"I can believe it. He's been a bit more vocal lately. Well, I'm about to head home and get some dinner."

"Oh okay. Well, if you're up for it, come through later. There's a pool tournament tonight and you know we go all night long."

"I'll think about it."

"C'mon. You know I love to see you whip ass up in here," he cackled.

"You funny. I love you. Hey! And no more drinks! You promised!" I reminded him as I walked out.

"Love you too Baby Girl! See you later."

TWENTY-THREE
Justin

For the third time this week I took the elevator to Bianca's floor and knocked on her door with no answer. I wondered if she had been avoiding me. I nixed that thought and took to the stairs to my floor although I was exhausted from a long day doing landscaping. It was a lot of labor and hot as hell outside, but I had to do what I had to do. I was dead set on helping my mom and trying to knock out student debt. The temptation to stand on a corner and make easy money had crossed my many times over pushing a lawnmower across some well-off person's lawn. But I wasn't about that life.

I opened the door to the apartment shaking my head realizing what they charged to get an education was the real hustle. No street corners or weight needed. Gotta love America. It costs an arm and some ass to try and make it out of the ghetto. I closed the door behind me surprised to see my mom and Bianca sitting at the dining table snapping peas and chatting like they were best friends.

My mom welcomed me home and Bianca just looked up at me and smiled. Seeing her domesticated and friendly with my mom arrested me on the spot. I wasn't by any means a chauvinistic man but seeing a strong, beautiful woman gentle and meek did something to a man. I wasn't stupid. I knew Bianca wasn't meek by any measure but seeing that she could be calm, and tender made my mind travel to a future I had left a long time when we'd broken up. For now, I would just chill and see where things went.

"Hey beautiful ladies," I responded. "Y'all sound like y'all in here gossiping."

My mom smacked me in the arm after I greeted her with a kiss. "Hush your mouth. I don't care about people business 'round here. I was telling Bianca about the time your grandma caught you eating the pies. Remember?" My mom laughed so hard she shook. Bianca was smiling too and chuckling.

"Now mom, why you in here trying to embarrass your firstborn?" I pretended to be bothered. "I hope you didn't bring out the photo album."

"That's a great idea! Go get it. It's at the top of my closet!" She half-turned in her chair pointing to her bedroom.

"You can't be serious." This time I wasn't pretending.

She cracked up again and went on snapping her peas.

I looked over at Bianca who had just smiled through the entire exchange but hadn't said a word. "Hey B."

"Hey, Justin. How was your day?"

Shitty but suddenly I wasn't in the mood to complain. "I guess that depends on what's for dinner." I turned to my mom, but Bianca was the one that replied.

"Meatloaf and mashed potatoes. Oh, and peas."

My mom nodded and pointed to her bowl. "I told her to always add a vegetable, so we decided on peas."

They began talking amongst themselves as if I weren't even in the room. Women. I left them babbling about Lord knows what and showered. I was all kind of nasty and grimy and it felt good to be clean and about to be served dinner by a beautiful woman.

The table was set, and I walked into the kitchen where I had heard them still chatting away. Bianca placed two wrapped plates of food into a bag and thanked my mom for having her over.

"Anytime baby." My mom grabbed a few napkins and stuffed them in the bag. "I hope your dad and Brandon enjoy it. Your meatloaf is much better than I thought it would be." She laughed again.

"I'm sure they will. Those two eat pretty much anything I cook."

"That's what happens when people really love you. They tolerate things they normally wouldn't. Even bad food." My mom cracked up so hard I thought she was gonna fall over. "But in your case, they are just right. You cook better than you think."

"Thanks, Mrs. Saunders! And you're right. They're both very supportive of me cooking. I don't know. It kinda brings me some peace."

"That's because you love them too. It always does the heart good to take care of the people you love."

Their conversation ain't have nothing to do with me, but I had heard every word and had had some questions. Bianca said goodbye to my mom and walked right past me to the door. "Bye Justin!" She called out.

I caught up to her in the hallway and tugged at her elbow. "Whoa, whoa, whoa. B, where you going so fast?"

She looked down at her elbow then back up at me giving me a silent warning to release her. I didn't.

She gently pulled her elbow from my loose grip. "I'm taking food to my dad and Brandon."

"So, I heard, but who is Brandon?"

She turned and faced me fully. Her hazel eyes twinkled, and I knew what that look meant. That was the bait to lure you in before she chewed you up and spit you out.

"With all due respect Justin, I don't need to explain anything to you. But I'm going to just assume that you are only asking for safety reasons. Right?" She nodded.

I sure as hell wasn't, but I'd play along. "Yeah. Just want you to be careful. That's all."

Her smile was all teeth and satisfaction. "Yeah, I thought that's why you were asking. But just so you know, I can take care of myself. Brandon is sweet and respectful and no one you need to worry over."

I wasn't satisfied with Bianca's answer, but I guess I didn't have a choice but to be. She went about her business, and I went back inside ready to eat. In the kitchen, Jordi was serving dinner. He passed me a plate with more peas than Mom would normally serve. "All these peas Jordi?"

"What you complaining for? Your girl made 'em. So, you should be the one to eat 'em."

"She ain't my girl."

"You should tell yourself that. The way you always in her face, I don't think you don't know she ain't your girl." Jordi added so much gravy to his mashed potatoes, it leaked over the plate and onto the floor.

"Look at you. You better clean that up before Mom walks in here and sees that." I grabbed a glass from the cupboard and poured myself some juice. "And I don't be in nobody's face."

"Yeah, yeah, yeah," Jordi replied nonchalantly as he cleaned his mess and I walked to the dining room.

Mom was sitting in the living room with her leg propped up watching some talk show. I joined her instead of sitting at the dining table. "What you watchin' Ma?"

"Twin sisters separated after their first birthday are being reunited. They were too young to remember each other." She'd said it so nonchalantly I wondered if she'd even been interested in it at all.

"So, Ma?"

She grunted in response, not bothering to take her eyes off the television screen.

"So how long was Bianca here for?"

"When? Today? For a few hours. Yesterday, just a few minutes to check on my foot."

I stopped eating. "She was here yesterday and today?" How in the hell didn't I know that?

"Mmm-hmm. She's been here every day since the fire, checking in on me."

I looked at my mom and wanted to shake her and open the faucet for more information instead of the drops she'd been giving me like an annoying leak. I cleared my throat and probed some more without being obvious.

"What did she say about your foot?"

Just then Jordi walked by and shook his head at me. "Whooped and don't even know it."

I tossed a sofa pillow at him. "Mind ya business."

"Jordi get your ass back in that dining room. You know I don't want you eating in your bedroom. I ain't tryna deal with no mice. And Justin you too old for the nonsense. You know better than to throw my pillows."

Jordi and I looked at each other dumbfounded. The woman hadn't taken her eyes off the television once and had managed to see everything. We shrugged and did as told. After I picked up the pillow and finished eating, I sat beside my mom again.

"How's your foot feeling?"

"It's getting better. Now, why don't you ask me what you've been trying to ask for the past hour?"

I shoulda known better than to try and get one over my mom. "Who's Brandon?"

"Her friend."

"Well, I know that, but what kind of friend?"

My mom turned to me, and this time gave me her full attention. "Son, if it bothers you, do something about it. Go to the source."

She was right. I nodded. In my twenties and still doing some kid shit. But I thanked my mom for giving me wisdom instead of judgment.

"I don't know if they are more than friends, but I can say she is being a very good friend to that young man just as she being to me."

I didn't know exactly what that meant but my mother said it in a way that denoted approval and that settled me. A few hours later I went down to Bianca's apartment. She was home this time.

"I would say I'm surprised to see you, but I'm not." She laughed and left the door open, her way of inviting me in as she walked back into the apartment.

I entered and closed the door behind me. "I wanted to talk to you about something."

She went and sat at the kitchen table in shorts and a tank top looking like she smelled like a fresh summer day. I wanted to bury my face in her neck again and find out for myself. Picking up a piece of paper, she folded it then stuffed it in an envelope before licking it closed. I watched her in fascination. B had always been crazy sexy cool to me and now wasn't any different. Her wild hair matched her attitude, and her soft lips matched her heart. She was a force to be reckoned with but there was a soft vulnerable side people never saw and one I saw even when she tried to hide it.

I let myself remember how much I loved the core of who she was. Underneath all of that anger was a beautiful soul. Even more so now. I don't want to say she'd changed. Essentially, she hadn't. In truth, B had blossomed, and it was incredible to see a beautiful young black girl grow into a beautiful black woman. Yeah, she had had some growing pains but the woman she was becoming was overcoming all her past shit. I wasn't just in love with her, I was amazed by her. She was strong. She was smart. She was loyal.

Bianca stuffed the sealed envelope in her backpack and walked to the couch. "So, what's up? You wanted to ask me something?" She turned the TV on with the remote and began flicking through channels as if I was part of the furniture. It irritated me.

"Bianca."

"Hmmm." She didn't even look in my direction.

Without another word, I walked to the door. Then turned back frustrated. "Who is Brandon?"

She slammed the remote down. "You have no right to ask me about anyone. You broke up with me! You left me! So, who I take dinner to is none of your business."

I felt all this anger rise up in me, but who the hell was I to question anything about her life? It wasn't like I hadn't moved on with someone else. I stomped my way out of the apartment wanting to punch the wall, but I remembered spraining my hand the last time I'd done that and stopped myself. I got to the elevators and pressed the button. It took forever and I was about ready to take the stairs.

"Justin."

I turned and saw her standing at her door. As soon as my gaze locked on hers, I don't know what overcame me, but I ran to her. I got to her door and kissed her savagely pouring all of my anger, frustration, love, and hope into it. When she kissed me back just as passionately, I let myself love her. Completely. Her hood and her good. My mom said when you love a person, you'll do things just for them you wouldn't do otherwise. Like, come knock on her door damn near every day like a stalker and shit.

In that moment though, I didn't care. I just wanted her. Every inch of her body. Every smile. Every confidence. Every deep conversation. I wanted her to be my lover. My best friend. My wife. And every day for the rest of the summer I made Bianca my all. My future. My love. My life.

TWENTY-FOUR
Bianca

As soon as I walked into my apartment, I heard the phone ringing. I ran to answer it. "Hello," I answered loudly.

"Damn B. You tryna bust my eardrum?" Justin asked.

"I was runnin' to answer the phone before you hung up. Sorry," I laughed.

"So does that mean you aren't gettin' ready yet?"

"I just got in the house. That's why I was runnin' for the phone."

"Don't make me leave to dinner without you. I'm starving and ain't waiting for you." Justin joked,

"I'm about to jump in the shower in a few."

"Alright. I'll see you in about forty-five minutes or you getting left."

I cracked up. "Whatever. Don't make me whoop your ass. You know I will."

"Yeah, 'cause you crazy as hell."

I laughed again. "I sure am."

We laughed and I promised to be ready on time.

As soon I hung up, I took a shower. After rubbing a light layer of baby oil all over my body, I slipped into a white, sleeveless dress. It was form-fitting and made my boobs sit up. I laughed at myself trying to push them down a little. I heard a knock at the door and rushed to slip on my new red heels and grabbed my matching clutch bag.

Right as I reached for the door, I twisted my foot and lost my balance, landing onto my dresser rattling it.

Oh shit. I almost bust my ass.

I regained my balance, stood for a moment making sure I was steady. I prayed I wouldn't embarrass myself and fall in public. After a little walking test and not stumbling, I safely went to answer the door.

Justin's mouth gaped open. "Damn Babe. You look good."

"Thank you," I grinned from ear to ear.

"You ready?" Justin asked.

"Yup."

"Let's go."

We'd been driving for a few minutes and Justin had already looked over at me a bunch of times. "You need to pay attention to the road, Justin. You're driving."

"I know. I am. You just look so damn good. And you're wearing red high heels, Bianca. What did you expect?"

I laughed. "So you approve?"

"Approve?" He looked out the road then quickly back at me. "You just don't understand woman. I'm feelin' some type of way."

"You're not the only one."

"Glad to hear to that. Matter of fact, that's exactly what I wanted to hear."

"Why? What do you mean?"

"You'll see."

"See what?"

"How's your dad?"

"Did you just change the subject?"

"I did but I do want to know. How's your dad?"

"He's gotten a lot better but still not walking on his own. I think he's holdin' back on his speech but he's not silent like before, so I won't complain."

"Little progress is still progress, right?"

"Yup, and that's exactly how I look at it."

"Okay, and here we are," Justin said as we pulled up into the parking of The Charter House Restaurant.

"Oh, nice. What you took somebody here before?" I was surprised he'd brought me to such a fancy restaurant.

"Now see, why you had to ask that? No. I've never brought anyone here. My bro, Manny took his girl here and he told me about it, so I wanted to bring you."

"Oh okay. I'm sorry. I shouldn't have said that. It just came out." I mentally slapped myself.

"It's okay. You asked because you wanted to know."

I couldn't help but to be straight up. I didn't know how to be any other way. "Yeah, I did. You didn't have to answer, but you did so thank you for understanding."

He grabbed my hand and kissed it before we went inside the restaurant and were seated.

"This place is elegant, Justin. Looks expensive. Do you want me to go half on the bill with you?"

Justin shook his head at me, practically scolding me. "No, I do not. I got it, B. Just let me wine and dine you girl."

I winked at him and brought out a smile. "Okay, big spenda'. I'm lovin' this whole vibe."

"Yeah, me too. What I'm lovin' more is lookin' into those beautiful hazel eyes of yours."

"You got me blushin' again," I said as I peeked from behind the menu. I nibbled my bottom lip while I was concentrating on the menu.

"Don't do that," Justin said.

"Do what?"

"Bite your lips like that."

"Should I do it like this?" I bit my lip seductively.

"Oh, so now you like teasin' me?"

"I was just showin' you how I scratch my lip." I joked.

"Okay. Okay, B."

After dessert was served, a man walked up to our table and began singing Johnny Gill's song, *My, My, My.*

"Justin, what's goin' on?" I whispered.

"Just listen. Shhh."

I listened to the man's rendition, and couldn't stop smiling. I didn't even care that people were staring at us. When he finished, the entire restaurant clapped for him. Justin got up and came to my side of the table and got on one knee. I was so confused.

"Justin, what are you doing?" I whispered.

"Bianca you have grown into such an amazing woman. You have grown in ways that leave me lost for words. I love you and I am in love with you. I am proud to be your lover and your friend and now I am asking you to be my wife. Will you marry me, Bianca?"

My eyes were filled with tears of joy. I leaned in to kiss him as I said yes. He slid the ring on my finger and applause filled the room.

On our ride back home, I kept looking at the ring on my finger. When he'd proposed I was too shocked to have paid it any attention. Now I couldn't take my eyes off it. Simple and beautiful. I giggled to myself. I was engaged. It was so surreal.

"This ring is beautiful, Justin. It fits perfectly."

"Thank you. I'm glad it fits. It was my mom's ring. My dad saved all of his money and brought that for her. When I told my mom that I was going to propose, she insisted I take her ring. She said you were special. She even got it cleaned for me. That ring holds significant meaning. Not just for my parent's love, but now, for ours."

"Oh my God. Your mom did that?" My eyes watered.

"Yes. She said my dad would have wanted me to put that ring on my bride's finger since he's not here to physically take part in it. It's like he's right here with us."

"I have to thank her for doing this. I know this ring has sentimental value to her and that was so selfless of her."

"She wants us to be just as strong as she and my dad were."

"And we will."

"You know it." He nodded and reached his hand over and slipped it in mine and held hands the rest of the way home quietly and basking in our joy.

We went back to my apartment, and I changed out of my dress and got comfortable. As I walked past Justin to sit beside him, he pulled my arm so I could land on his lap. We kissed with such passion. I felt completely free to release all my feelings. There was no need to hide or hold back. Justin was mine. I was safe to be vulnerable with him.

We went into my bedroom, and undressed each other, our clothes falling to the floor one by one. He took a hand full of my hair and gently pulled my head back so he could kiss and lick my neck. He felt so good my eyes fluttered closed without thought. I moaned in satisfaction.

"We just gettin' started, Baby." And he meant that.

We made love on and off throughout the night completely lost in each other. Afterward, he laid on my breasts as I ran my hand over his head. I could hear his heavy breathing and knew he'd fallen asleep. I laid there replaying our dinner date in my mind. I was engaged to be married to my best friend and the love of my life. I grinned so hard I probably looked like some freaky clown. But I didn't even care. I was happy. I instantly thought of my mom and how I wished she would've been there to share that moment with me. I prayed she was, even if I couldn't see her.

TWENTY-FIVE
Tianna

I had rehearsed a hundred times what I would say if I ever saw Justin again. It had been months since we'd spoken. He had returned home for the summer, and I had only had his dorm phone number. Although admittedly, had I had other contact information for him I doubt I would have used it. How did you tell a man who probably thought the worst about you that you were carrying his child? After everything he'd overheard Lou say about me, I wouldn't blame him.

I walked out of my History of Modern Art class and subconsciously tugged at my t-shirt. At sixteen weeks, my baby bump protruded from my slender frame. I had grown out of most of my clothes but refused to buy maternity clothes despite *Mami's* insistence. It would make this whole ordeal too real and still had difficulty accepting that I was with child, even with a swollen belly. I'd buy oversize t-shirts and sweatpants and be done with it.

I headed to the student center to kill some time before my next class started. I bought a carton of milk and a banana and sat on the couch that looked like it needed to be scrubbed clean. Thankfully, I hadn't been as tired as I had been before, but my indigestion felt as if a miniature Satan was lounging inside of my chest, the heartburn was so severe. After little relief from the milk, I pulled out my notebook and went over my notes for my Issues of Contemporary Art class. The professor liked choosing a random student to embarrass if they didn't know the material or praise if they had. I didn't take too kindly to possible public mockery, so I opted to be over-prepared.

"Tianna?"

I looked up to see Justin standing a few feet away. The second I recognized him, my heart and mind crashed like a faulty computer. Every word I had rehearsed disappeared from my memory bank in an instant. The longing to run into his arms clobbered me upside the head. I missed him more than I wanted to admit to myself.

"Hey," I replied almost breathless.

He looked back as if he wanted to bolt but instead approached me slowly. He scratched his head and looked down at his feet before making eye contact. "You came back."

I wasn't sure what that meant, but I simply nodded.

"I haven't seen you this semester, so I just assumed you weren't coming back to school."

"I try to keep a low profile." The change in his expression was slight but I could see he took offense to my reply. In truth, my desire to be incognito was about my growing belly and nothing to do with him directly. And I guess if there was a time as good as any to talk to Justin, now would be it. "I wasn't avoiding you. That's not what I meant."

"It's cool."

"Justin, there's something I have to talk to you about. Privately."

He looked at his watch and around the student center before he nodded. He seemed uncomfortable but then again so was I, so how could I find fault in his demeanor?

"Ok. I'm done with classes for the day. We can go to my dorm lobby if you want or the cafeteria?"

The lobby? He didn't even want to be alone in the same room with me. That stung fiercely. Lou's poison had done its job and humiliation wrapped itself around me like a snake. Nevertheless, for my own sake, I preferred no one else around. "I think it's best we have this conversation alone."

"Tianna, I don't mean to be rude, but it's not a good idea that we are alone anymore. Please respect that." I stood to my feet, a hand to my belly cutting off his rant and the scene he was beginning to make. He looked at my belly and then back up at me. "Wait, what?" He pointed to my stomach at a loss for words. "Are you pregnant?"

"It's yours."

Two words. That's all it took to change Justin's world. I could see a range of emotions playing out on his face and in the end, anger reigned supreme. "How far along are you, Tianna?"

Tears began collecting in my eyes and my throat restricted, but I fought against it. "Almost seventeen weeks," I replied hoarsely.

"Seven—seventeen? Did you just say seventeen weeks?" His ire began to rise. A few of the students nearby turned in our direction.

"Yes." I had already carried enough shame and guilt and now I added humiliation. "Now, can we please talk about this in private?"

Justin stormed out of the student center without a word. I contemplated following him but didn't. Instead, I settled my nerves before I picked up my messenger bag and headed for class. I abruptly stopped when I spotted Justin pacing outside the glass doors. I took a deep breath preparing myself for an encounter with him and exited the student center. He saw me, grabbed my hand, forcing me to trail behind him. A few feet later and winded, I snatched my hand back. "You don't need to drag me like that." It pissed me off to be treated like a wayward child. Just then the clouds opened up and poured down the rains it had been predicting all week as if in anticipation for this moment.

Justin's nostrils flared before he gripped my wrist, and we were back on the move as if speeding between the raindrops. I couldn't keep up with his pace and began to struggle against his hold needing to slow down but he was relentless. Several yards from his dorm building my strength had waned and I fell to my knees, my wrist still clutched in his hand. My flesh stung at the impact of being dragged across concrete before Justin realized what was happening.

He finally released me, and the rest of my body landed with a splat to the ground. He frantically knelt before me. "Ti. I'm sorry. Are you ok?"

I could see the remorse in his eyes, but I was too tired, pained, and wet to care. All my energy was dedicated to catching my breath and relieving the pain radiating in my knees. The rain was more annoyance than anything. Justin offered me his hand, but I refused it and tried to stand up on my own. I was only four months pregnant but the extra weight I had gained felt as heavy as a suit of armor, especially when I was tired. Wet clothes weren't helping. Unable to get up, I rolled over and sat on my ass. He stretched out his hand again, looking up at the sky and squinting at the steady drops pouring down on us, but I slapped it away.

I think I heard him growl but maybe that was me. He raised his hands and backed away from me in surrender. I wanted to get off the wet, dirty ground. I was tired and I was hungry. Unable to control myself I began to cry. I hated being pregnant. I hated my body being invaded without permission. Again. I didn't want to be emotional all the time. Or exhausted all the time. Or craving weird shit all the time. I couldn't even get up off the ground without help. I wasn't even a big young woman. My frame more closely resembled a stick. Now I looked tetherball with the agility of gelatin. It was ridiculous. I was ridiculous. My tears turned to hot, angry ones and this time the growling definitely came from me. I rolled over, brought one leg up at a time until I was standing, and wiped the rain from my face.

Justin grabbed my messenger bag and held it in his hand "I could have helped you up, Ti. Why are you so damn stubborn?" He was motioning for me to rush so we could get out of the rain.

"I don't want your help." If my eyes could have shot daggers, they would have.

"That's very obvious," he replied looking down at my belly.

I snatched my bag from him. "I offered to talk to you in private. You're the one that had a meltdown."

He pointed in my face, anger filling his face ready to cuss me out before he checked himself. "Know what? I'm not gonna let you take me there. Hurry up and get out the rain, Tianna."

He snatched the bag back and walked ahead of me to the door and held it open for me. I purposely walked slower just to make him wait longer. Some real corny shit that I could've blamed on hunger or hormones, but it was just some plain old immature nonsense. And he knew exactly what I was doing too. He laughed humorlessly and shook his head. "You are something else, you know that?"

We took the elevator up in silence, both dripping wet. After he unlocked his room door, he let me in and sat my bag down before he disappeared. I stood by the door not wanting to drip all over his floor. I looked down at my knees that stung fiercely. I patted them to help ease the pain. Maybe I could go check them in the bathroom first. I opened the door only to run into him.

"Running off already?" He slammed the door behind him.

"No. I was going to go to the bathroom to clean myself off."

He held up a towel and a first aid kit. "Sit down."

I felt like the unruly child again and remained standing. "Tianna, please sit down and stop being a brat."

I didn't have the energy to argue with him and obliged him. He pushed up my pant legs, but they stopped short of my knees. "You're going to have to take them off."

My eyes widen with surprise. "So much for us not being alone together."

I had never seen Justin embarrassed before, although he recovered quickly. "Do you want the help or not?" He stood to his feet and handed me the towel. "I prefer we get you patched up before we talk, Tianna. I'm not playing games with you."

I stared at him feeling myself shutting down. Nonchalantly I spoke. "Do you think I am playing games? Do you think I want to be knocked up and going through all of this? Do you think that I wanted to be dragged across campus in the rain and have my knees scraped up? Is that what you think?"

Justin rubbed his head and faced the opposing wall. He sighed and spoke softly. "Take your wet clothes off Ti so you don't get sick, and I can tend to you. You can cover yourself with the towel or take whatever you need from my drawer. I'll go change in the bathroom and give you some privacy."

And just like that, he sent a wrecking ball through my feeble wall. Even upset, he was a caring man. His compassion always broke me down and so I did as he suggested. I removed my clothes tranquilly, laying them out on the chair to air dry. I sat on the bed wrapped in the towel awaiting him. I didn't feel comfortable slipping into his clothes. It felt too intimate. After several minutes of overthinking it, I wondered if sitting on his bed mostly nude would look like I was trying to seduce him. He already believed what Lou said about me.

I tossed the uncomfortable feeling of borrowing his clothes aside and jumped up heading to his bureau forgetting my sore knees. I took two steps before I felt the agonizing pain. I clutched my knees losing my grip on the towel. Justin walked in just as it hit the floor exposing me in just my bra and panties. I instinctively used my arms to cover my already covered parts.

Justin stopped and stared at me. First at my face, then at my protruding belly. His eyes remained glued there. I tried to bend down to pick up the towel to cover myself snapping him out of his trance. He rushed over and picked it up for me, handing it to me and giving me privacy.

I situated myself on the bed red-faced and blanketed myself. I cleared the frog in my throat to signal him that I was decent. He got to work quickly and avoided looking up at me. He cleaned up my scrapes with alcohol pads. It stung and he instinctively blew on them to ease the pain. I watched him a little awestruck. Was this how he'd be with our child? Gentle and caring?

He carefully bandaged my knees and shins. He then handed me some clothes and insisted that I get dressed. I didn't argue and accepted his tee and shorts.

The silence afterward begged to be broken and I honored it. "I didn't know how to find you."

Justin remained quiet and situated the first aid supplies back into the box.

"I would never keep the baby from you." My words were just as random as my thoughts. I didn't know what to say or how to fix this. I didn't even know what I did wrong other than be born a woman and accidentally get pregnant. The injustice of it angered me. I had no control of my gender and the last time I checked; he was in control of his sperm. "I don't understand why you are upset. I'm the one that's pregnant!"

He slammed the kit against the wall. "You shut me out! You abandoned ship! This is your fault! If you would have just talked to me, I wouldn't have-"

He stopped yelling mid-sentence.

"You wouldn't have what?"

He stared at me, and I could see tears forming in his eyes. "I wouldn't have gone home for the summer. I would have been right here with you making sure you and our child were cared for. Your decisions don't just affect you, Tianna!" He punched the pillow and went silent for a minute before his rage subsided. "My life changed over the summer," he said softly.

"As did mine. Ten years ago, and again four months ago. I know all too well the trickle effect of a person's decisions." The audacity of him. I was sitting in his room pregnant, formerly molested basket case with an adulterous father. I stood up and grabbed my clothes. I didn't care if he'd see me mostly naked. Wouldn't have been the first time. I took off the clothes I'd borrowed and tossed them on the bed.

"Tianna, wait. I'm sorry."

I grabbed my tights and cursed that they were still dripping wet. I didn't care. I'd just wear them wet. Justin slipped his hand into mine gently and removed the tights from my hand and tossed them on the floor. He fell to his knees, leaned his head against my belly as he held onto my waist, and cried. "I'm sorry." He repeated it several times before I crouched down before him and embraced him, my apologies and tears mingling with his.

After that day, Justin saw me almost daily. At first, we'd just meet up for breakfast or lunch in the school food court. Sometimes we'd have dinner together. He was obsessed with my health and the baby's well-being. Then he started calling me every night. He'd purchased a book about pregnancy. Nightly he would read how the baby was growing daily and what the birth mother was experiencing and what to expect. I would listen quietly and came to love those calls. Between Justin and *Mami*, I was the most doted on pregnant woman on the planet.

I was nervous to ask, but I invited him to my prenatal appointment. He played it off like he'd go as support for me. I told him *Mami* always accompanied me, and I was just being courteous extending him the invitation. *Mami* would be more than happy to go if he wasn't interested. He quickly accepted the invitation telling me *Mami* wouldn't need to.

At the appointment, he kept asking me lots of questions. I had the answers to half. He peppered the obstetrician with the rest. When the doctor lifted my shirt and placed the gel on my stomach, Justin looked on curiously.

"What's that for?" He asked. I shook my head at Dr. Grover not to respond. She simply smiled at me and agreed. After a few seconds of searching with the probe, a rapid wish washing sound filled the room. Justin looked at us confused. "What is that?"

Dr. Grover smiled at him. "That's the baby's heartbeat. You have a strong healthy baby baking in the oven, Dad."

He listened intently smiling from ear to ear. "That's amazing. Can we see what it is?"

Dr. Grover laughed. "Tianna didn't want the gender revealed during her ultrasound."

Justin didn't seem to care. He was grinning listening to the heartbeat. Afterward, he took me to get lunch at the mall and we strolled around for a while as the doctor suggested to stay active. I was exhausted by the time I dropped him back off at school. He asked me to come in and rest, but I declined the invitation. Our relationship was uncertain. Since we'd reconnected, there had been nothing romantic between us. I suppose he only tolerated me because of the baby. What man in their right mind would want to be in a relationship with a woman he believed enjoyed being molested? My feelings for him hadn't changed, but I tried to protect myself as best as I could and kept our interactions friendly.

A few days later, Justin invited me over for a surprise. I couldn't imagine what it could be, but he seemed excited, so I indulged him. I walked into a large bowl of chili waiting for me. My craving for it had bordered on obsessive. I could eat it for breakfast, lunch, dinner, and in between. I ate until I couldn't fit another spoonful.

Not surprisingly, right after stuffing myself, I needed a nap. Justin permitted me to rest on his bed. While I was lying there, he sat beside me on the bed. "Are you comfortable?"

I laughed at his doting. "Yes. Thank you."

"Ok, close your eyes and lift your shirt."

I raised a defiant eyebrow. "Excuse me?"

His laughter bounced off the brick walls. "Just trust me."

Those were dreadful words, but coming from him, I didn't feel my anxiety spike. I made myself vulnerable and did as he asked.

"Keep them closed no matter what."

I nodded as he lowered my shirt to cover my chest keeping me modest. I felt a warm wet towel on my belly, and it felt nice. He dried it off and applied an absorbent amount of lotion. Suddenly I felt something pressed against my baby bump and I heard the faint sound of the baby's heartbeat.

"Is that what I think it is?"

"My son's heartbeat."

I laughed out loud. "And what if it's a girl?"

The pressure from the monitor gave way. "A girl?"

I could tell he was appalled. "Yes. A girl. You do not know there's a fifty percent chance it's a girl, right?"

"Nah. This here is a future Saunders namesake. He's going to carry on my legacy. And my dad's legacy." He kissed my belly. He began talking to the baby, telling the baby about him growing up and his family. I opened my eyes and looked down at him staring at my belly. He looked up at me and caught me smiling. Something in his eyes changed. He leaned forward and kissed my forehead. When he pulled back our eyes locked. My heart began pounding wildly. My feelings for him rushed to the surface. I wanted to throw caution away, kiss him, and risk rejection. Instead, he took the leap and kissed me softly. I made room for him on the bed and nestled myself in his arms.

"If it's a girl, she can be Daddy's little princess." I joked.

"A princess? Yeah right! I can't handle a little Spanish girl. She'll be all attitude. Her momma is enough."

I laughed so hard my belly shook like Santa's. "If anyone can handle two of us, it's you. She'll be your princess and I'll be your peace." I felt Justin stiffen and looked up at him. "You ok?"

He gave me a weak smile then stared at the ceiling. "Yeah. Just thinking about life as a father."

It didn't escape me that he didn't say husband, but I tried not to read too much into it. As the days got colder, Justin and I grew warmer. Long gone were our days of fun and passion, replaced by maturity and companionship. A few days a week when his roommate wasn't there, I'd spend the night. *Mami* and Pop had allowed him to spend nights over with me, but he was restricted to the sofa bed.

They didn't care I was carrying his baby. Until we got married, we weren't playing house in their house. We didn't mind. Most nights he'd carry me upstairs to my bedroom after I fell asleep next to him.

He stopped by the studio the day before Thanksgiving to say goodbye. He was going home for the weekend to spend the holiday with his mom and brother. I had been painting a lot more in preparation for my gallery exhibit grade and if I weren't with him or in class, I was at the studio. He kissed me then rubbed my belly greeting the baby. I loved when he did that.

"Whatcha working on?"

I was about to explain but then remembered he didn't know a lick about art, and it would be a waste of time. "Captivating pieces for my show."

He eyed me and then laughed. "Always the smartass."

I shrugged and kept painting. Every time he came to the studio he would walk over to the wall and admire the first piece I had ever painted in front of him. I vividly remembered us making love so sweetly after that. I think that was the day I got pregnant, but I never confessed it.

"Have you thought of a name for it yet?"

"Did you just refer to the baby as in 'it'?" I yelled back at him as I added paint to my brush.

He came behind me and kissed me on my neck. "Stop talking crazy. The baby's name is Justin Junior. I'm talking about the painting, Ms. Leonard."

I chuckled and faced him. "I had an idea for a name, but I wasn't sure."

"Word? Let's hear it." Justin plopped on the stool and pulled me onto his lap rubbing my belly.

"Well, my life changed that day. More than I had ever imagined. A new life. So, I thought maybe Resurrection."

Justin stayed quiet so long I began to doubt the name. "You don't like it?"

"Resurrection," he repeated. "I think it fits it's perfectly."

I took Justin's hand and moved it to the side of my belly and pressed down where the baby had been kicking me all day. I pressed a little harder. The baby reacted and this time Justin felt the kick.

He turned me around, lifted my shirt, and rubbed my belly. When it moved, he marveled at it and leaned in closer talking to the baby. The baby kicked for a few more minutes. Justin instantly missed the experience.

"Ti, do you think your parents will mind one more person for Thanksgiving dinner?"

"What do you mean? When *Mami* invited you last week, you were adamant that you had to go home. Your Mom and Jordi are expecting you."

"They'll have me home for winter break. Right now, my family here needs me."

My heart burst open. "Family?"

"You and the baby are my family. Always."

I was overcome with emotion. "I love you, Justin."

He kissed me tenderly. "I'll always be here, Ti."

I exhaled at his promise. Resurrection.

TWENTY-SIX
Bianca

I hadn't seen Justin since he'd gone back to school, and I missed him like crazy. He hadn't been calling as much because he said his classes were piling a lot of work on him. My baby was about to be a college graduate and that was great, but I felt neglected. He barely answered his phone or called. They needed to calm the hell down giving him so much work. That didn't make sense to me. Stupid ass professors.

I changed my thoughts to something more positive and reminded myself that Justin would be home tomorrow for Thanksgiving break. When his phone number popped up on the caller ID I smiled.

"Hello."

"Hey B."

"Baby, I was just laying here thinking about you. I miss you so much. Can't wait to see you tomorrow. I'm going to love spendin' Thanksgiving with you, your mom, and Jordi. She's teaching me how to make peach cobbler."

"Um, yeah, about Thanksgiving," Justin said with hesitance in his voice.

"What?"

"I'm not comin' home. I'm gonna stay at one of my friend's house. I still have a lot of schoolwork I need to finish. I'm sorry B. I know you was lookin' forward to us spendin' time together."

"Wow. This is some bullshit, Justin. You tell me this the day before? So, what does this mean? I'm not gonna hear from you either?"

"Well, I don't know about the phone situation over there. But I will find a way to call you. Don't even worry about that."

"I'm so pissed right now."

"My mom and brother are gonna be too. I'm 'bout to call them and break the news to them. I'm sorry B."

"I don't know what to say. This news ruined my day and my holiday."

"I'll make it up to you. I'ma make Christmas break extra special. Okay?"

"I guess I have no choice but to be okay with it. I know you need to handle ya school stuff. I'm just missin' you that's all."

"Thank you. I'm glad you said that. I love you."

"I love you too."

"Well, let me call my mom. I know she gonna chew me up."

"Yup. You know she is."

"You have a good night. I'll talk to you tomorrow."

"Okay. You too."

I really wanted to go off way more than I had but I didn't want to come off as selfish or inconsiderate. I understood he needed to handle his responsibilities in school, but now I had to wait another whole month to see him.

Thanksgiving came and went, and I heard nothing from Justin. I began to get curious. Was it school or something more? He hadn't answered any of my pages, so I literally had to wait for him to call. He called three days after the last time I had beeped him.

"Hello."

"Hey B, I'm sorry I haven't called. The phone is hard to get to here. The brother is always on AOL."

"AOL? I don't give a damn about no internet. I'm feelin' some typa' way, Justin. Somethin' don't feel right."

"What do want me to do? Tell them to get off the internet in their own house? I can't do that Bianca."

"I'm not asking you to. You go back to school tomorrow so there should be no problems getting in contact with you. Even before that, I was barely hearing from you. It feels like somethin' is goin' on. I've never had a problem with getting in touch with you, or for that matter, you keepin' in contact."

"I'm just busy."

"I hope that's all it is. You know a woman's intuition be tellin' her stuff. And it's givin' me weird vibes that I do not like."

"Everything is fine."

"I hope so."

"It is."

"Okay. You've never given me a reason to not trust you. Maybe it's me missin' you that's gettin' to me."

"I'll be there in a few weeks. Time is goin' by quick. I'll be home before you know it. Just hang tight future wifey."

I exhaled and eased up on him curbing my impulse and choosing to trust him. "See, you know exactly what to say to make me feel better. I love you."

"I love you too. I'll talk to you soon as soon as I get back in my room tomorrow."

"Okay."

After we talked, I felt much better. Hearing him say my future wife made me think about the night he proposed to me. I immediately got lost in the memory and brushed my intuition aside.

The weeks flew by, and Justin was coming home for Christmas break. I asked Mrs. Saunders if I could be the one to pick him up. I wanted to surprise him. She didn't mind at all, in fact, she encouraged it. She had made him some chocolate chip cookies to eat on the way home and had asked me to take them with me. I was so excited to see him. I left early to avoid holiday traffic and because I couldn't wait to see him.

When I approached the exit to Justin's school, I quickly peeked at my engagement ring. For the thousandth time. I cheesed so hard as I had every time I stared at it. I still couldn't believe my black ass was engaged. Even my dad looked at me shocked when I'd told him. I didn't need him to say a single word because I knew exactly what he was thinking and replied to his unspoken thoughts. I told him that Justin loved me, crazy and all, and my dad cracked up so hard. Felt good to see him laugh. It was a rare occurrence.

As I was driving the scenery began to change. I got a little anxious driving out to West Bubba Fuck. I definitely wasn't in Camden anymore but I focused on the destination and who was there. Even out of my comfort zone, my heart raced with excitement to see my fiancé. I cracked up and said it out loud with a terrible French accent. I hadn't seen him in three months, and I wanted nothing more than to hug and kiss him. Among a few other things. It had been way too damn long.

When I arrived at the campus I circled the parking lot several times not knowing which building he lived in and ended up parking where I could see the doors to both buildings his mom had described. Every time I saw the door open, I stared waiting for Justin to walk out. I smiled thinking about what his reaction would be when he saw me. My romantic side pictured him picking me up and kissing me passionately. I shook my head and told myself to stop acting crazy. Further proof that it had been way too long since I'd had some.

I pulled down the mirror to make sure my lip gloss was still poppin' and fluffed my curly hair a little bit more. Just as I was pushing the mirror back up, I heard laughter and I turned toward where it was coming from. Justin was holding a pregnant girl's hand as she walked down the steps. Always the gentleman. I watched him proudly as I took off my seatbelt and let it slide back into place. My baby was one-of-a-kind. Smart, sexy, and sweet.

I smiled as I got out of the car and zipped up my coat. It was freezing out here in the boonies. When I looked back up waiting for him to notice me standing there, I saw him rub the pregnant girl's belly. An alarm in me went off. That looked a little too cozy for my liking and where there was smoke, you know there was fire. I got back into the car quickly and waited to see what would happen next.

See, the problem with wanting to take in the show is that you're gonna get a show. You're gonna see some things. And feel some things. And realize some things. And wanna hurt some things.

I sat in the car and watched that negro bend down and kiss that girl's stomach. I watched him talk to her belly. I even watched them laugh together. And through that all, I maintained. Oh, best believe I was pissed, but I still maintained and contained. Until that motherfucka sniffed her neck and worked his way to her lips just like he had done with me more times than I can remember. And when he tapped her nose playfully like he had done to me, I was so hot I didn't need my coat anymore. I exited the car ready to light shit up. Justin looked up and his smile immediately disappeared.

"What the fuck is goin' on Justin?" I asked as I marched toward them ready to hook off.

"Wait, B. Hold up. Let me explain."

"Who the hell is she?" I pointed at the pregnant bitch and ignored her look of surprise.

"Where's my mom?"

"Answer the damn question, Justin!"

"Is my mom with you?"

"Do you see her? I came to get you. It was supposed to be a surprise. And look! A surprise for both of us! Bitch, get away from my fiancé!" I screamed. I lunged at her, and she instinctively covered her stomach. It stopped me from attacking her. I wasn't about to hurt a baby.

"Bianca no!" Justin jumped in front of me to stop me from advancing on her Pocahontas-looking ass although I had already checked myself.

"Who is she, Justin? You betta start talkin' now! You propose to me, and I come here and you wit' some girl! "

"Please let me explain. I didn't mean for this to happen. You have to believe me, Bianca."

"Is this why you haven't been callin' me or answerin' your phone? Were you wit' her on Thanksgiving break? She the damn Indian and you the fuckin' Pilgrim? Answer me! And I swear if you lie to me again, you will never have to worry about me again. Were you?"

"Please understand that I was not trying to hurt anybody. Yes. I was with her on Thanksgiving break. I'm so sorry Bianca. I wasn't trying to hurt you or her."

"Who is she? How long have you been wit' her? Is that your baby? I can't believe dis shit is happenin' right now. Yo, I need to walk off before I knock you in ya head, Yo. Fa real. I'm beyond pissed right now." I had so many questions and thoughts going through my head I couldn't grasp anything.

"Justin, who is this?"

Prego had the nerve to be asking questions. No bitch. You the side piece. You don't get to ask questions. "Look at her. Just as dumb as cat shit. Does she know about me, Justin?" Not that I cared. I still wanted to beat her ass anyway.

"No."

"She doesn't know that you're engaged to be married?" I turned toward her to enlighten her since she seemed to be stuck on stupid.

"I'm his fiancée Bitch." I held up my hand and showed her my engagement ring. "The real question is, who the fuck is you?"

"B, stop it. She doesn't know about you."

He kept trying to protect her and it pissed me off even more. I walked away before my fist started flyin'. My adrenaline was rushing, and I wanted to flip the hell out on Justin and that girl.

"Bianca, where are you goin'?"

"You betta leave me the hell alone right now!" I stepped away and paced trying to remember the skills I'd learned to manage my anger, but I was already enraged. I tried deep breathing but I couldn't get a grasp on inner peace and calm. I wanted to wreck shit.

"B, It's cold. Let's go. We can talk in the car." Justin turned to Pocahontas and whispered something close to her ear. The look on her face was weird. No anger or outrage. She didn't even say anything. She was just standing there like a freaky ass robot until he placed his hand on her stomach and I saw her flinch. Justin noticed too and moved in closer to her shaking his head. That set me off again.

"What the fuck you sayin' to her Justin? Don't wait for me to walk off and talk! Talk in front of me!" I hollered as I walked back toward them.

He walked toward me and cut off my advance. "Let's go."

"Nah. Ya ass ain't sittin' upfront wit' me. That ain't happenin'. Sit in the back. That's too close to me right now. If you could ride home on the hood, that's exactly where you'd be. I can't stand liars! She's fuckin' pregnant, Justin! How could you do dis shit to me?"

"I didn't know she was pregnant until I got back from summer break. That's my word."

"Ya word? What about ya word when you was stayin' at ya boy house? Ya word don't mean shit to me no more. I can't trust you. Marry her!"

"I don't wanna marry her. Can we leave, please? It's cold as hell out here."

"Sit in the back seat, Justin." I was serious. "Do not sit next to me."

"You ain't my chauffeur. I'm not sittin' in no back seat."

"That's the least ya ass can do! Respect that I don't want to be near you right now. Wait, you know what. I'll find my own way home. Go ahead. Take ya mom's car. I refuse to sit next to you." I threw the car keys at him with all my might.

He tried to catch them, but it was too late, and they smacked him right in the eye. "What the fuck is wrong with you?"

"No, what is wrong with you? You the one out here cheating and getting girls pregnant." Hearing it out loud broke me. I ran up on Justin and got in two punches to his head before he snapped.

TWENTY-SEVEN

Justin

Bianca was pissed and had every right but I be damned if she thought she could put her hands on me. No grown-ass man should tolerate disrespect on any level from anyone. Not even the woman that gave me life has put her hands on me since I was ten years old. Bianca had done really lost her mind this time. I picked up the keys from the ground and unlocked the trunk. I tossed my bags in and slammed it shut. I put the keys in the ignition and started the car.

"Get in the car, Bianca."

She crossed her arms and rooted herself where she stood as if she was an immovable tree. "You must think I'm that dumb bitch over there." She pointed to Tianna. "Don't tell me what to do."

I looked over at Tianna. Her expression was unreadable before she turned and walked away.

"Tianna!" I called after her, but she kept on walking. "Ti! Please wait let me explain!"

"Ti?" Bianca yelled out. "Well, ain't that just real fucking cute! Sorta like B huh? Couldn't even think of a different name for your whore, huh?"

I was not a violent man, and I would never hit a woman but for a second, I understood why a man would. I checked the urge and exhaled slowly.

Women are a gift. I reminded myself.

I'd heard it as clearly as the day Dad had said it to me. I released the rage and focused on diffusing the situation. What would my dad do? I remembered the time my mom had gotten angry at him and

231

dumped his dinner on his lap after he had complained about it. He jumped up shocked. He asked her to stop acting crazy, but she had been determined to get a rise out of him. So, when he instead turned around and simply walked away from her, she'd started beating on his back like a drum. Finally, he'd had enough and snatched Mom up, tossed her in the shower, turned it on, and told her to cool down. He chose to keep his peace rather than hit her. I'd do the same.

"Bianca. Stop making a scene and get in the damn car."

"No."

There was no shower out here, but the car would suffice. I marched over to her stubborn ass, picked her up, and tossed her over my shoulder. She began to yell and kick and punch my back. She tried to elbow me in the back of the head, and I started spanking her ass. Hard. She bucked and her hands flew to cover her backside that was most likely stinging.

"You wanna keep acting like a child, Bianca? I'll treat you like one. Cut this shit out and sit your ass in this fucking car." I dumped her in the front seat. "Stay here and don't piss me off any more than you already have. I'm not playing with you."

She rolled her eyes and faced forward but stay put. I slammed the door and caught up to Tianna who hadn't gotten very far. She was in her third trimester and was already pretty big. Her feet were constantly swollen, her headaches sometimes debilitated her, and she tired easily. I wanted to walk her to her car to make sure she'd made it safely.

"Ti, let me explain, please." She continued walking not even acknowledging my existence. I walked alongside her doing a piss poor job of making things right. "Tianna, I'm sorry. Bianca and I got engaged over the summer. I didn't know you were pregnant. You shut me out." I stopped trying to find how to make myself right and tugged at her elbow. "Tianna, please."

She finally stopped and faced me. "The decisions we make affect more than just ourselves."

She turned my words back on me and stabbed me in the chest with them. I stared into her vacant eyes. She wasn't crying. She wasn't angry. She didn't ask why or expressed what she was feeling. She said nothing. She did nothing. It scared me how far gone she seemed. Almost like a zombie. I felt the disconnect and felt like a part of me was missing.

Even more than that I felt disconnected from my child. I wanted to rub her belly and tell our baby that daddy was there and would never leave but I had done enough damage and didn't dare invade her space again. A car honking obnoxiously pulled me from my sea of sorrow and regrets. Instantly my rage returned. Bianca pulled up beside us and honked like she was in a parade before she flipped us the bird and drove off.

Tianna paid her no mind and continued her slow gait to her car and this time I let her. There was nothing I could say that would fix this. At least right now. I had seen Tianna shut down and I didn't have the power to stop it. I'd do more harm than good trying to push my own agenda. I recognized that I was being selfish.

I began walking back toward the dorm to call a cab home when Bianca pulled up, stopping within inches of me as if she was about to run me over. I jumped out of the way and jumped onto the curb. "Are you fucking crazy?" I yelled.

She got out of the driver's side and pointed at me. "You lucky this is your mom's car and that I have gotten a lot of help because trust me, the old Bianca would have run your bitch ass over and left you here, flat as a muthafuckin' pancake."

She jumped in the backseat of the car, and I didn't bother to question why. I was battling so much anger, regret and shame, I just wanted everything and everyone to just cease moving to give me a second to just process what had just happened.

We got home in record time. I didn't realize how fast I was driving until Bianca muttered something about my black ass getting a ticket and saw the speedometer was clocking in at ninety-five miles per hour down the highway. When we arrived at the apartment building, she stormed off and I let her. Truth was I didn't want to talk to her when she was violent and angry. We'd get nowhere and I needed to explain things to her when she was calm. There were so many things she didn't understand. Hell, there were so many things I didn't understand my damn self. I knew I fucked up. Instead, I grabbed my bags from the trunk and went home.

Mom hugged me tightly. "Welcome home, Son. How was the semester?"

"I did well, Mom. Thanks."

She beamed up at me with her bright smile. "That's my baby. You get your handsome good looks from your daddy, but you got all that brainpower from your momma."

The pride in her words and expression shamed me. I sat her down and told her everything. Other than a few facial expressions of surprise and questioning looks she remained quiet until I was done recounting my mess.

"I'm gonna be a grandmother?" She asked. I hesitated afraid of her disappointment before I nodded and waiting for her response. She brought a quivering hand up to her mouth while tears filled to the brim in her eyes.

"Momma, I'm sorry I didn't tell you sooner. I didn't know what to do. To be honest I still don't. I feel torn. No matter which way I turn, I am going to hurt somebody."

My mom placed her hand over mine. "Justin, your features may resemble your father's and your thinking similar to mine, but your heart is an empty field. Unique like a snowflake. Only you get to decide what you plant there and how to nurture it to make it grow. You get to decide what is best for you. And do so confidently and unapologetically. No one has to live your life but you. No one is responsible for your happiness and well-being, except you. Each one of us is responsible for our own contentment in life. And part of that is admitting when you are wrong and doing what you can to fix it.

You gotta fix this. Neither one of those young women deserve to be hurt any more than you already have." She was right.

I excused myself to my room and thought about life for hours. Guilt beat down on me like it was Mike Tyson. While I refused to play victim, I couldn't get past that life had handed me an unfair hand. I had always tried to be the person dad wanted me to grow up to be and I wondered if he was looking down at me disappointed. I wanted to punch something. But violence and anger weren't the answer. How many times had I stressed that to B? Too many times to count.

Yet, everything in me wanted to punch the damn wall and keep punching it. Yeah, I'd fucked up. I made some stupid decisions. A lot of them if I was honest with myself. How many times had I told Tianna that our decisions affected more than just ourselves? And again, here I was shattering lives like I was a bat being swung in a glass house.

I was plenty pissed about B putting her hands on me, but I wasn't blameless. I hurt her and I hated myself for it. She hadn't deserved my betrayal or deceit. But I wasn't going to condone her putting her hands on me or Tianna.

I thought about Ti and our baby. I could almost see her in her bed crying and falling back into that state of isolation like the first time I held her. Could our baby hear her tears and feel her emotions? Did she go numb again and not feel at all. That was worse. Our baby needed her to be healthy and well. I needed and wanted her to be healthy.

What the hell would she care about what I wanted? I had promised to never be like everyone else in her life who'd let her down and now I could be the drum major to the damn parade of her betrayers. For now, she had Tanya, Tommy, and Abe to care for her. Bianca had no one.

I hated the see-saw I was on. Bianca was the love of my life, and she'd had my heart since I was fifteen years old. Tianna was my best friend and carried my child. She inspired me to reach higher. But Bianca kept me grounded and rooted.

I could never leave my child. And I could never leave my true love.

"Dad, what do I do?"

Women are a gift.

I thought about how my dad loved my mom and how he had pleaded with me the day he was dying to watch out for her. For years I thought he meant on the way to the hospital, but I later realized he meant to take care of her while he was gone. Even while he was dying, she was who he thought of. His soul mate and his life partner. I cried amazed at the man that he was. Even in death, he was still bestowing wisdom upon me. My dad was a strong black man. A wise black man. A confident black man. A proud black man. A loving and honest black man.

Seeing my dad that way made me see myself and my path more clearly. I saw myself walking the path with only one woman and I hoped and prayed that she would forgive me and take my hand.

The following day, I went to B's apartment with hopes that she calmed down and would allow to me explain myself. I owed her that. Just as I was about to knock on her door, she opened it as if she were on her way out.

"What are you doing here?" she asked as she proceeded to shut the door.

"Can we please go inside? I need to talk to you."

"I don't have anything to say to you."

"Well, I have some things I need to say to you. Please let me get this out, Bianca. After I finish talking, if you still like you have nothing else to say to me, I'll respect and will never bother you again. All I'm asking for is a few minutes of your time and listen to me. Please."

She rolled her eyes, opened the door. "Five minutes."

I walked in and got right to it. "Look, I know you are mad at me, and I know you're hurting. Bianca, I did not mean to hurt you. I'm so sorry. Things happened so quick, and I was overwhelmed."

"I'm not understanding, Justin. Don't come in here with your lies. I don't have any more time for this shit. My heart hurts and I'm trying to hold it together. I don't want to snap, so don't play with my mind or lie to me like I'm stupid."

"I would never play with your mind. B, you know me."

"No. I thought I knew you, but apparently, I don't."

"I didn't know she was pregnant until after I got back from summer break. We were seeing each other when you and I were broken up. We parted ways right before I came home for the summer. When I went back to school, she had a little belly already. She didn't tell me anything. I swear."

"So, I'm just supposed to believe you?"

"Yes. I admit that I was wrong for not telling the truth sooner, but I am telling you the truth now. I'm trying to make this right. I'm hurting because I hurt you and her."

"Her! I don't give a fuck about her, Justin! Don't talk about her to me!"

"Bianca, please. She didn't do anything wrong just like you didn't. I want to make this right. I'm asking you to forgive me and work through this with me. I don't want to be without you. Whatever it takes to make this work, I'll do it. But please don't ask me to not be there for my baby because I won't do that."

"I would never ask you to abandon your child."

I exhaled relieved she'd not make me choose. "But I don't think I can deal with this type of situation. You cheated on me. And now a baby is coming into this world that isn't even ours."

I couldn't pretend to not understand her side. I know I had no right to ask her for anything, but I'd regret it for the rest of my life if I didn't. I'd risk rejection. What I couldn't risk was the chance to try and make it right.

"I know it's crazy but please believe me B. The baby was conceived when we weren't together. And now that a baby will be a part of my life that doesn't change how I feel about you. And it doesn't have to change us. I would want you can be a part of every part of my life. Including raising my child."

"Raising your child?"

I could see her temper flare and calm and had to be cautious with my words but let her vent and ask whatever she needed to make her understand.

"I was supposed to have your first baby. That's how it was supposed to be." She turned and faced the opposite direction. "This is a lot to take in."

I walked around so I could face her and have her see the sincerity in my eyes. I tried to hold her hand, but she snatched it back. "I know. I know it is. And we can still have our own children. B, I still want to marry you. I want to spend my life with you. You are my gift and I'm so sorry that I hurt you. I'm sorry that I lied to you. I was so caught up and in love with my baby. At first, my attention was on the baby and making sure Tianna was taking care of herself. Then I just got caught up, but B I promise you, it's always been you. My heart is here with you. My future is with you."

"And how do I know you are being serious? I just can't take your word for it. I don't trust your word."

"Then trust the man you've known for a long time. I'm still that guy. Yes, I messed up. I admit that. But the same guy who was with you when you were crying and scared, and with you when your dad was hospitalized, and the one who showed you how much I love you over the summer, is still right here. I'm still him. You need to know that it's all about my baby and you. I promise you."

"Even if I said yes, do you expect her to just be ok with her baby being around me? That's bullshit and I don't want no part of baby mama drama."

"You're a part of my life. If you're going to be my wife, you have every right to be there for my baby. She's not like that. I will make sure there is no baby mama drama."

"Oh my God. This is just too much."

I felt her slipping away from me and I mentally grabbed ahold of her. "Do you still love me?"

"You know I still love you."

"That's not what I asked you. Do you still love me?"

"Yes," she answered while tears filled her eyes.

"Bianca, marry me. Forgive me and marry me."

"Justin," she cried.

"I love you. I will never hurt you again. Tell me, you're not going anywhere, and we can work through this. I'm about to graduate. We can get married right after I graduate. Get our marriage license and get married at City Hall."

"What? Are you serious?"

"Yes, I am. I'm not playing any games. I know what I want and who I want. I love you B. Now, answer me. Can we get through this? Will you still marry me and spend the rest of your life with me?"

"I want to say yes but I'm scared of getting hurt again. I don't want to go through anything regarding that girl or for that matter, any girl."

"You got me, Bianca. I don't want anyone but you. I'm telling you; we can get through this, and I'll treasure you just like my dad treasured my mom."

She looked down at the floor before looking into my eyes, tears streaming down her face. "Yes. I'll still marry you."

I took her in my arms and held her tightly. Never in my life had I been so grateful for a second chance.

TWENTY-EIGHT
Tianna

Sometimes life just blindsided you. I was never a person of many words to begin with and there weren't many things that left me speechless and dumbfounded, but it had been days since Justin's unknown fiancée showed up and my world tilted on its axis, and I was still astounded. Justin was engaged to be married. Had been the entire time he'd been back at school.

I combed over every interaction with him that I could remember, and sure enough, the signs were there. I was just too trusting to notice. The day he found out I was pregnant he told me that our decisions affected the lives of others. I see now why he cried.

In retrospect, it took us weeks afterward before we were intimate again. And if I were honest with myself, he seemed more invested in the baby than in our relationship. I just figured it was first-time dad excitement and didn't give it much thought. But it was clear now that it was his engagement that had held him back.

Justin had called the day after the blow-up, but I hadn't taken the call. I had nothing to say. I didn't understand why I was bothered that it was now three days later, and he hadn't called back. Funny thing was I still had nothing to say about that entire situation so what did it matter?

I cleaned and dried my brushes after painting a dead rose in a vase. I hadn't even thought about what I was creating. It just evolved from the dark paint choices. I sat down taking the pressure off my swollen feet. I had never been so heavy in my entire life and catching my breath from simply walking or standing was new to me. My nose had naturally spread a little to help accommodate the need of the growing child within me. Everything I had the baby took from me. My body. Food. Air. Justin.

I wasn't jealous. It was an observation that manifested when lying in bed at night and tears refused to shed. I felt more like an incubator than a mother. The more I thought about it, the more I believed it and came to terms with it.

The baby kicked and I rubbed the spot. The bigger the baby got, the harder the kicks. I wondered if I had a future soccer player growing inside of me. I immediately squashed the thought. Whatever the baby was going to be was not something I would let myself think about. I had too many other pressing thoughts at the current moment to daydream about a future I had already turned away from.

"I've never seen a black rose before."

The unexpected voice startled me, and I dropped the brushes. Justin rushed over and picked them up before I could make it off the stool. He handed them to me, and I accepted without making eye contact.

"I take it you received my message. Thank you for coming. I wasn't expecting you until later."

"I didn't call again to respect your space. I assumed you didn't want to talk to me but thank you for wanting to meet up with me."

I didn't respond. I had no desire to exchange pleasantries or talk about what was already over. I don't know how I knew, but with everything in me, I knew Justin had chosen a future with his fiancée. I was never chosen. I'd lost my worth long ago and more than I cared to remember. And because of that, I had never been good enough to have been chosen. That had been the story of my life for my entire life. It sickened me that the only person who had chosen me was a pedophile. Over and over again he'd chosen me. I checked the disgust and tears that threatened to erupt from within me. The faster I got this conversation with Justin over with, the better.

"I don't wanna take too much of your time." I waddled over to my bureau and tossed the brushes inside, not handling them with the care I usually would. Maybe it was my anxiety. Or perhaps my lack of caring much about anything lately.

"It's no bother to me. I'm here for as long I need be, Tianna. We have some things to talk about. I need to apologize and explain."

"You need to do neither. I wish you and your fiancée well."

When he didn't refute it, my heart unexpectedly broke. It caught me so completely off guard I began to gasp for air but turned my back so he wouldn't see how much I hurt. I composed myself and turned to the only topic that mutually concerned him and me now. The baby.

"I have been doing a lot of thinking and I have made a decision about the baby."

"Ti, you cannot keep my child from me. I have rights," he interjected. I waited a few seconds before I continued my thoughts disregarding his outburst.

"Please call me Christianna. As I was saying. I have made a decision about the baby. It is up to you how you wish to proceed."

"Proceed with what? What are you talking about? And we've come to that? We're strangers now? No. Even worse than that. The day I first met you and didn't know you from Sally you told me friends and family called you Tianna. I guess I'm neither."

I ignored his barrage of questions and trying to get to middle ground. There was no middle ground. All of the ground had been blown up and there was nothing left for either of us to stand on. And we'd both had laid the bombs that had been detonated.

"I am signing away my full rights to the baby. If you wish to have full custody, I will sign whatever I need to for you. If you do not, I understand and will place the baby up for adoption."

An array of emotions broke through across his face. Sadness, shock, confusion, hurt, and anger.

"Like hell you will. What is the matter with you? That's our baby. Not a toy, Christianna."

He said my name with sarcasm and I almost cared, but I checked that too. Justin no longer could say or do anything to make me care about his words or actions. They held no weight with me. He'd lost that privilege. "Does that mean you will accept full custody?"

He didn't respond but instead stared at me with bewilderment in his eyes. "Did I hurt you that bad? You just want to give up your child to whoever will take him."

"The success rate of children adopted in the United States is in the high ninetieth percentile. While there is an adjustment period and a legalization process that can often be an uncertain time, in the long run, that does not hinder the overall health and contentment of adopted children afterward."

"Are you serious right now?"

"The most common type of adoption is a stepparent to a child. Preliminary studies show that adopted stepchildren fare better than stepchildren never being adopted. It has also been shown that stepchildren tend to exhibit more negative behaviors to those who have been legally adopted by a stepparent. I would go as so far as to say that a stepparent that willingly adopts their spouse's child is more inclined to treat that child as they would their own biological children. Children are very perceptive and can sense genuine love or lack thereof. On that matter, I speak from personal experience."

"Tianna! This is not Philosophy class! Stop it!"

I wouldn't let the tears rush up. I willed them back with an iron fist. "If she loves you, she will love your child. And she will accept what is a part of you. An innocent that is not at fault. Love is patient and kind. It is not boastful. Nor does it hold a record of wrongs. Love is not selfish or self-seeking. It is pure. And I wish you all much love and happiness as a family."

I walked out of my studio leaving him behind in it and not bothering to lock the doors. As I drove home, I pondered why scripture, which I hadn't thought about in years, surfaced and flowed from my mouth as if I had just read it from the Bible yesterday. More so I thought about the life I had temporary responsibility for.

It may not have seemed like it to anyone else, but despite all I felt and said and decided, I loved the child growing within me. I loved him enough that I wanted him to have more than a mother like me. He deserved better. He deserved more than a battered heart and worn-down woman as a mother. He deserved a strong and fearless mom.

As weird as it sounded, Justin's fiancée was better suited. I couldn't fault her for being upset to see her fiancée cheating. I couldn't fault her for thinking the worst about me, just as Lexy Carstarphen had. Bianca would probably never know that I was not directly at fault for her hurt and I could live with that. What mattered was far simpler. Although I didn't know Bianca at all, one thing I most certainly recognized was a woman that loved hard and was relentless.

She refused to be silent in the face of her injustice. She wasn't afraid to stand up for herself. When she nearly attacked me, something in her eyes changed when she looked at my belly and she stopped herself from hurting my child, even in her anger. I wouldn't deny that she wasn't definitely a hood chick but that wasn't always a bad thing.

What if she would stand up for injustices for my child one day? What if, despite her anger, she would always protect my child? What if she relentlessly loved my child? What if she taught my child to stand up for themselves and be of strong character? Yeah, Bianca had hood in her, but it also equated to good. The more I thought about it, the more I was convinced Bianca would make a better mother to my child than I could. I refused to see it any other way.

TWENTY-NINE
Bianca

Although I'd forgiven Justin, I struggled with him having a baby with someone else. I believed Justin loved me without a doubt and I loved the fact that he wanted me to be a part of his baby's life. I was afraid of baby mama drama until Justin told me that Tianna wanted me to adopt the baby so he and I could raise the baby together. She didn't even know me but wanted me to be a full-time mother to her child. I didn't know how to feel about any of it.

I walked into group therapy surprised to see Brandon sitting with the Misfits, minus Dani who'd 'found her calling' as a waitress at Hooters. We'd all had a running bet to see when she'd quit or get fired. It was pretty messed up but that's the kinda nonsense we did, yet never out of malice. We'd told Dani and her nutty self just cheered us on.

It had been a while since we had all met up and therapy got deep. Brandon had been healing with little hiccups physically but admitted that he had avoided crowds and bars. Even sitting amongst us made him nervous but he wanted to overcome it. My heart broke for him. He used to be such a goofy and hype guy. And when I visited him alone, I still saw that guy but here he seemed so different. Subdued almost.

Everyone else began pouring out their recent lives too. I decided to keep my drama to myself. I wasn't ready to share that yet. I was trying to not think about it at all. I had gotten so into everyone else's share time that I had forgotten my troubles for a while. Up until Isys shared that she had been pregnant and suffered a miscarriage. She began to weep. I didn't know what to do or say. I secretly felt guilty. She was crying over the fact that she'd lost her baby and Tianna was giving me hers and I was almost sure I didn't want it. I left therapy more confused than when I had gotten there.

I went home and soaked in my bathtub until the steaming hot water turned cold and I was wrinkled. Afterward, I untangled my wild curls and attempted to tame them with my Pink Lotion. I was inhaling the smell as I had always done since my mom had died. It reminded me of her sitting behind me and complaining about the knots in my hair. She'd always complain about how much hair I had. She called it a mop and would tease me that she was going to turn me upside and clean the floors with me if I didn't stop fussing while she ripped my hair out by the roots.

I cracked up to myself. My poor mom didn't know what she was getting into when she had a baby with a black man. Her blonde hair was thin and straight, and she couldn't braid hair for shit. She'd tried once and my two ponytails looked like two pieces of dookie hanging from the side of my head. And she had the nerve to send me to school like that. I'd gotten into two fights that day after kids were teasing me. She promised to never do that again and kept her promise.

I was pulling out some pajamas from the dresser when my phone rang. Uncle Ricky had called me to tell me about a few pool games going on that night. At first. I declined, but it was only seven o'clock and I knew I'd think about nothing but my troubles and I didn't want to dwell on it. I needed to take my mind off all the baby stuff and decided to go see if I could rack up some money.

Justin called right after and insisted that he go with me so he could see me play. It had been years since he'd seen me play. My skills had grown a lot since then. We made it a date night and I was excited about getting us back on track. I put the PJs away and pulled out some clothes. I purposely chose heels. They distracted my mostly male opponents, but I also wanted to seduce Justin. He liked when I teased him. I was anxious to gettin' us back on solid ground. Sex had never been an issue between us, and I longed for that intimacy. Tonight, I'd seduce him.

Just as I thought, it hadn't taken much. As I played, we kept cutting eyes at each other saying more than words ever could. He'd wink or smile. A few times I caught him blushing. Oh, how I loved that man.

As I bent over to position myself to take my first shot in the next game, I looked up at Justin. He licked his lips before his beeper stole his attention. He looked down at it and his facial expression changed immediately. He walked over to me, "I have to go."

"Why? What's wrong?"

"I just got a page from Tianna's house with 911 after it. I need to get home so I can see what's going on."

"Give me one second while I cash out and opt-out of the rest of this game, okay?"

"You're going with me?"

Part of me wanted to stay out of all of that, but a bigger part of me wanted to be by his side through everything. "You said we'd be together through everything right?"

He nodded. "Through everything," he said and hugged me before I walked away to tie up my end of the game.

After a phone call to Mrs. Leonard, Justin learned that Tianna was rushed to the hospital with a severe headache that had her so dizzy she'd nearly collapsed. Her doctor ordered her to get there as soon as possible. Justin grabbed the car keys, and I could see that he was upset.

"Do you want me to drive?" I asked.

"No. I can drive."

"Okay."

He drove like a bat out of hell and scared the shit out of me, but I kept quiet understanding his urgency. When we got to the hospital Tianna's mom stood in the hallway.

"Hey, Mrs. Leonard. How is she? How's the baby?" Justin asked.

"They are about to do an ultrasound. They ruled out preeclampsia and said it may be stress. She needs to take it easy and stop worrying herself so much. It's not good for her or the baby," Tianna's mom explained.

She looked at me nastily then turned away. I wanted to snatch her by her hair, but I didn't. The old B would've punched her in the face though. I put my feelings aside and focused on being Justin's support. I was there for him and didn't care about anyone else.

A woman in scrubs was about to enter the room and Justin rushed to her. "Can I go in and see her?"

It surprised me to see Justin so worried and anxious. He was usually so chill. He was practically breathing down the nurse's neck.

She slowed her pace and looked at him strangely. "I'm sorry who are you?"

"I'm the baby's father."

I could see her demeanor ease and she nodded. "We're about to do the ultrasound."

"I'm going in," Justin said to Mrs. Leonard. "B, come on."

Mrs. Leonard intervened. "Justin you are seriously not going into my daughter's hospital room with her. Right?" She looked like she was about ready to kick his ass.

"Mrs. Leonard, no disrespect but this is my fiancée and the woman that will be a mother to my child. So yes, I'm taking her inside."

She began muttering something in Spanish and I understood a little because Milly from around the way had taught me all the cuss words.

"Oh no she didn't just call you a pen day ho." I turned to her shooting daggers at her with my eyes.

"A ho what?" Justin asked.

"A pen day ho. I think it means you ignorant."

Justin ignored it and grabbed my hand leading me into the room. When we entered the room, Tianna looked at us confused. "What are you doing here?"

"Your mom contacted me."

Tianna nodded but didn't say anything.

"And she just called me a ho or something. I don't know what that means, but I don't want any problems with your mom."

Her brow dipped in confusion. "My mom called you a ho?"

"A pen day ho," I corrected. Tianna then looked at me and I remembered where I was and who I was talking to. "I'm not here to upset you. I'm here for support for Justin and the baby." I had to make that crystal clear so she would check herself and dare not get funky with me. But at the end of the day, this was still her baby and her situation.

"You mean a *pendejo* and that means an idiot." Tianna exhaled slowly. "Sorry about that."

Justin looked to the floor for a second. I could tell he was uncomfortable, but he still held my hand and stood his ground. And just as he always did, he lifted his chin and faced life. "Christianna, we don't want any issues, and come here in peace."

"You're fine." She rested her head on the pillow and closed her eyes.

Justin and I looked at each and he offered me a reassuring smile. At that moment I knew I could love him forever. He had my back and I promised myself to have his. He offered me the only seat available in the room, but I refused it. I was right where I belonged; by his side but I didn't need to sit front row and center. Nah. After he took the seat, I stood behind him and placed my hands on his shoulders being his support.

The technician slid her stool closer to Tianna squirting some jelly-like substance onto her exposed belly, "This is going to be a little cold."

Tianna kept her eyes closed and nodded.

"Let's see what we have here," said the technician as she slid the apparatus across Tianna's stomach.

On the screen, all I saw was a bunch of black and white mess. Justin was so focused on the screen I wondered if he could make out what I couldn't. Then I heard the distinctive sound of the heartbeat, and I was so enraptured by it I stopped paying attention to everything else.

After the technician clicked a bunch of times and moved the apparatus around Tianna's stomach for a few minutes she cleaned it off and handed Tianna some towels to clean her stomach.

"He looks good Mom. I'll send the results to your OB, and they'll go over them with you. Ok?"

Justin sat up straight in his chair. "Wait did you just say he? It's a boy? I'm, I'm having a son?"

The tech turned all shades of red. "I'm sorry, I didn't know you didn't know the gender." She looked at Tianna who'd opened her eyes but didn't seem to care. "I'm sorry. I could have sworn you referred to the baby as 'he' and that you knew the gender."

Tianna exhaled deeply. "You don't need to apologize. I didn't know. I just had a feeling, so I refer to the baby as a boy."

"Well, you have good maternal instincts because you were spot on."

I saw Tianna freeze up before she hid back in her shell. I wondered what was going through her mind. Did she not love her baby? How could she not hear that heartbeat and feel a baby inside of her and not love it? Justin looked about ready to explode with excitement. So, I chose to unite with his energy. I kissed the top of his head and rubbed his shoulders. He grabbed my hand and placed a quick kiss on it.

Tianna saw it and turned to face the technician. "We're all done here, right? Can I change back into my clothes?"

The tech advised her to wait for the nurse to come in and instruct her further. She nodded and thanked the technician before she went back into her shell like a turtle. I almost felt bad, but I didn't. I had a right to be happy and in love. I hadn't done anything wrong. I wasn't flaunting my relationship in her face. I was just being genuine, just as Justin was.

But I wasn't heartless either. Now that Justin knew the baby was ok, I didn't need to be in Tianna's room anymore. Granted, I didn't want to be around her mom, but I was willing to leave, just to be nice to Tianna. I didn't owe her anything but for my sake and Justin's I chose peace over standing my ground.

I whispered in Justin's ear that I would wait out in the hall. He looked up at me surprised. "It's ok. I don't want her to be uncomfortable," I whispered.

His face relaxed and he nodded approvingly.

I stepped out into the hallway and was relieved Tianna's mom was sitting down the hall in one of the orange chairs. I took the time alone to process what had just happened. I could still hear the baby's heartbeat in my head. I wanted to hold it and nurture it. It touched me knowing one day I would hold him and love Justin's baby.

Justin's baby. I referred to him that way because I was detached from him and his existence. I didn't want to blame the baby, but I wasn't sure I was capable or even wanted to embrace him. I was ok thinking of him as Justin's baby. Justin's situation. Justin's responsibility. Thinking about it that way had begun to change. It didn't feel like just Justin's baby anymore. I felt like a cord had lodged itself from the baby to me. I connected with an unborn child that wasn't mine and it was emotional and felt crazy, but it was real.

When we got to my place, we sat down and cuddled. A new connection had been solidified between Justin and me. I had always believed that I would support his fatherhood situation from a distance, but now I didn't want to. I wanted to be involved as I could be. That was what a wife was called to do. We were life partners, so it wasn't just Justin's situation. The minute I said I'd marry him it became our situation. I embraced his son, and it took our relationship to another level. We made love and I gave him all of me like I never had before.

After my shower, I found Justin sitting in my bedroom waiting for me. "You're wonderful, you know that?" He commented.

"What? Where did that come from?"

"At the hospital. First, you walked out of Tianna's room so she wouldn't feel uncomfortable. And because I know you B, you heard my son's heartbeat and saw him on that monitor, and it did something to you."

"It did," I admitted. "Seeing him on that monitor and hearing his little heartbeat made him so real to me." I paused and reflected on that moment for a minute. "He's innocent in all of this."

"I'm the luckiest man alive. You're a gift, B. I love you future Mrs. Saunders."

"I love you too. I love the sound of that," I said as I walked over to hug Justin.

The remainder of the night, we talked about setting a date for our wedding, and possible locations to move to after he graduated from college. We agreed that he would come live with me in my apartment until we found the perfect home. It was crazy how my life had changed so much, and now Justin and I were planning for a house, a wedding, and a baby all at once. But change didn't scare me. I was from the hood, so blessings were far few and in between and were snatched up when they came along. I had every intention of grabbing each one and holding them close.

The idea of holding the baby and being married made me smile. I cozied up to Justin even more wrapping my arm around him and laying my head on his chest listening to his heart beating. The baby was a few months away and I couldn't hold him close, but Justin was right here, and I was more than satisfied to start with him.

"I love you, Justin."

"I love you more, B."

THIRTY
Justin

I was surprised Tianna paged me as I packed my bags to move in with Bianca. Now that Bianca and I would be raising Justin Jr. together, our future together came at us at warp speed. We'd decided to get married in June, as soon as I finished my last semester of school. I'd be a college graduate with a bachelor's degree in science and studying for the MCATs. If everything went as I hoped, I'd be starting medical school. A poor black kid from the ghetto could do anything he set his mind to. Tianna always pushed me to dream bigger. When I said sports physical therapist, she said sports medicine doctor.

I zipped my luggage closed and went to the living room to reply to her page. She answered on the first ring.

"Hello." She sounded out of breath.

"Hey Ti, I mean Christianna. It's Justin. How are you?"

"I want to punch you in the face for doing this to me," she said, followed by a groan.

I knew it would come sooner or later. I suppose her wrath toward me was inevitable and everything that she'd kept buried inside would one day erupt. And just as I had endured Bianca's rage, I would man up and allow Tianna to unleash her tongue lashing. I'd say my piece and brace myself for hers.

"I'm sorry Ti. I truly never meant to hurt you. For the rest of my life, I will regret breaking my word to you. Please believe me, I will make up for it. Even if it's just through Justin Jr."

"Please shut up. I'm in labor. And these contractions are all your fault. I hate you."

"You're in labor? How? You aren't due for a few more weeks! The baby can't come yet!"

"Would you like me to tell him that? You think he'll hold tight for a few more weeks out of obedience to his father? *Pendejo*," she whispered.

Always the smartass and now in Spanish, but I let it slide. I admit I panicked a little. I'd been anxious for so long and couldn't wait to meet my son and here the time was, and I wasn't even ready. But he was coming whether I was ready or not.

She groaned again and I could hear her breathing through the contraction. "Breathe in and out, Ti. You're doing great. Is your mom with you? Are you on your way to the hospital?"

She inhaled and exhaled forcefully for a few seconds before she responded. "Stop asking me a million questions. *Mami* and Pop are not home. I had to call you first, but Abe is waiting to drive me. And in a panic that I'm going to get 'womb juice' on his seats. Why are males so stupid?"

I wanted to laugh but I was sure that would piss her off. "Ok. Let me call Bianca and then we'll be on our way."

"Ok. I'll see you soon."

"Keep doing your breathing. You got this."

"Justin."

"Yeah," I replied wanting to rush off the phone and get to her in person as soon as possible.

She was silent for a moment before she spoke softly. "I forgive you." I could hear the emotion in her voice, and it caused my own to surface.

Forgiveness had the power to set people free from self-abounding chains. I had battled guilt regarding both Bianca and Tianna, but shame cloaked me when it came to Tianna. She had already experienced so much betrayal in life, and I had added my fair share to it. Yet here she was extending me grace when I hadn't deserved it. I swallowed the lump in my throat.

"Thank you, Ti."

"I am doing what's best for the baby because I think you're a great dad."

"I'm gonna try to be."

"No Justin. You already are."

Had Bianca not already had my heart, it would have been Ti's. She was true beauty personified, and it had nothing to do with how she looked. She was a rare one. "Tianna, I know this might not mean much coming from me, but you are the strongest person I know. You have every reason to hate me, and the world, but you don't. You are gracious beyond understanding and worth so much more than you realize. It may not be in the way we had planned, but I do love you."

Her silence paralyzed me. I didn't want to hurt her more than I already had and wished I could have snatched back the words until she spoke, her voice shaky and sweetly. "I love you too. No matter what, I will always treasure the friendship you gave me when I needed it most."

She hung up before I could respond but I didn't mind. I couldn't imagine how much it cost her to say that. I was grateful she'd found it in her heart to forgive me. No matter what happened, she'd always be Justin's biological mother and someone I'd cherish. But right now, I had to call Justin's other mother. The one that had begun to love him as if he were her own. I was even more grateful that Bianca had forgiven me, and we were starting a whole new life together. I paged her our emergency baby code and she'd called me back within minutes.

"Hey, Babe. What's wrong?"

"Tianna went into labor. We gotta go to the hospital."

"Labor?" Her voice rose an octave. "But the baby isn't due for a few more weeks. Is the baby, ok?"

"That I know of, they are both fine. Jr. just couldn't wait to meet Daddy is all."

Bianca laughed. "I don't blame him. His dad is all that and a bag of chips."

"Damn right I am, woman."

Bianca's laughter hit me right in the gut as it always had. I loved that woman beyond reason. Thinking about how I almost lost her scared the hell out of me. My dad must have really been looking out for me in heaven to have allowed both women to have forgiven me. He was right. Women were a gift. And I had been blessed with ones I knew I hadn't deserved.

"Where are you? Can you meet me in front of the building in a few minutes?"

"I'm at an appointment with my dad and not near the city. I'll just meet you at the hospital in like an hour or two. Labor can take a long time."

"Sounds good."

"Are you ready to meet your son?"

The idea terrified and thrilled me at the same time. My life would never be the same, but I was as ready as I could be. "Are you ready to meet yours?"

"I can't wait," she replied.

"You never stop surprising. I mean sometimes I wanna put you in jail and throw away the key but most times I want to lock myself up with you. I don't know how I could ever do any of this without you."

I could hear her sniffling. "You don't ever have to. I'll see you at the hospital. And don't forget the outfit we picked out for my Boopie to come home in."

"Now I done told yo ass to stop all that Boopie shit. Trying to make my son soft. He needs a nickname like Beast or Hulk."

"Nigga, he ain't no damn comic book character and I can call him whatever I want. If I wanna call my son Boopie, I will."

I just shook my head at all that feminine Boopie shit, but what mattered most was how quickly she claimed him. "Your son. See? That's why I'm completely stuck on stupid over you. Not many women would accept a baby from another woman and then love him like you already do."

"And don't you ever forget it. I love you, Mr. Saunders."

"I wouldn't even dare. And I love you more, future Mrs. Saunders."

A few minutes later I placed the bag Bianca had packed for the hospital and placed it in the back seat, baby outfit and all. I started the car and pulled out of the parking lot. At the light, I saw Jordi standing on the corner with Rah Rah and his boys. Rah had been a good kid growing up but when the streets came calling, he answered. Not the crowd I wanted Jordi around. That was even more evident when a girl walked by, and all the guys started hooting and trying to kick it to her.

She kept walking and Rah called her a stuck-up bitch. Jordi, not to be outdone, grabbed her ass. She turned around and shoved him. He started laughing and tried to hug her, but she shoved him harder and walked away. All the fellas laughed at his disrespect. My dad would roll over in his grave.

I honked the horn like a madman. They all looked over at me like I was crazy. The light had changed and the car behind began their own honking. I motioned them to go around not giving a shit. I needed to hem up my brother. I waved him over and he rolled his eyes before jogging over to the car.

"Hey bro. Wassup?"

"It's cold out here. Whatchu doin' out here? And why ain't you in school?"

"Just chillin' damn. School is boring. I can miss a day every now and then. Ain't no big deal. Everybody ain't trying to be a doctor like you."

"Get in and take this ride with me." I wouldn't let him bait me and I sure as hell wasn't leaving him out here with those knuckleheads.

"Where to?"

"Just get in Jordi. Now."

He huffed before he got in the car. "Does Mom know you have her car?"

I pulled off and headed toward the highway. "Don't change the subject. You know your ass belongs in school. Ain't nothing for you out here baby brother except death or jail. Why would you put Mom through that?"

"I'm not putting her through nothing and stop coming down on me all the time! Damn! My grades are fine. I'll graduate and I don't wanna go to college, so just leave me alone. I don't wanna be you, Justin. Why can't everybody just understand that?"

"I don't want you to be me. I want you to be the best you, you can be. And hanging out here disrespecting females and cutting class ain't something to be proud of."

Jordi slapped his lap and laughed. "You have gots to be joking me. You out here with two bitches. Engaged to one and got the other one pregnant and you talkin' to me about respect. You got some balls, Justin. How you gonna tell me anything? You buggin', Yo. For reals."

Jordi was right. I was far from perfect or hardly the best example to follow but I surely had learned from my mistakes and was reaping what I had sown. "I never pretended to be perfect."

"Coulda fooled me. Mom's good son. It's cool. I'll be the hood son. I'm aiight with that."

I took my eyes off the road for a quick second and looked over at him as I merged onto the highway and then the fast lane. "We are both just her sons. No labels needed."

Jordi looked out the window and remained quiet. I wrestled with how to reach him. I didn't know what to say or how to bridge the gap between us. What would my dad say if he were here? Truth was I had no idea. But I knew we both loved dad and that was one area we always found common ground in. I'd use that.

"Do you remember when Dad used to sit you on his lap and let you steer the car? Back before seatbelts and car seats were mandatory?"

Jordi shrugged and kept his gaze fixed out the window. "A little."

"How about the time he caught you watching his porn video?" I laughed remembering how outraged Mom was when she found out Dad even owned porn and that her six-year-old son was watching it. "Mom nearly had a damn heart attack."

Still, Jordi said nothing.

"How about the time Dad-"

"Would you stop it? I don't wanna talk about Dad. And where the hell are we going?" He snapped.

I stayed quiet for a few minutes before I risked his wrath. "Dad did what he thought was right. He was an honorable man. Forgive him, Jordi."

"No!" He screamed! "He left us! He shoulda just minded his own damn business like he used to tell me when I'd get in trouble in school. He shoulda came home and eaten chicken with us! He shoulda chosen us! He wasn't the hood superhero. He was supposed to be our hero and he failed. And he left us! What kind of father leaves his children? And in that fucking ghetto to try and survive in. He left his wife. He left his sons. He betrayed us and you praise him like he was a saint. He wasn't a saint or a hero. He doesn't deserve my forgiveness!"

His tears flowed so heavily I pulled over overcome with emotion. Jordi wiped the tears angrily then pulled a glass bottle from inside of his coat. He removed the cap from the bottle and brought it to his lips and drank.

"Since when do you drink whiskey?" He didn't respond. It was perfect timing. I was on edge. "Let me have some."

He looked at me strangely before handing me the bottle. I drank a little and handed it back to him. I pulled back out on the road and drove in silence for a few minutes. He finally calmed down. I think he needed to get all that out. I was glad he did it in a safe zone and was with me. I'd take all the verbal punches and just let him grieve how he needed to. After a while of him being quiet, I felt free to share with him.

"Christianna is in labor. We are going to the hospital. You're about to be an uncle."

I could feel him burning a hole into the side of my face. "Are you nervous?" He asked.

"Hell yeah! I ain't even the one that gotta push a baby out of my vagina but I sure do feel like a twat." Jordi surprised me when he chuckled. "I don't even know why I'm so nervous but if you tell anybody, I'll kick your ass."

He laughed again. "Speaking of kicking your ass, how in the hell hasn't Bianca kicked yours? She crazy as hell."

"She almost ran me over with this car so trust me, I know she crazy." We laughed out loud. "Honestly, I have no idea what I said or did to earn her forgiveness, but I won't take it for granted."

He nodded and we drove in silence for a few minutes before he spoke. "An uncle." He shook his head and stared out the window again. He tightened the cap on the bottle and shoved it under his seat and straightened himself out.

I knew all too well what that was. That was change. Justin Jr. wasn't even born yet, and he was already making a positive difference in people's lives. I was already a proud father. "Yep, an uncle. Matter of fact, you'll be his only uncle."

"His only uncle? His mom doesn't have any brothers or sisters?"

"She has one brother but—" I hadn't truly come to terms with Tianna's decision of giving up her rights so vocalizing it hadn't been easy.

"But?"

"She gave full custody of Justin Jr. to B and me. B doesn't have any siblings, so baby brother, you're the only uncle."

"Whoa," Was all he said. A few minutes passed before he laughed. "I guess that automatically makes me the favorite then, huh?"

I laughed out loud. "No doubt."

He smiled at me, and I choked on my emotions. I hadn't seen him smile in so long I'd forgotten how much he looked like dad. But more than that I loved seeing this side of him again. I missed my kid brother.

"Don't tell Mom I told you this, but she's been hiding baby clothes in her closet. I caught her the other day and she told me if I ratted her out, she'd whoop my ass. But since Little J is already on the way, her secret's about to come out anyway."

I chuckled. I knew that woman was more excited than she'd let on. She'd nearly cried when I told her she'd be a grandmother. I just wasn't sure if those were tears of anguish or joy. I was glad it was indeed joy.

"I'm gonna teach Little J to call her Grandmaster Ma."

"Why you tryna get my son beat? Keep that shit up and you won't be the favorite uncle," I joked.

Jordi sobered quickly. "Man, don't play like that. That's my little dude right there."

I cracked up at his expression. It amazed me how much a baby could change people. The closer we got to the hospital, the more excited I became. "We should be there in like ten minutes. School is not that far from here and the hospital is five minutes closer than the school."

"Ok, cool. But I'll wait in the waiting room. I ain't tryna watch nobody have no baby and shit. I don't wanna see no pus—"

I backhanded him in the chest. "Watch your mouth."

He smirked. "No snatch you done already marked like a dog." He finished.

I chuckled and shook my head. "Ain't nobody invite yo ass into the room anyway. It'll be me and Bianca."

"Man, that's some Jerry Springer type shit but I'm glad y'all worked it out though." He bent forward holding his stomach as he cracked up.

"Boy, hush up." He always had something smart to say. I smacked him in the back of the head, and he laughed harder. That was when I noticed the flashing lights behind me.

I slowed down and switched to the right lane to let the police officer ride past. Instead, he switched lanes right behind me and when I slowed down to a complete stop, he did as well.

I asked Jordi to take Mom's registration and insurance cards from the glove compartment. He handed them to me.

"What did you do?" He asked.

"I don't know. Nothing that I can think of." It took several minutes before the police officer walked over to my window. I put the window down.

"License, registration, and insurance cards."

I handed the documents over to the police officer. "What did I do officer?"

He didn't respond as he looked over the documents Jordi had given to me. Forgetting about handing him my driver's license, I lifted myself up from the seat and to pull my wallet from my back pocket when the officer pulled his gun on me.

"Don't move!"

I froze in place.

"Put your hands on the steering wheel where I can see them!"

"Passenger! Hands on the dashboard!"

"What the fuck?" Jordi yelled.

"Just do it Jordi. We didn't do anything wrong. Let's just follow the law." I urged him quietly. I was grateful when he obliged without his usual contention. If I could avoid a ticket or a moving violation, I'd try.

"What were you reaching for?" The officer asked.

"Just my license," I assured him. "It's in my wallet in my back pocket. You asked for my license."

"Where are you headed? Your car is registered at a Camden City address. You're far from your neighborhood boy."

That angered me but I kept a cool head. "I'm on my way to the hospital. My baby is about to be born. You can check my backseat. There's an overnight hospital bag and a newborn outfit in there. I'm about to be a dad. Maybe I was speeding a little excited to get there."

The officer reminded me to keep my hands on the steering wheel. He opened the back door and quickly looked through the bag then suddenly stopped. He opened my door forcefully and told me to get out of the car.

"What did I do?" I asked confused. He pushed me against the car and told me to place my hands on my head. He kicked my legs wider apart and began to frisk me with one hand, his gun still in the other.

"Do you have any weapons or drugs in the car?"

"No officer. I'm on my way to see my son being born. You can call the hospital if you want. They can verify. Christianna Leonard is the mother."

"Answer only the questions I asked. You got that?" He yelled!

"Yes. Yes Sir." My heart began to race. I didn't know this had escalated so quickly and nothing I said seemed to matter.

"I see an open bottle of alcohol in the car. I'm going to ask you again, are there any weapons or drugs in the car."

"He said 'no' damn it!" Jordi hollered. "What kind of bullshit is this? He just wants to see his baby being born. We didn't even do anything wrong! That's my bottle. It slid to the back."

The officer backed up from me and demanded Jordi get out of the car. Panic started to set in. My brother was a hot head and I needed to protect him from himself.

"Officer. He's only eighteen years old. Young and dumb. I promise he'll be quiet. Jordi keep quiet!"

"Get out of the car now!" The officer repeated. "Walk around slowly and stand by him! Hands on your head and don't move!"

Jordi did as instructed. It seemed like an eternity before I felt him standing next to me.

"Both of you turn around and face me!" He demanded. We obeyed.

"This ain't right Justin," Jordi said so only I could hear.

And he was right, but I needed to diffuse this situation that had gotten way out of hand. I needed to protect my brother. I needed to see my son. I needed to get my college degree. I needed to marry the love of my life. I needed to keep my promise to my dad to take care of my mother. We could fight justice another day. Today we needed to get back in the car in one piece.

I raised my hands high in the air slowly to show I wasn't a threat. The officer began to yell at me to stop moving. I dropped to my knees in submission. "We will do what you ask Officer. We are no threat."

I heard the unmistakable pop of a gun. One pop. Then two. Then three. Jordi fell beside me to the ground. He looked up at me in shock. I looked down to see blood flowing from his leg. I looked over at the police officer in both shock and rage. He'd shot my brother. He stared at me with his bright blue eyes wide in fear. Did he not realize he held the gun? What did he have to fear? I looked back down at my baby brother and tears began to flow from my eyes. Never in my life had I felt so helpless and enraged at the same time. The motherfucker shot my innocent brother. He wasn't even driving.

January's frigid temperatures began to encapsulate me. It felt as if the cold had seeped into my stomach. I put my arms there to try and warm myself. Instead, I felt something foreign and looked down to see blood on my hands. Jordi sat up and pulled me to him. I fell over into his lap unable to make my limbs move as I willed them

Fear and tears filled his eyes. "Justin? Justin?"

I looked up at him and smiled. He was ok. He'd been shot but he was ok even if I was not. I preferred it that way.

"Baby brother."

Tears streamed down his face. "Come on Justin stay strong." He took his coat off and wrapped it around me. "Call an ambulance!" he screamed at the police officer! He turned back to me, horror written all over his face. "Please don't leave me like Dad did. I'll forgive him. I promise. Just please don't leave me. Fight through, man. I need you here. Little Man needs you here. Mommy and B need you here."

"Tell Bianca I love her. It's always been her. She is my wife, and we don't need a paper to tell us that. Tell Mom she is the best mother a kid could ask for. And not to cry. I'll be right next to Dad watching over her. You bring her to the hospital, and you make sure she's ok? Take her to see Little Man." With the little strength I had left, I yanked his shirt bringing him closer to me. "Promise me you'll take care of my girls, ok?"

He nodded not bothering to wipe the tears.

"Take care of Little Man. I love him more than I love myself. I'm trusting you to take care of my son, baby brother. I love you."

I don't know how much of those words I managed to speak clearly or if I'd even spoken them out loud at all, but I'd meant every word. I looked up to the sky and closed my eyes seeing me and Bianca laying in our bed. Jr. squealed with joy jumping in between us as we tickled him before I could no longer see their faces, feel their love, or hear their laughter, and fell asleep quietly.

THIRTY-ONE
Bianca

My emotions were all over the place. Justin Jr. was coming sooner than we had expected and I couldn't wait to hold my son. My son. How had I gotten to this place in life? Just thinking I was about to be a mom was crazy to me, but I was excited to share this journey with Justin. Tears of joy slid down my cheeks. That was a rare thing, so I let them run free.

Once inside I received my support person pass and I went to Tianna's room. I wish Justin would have been out in the hallway so we could have walked in together. She and I had come a long way, but it wasn't like we were friends. I chucked the uncertainty and did what I needed to do. Besides, it wasn't about me at all. Remembering that Justin Jr. was on his way re-centered my focus. I walked into the hospital room all smiles a little surprised Justin wasn't already waiting.

"Hello Christianna," I said when I walked in.

"Hello, Bianca." She looked behind me and her brow bunched in confusion. "Where's Justin?"

"He's on his way. We weren't together when you paged him. He told me to meet him here."

"Oh, okay."

"Are you okay? Are you in pain?"

"Contractions are consistent." She stopped and closed her eyes in visible pain as she inhaled and exhaled through a contraction before she continued. "I'm waiting for them to give me the epidural. I'm definitely going to give birth. My water broke so this is no false alarm."

"Oh shit. Okay. I just got super nervous."

She looked at me like I was crazy. Here I was saying I'm nervous when she's the one in labor. I needed to pull myself together and not in front of her. "I'm going to take a walk and find a phone to page, Justin."

She nodded and rested her head against the pillow. I rushed out of the room in search of a telephone. Where was Justin? My nerves were getting the better of me, but I knew once he arrived, I'd feel much better. He always knew how to calm me.

Needing time and space, I left the maternity floor altogether and took the elevator to the emergency room floor. On my way to the reception desk, I passed three police officers standing by an examination room. Someone must have been hurt and in trouble. Once at the desk they let me use the phone to page Justin. I waited a few minutes to see if he'd call. After a few minutes without a call, I decided to return to Tianna. He may have already been upstairs, and I didn't want to miss the baby's birth. I walked back toward the elevators.

"Bianca!"

I turned around startled. Jordi emerged from a room with a limp. I stopped in utter confusion. "Jordi?" I rushed over to him. "What are you doing here? Did you come with Justin?" I looked behind him to see if Justin was in the room, he had just exited.

He looked at me and shook his head no, tears beginning to stream down his face. I took a step back from him taking in what I had initially missed, alarms beginning to go off within. He had been covered in blood and was distraught, hardly able to speak. I tried to make sense of his muffled cries and began asking questions to get some logical information.

"Jordi, slow down. What happened? What's wrong with your leg?"

He fell into the nearby chair and wailed, his words making no sense. The police officers watched us strangely but said nothing.

"I don't understand what you're saying. Please. Tell me where Justin is? Is he with you?" Jordi's sob echoed throughout the hallway. I looked at the officers needing answers. "What happened to my brother-in-law?"

"Don't talk to them!" Jordi roared. "Those fucking bastards! Don't talk to them!"

His words were clearer, but I still didn't know what was going on. I knelt before him and softened my tone hoping to calm him down. "Jordi please listen to me. I need you to calm down and tell me what happened to your leg? Tell me where Justin is."

He lowered his tone, but the tears still flowed furiously. "B, first they took my dad, now Justin."

My heart started to pound uncontrollably. "Took Justin where? What are you talking about? Where is he?" My voice began to spike.

"They killed him, B. They killed my big brother," Jordi looked me in the eyes and sobbed. He pointed at the police officers. "Those bastards killed my big brother." He wailed.

But that was impossible. I had just spoken to him, and he was alive and excited. Jordi must've been high or drunk and talking crazy. I shook him trying to get him to snap out of it. "Jordi, where is Justin? Tianna is upstairs in labor. We're waiting on him!"

"Didn't you just hear me dammit! They killed him! Justin is dead!"

I shook my head at him and fell to my knees. It wasn't true. He was mistaken. Yeah. That was it. Jordi was mistaken. He was just mad at Justin, like always. "Stop it Jordi! Justin is not dead. I just talked to him. We're supposed to meet each other here! Stop being so mean to your brother! He loves you!"

Jordi's eyes turned somber, and he quitted his rant. "Bianca, I loved my brother. I wouldn't lie about this. A cop shot me and Justin on our way here."

"I don't understand," I said now knowing he was telling the truth but not wanting to accept it.

"Justin said we were ten minutes away from here when we got pulled over. It happened so fast B. One minute we were laughing and then next minute I was holding my brother as he died in my arms." Jordi looked a million miles away before he closed his eyes and began banging his head against the wall. He exploded. "That fuckin cop shot us for being black!" He was so enraged the police officers began to give him verbal warnings, but I couldn't think about anything but Justin.

I looked up at Jordi and shook my head repeatedly. It wasn't true. I refused to believe it. "No. No. Take it back."

"He died in my arms B. I can't take it back. I wish I fucking could, but I can't. I saw him take his last breath with my own eyes." He roared so loudly I felt it.

My body crashed down on the floor. Justin and Justin Jr.'s names echoed loudly in my head. I felt like I was about to lose my mind. My love was gone. How could this be? No. He's going to call back. He's going to walk into this hospital, and we will witness the birth of our son. I won't believe Justin is dead.

"I just talked to him. Our baby is coming. Please walk in here. I don't know what to do without you. Please," I spoke aloud in a daze.

"Bianca, get up. Justin wouldn't want you on the floor."

I walked down the hall like a zombie needing to see for myself that he was gone until I heard someone call me my name. I turned and saw Mrs. Saunders running towards me, her face covered in grief and tears. "Tell me it's not true," she screamed. "Tell me!"

But I couldn't. I shook my head and shrugged, fresh tears streaming down my face. She fell to the ground and Jordi rushed to her side. "I need to see my son. I need to see my son!"

It was all happening so fast. I went into a state of shock and the next thing I knew I had escorted Mrs. Saunders to see Justin's body. I don't remember much of it other than that that he looked so peaceful. I told him that he'd be my forever love.

I sat in a chair in a daze floating between pain and bewilderment and denial. A nurse approached me. "Are you Bianca? We have a patient in labor and delivery that is asking for you." She looked at me confused. "She was worried something happened to you."

I was so out of it I had forgotten about Justin Jr. I gathered myself and shook my head at the nurse. "Yes, I am Bianca. Did she have the baby yet?"

The nurse shook her head. "Not yet. You still have time to be there."

"Ok. I'll be there in a few minutes."

She smiled and nodded before she walked away.

I stood up and wiped the tears from my eyes. Justin was relying on me to be his life partner and though his life was taken, mine had not and I'd accomplish alone what he had planned we would together. I put on a mask for Tianna. I couldn't share Justin's death with her while she was in labor. I went into the bathroom to pull myself together before I went back into her hospital room.

Mrs. Saunders waited in the waiting room somberly while Jordi was dealing with the aftermath of being shot. I bent down in front of her. "Would you like some coffee or something to eat?" She kept her face covered with her hand and shook her head no. "I'm going in with Christianna now." I kissed her on the top of the head and braced myself.

As soon as I walked into the room, Tianna asked, "Did you talk to Justin?"

I shook my head. I don't know how I held it together, but I did.

"They gave me my epidural while you were gone. My contractions are getting closer together and I've dilated more. I'll be ready to push soon. I hope he makes it here in time."

I offered her the best smile I could manage and avoided answering her one way or another. It was hard standing there pretending like Justin was still alive. I wanted to burst into tears and tell her the truth just so I could grieve. I wanted to release this pain that needed to come out.

The nurse came in and checked Tianna's vitals. She told her that she was going to get the doctor because it was officially time to push Justin Jr. out. Tianna asked if she could wait a little longer for Justin to arrive and the nurse joked that dads were always late and would probably only pass out anyway.

It infuriated me and when she walked out, I followed her out and caught up to her. I tapped her on the shoulder, and she turned around surprised before I let her know about herself. "Let that be the last time you ever diss a patient's loved one when they are in pain and distress. It's unprofessional, not to mention rude. And just so you know, the father of her son was just senselessly murdered while on his way here, on time and ready to be her support. And she has no idea."

The nurse looked like she'd been hit by a mac truck. "Oh my gosh, I'm so sorry. My deepest condolences. I didn't mean to offend. I'm very sorry for your loss."

I stopped myself from punching her in the face. "Please make sure that another nurse is available during her delivery. Your bedside manner and care are not welcomed."

"I am the nurse assigned—" She tried to get bold with me, but I got bolder and cut her off.

"And the last time I checked, the assignments to patients weren't carved in stone. And even if they had been, so were the ten commandments and we see how well those rules were followed. I suggest you go erase the board and add someone else's name next to Christianna's. Don't come back into that room."

Her face turned all kinds of red. "Are you threatening me?"

"I will report you to everyone down from the janitor to the president of this hospital. And when I'm done, I will be sure to make an appearance with the local news station that I am sure is outside waiting for interviews from the family of the young black man that was murdered by a white police officer and is now being made fun of by a white nurse, hours after his death. I'm sure the hospital would love that type of publicity."

"I did no such thing."

"But didn't you Karen?"

"My name is Rachel."

"Rachel, you most certainly did walk into that hospital room and saw that young woman and assumed that her baby daddy was absent or a low life just because she was young, brown, and unmarried."

She remained quiet and looked away.

"Once again, you are not welcomed in that room while she is a patient here." I walked away from her proud that I hadn't needed to get violent to make myself heard and understood. I wouldn't allow her or anyone to disrespect Justin in life or death. I exhaled and walked back into the room."

"I thought you were Justin," Tianna said disappointed

I smiled at her before I walked over to the window.

"He's going to miss it."

I was quiet as I looked out of the window.

"Is everything okay? Have you heard from him?"

I shook my head no.

"Oh okay."

I could hear the disappointment in her voice, and the deceit began to weigh on me. I needed air and headed for the door.

"Where are you going?"

"I need to use the bathroom. And I'm going to the vending machine."

"Don't be gone too long. They are most likely on their way back to get me started. I don't want to be alone, especially if Justin hasn't made it here by then. I spoke with the nurse and doctor, and they know that I'm giving the baby up for adoption and not to give me the baby. So please be here to hold him."

"I'm not going far. I'm going to be right outside this door, so I'll see them when they come. I'll be here."

"Okay."

The moment I stepped into the hallway my tears released. I walked down the hall to the waiting room to check on Mrs. Saunders. She looked lost in thought.

"Mrs. Saunders, the doctor should be here any minute. It's time for Christianna to start pushing."

"My Justin is gone," Mrs. Saunders cried. "His Justin is coming." She began to sob quietly.

"I'll let you know when our Justin Jr. comes out, as soon as I can."

She didn't reply and continued crying. I went back to the room and just as I walked in, the doctor and a different nurse followed behind. I was glad because it looked like Christianna was about to ask more questions. Instead, the doctor filled the room with questions and instructions as the new nurse set up beside him.

Once they positioned Christianna, they told her that she could start to push. I stood nearby with a clear view of everything. They told her to stop and take a moment. Tianna was breathing heavily and had a tight grip on the top of her knees.

"Do you need my hand to hold or squeeze?" I asked. I thought about what Justin would do if he were here.

Tianna screamed as she pushed and put her hand out reaching for me. I rushed over and gave her my hand. The nurse told me to encourage her and so I did.

"Okay. It's time to push again. Give me a nice big push. Now," the doctor instructed.

Christianna squeezed my hand so tightly it felt like it was about to be shattered into a million pieces, like my heart. "Push Tianna. That's good. You're doing great."

Another round of rest and I wiped her forehead and pushed her hair back. She panted and began to cry.

"You got this Ti!"

She looked at me strangely and nodded before she sat up and pushed again on the doctor's count.

"The head is out! Take a moment Christianna. Inhale, and then push again real hard on the next contraction. The hardest part is done," the doctor said. Tianna did what the doctor ordered and pushed again with all her might.

Justin Jr. made his entry into the world crying loudly. A nurse handed him to me first. I looked at his pale face and head full of hair and cried. Tears of joy and tears of pain.

"Welcome to the world Justin Saunders Jr. You are already very loved, and no one loved you more than your daddy," I whispered in his ear and held him close until the nurse took him away for cleaning and medical care.

THIRTY-TWO
Tianna

A baby's wail filled the room and I wasn't expecting it to trigger me so much. I looked at the wall instead of the source of the cries. I couldn't believe Justin Jr. was finally here. It seemed like I had been pregnant for years. I could hear Bianca sniffling and talking to him sweetly. I closed my eyes and let exhaustion take me. I woke up and found her sitting by my bedside. She looked tired and like she had been crying. She sat up half dazed.

"Hey, how are you feeling? You okay?" She asked.

I lied. "Yes." I wanted to ask about the baby, but I didn't dare. Justin Jr. was Justin and Bianca's baby and I know I made the right choice. I tried to make light of the situation.

"Where's Justin? Is he in the nursery monitoring the nursery staff?" I could definitely see Justin watching them to make sure they were doing their job to the best of their abilities.

Tears filled Bianca's eyes. "No."

"What's going on? I feel like something is wrong." I sat up straight beginning to worry.

"I wanted to wait until after you delivered the baby to talk to you."

"Talk to me about what?"

Bianca began to sob, and my heart constricted. "Bianca, you're worrying me now. Please tell me what's wrong."

"Justin and his brother were on their way here. They were stopped by a police officer who shot them both. Jordi survived, but Justin didn't."

"What?" I'd heard what she'd said but maybe the anesthesia was messing with me. Bianca began to cry and seeing her so broken made my stomach clench. I wanted to vomit. I refused to believe her crazy ass. "You're lying. You just didn't want him to be here with me. Even though I gave him up and gave up the baby! You were just jealous! And now you're making up all of these lies! You have everything Bianca! You don't need to be cruel! Where is Justin?"

She shook her head in disgust and got up to walk out.

"Don't you dare walk out that door! Tell me where Justin is!" I began to sob. Tianna the protector couldn't save me. Nor Pop. Nor Abe Nor *Mami*. My heart shattered like glass. "Why didn't you tell me the truth when I asked about him?" It hurt so much I couldn't think straight. My best friend in the world was gone.

"You were in labor, Tianna. Why would I come in here and tell you something that traumatic? I don't know what effect your emotions would have had on your labor, you, or the baby?"

"So, you felt that lying to my face was right?" I was so angry I wanted to hit her over and over again.

"Really? Did you just fuckin' hear what I said!" She yelled! "I did what I felt was right. I did what Justin would have wanted me to do! I don't need you to like it or agree to it. How dare you sit here and question me as if I've done something wrong. You're not the only one hurting Tianna! This is bigger than you, and when do you believe was the right time to have said something? There is no right time! I lost the love of my life so excuse me if I don't have the proper etiquette in breaking tragic news to the woman pregnant with my fiancée's child!" She stormed to the door.

"Wait! Bianca. Please." I got so caught up in my own hurt I did not consider hers. I always saw her as this tough woman and never considered that she was as much flesh and bone as I was. Grief didn't discriminate against age, gender, zip code, upbringing, denomination, or race. "I'm so sorry," I got out trying to hold back my sorrow. "My deepest condolences to you. I know you loved him and how much he loved you. Please forgive my outburst."

"I'm not your enemy Tianna. There doesn't have to be bad blood between us."

I wanted to hug her and needed to be hugged in return but didn't dare ask. "I can't believe this. I'm in shock."

"You, me, his mom, and his brother. They are here too. They're at the nursery right now seeing the baby."

I just stared at her not knowing what to say or do. Instead, she filled the silence. "I don't know if I'm coming or going right now. My mind is all over the place."

"I'm so sorry, Bianca. I really mean that."

"Thank you." She wiped the tears. "Will you be ok. I'd like to see the baby and sit with him for a little while before I leave."

"Justin would have wanted that."

She nodded and cried as she walked out the door a broken mess. My heart ached for her as much as for my own. A little while later, I showered then cried myself to sleep.

The next day the doctor suggested I walk around the floor and get some exercise in, and I followed his care instructions. I wanted to be released as soon as possible, I came upon the nursery and looked in. Only a few babies were in the nursery, and I instantly felt guilty that Justin Jr. was one of them.

An older woman came up to the bassinet and rolled him out to me. "He's been waiting on you," she said with a tender smile.

"I don't, I mean I didn't ask for him. I was just walking by."

"Oh, don't be scared. I'll let you in on a little secret. When I was a first-time mother, I used to diaper my children with cloth diapers, and I don't know how many times I stuck my oldest with the pin. I used to cry just as much as he would I'd feel so terrible. True story. But he's my toughest child. So don't you worry. The only ingredients you need to be a good mother are love, patience, and prayers for when you're low on patience." She laughed at her own joke. "I'll tell you another secret. It's the love a mother has, that manifests all the other things good moms are made of."

She handed the bassinet over to me and went to tend a crying baby. I looked at Justin Jr.'s face and cried. He was all cheeks and a head full of hair. I touched his sweet face and rolled him back into the nursery. I couldn't break my promise to Justin.

"She's right ya know?"

I turned and found Bianca standing behind me. I was not in the mood to argue with anyone. "I wasn't trying to take him. The nursery mom made a mistake and thought I came looking for him. I'm just getting my walking rounds in so I can be discharged." The last thing I wanted was to get into anything with anyone. She leaned her head to the side and stared at me. She was a petite little thing with an attitude larger than life. Reminded me of my mother.

"I overheard everything. You don't have to explain."

I nodded and continued to my room and left her behind in the nursery. A while later she knocked on my door. I invited her in wondering how this exchange would go. I wasn't one for small talk or deep conversations with just anyone, but I'd be polite. "How are you doing?" I instantly regretted the question.

"Honestly, not good but seeing Justin Jr. helps. He is such a blessing."

I tried to not ponder that thought to keep myself detached although, I was glad she had found a measure of comfort.

"I actually came to talk to you about something important."

I had no idea what she needed to talk to me about, but I opened myself up to listen. "Ok."

I know you don't know much about me, but my mother was killed by a drunk driver was I was thirteen. I ran away from her and into the street and she ran after me, pushing me out of the way and saving my life because that's what good moms do." She began to tear up. "They risk their own lives and hearts for their children's well-being. They will hold a thirteen-year-old girl's hand if they sense danger that others can't see or understand just to protect their children. They discipline even if it means they come off as the mean parent just to make sure their children become responsible adults. They will do anything to make sure their children are well. I believe it isn't until we become mothers that we can truly appreciate all that our mothers have done for us. Or until you've lost them. The void they leave behind is inexplicable and unfillable by anyone else."

Every word she said punctured my heart. My heart broke for her loss. My heart ached wishing she had described *Mami*. I had no idea what Bianca was getting at, but I was overcome with emotion. "Why are you telling me all of this?"

"Because only a mother who loves her child will look at her baby the way you looked at Justin Jr. and I think he belongs with you."

My anxiety skyrocketed and I quickly shook my head opposing her. "I promised Justin and I won't ever break my promise to him."

"Christianna, you promised Justin you would do what you thought was best for Justin Jr. and at the time it was Justin raising him. But Justin is not here with us anymore. You are what's best for him."

I didn't know what to say.

"I can't force you. But I can suggest that if you decide no to that you would consider Mrs. Saunders to take custody."

I instinctively shook my head. I wanted my baby. I allowed myself to admit it. "No. Please. I'd like to keep him." I bawled.

She nodded once, left, and returned with him. For hours watched him sleep, talked, and cried. I learned she was all alone, and I instantly brought her into my heart. The following day she picked me up from the hospital and drove me and the baby home. I had banned *Mami* and Pop from the hospital so they wouldn't get attached and when I unexpectedly brought the baby home *Mami* cried. Pop held him close and smelled his hair.

When Bianca tried to leave, I invited her to stay. I made Abe stop staring at her like she was a pork chop. She left after feeding Justin Jr.

and rocking him to sleep. Several times I saw her cry and I gave her time alone with him. It was how she coped with the loss of Justin.

THIRTY-THREE
Bianca

The group session was draining but I was glad I was able to release. The Misfits and Lisa had been so much help to me afterward. Brandon had returned my kindness and brought me take-out a few times, apologizing that he didn't know how to cook. I thanked him regardless. It was the thought that counted. I was appreciative of him and everyone else. Isys clung to me the most. We grieved our loss together for a while before she moved away with her boyfriend. They wanted to start fresh somewhere else. I missed her.

I walked into my dad's room on his birthday, and he smiled at me. A while back when I had broken the news about Justin, he cried and reached for my hand. He held it for a while, and I was so grateful that he'd survived his stroke. I needed him just as much as he needed me. Since then, he always smiled at me when I walked into his room, and he'd wave me over for hugs and kisses on my forehead. I would do the same.

He pointed to my purse, and I knew what he wanted. Today I had to disappoint him. "Sorry, Dad. I don't have any pictures of the baby today." I saw his shoulders slump and wanted to hug him to make him feel better. He had taken to collecting Justin Jr.'s picture and making a collage on a board I had hung in his room. I had framed a picture of me holding Justin Jr. and placed it by his bed. He loved that photo.

But I had a better surprise for him on his birthday. After he'd eaten lunch, I shaved his face clean and brushed his hair down. I'd bought him a nice polo shirt and changed him into it. He nodded his thanks and I kissed him on the top of the head. "I love you Dad. Happy Birthday."

"I love you too," he forced out slowly. I beamed at him. I loved when he made the effort to progress. A little progress was better than none, Justin had once said.

I heard a knock on the door and winked at my dad. "I have a surprise for you."

He looked like he was ready to bolt, and it made me crack up. Uncle Ricky came in all loud and crazy and I had to shoosh him. It wasn't the bar. He waved me off and told me to hush. I chuckled. He sat with my dad for a while, and I saw my dad laugh a few times. Uncle Ricky was shot out for real and was always cracking somebody up.

"Hey, Baby Girl! I was telling your dad how you be whipping tail down at the bar and when he's ready to get the hell up out of here, he can come see his student racking up the dough."

I laughed. "I think I'm a little rusty but definitely. It'll be fun Dad."

My dad looked at me and nodded with pride in his eyes. Truth was I didn't know if my dad would ever leave the facility, but we had to speak things out into the world and that's what we did. A half-hour after Uncle Ricky left, I heard another knock on the door. I invited Christianna in and she pushed the stroller inside.

My dad looked confused, and I knew he was going to be surprised. She took Justin Jr. out of the car seat and handed him to me. I walked over to my dad and sat in the chair by him. I unwrapped the blankets from around the baby so my dad could get a good look at him. As soon as recognized him, he teared up and nodded frantically.

"Jr.," he stuttered out.

I nodded. "Yes. This is Justin. Jr." The baby had filled out and was a fat ass baby boy. I looked over at Christianna who looked out of

place. "Dad that's Christianna. Justin Jr.'s mom. And this is my dad, "
I said to her.

When I had told her that I hung the pictures of the baby on my
dad's walls and how much he loved that, she insisted on bringing the
baby in person. I was grateful for her kindness.

"Nice to meet you, Mr. Williams."

He nodded at her and waved her over with his good hand. She
came closer and stood nearby. He pointed to the baby and then to his
heart. I choked up but held it back.

"Anyone that Justin loved is family to Jr.," Christianna said.

My dad agreed by shaking his head quickly. I laughed.

"Would you like to hold him?"

My dad looked scared as hell, and I got up quickly before he could
protest. I situated the baby in his good arm and kneeled before him to
be a support. After a few moments, he embraced the experience and
just started at the baby. He looked up at Tianna and blew his cheeks
out saying the baby was chubby.

She laughed. "Yeah, he's a greedy little baby."

My dad chuckled and my heart burst open. Not since Justin died
had I felt joy. I missed him so much and still cried myself to sleep
most nights, but life went on and it was ok to enjoy the blessings. I
had to snatch them up just like I had promised myself.

After a while, Dad was tired from all the excitement and we'd left
to allow him to get his rest. I was thankful for her coming all this way
for my dad's birthday so when she invited me to her house for
dinner, I couldn't refuse her.

I baked a peach cobbler and took it with me. That's what they did
on TV when you got invited so I just tried to be well-mannered.
Tianna's brother Abe had welcomed me in, and I cracked up to
myself when he tried to give me a flirty look. Nah son. I'm good.

Tianna greeted me and walked me into the dining room. The baby
was sleeping in the swing nearby all cheeks and thighs. Every time I
saw him my heart would burst, I loved him so much. She sat me

down at the table and called everyone in. None of them looked excited and I felt awkward.

Her parents greeted me. Her father was sweet and a kind man. Her mother made me nervous. Although she had greeted me kindly, I couldn't tell if it was genuine, but I was still polite and greeted them in return. Tianna disappeared into the kitchen and Abe took the time to vent his frustration.

"Why is she doing this? Ma, you know Ti can't cook. Why would you agree and then force us to eat it?"

"Abraham Lincoln Leonard, mind your manners," Mrs. Leonard replied appalled. I covered my mouth trying to hide my amusement.

"Wow. You just gonna put all my government out there in front of company, huh? That's real foul Ma."

Mrs. Leonard hushed him and apologized. "Bianca, I'm sorry. I don't know where he gets his attitude from."

Just then Mr. Leonard choked on the lemonade he'd taken a sip of and began coughing. He covered his mouth with a cloth napkin and held up his hand to signal he was ok. After he cleared his throat, he apologized. "Excuse me. I'm sorry."

"Thomas Jefferson Leonard, I know you were not just being smart."

"No baby. The lemonade was a bit tart. That's all." Mr. Leonard responded.

"Mmm-hmm," she replied and cut her eyes at him.

I heard Abe chuckle to himself. I lowered my face and tried hard not to laugh. These people were freaking nuts. Crazy ass names. Cracking on each other. I couldn't see how Christianna fit into this family. She was so quiet. Right on time, she returned with a bowl of corn on the cob, and I offered to help her. I followed her into the kitchen and saw her about to cry. "What's wrong?"

"I don't know what I'm doing." She showed me her overcooked chicken and runny mashed potatoes and I cringed. "I was trying to learn how to be a mother. I have no idea what I'm doing. I'm going to fail as a mother."

"Well, first of all, Little Man only needs milk so there's no rush to learn how to make chicken. But let's fix this really quick."

She looked at me like I was crazy but moved aside. I cut up all the chicken and quickly made a chicken salad out of it. "Do you have pickles, tomatoes, and lettuce?"

"I think so." She pulled out tomatoes and lettuce but no pickles.

"Grab the toaster and toast a few slices. Toss out the mashed. We don't have time for fries. Do you have any potato chips?"

She rushed to a cabinet and pulled out a few bags. "It's Pop stash." She winced but grabbed them anyway. I quickly taught her how to stack a chicken salad BLT sandwich and how to cut it. We plated it and added some chips to the side and hoped for the best. She carried out two plates, as did I. Her family looked at the food strangely.

Abe protested. "Ti, you've been in the kitchen for hours just to make sandwiches?"

She popped him on the back of the head. I felt the table jerk then heard him wince and bent over to rub his leg. I wasn't sure but I could swear Mrs. Leonard kicked him under the table. These people were definitely throwed all the way off.

"Everything looks delicious," Mrs. Leonard commented. "I can't wait to taste it."

"Especially these chips," Mr. Leonard said with a hint of accusation.

Tianna and I looked at each other and smirked. She went back into the kitchen and returned with her plate and minus her apron.

Her father said grace and blessed the food.

"Ok, everyone. Eat up. Bianca brought over a pie for dessert." Tianna announced before she took a bite of her sandwich. She moaned and seemed surprised by the taste.

"Ti, why you acting like you ain't ever tried your own cooking?" Abe hadn't touched the sandwich and picked at the chips.

In fact, no one had; other than Tianna. It was obvious they didn't trust the food. I felt bad for her, so I picked up a part of my sandwich and ate it. It wasn't my best chicken salad, but it was good enough. "Pretty good, Tianna," I said.

Mr. Leonard tried it next and didn't say a word. Just scarfed it down. The rest of the family followed suit. After dessert, Tianna and Abe went to clean the kitchen and I spent time with the baby. He was getting so big so fast. I couldn't look at him without thinking about Justin.

I fed and burped him, singing a lullaby until he fell asleep, and then I just stared at him. My heart ached missing his father so much yet a part of me marveled at the fact that I was holding a part of Justin in my hands. I treasured the son he'd helped conceive.

"You are good with him."

Mrs. Leonard stood nearby watching me.

"I try," I said and gave my attention back to the baby.

"Can I sit," she asked motioning to the vacant part of the couch.

I nodded. Shit. This wasn't my house. She could sit wherever she pleased.

"I know you probably don't care much for me. And honestly, that's ok. I don't mind that."

Well damn. This woman was outta control. I put the baby in the bassinet and was ready to go.

"You aren't a mother yet Bianca, but maybe one day you'll understand that a mother would do anything for her child. A mother will protect her child and risk the hatred from other people to make sure her child is safe and loved."

I thought about my own mother, and I froze in place listening to Mrs. Leonard.

"I love my daughter. And all I saw was her struggling and in pain. And it didn't really matter if you were blameless. Her seeing you and Justin at the hospital together hurt her and I didn't want her to hurt anymore."

"Mrs. Leonard, I did nothing wrong but love Justin. I knew him since we were young. I never intended to hurt your daughter. I was just being who I am."

"I know that now. But I didn't know you then." She stood up and walked over to me and exhaled deeply. "I was at the hospital when you told Tianna that she should keep the baby. She had banned me from going, but what kind of mother leaves her daughter in the hospital alone and grieving? Granted she doesn't know I was there, but I did check in on her and the baby. And maybe I was supposed to be there just to hear you tell her it was ok to love her baby."

I was shocked but didn't say anything.

"And if I had to guess, you were the one who made that delicious chicken salad." She winked. "I know my daughter. She can't cook and would have never thought of chicken salad."

I turned red for getting caught. "I was just trying to help save her. I didn't mean to be dishonest."

"I know. She's blessed to have a friend like you."

Her words clobbered me over the head. Friend? Tianna and I were many things, but I had never considered us friends. It was weird but I couldn't help but be intrigued by it. I left their house filled with food and questions, namely the idea of a friend.

THIRTY-FOUR
Tianna

A few days later, Pop had taken Justin Jr. to his mancave to feed him and spend time guy time with Pop-Pop, leaving *Mami* and me alone in the living room. I closed my eyes and thought about Justin in philosophy class. It seemed like a lifetime ago and I missed his laughter. Tears sprung and I quickly wiped them away.

"I miss him too," *Mami* said.

I was surprised at her sentiments. "You aren't mad at him for lying?"

She sipped her tea and brought her mug down contemplating before she responded. "I don't think I ever told you how I met Tommy."

I shook my head no and sat up intrigued. I'd never thought about it.

"I was eight months pregnant with you and walked into a small church looking for answers to all of my pain. I was only nineteen years old. Your biological dad found out I was pregnant and booked on me. Told anyone that would listen that you weren't his baby and just up and disappeared. I was a mess.

Anyway, long story short, Tommy saw me in the church lobby with my big belly and asked if I had swallowed a watermelon. I looked at him like he was crazy. He laughed at his own corny joke, and I walked away and left him standing there like the idiot that he was. The next Sunday, I contemplated not returning but it was the only church within walking distance, so I went back.

288

I sat in the back row and listened to the sermon. At the end of service, I spotted him and hid in the women's bathroom for a few minutes to avoid him. When I got to the parking lot, he nearly ran me over with his car. He jumped out and apologized. He insisted on driving me home and to shut him up, I let him. Plus, it was hot, and I was tired. He talked the whole ride, and I was glad it was only a few blocks away. The following Sunday I had gone back and that was the Sunday that I had given my life to the Lord. After service, he came up to me and asked me to marry him."

"Wait. What?"

"Yep. He asked me to marry him. I said no of course. He said God had made it clear I was his future wife. I told him that he only wanted me because I was the only single young woman our age that wasn't after him. At first, he laughed it off but as the weeks continued, I kept true to not wanting anything to do with that fine man. Your biological father was fine too. And every girl in school wanted him and every girl in school apparently had him. He was a cheat and I had had more than enough of fine men.

Well, Tommy didn't know how to take no for an answer and continued to pursue. I joined the choir, so he joined the choir. Turned out he had the voice of an angel, and I hadn't, but I didn't care. I just wanted to praise the Lord. One night at choir rehearsal I went into labor. Tommy volunteered to drive me to the hospital and stayed in the waiting room while I delivered you. A few weeks later I returned to church with you in tow and there he was again. He'd feed you and put you to sleep during service. And still, I denied him.

Until one day I was leaving church and one of the young men called me a skeezer."

"A what?" I asked.

"A woman of low worth. Said I was using Tommy and was nothing but a whore looking to trap a good church man. I never returned to that church. One day I was walking down the street with you in a stroller and Tommy was waiting outside my house leaning against the car. He saw me and turned the car radio on. James Ingram began singing, *Baby Come To Me.* He told me that he'd beaten up the guy who had disrespected me. He had also left his parent's church because he knew I'd never return there. We were married a few months later."

"*Mami* what does any of this have to do with Justin?"

"I was never mad at Justin. He was caught between the woman he loved and the child he loved. Had he known you were pregnant sooner he would have asked you to marry him out of obligation. You would have been stuck with a man who loved someone else. I told you about Pop because I want you to know that the man God has for you, will find you. And he will love you as you deserve. There will be no competition. It will be you and only you."

I felt the need to come clean and wash away all the dirt that had caked on and start over. "*Mami,* the reason I was so mad at Pop was because I saw him with another woman."

She looked surprised. "You did?"

I confessed the whole story and she listened. Then what she said surprised me even more. "What happens in a marriage is between a husband and a wife. But let me give you some advice as a woman. Tommy was wrong and I did find out about his co-worker. But I did my fair share of damage Tianna. My wrong doesn't excuse his, just as his wrongs don't excuse mine. But when two people love each other and they are willing to fully forgive and work on their relationship, with God in it, they can absolutely mend broken hearts. I have forgiven your father and he has forgiven me. We are better than ever before."

I didn't know what to say. I didn't know about marriage, but I did know about forgiveness. Justin and I had had our share of wrongdoing and forgiveness. I was glad we had managed to forgive before he died.

Just then Pop walked back in with the baby. "Little Man needs to be changed and that's where I draw the line."

Mami jumped up eagerly. "I'll take him. Ti needs to talk to you anyway." I shot my mom a look that could have immobilized her had I had had superpowers, but she just ignored me and took the baby upstairs.

"What's up Ti?" Pop plopped down on the couch beside me and picked up the remote.

I braced myself for a conversation I never thought I had to have but was long overdue. I went on to tell him about the other woman I saw him with. He apologized and cried. He said he had wondered for years why I hated him and how it had broken his heart. Hearing him cry, tore me up inside and I immediately forgave him and wished I had done so a long time ago. I missed so many years of his love and guidance because of my tendency to jump to conclusions and shut everyone out.

After that, I took a deep breath and asked him what happened with Lou on the day of the wedding. He paused and stared at me for so long I began to wish I hadn't asked.

"Baby girl, I'm sorry. I didn't know. I didn't know," he repeated sobbing. "I had heard a scuffle upstairs and went to investigate. Justin had punched Lou in the face and was threatening to have him arrested. I pulled Justin back and told him to get the hell out. And then he looked at me in disgust. Out of breath, he went on to tell me all the disgusting things Lou had said to you. And I believed Justin because a few years earlier someone else had accused Lou of the same thing, but no one had believed that girl because she had been sexually active already.

Then things just made sense. How you hated being around Tanya's family. How you stopped letting men hug you. You became drawn and to yourself. And I beat that man senselessly for hurting my baby girl. And I'd do it again."

I let the tears fall. "You didn't know?"

He looked at me sadly. "Ti, how could you think we'd know and allow that? Of course, we didn't know."

"Not even *Mami*?" I was full-blown crying by this point.

"Not even *Mami*. Tianna, I beat Lou down, but it was your Mom who almost killed him. When the police came, I took the full blame so she wouldn't get arrested."

I couldn't have been more shocked. I thought about Bianca's words. A mother would do anything to protect her children. Her love is unmatched. *Mami* walked in singing to the baby a Spanish lullaby and I was overcome with emotion. After she put the baby in his bassinet, I walked over to her and hugged her, and wouldn't let go. "You didn't know."

"Oh baby," she said. "I love you more than you could ever know. I would never do anything to intentionally hurt you. Ever."

"I'm so, so sorry."

"I'm sorry too, Tianna. I'm sorry I didn't protect you."

"You didn't know *Mami*." The words brought the much-needed healing I didn't know would set me free. Life began to change so dramatically after that.

A few weeks later, I received a letter from Stroked Magazine announcing me as the winner of the art contest. I had no idea what they were talking about as I hadn't entered any contests, but as sure as paint was wet, a digital copy of my painting *Resurrection* had been included along with the prize money check. My art was also being featured in their magazine and a replica would be displayed in their lobby for a year.

I read the letter twice unsure how any of this had happened but completely amazed I had won. Bianca had begun stopping by more frequently and I could sense a change in her. She seemed friendlier and would sit and talk with me, as much as she would with the baby. At first, I thought it was pity but over time I saw she was just being herself. She'd entered into the living room and caught me stupefied.

"Why is your mouth hanging open like a fish?" She walked over to the bassinet and scooped the baby up grinning and stuffed her nose in his hair as she always did. "I love how his hair smells," she cooed.

"I know. You say that every single time you sniff his hair like a weirdo."

She burst out laughing. "Girl, shut up. It smells good." She kissed his sleeping face and laid him back down. Afterward, she walked over to me and plucked the letter out of my hand that I had read at least four times by this point wondering how in the world it had happened. I needed to talk to Sarah. No one had access to my art besides me and her.

"Resurrection won?" Bianca brought her mouth to her hand in shock. "He was right."

"Who was right? What are you talking about? How do you know about Resurrection?"

She looked at me and laughed, her eyes getting glassy. "Justin submitted it for you. After you gave him custody of Little Man. He was so sad about you giving him up. I remember being mad at him for caring so much but he wouldn't let me hate you. He never disrespected you or allowed me to talk negatively about you. He said you were a good person that had gone through a lot in life. He never blamed you for giving him custody. Matter of fact, he said you were destined to resurrect. So, he submitted your artwork on your behalf. I thought you were just a terrible person to give your baby up, but he was right. I should have known he was. He always saw the best in people and places and things. He said that that painting was amazing and reminded him that women were a gift to this world."

I was stuck and didn't know how to respond. Even after he was gone, Justin was still impacting my life. I hugged Bianca and cried with her.

The following Sunday was Easter, and I hadn't been to church in years, but I felt a calling to visit. I sat in the back row and listened to the preacher talk about Resurrection. I'd heard the Resurrection story all through my upbringing but never had it impacted me like it had that day. Jesus was beaten and bruised and even died on that cross, but that wasn't the end of the story. There was a bigger plan for it all. None of it had been in vain. Death wasn't the end. Death had been necessary to bring forth life.

Although I was far from being Jesus, I had had my own resurrection. I had given my life to the Lord again and found peace from my past hurts. I missed my best friend, but I chose to remember all the wonderful gifts he'd given me. He loved me when I thought no one had. He'd inspired me to paint again. He gave me Justin Jr. and had even given me Bianca. It took a while, but I had grown to love her as my sister and *Mami* was more than happy to love on her as her daughter. She had become Little Man's unofficial aunt and his official Godmother. We found healing and comfort in each other. It hadn't mattered where we had grown up. What school we had attended. That her hair curled tighter than mine. That our hobbies and beliefs were different.

We faced adversity, stereotypes, injustices, and heartbreak and rose up against all of it. I was proud to call her my sister and me, hers. When it came down to it, we were both just two women with both hood and good in each of us overcoming whatever life threw at us.

EPILOGUE

Bianca

One of my professors in nursing school had given me a great referral to a new nursing home. After a tour and asking lots of questions and checking with the Better Business Bureau I'd moved my dad to Dayton Manner and never felt more sure and secure about leaving him in their care. I saw the love and humility they had for their patients and regretted not having moved him sooner.

Justin Jr.'s visits to see my dad had become frequent and the little rascal loved visiting him. It tickled my dad when he'd hear that sweet little voice him calling him Pop Pop. Little Man would climb onto his lap and raspberry kiss his cheeks, leaving saliva behind. My dad would swat me away when I would try to take him down. That little boy had the power to lift spirits. Dad would turn up his mobility a few notches just to try and keep up his energy. I loved seeing them laugh and having fun together.

And just as I loved their connection, I valued my Misfits equally. Years later I was still going to anger management group sessions and volunteering to help others. The group had changed a little, but we were still close. After Isys had moved away, Eddie joined our group and clicked with us right away. Lisa had encouraged us to start giving back and so I began volunteering there. I wanted to give back to the place that had been instrumental in helping me face my traumatic experiences and led me on the road to healing in the most unimaginable ways.

Once I got home, I turned the radio on and turned it up loudly. Whenever I would feel anxious, I would no longer use my anger as an outlet to justify my actions in other matters but would dance, sing, or whatever I needed to, in order to release it. Jordi and I had started working out together and he'd hung up a punching bag in my bedroom and I would pound on it until I exhausted myself.

After a few rounds, I took my gloves off and wiped the sweat from my forehead. I guzzled down a bunch of water and just as I did every day, I went into the hallway and stared at the wall of photos Ti had helped me hang up. Front and center were photos of my mom and Justin that I had hung beside each other. Surrounding them were pictures of my dad and Little Man. Pictures of me graduating college and Ti in front of one of her paintings. I had a group picture of the Misfits and one of Justin and Jordi cracking up. He'd made me a copy after I saw it in Mrs. Saunders's living room and stared at it forever. I missed Justin's big bright smile.

I brought my attention back to the center where my two lost loves faced me. "I love you both. Take care of each other," I said with love. I kissed my fingertips then transferred the kisses to them.

A quick look at the time and I jumped. I rushed and showered. Afterward, I got dinner started. My newest love was on his way to spend the weekend with his Godmother, and I couldn't wait to see him. Being the God mom to Justin Jr. meant everything to me. I was grateful that Tianna asked me to be a part of his life. I had changed my mind about raising Justin Jr. for many reasons. He deserved to be with his mother and truthfully, I couldn't bring myself to do it without Justin; that was our plan. I was too hurt then to move forward with it on my own.

I have come a long way since then though and am glad to be in a better place moving forward and accomplishing my goals. Tianna was a major part of that. She and I became best friends. I actually consider her more like my sister. It's crazy how things turned out because I would have never thought she and I would ever be friends. Justin's death brought us together and I know he is proud of both of us.

Two chicks from different sides of the track, but all in all we aren't really so different. I'll always be that hood girl born and raised in North Camden. But I was happy that Justin encouraged me to want more. It was ok to be a hood girl. But he also saw in me a good girl. And anyone who didn't know Tianna, well saw the good girl, because she was a good person. Loving and loyal. But she was more than that. She had that hood in her too. That hustle drive in her spirit. That mindset to overcome whatever came at her and just keep going.

She and I had the same goals. We just traveled different roads to get there, and we were ok with that. We encouraged each other to be who we were and be supportive. She wasn't better than me and I wasn't better than her. Mutual respect was the foundation of our friendship.

Well, I was still better than her at cooking, but she'd come a long way. In the kitchen, I put some water to boil and put spaghetti to cook. I turned the radio up, lip-syncing and dancing around with a slotted spoon as my microphone. The doorbell rang and I turned the music down to answer the door. I looked out of the peephole and saw Tianna, Little Man too short to be seen. It was my weekend with him, and I couldn't wait to hug him.

Tianna

Bianca opened the door and yelled like she always did when I dropped Jr. over. And he looked forward to every second of the shenanigans. He was giggling before she opened the door and was now laughing so hard, he could hardly breathe. She snatched him up and gobbled at his neck and he laughed some more.

She finally set him down and kneeled in front of him. She always talked to him at eye level and with respect as if he were a grown man. "Hey, Jr. How are you?" She asked straight-faced.

"Hi Momma B," he replied, remnants of his chuckling trailing behind his words. "I'm good. Thank you."

Bianca looked up at me and raised an eyebrow. I matched her expression challenging her influence over Little Man. She looked at Jr. and scratched her forehead. "Let's try this another way. So Little Man, how you doin'?"

"I'm chillin'."

"There ya go! That's what I'm talkin' bout!" She gave him an overexaggerated bro hug and he continued with the giggles.

"Momma B, you silly," he said then ran off into the bedroom. She pretended to chase him, and he squealed loudly.

She looked me up and down and grinned. "Look at you girl! Work it! You look beautiful! Who you tryna give the panties to?"

I laughed out loud and hushed her up. "That would be a negative. You know I'm nun status."

"I forgot ain't nobody but Jesus your Boo!" She cracked up at her own joke.

"That's right! And proud of it, smartass."

"Oh! You kiss your Boo with that mouth?" She laughed again as she walked to the kitchen then lifted the lid to a pot on the stove.

"Speaking of mouth, can I borrow your red lipstick?" I walked to her bedroom.

"It's in the bathroom!" She yelled.

I did an about-face to the bathroom and checked my makeup and hair in the mirror. I applied the lipstick and exhaled. My third official gallery exhibit. It was a combined effort, but I was still grateful every time one of my pieces had been selected. Book illustrator paid the bills, but painting was my passion.

I cuffed my clutch handbag under my arm and hugged and kissed my baby boy goodbye, warning him to behave.

"Bye Mommy. I love you."

"I love you more!" I said and squeezed him tightly.

I walked out into the living room as Bianca was serving dinner. "How do I look?"

"Beautiful. With those long-ass legs, you could have been a model! But no. You want to color all the time."

I laughed at her and blew her a kiss as I walked out the door. "Wish me luck!"

"Luck!" She yelled behind me as I closed the door.

I drove over the Ben Franklin Bridge to the Philly Flow Art Gallery off Broad Street near City Hall and valet parked my car. I walked into a beautiful ambiance of romantic lighting, champagne-filled flutes, and amazing art. I walked around studying each piece enamored of the talent. Some of the artists were familiar but most I had never heard of. I suppose they were probably saying the same about my piece.

I avoided mine altogether nervous how others would critique it not knowing I was the artist. Instead, I just enjoyed the experience. I came upon a painting that intrigued me and I stepped back to take a better look at it and right onto someone's foot nearly losing my footing in my heels.

He quickly caught me and set me straight on my feet. "Are you ok?" He asked.

I straightened my gown to make sure nothing had popped out and assured him I was before I apologized for stepping on his shoes. "I'm so sorry. I was so intrigued by the painting I lost myself for a moment."

"Hello, Tianna."

I looked up at him and lost my breath. "Elijah. What are you doing here?"

"My favorite artist has a piece in this exhibit, and I came to purchase it. I have to collect them all while I can still afford them," he joked.

My hands began to shake. He was still as fine as he wanted to be, and I had no business noticing and acting like a teenager. I gathered myself and focused on the art. I had a level of confidence in discussing art that kept my nerves at bay. "That's wonderful. What's it called?"

He held a hand out and invited me to walk with him. "How about we go see it together?"

I lifted my chin and walked boldly through the gallery-like I owned it. I hadn't forgotten that he'd gotten me pregnant then ran off to Daddy. I should've grabbed a flute of wine and bust him upside the head with it. I shook my head and erased the thought. Bianca had had a bigger influence on my life than I had thought. I laughed to myself. Nevertheless, I would be cordial but that's where it would end.

Or so I thought. He brought me to my painting and stared at it smiling. "You have always been gifted, Ti. I'm glad you chose to continue walking in your purpose and gifts."

My purpose. I was still trying to figure that out, but I knew I was content in life. I was blessed beyond measure and grateful for it. "Thank you, Elijah. Your support is humbling. Now if you'll excuse me, I'm going to mingle. Please enjoy the exhibit."

He reached out to me and touched my hand. "Tianna, wait. Please."

I turned to him and smiled. "What happened in the past, is in the past. There is no need to rehash it."

He stepped closer so only I could hear. "I do not wish to rehash it. I wish to correct it."

"That is not necessary. I have moved on with my life."

"I have not. I flew all the way here just to talk to you."

My mouth went dry. "Why?"

"Because I need to right a wrong."

"Elijah, I—"

"She told me if I left, I could come back to you in a month otherwise she'd move us to North Carolina. I figured a month away was better than a lifetime. She lied to me. I tried to say goodbye and tell you I'd be back, but you wouldn't take my call."

I felt my eyes beginning to sting, broke eye contact, and looked down at my clutch. "It doesn't matter anymore. We can move on."

"I want my best friend back." He reached for my hand. "I still miss her."

"I'm not who you used to know."

"Then I want to know who you've become."

I didn't know what to say and remained quiet.

"It wasn't a coincidence that I came across your art piece that won. Resurrection. When I saw your name, I was blown away. Since then, I have followed your work and I have prayed about you every day."

I couldn't comprehend all that he was saying. My heart wouldn't allow me to absorb it. "Elijah that was years ago."

"I chose you and want only you."

I searched his eyes for deceit but saw only vulnerability. "Me?" I whispered.

He slipped my hand into his. "Only you."

"I fell and had a miscarriage so if you are looking for your child, I'm afraid you've come a long way for nothing." I refused to let the tears fall. I was too young and stupid then, but it had only been since I'd had Jr. that I began to grieve the baby I had lost.

He stepped closer to me. "I know and I'm sorry."

I thanked him and took a step back. He was all in my personal space messing with my common sense and had me tripping. His cologne. His tuxedo. The warmth in his eyes. It was all too much.

He cleared his throat and stepped back stuffing a hand in his pocket and looking down at his shoes. "I'm sorry. I don't know what got into me."

I watched him and saw how nervous he was, and it touched me. I supposed I wasn't the only one who had been deceived, betrayed, and had lost. His mother had lied to him. He'd lost me and his child. He wasn't the only one who needed to correct past wrongs. I reached out and placed my hand on his. He looked up at me surprised.

"I'm sorry I didn't give you a chance to explain. I was young and broken. It's not an excuse, but it is my truth."

"That makes two of us."

For the rest of the night, we chatted and discussed art and life. Just like old times, he told me stories and I laughed. We reminisced about high school and Leon being afraid of him. We exchanged numbers at the end of the night, and he kissed me on my cheek before we parted ways, him promising to call me the next day.

Whether he planned to or not didn't much matter. I was gratified in knowing the truth about our past. I drove home and thanked God for all the ways he had blessed my life. He mended an old wound. Elijah hadn't left me. Back then he had chosen me. *Mami* and Pop had never betrayed me. They'd chosen me. I was indeed loved, and my past and mistakes didn't define me any more than my address or my race had. Most importantly God had never loved me any less and He'd chosen me for many things even before I existed. That brought me the most comfort and I dwelled in it.

I turned up the radio as Nas and Lauryn Hill sang *If I Ruled the World.* When the third verse came on, I handed the mental mic to Justin and pictured him up sitting shotgun and rapping until his heart was content and I smiled the rest of the way home.

Bianca

Saturday night had gotten here too fast, and Tianna would be here in the morning to pick up Little Man. I could stare at him for hours. He wasn't Justin's twin, but when he laughed, I saw Justin in his face and so naturally I kept that beautiful boy smiling. He soothed my aching heart. It had been over two years since Justin had been taken from me and I still missed him immeasurably.

But I had learned to find joy in our memories and instead of bitterness in a future we'd never share. I would tell Little Man stories about his dad, and I knew he didn't understand or wasn't paying attention, but I promised myself he would know the wonderful man his father was.

I bathed him and put on his PJs. I kissed his cheeks until he pushed me away and laughed. I loved that little boy with everything I had in me. He climbed onto my bed as he always had and began to jump. I snatched and tickled him until he couldn't breathe. He loved when I did that. I let him go and he started jumping again laughing. I looked over to the other side of the bed and felt Justin lying there beside us. I closed my eyes and pictured him there. He smiled at me and told me loved me. Then he proudly watched his son jumping on the bed before I no longer felt him.

"I love you too," I whispered.

Little Man, jumped on top of me and kissed my forehead. "I love you too Momma B." Tuckered out, he laid on me and fell asleep hugging me and filling up every crevice of heartbreak one kiss and hug at a time. He would forever be my good boy born from my hood boy.

Thank You so much for reading Hood Girl, Good Girl

If you enjoyed this book, please consider leaving a review on Amazon or any of the major bookstore retailers.
Be sure to check out these other books you may enjoy.

Releases March 2022

Releases September 2022

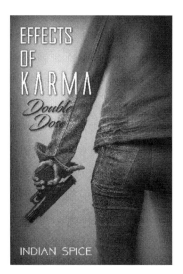

AVAILABLE NOW

ACKNOWLEDGEMENTS

Of all the books I have written, this one has been my favorite by far. I have been asked many times if either of the heroines are based on me and my life. While their stories are not my story, I can identify with both heroines. The whole purpose of the book stemmed from the idea that we all have good in us and not so good in us. And that hood does not equate to bad. The biggest step in eradicating prejudice and racism is by eradicating and ignorance. I wanted to introduce the hood through the lens of something other than rap videos, and television promoting the violence, drugs, and guns found in urban cities. The hood is more than that.

The idea germinated in my head and quickly blew into something larger and along the way, I have had some wonderful people help me bring this to life.

First, I always give honor and glory to my Lord Jesus Christ, for without him I have nothing and am nothing.

Indian Spice, thank you so much for co-authoring this book with me. More than words can ever say, you have been such a blessing. I know I was a pain in the butt but what else is new? We did it Sis!

To all my Hood Girl Good Girl Models, Tosha, Chasity, Daminiq, Jasmyne, Delma, Kim, Teresa, Tiarah, Jada, Fay, and Cailyn. You women were all beautiful and amazing! Thank you and love you guys.

My sisters and Daminiq, thank you for always believing in me and supporting me. Y'all always have my back and I'm so grateful.

For all the musicians and artists that are working with me on the soundtrack. Y'all have no idea how you are making a big dream come true for me! Thank you! Thank You! Thank You!

And to my children! You three are such amazing children. Between listening to me read it out loud, to Cailyn reading it back to me, to giving me quiet time to write and edit, I can't thank you each enough for letting Mommy focus on her goals. I love you each very much and you are my world.

Cynthia Marcano

First of all, I am grateful that I was chosen to be a co-author in this powerful novel with Cynthia Marcano. Thank you for taking my writing to another level. You are a phenomenal woman and friend.

For me, this book was written to bridge gaps in topics that need undivided attention. The reality is, we all are battling something, going through something, and trying to heal from something or someone. I would like to acknowledge everyone on the path to getting their lives back. Those who are doing what's necessary to heal and become a testimony to inspire others.

And lastly, to my parents, thank you for being so supportive all of my life. I kept some of the most traumatic experiences to myself but your love and support helped me tremendously without even knowing how much I was hurting on the inside. I thank God for giving me great parents.

Indian Spice

About The Author

Cynthia Marcano is a native Jersey girl enamored of Jesus, reading, and cake, born and raised in Southern New Jersey to Puerto Rican parents. She loves to incorporate South Jersey culture with life as a Christian and Hispanic woman into her fiction writing. She founded Feeding Thousands Publishing in 2015 and just launched Urban House Publishing in 2019.

When her nose isn't stuck in her laptop designing graphics or in a book, reading Christian Fiction you can probably find her volunteering and praising God or at home avoiding the dishes and spending time with her three beloved children.

She Will Rise, a brand devoted to encouraging others through heartbreak and loss was launched in 2019 to empower women into business, inner and outer beauty, and self-love. Through her organization, she leads women on self-discovery and self-love "journeys."

www.CynthiaMarcano.com
Facebook - @AuthorCynthiaMarcano
Instagram - @MsCynMar

About The Author

Indian Spice is an author, poet, and spoken word artist, born and raised in Camden, New Jersey as Tosha D. Jenkins. Writing has always played a daily part of her life. Indian Spice found it to be therapeutic in her life's journey and feels compelled to share her gift with others. Finding it to be a great tool for inspiration and encouragement. Being a self-published author of four novels, only prompts her to write more and dabble in her versatile creative mind.

Indian Spice debut to the world as a poet and spoken word artist first before becoming an author. She has opened for many events and artists throughout the years and loves being on stage projecting her voice of powerful truths and words to the people.

Currently, Indian Spice is working to publish more novels through her publisher, Urban House Publishing.

Indian Spice wants to continue to share her gifts with the world, hoping that it will generate a positive impact on the hearts and minds of humanity. Sharing her light is not a want but a must. You can find all of her literary work on Amazon Author Central under Indian Spice

www.indianspicecreations.com
Facebook: @Spice Jenkins
Instagram: indianspice_creations

Made in the USA
Middletown, DE
30 June 2021